MIRANDA
AND
CALIBAN

MIRANDA
AND
CALIBAN

JACQUELINE
CAREY

A TOM DOHERTY ASSOCIATES BOOK  NEW YORK

This is a work of fiction. All of the characters, organizations, and events portrayed in this novel are either products of the author's imagination or are used fictitiously.

A Tor Book
Published by Tom Doherty Associates
175 Fifth Avenue
New York, NY 10010

www.tor-forge.com

Tor® is a registered trademark of Macmillan Publishing Group, LLC.

Library of Congress Cataloging-in-Publication Data

Names: Carey, Jacqueline, 1964– author.
Title: Miranda and Caliban / Jacqueline Carey.
Description: First edition. | New York : Tom Doherty Associates, 2017. |
  "A Tor book."
Identifiers: LCCN 2016043546 (print) | LCCN 2016051787 (e-book) |
  ISBN 978-0-7653-8679-3 (hardcover) | ISBN 978-0-7653-8680-9 (e-book)
Subjects: | BISAC: FICTION / Fantasy / Historical. | GSAFD: Fantasy fiction.
Classification: LCC PS3603.A74 M57 2017 (print) | LCC PS3603.A74 (e-book) |
  DDC 813/.6—dc23
LC record available at https://lccn.loc.gov/2016043546

ISBN 978-0-7653-9704-1 (international edition)

Our books may be purchased in bulk for promotional, educational, or business use.
Please contact your local bookseller or the Macmillan Corporate and Premium Sales
Department at 1-800-221-7945, extension 5442, or by e-mail at
MacmillanSpecialMarkets@macmillan.com.

First Edition: February 2017

Printed in the United States of America

0 9 8 7 6 5 4 3 2 1

*To all my fellow lovers of the
Bard, forgive me my trespass.*

MIRANDA
AND
CALIBAN

ONE

MIRANDA

I awake to the sound of Papa chanting in the outer courtyard. It is a morning like any other morning. I lay abed watching a bar of sunlight creep across the dusty tiles of the floor.

Papa forbids me to interrupt him at his art. When I was little, sometimes I would take fright upon waking alone and forget; and then he would have to punish me, which grieved him. But now I am six years of age and old enough to know better, for I mislike nothing more than to grieve him.

Beneath the deep, distant tones of Papa chanting the music of the spheres, I hear a faint pattering sound close by and roll over on my pallet to see a little green lizard creeping down the wall. It stops and stares at me. Its eyes are like shiny black beads and its throat pulses. I hold my breath and count, one, two, three, before I reach out with one finger to stroke it.

The lizard skitters away. Disappointed, I trace the flowing lines carved into the wall instead.

Papa says the lines are Moorish writing, which is different from the Latin writing he teaches me. He says that Moors built this palace, but they went away and left it behind when their magic grew weak, too weak to summon the spirits of the island to do their bidding.

I think it was a long time ago, for the palace is old and crumbling now. Still, it is my home; and Papa's magic is strong. The air shivers and chimes as he calls upon the spheres.

There is a calm note in his voice this morning, not a stern one; and I am glad to hear it, for mayhap it means the studies he conducts late into the hours of the night in his private sanctum went well, and he will be pleased to see me and attend to my studies today. Mayhap he will even pet my hair and praise me.

When the last note of Papa's voice fades, I throw back my bed-linens and rise. The dusty tiles are smooth and pebbled beneath my bare feet. I had shoes, once; cunning little kidskin slippers embroidered with seed pearls. I have them still, tucked away in a chest, but they've been far too small for ever so long.

I don't mind. Even in the winter it is not so very cold that I cannot bear it, and I think I should hate to wear shoes, now. Indeed, on warm days I should like to shed my clothing and run as free and naked as the wild boy, but Papa says we must be civilized or all is lost; and so I wear an old nightshirt of his to sleep and cast-off robes cut down to size by day.

Thinking of the wild boy, I go to the window and look into the walled garden. I've caught a glimpse of him lurking more than once, crouching like a toad in one of the wall's many gaps.

Not today, though.

I make use of the privy in the garderobe. When I have finished and emerge, a lumpish spirit scuttles past me; one of the household spirits Papa has bound to our service, an earth elemental smelling of freshly turned soil.

"Hello!" I call after it. "Good morrow!"

The earth elemental shows its stony teeth in a deferential smile, but it doesn't answer. They never do. It empties the chamber-pot beneath the privy cupboard into a pail and scuttles away.

I sigh, don my robe, and make my way through the empty halls of the palace to the garden outside the kitchen.

Mayhap it is mean-spirited of me to feel lonely. After all, I do have Oriana for company, as well as Beatrice, Bianca, Carmela, Elisabetta, and Nunzia. And I suppose I must count Claudio, although I like him no better than he likes me. He makes muttering sounds deep in his chest, cocking his head and eyeing me with suspicion as I examine the nests one by one. He is a handsome fellow to be sure, black with a fine speckling of white and a proud red comb, but I have reason to be wary of his sharp beak and spurs. I find an egg. Claudio scratches in the dust and mutters.

Bianca is my favorite. She is all white and she does not peck at all, only clucks softly in protest as I inch my hand beneath her and find a second egg. On the east side of the garden, Oriana strains against her tether and lets out a mournful bleat.

"I shall return anon to milk you," I promise her, carrying my prizes carefully into the kitchen. It is only since the spring that Papa trusts me to gather the eggs, and it grieves him when I am careless with them.

Papa is already seated at the kitchen table when I enter, his head bent over a slate tablet on which he scrawls with a piece of chalky ochre. I wait for him to notice me, and curtsy when he does.

"Good morrow, lass," he says in greeting. "What does the day's bounty bring us?" I show him the eggs and his brow furrows. "Only two? Methinks someone may be ripe for the pot."

My heart quickens with alarm. I am not ready to lose one of my only friends. "Not yet, surely! 'Tis the heat renders them sluggish."

Papa considers me for a minute. His eyes are grey and piercing, and I feel their gaze like a weight upon me. At length he relents with a nod. "Very well. But you must begin keeping a tally of who is laying."

I curtsy again. "Thank you, Papa."

When I place the eggs in a bowl on the shelf, I see something unexpected; a chunk of honeycomb lying on a large green leaf. There is a bit of dirt in it as well as a squashed bee and several long black hairs, but, oh! My mouth waters at the prospect of sweetness and I reach for it unbidden, thinking to dip just the tip of one finger in the amber liquid oozing from the comb.

"Do not touch it!" Papa's voice is stern and I feel a painful prick on my extended fingertip like the sting of a nettle. I snatch my hand back, tears coming to my eyes, and curse my impatient greed. "What do you see?"

This is a test, then. I gaze at the honeycomb. The pale wax cells echo the decorations that adorn the archways of many of the palace chambers. Mayhap that is what Papa wishes me to see? Like draws like, he says; that is the cornerstone of his art.

But no, I think that is wrong. If the Moors wrought the likeness of honeycomb in plaster, it was to draw the bees who love it. And though there are many bees that buzz amid the myrtle and the jasmine in the gardens, there are no hives on the palace grounds, or at least none that I have found in my explorations.

No, the honey is an offering from the wild boy.

He has brought gifts before, many times, leaving them on the doorstep of the kitchen. Fish, usually; mullets and sardines, Papa says. Mussels gathered from the rocks. A handful of dates or ripe olives. Once before, honeycomb.

Why is this time different?

A squashed bee.

Three strands of hair.

I draw a sharp breath. The wild boy is swift and elusive, coming and going too quickly to be caught. But Papa should *like* to catch him; catch him and civilize him. He says if the experiment is to work, it must be done gently, with art and kindness. I should like to be kind to the wild boy if he would let me, but I have no art with which to lure him to me.

Papa does, though. Papa wears amulets strung on fine chains around his neck to help him command the spirits; and one that holds a lock of my own hair so that he might charm me to sleep or soothe my fears or punish me at need. He summoned Oriana with a tuft of hair he found caught on a bramble where the wild goats graze.

"It is the hair," I say, looking up. "Do you think it is *his* hair? Do you mean to summon the wild boy?"

Papa smiles at me in approval and it is as though the sun has emerged from the clouds. My heart swells with pride. "That I do, lass," he says. "I believe it is a portent. And if the thing is to be done, 'twere best it were done quickly, ere the malleable nature of a child hardens into a man's savagery."

"Do you reckon him savage?" I ask a bit fearfully.

Papa steeples his fingers. "There is an impulse in him that lends itself to generosity," he observes. "Whether it be the untrammeled nobility of man's true nature made manifest or a base and craven instinct to appease remains to be determined. It may yet be that blood will out, and if my suspicions regarding the whelp's dam are proved—" He cuts his words short, fishing a kerchief from one of his robe's pockets. "No matter, lass. Fear not; whatever may transpire, I'll allow no harm to come to you. Now fetch me those hairs, and have a care with them."

I extricate three strands of the wild boy's hair from the honeycomb. The strands are sticky with honey and coarser than mine. I bring them to Papa, who folds them carefully in his kerchief and tucks it away.

"Well done," he pronounces, returning his attention to the slate. "You may finish your chores."

I remove the wooden pail from its hook and return to the garden to milk Oriana. She stands patiently for milking and suffers me to scratch the shaggy brown hair around her ears when I have finished.

I tell Oriana she is a good girl. The chickens are content to roost in their cote, but Oriana chafes at captivity. Papa says that unlike the simple elemental spirits he summons, goats, like people, are too willful to remain bound and obedient without tending, and it is not worth his while to tend to a goat. If Oriana were not tethered, she would scramble over the crumbling walls and rejoin her wild kin until Papa summoned her back.

Will the wild boy feel the same way, I wonder?

I hope not.

I lug the milk-pail into the kitchen, then return to the garden once more to gather two handfuls of mustard greens.

Papa sets aside his slate to prepare our morning repast. He does not trust me yet to tend the fire or cook upon it. We eat boiled eggs and greens, and yesterday's journey-cakes of ground acorn meal smeared with honeycomb picked clean of grit and bees. Oriana's milk is set aside for making cheese. I eat slowly to savor the honey, relishing the way the comb collapses under my teeth, chewing the wax thoroughly before spitting it out and saving it for use later.

Afterward I wipe our trenchers clean and scrub the iron cooking-pot, which is very old, its curved walls growing thin with usage; and then Papa wipes his writing-slate clean and gives me a lesson in cyphering. Sitting close beside him, I smell the sharp odors of the chymicals he employs in his sanctum clinging to his skin and robes.

When the lesson is over, Papa gives me the lump of ochre so that I might begin keeping my tally of who is laying on the wall beside the door that leads to the kitchen garden.

"You must be incisive," he cautions me. I nod, although it is a word I do not know. "A gentle heart is a virtue to be praised in a young girl, but in matters of survival, cold reason must prevail over sympathies. Do you understand?"

I nod again. "I will keep a careful accounting."

It is the right thing to say. Papa rests his hand atop my head and smiles. "Good lass."

I bask in his praise, and hope that Bianca continues to lay well. "When do you mean to summon the wild boy, Papa?"

"In good time." His voice has grown distant and he withdraws his hand. "There are preparations that must be made ready. Occupy yourself gainfully, Miranda, and do not trouble me."

Thus dismissed, I rise, curtsy, and leave.

For the remainder of the day, I seek to occupy myself gainfully, but there is little to be done. Earth elementals till the gardens with their spade-like hands. Air elementals blow softly through the palace, sylphs scarce visible to the eye, setting the dust to scurrying. In the fountains, the transparent figures of water elementals cavort and cause the water to flow. Although I am surrounded by spirits, I feel very much alone.

It seems it has always been thus, though I know this is untrue. Save for the terrifying spirit that remains trapped in the great pine tree in the front courtyard, there were no spirits in attendance before Papa summoned them, and the palace grounds were desolate. It must have been a difficult time, I think, although I was too young to remember it well, and Papa shielded me from the worst of it.

There was a time before the island, too.

I think so, anyway. Papa does not speak of it and I do not ask because it grieves him. Sometimes I think it is a thing I have dreamed; but if it were not true how would I know to dream of such things? There was a great house with walls of stone, not carved plaster, and pictures that hung upon the walls. There were ladies with kind eyes and gentle hands who brushed my hair and tied it back with ribbons; ladies who helped me dress, who slipped my kidskin slippers onto my feet. Ladies who sang me lullabies, smoothed my bed-linens, and bade me to sleep with a soft kiss on my cheek or brow.

Yet if it were true, how did Papa and I come to live alone upon this isle?

Yet if it were *not* true, from whence came the kidskin slippers I keep tucked away in a chest?

Thinking on it makes me feel strange to myself. Papa is so wise. If he does not wish to talk about it, likely it is best I do not think on it.

I will think about the wild boy instead.

When the midday heat begins to abate, I climb the winding steps of the watchtower. It is a good place for thinking. From atop the tower, I can see far: the whole western side of the island from the rocky path leading down the hill on which our palace perches to the sprawl of land below, dotted with palms. Beyond it lies the sea, and what lies beyond the sea, I cannot say. The sea is ever in motion, crashing and churning. It frightens me, although I do not know why. I dream of it sometimes.

Today it is calm and shining, and the ripples break gently on the rocks. When the tide goes out, the sea leaves pools behind. I think I should not be scared to splash in those pools. From this mighty vantage, I have seen the wild boy do so before, a tiny hunched figure clambering over distant rocks.

I look for him there, but I do not see him. It seems I will catch no glimpse of him today.

Soon that will change. I cannot help but be hopeful at the prospect. Surely there is goodness in his nature to leave us gifts as he does. I think he must be lonely, terribly lonely.

Like me.

"I will be your friend," I say out loud, wishing the wild boy could hear me. "Only come and stay, and I will love you. I promise."

TWO

It is a good many days before Papa is prepared to summon the wild boy. He chides me for impatience when I can bear it no longer and ask him when he means to do so.

"Are you a magus to chart the heavens?" he asks me. There is a cutting edge to his voice that warns me I have overstepped my bounds, and something inside me shrinks at the sound of it. "Can you tell me when the stars will be favorable for this endeavor?" I shake my head no and Papa waves one hand in dismissal. "Then importune me no more."

I swallow my impatience and hold my tongue.

Of course there is a great deal more to Papa's art than the simple notion of like drawing like on which it is founded. I know this although I understand but the merest portion of it.

I know that God in His heaven is the highest of highs, and there are nine orders of angels that sing His praises. Between earth and heaven are the celestial spheres, and the planets whose emanations influence all that happens here on earth.

There are seven planets, which are called the seven governors, and they are the sun and the moon, of course, and Venus and Mercury and Mars and Saturn and Jupiter; and each of them have secret names, too. Those are the names Papa chants every morning at sunrise to draw down their influence.

I know that the planets follow a wandering path within their spheres and the fixed stars move with the turning of their spheres, and that some conjunctions are good and some are bad. Also there are things in nature which attract the planets as like draws to like, and that the good Lord God has placed everything in nature for man's disposal.

And that is what I know.

Oh, and there are stories written in the gathering of the stars. When Papa is in a rare good humor, he tells them to me.

I think waiting would be easier if Papa would only tell me how long until the conjunction of the planets will be favorable for summoning the wild boy, but mayhap it is a more difficult tally to reckon than how many eggs a hen has laid in a week. Although that is not always easy either. Unless they are broody, hens do not always stay on their nests.

Alas, when Papa tells me at last that he means to summon the wild boy on the morrow, he tells me that one of the hens must be sacrificed in the attempt; a white hen to attract the moon's influence.

There is only one pure white hen and that is my Bianca.

I cannot contain my tears, but Papa is gentle at first. "You've kept your tally well, child, but 'tis time a new brood were hatched and 'twere best done while summer's warmth lingers," he says kindly. "Think on it. In a month's time, you'll have chicks to console you."

That may be, but a chick is not the same as my sweet Bianca. "Would not one of the others serve?" I plead. "Bianca is yet a better layer than Nunzia." Papa's expression changes. I look down to avoid his gaze. "Forgive me, Papa. It is only that she is my favorite."

"I cannot change the laws that govern the planets and their correspondences, Miranda," he says. "And I should hope that your devotion to your father casts a longer shadow than your fondness for a mere hen."

Fresh tears prick my eyes at the thought that Papa should think such a thing. "Of course!"

Papa nods. "Very well then."

I spend hours in the kitchen garden and make much of Bianca that afternoon, holding her in my lap and petting her soft white feathers. She is content to nestle against me in the hot sun. Claudio struts nearby, pecks at the dirt, and looks askance at us.

I wish that Papa's spell called for a rooster, but that is a piece of foolishness. Were it not for Claudio, there would be no chicks in the offing. Such is the way of the world.

In the small hours of the night, a storm breaks over the island. Gales of wind howl through the palace; outside its walls, jagged spears of lightning pierce the heavens as the rains lash down. The distant sea must be wave-tossed and raging, a thought that fills me with unspeakable terror.

I cower beneath my bed-linens and think about the wild boy, wondering where he takes shelter from the storm.

I wonder if he is as frightened as I am.

Outside the palace wall in the front courtyard, the spirit trapped in the pine tree begins to wail, awakened by the storm. It is a terrible sound, keening and filled with fury and anguish. Papa should like to free the spirit, for he believes it is far more powerful than any of the simple elementals, but thus far he has been unable to find the key to the curse that binds it, and I am secretly grateful for it. I huddle on my pallet, pull the linens over my head, and wait for the storm to pass.

In time it does. The wind ceases to roar and the dinning rains lessen to a patter. The spirit in the pine falls silent, and I sleep.

I awaken to Papa giving me a gentle shake in the grey darkness before the dawn. "Miranda," he says. "It is time."

The air smells of wet stone and dust. I suppose dust is no longer dust when it is wet, but it has the same smell, which is different from the smell of soil or mud. Papa is clad in white robes trimmed with pale blue and silver embroidery. I cannot see the color in the dim light, but the silver thread glints and I know the other is pale blue. There are pouches strung from his belt and the hilt of a dagger protrudes from it. He carries his wooden staff as well as a little silver bowl that hangs from a chain. The latter sways as he walks, smoke trickling from holes that pierce the lid so that I know the bowl contains embers.

In the garden outside the kitchen, the patchy grass is wet beneath my bare feet. When Papa bids me retrieve Bianca, I weep silently, but I do not disobey. Bianca clucks in sleepy protest, but she suffers me to wrap her in the folds of my makeshift gown and bind her wings at her sides.

Holding her fast, I follow Papa through the palace gate and into the front courtyard where the great pine stands.

Another time, it would gladden my heart to be allowed to attend Papa in the practice of his art, but I cannot be glad today. Not with Bianca cradled trusting in my arms and the memory of the storm's fury and the pine spirit's cries ringing in my ears. At least the spirit remains quiet as Papa turns to face the eastern sky behind the palace and chants the music of the spheres.

Papa's deep voice makes the air tremble, and it trembles twice over as the planets in their distant spheres pour down their emanations in response and the rising sun turns the sky to gold. It is impossible to remain unmoved at the beauty of it; but when it is over he turns to me.

"Now you must give me the hen and tend to the thurible," he says to me, tucking his staff in the crook of his arm and putting out one hand.

I pass Bianca carefully to Papa. He tucks her against his side and gives me the hanging bowl's chain to hold. *Thurible.* So that is its name. I clutch the chain tightly and look away as Bianca begins to struggle. At least her end is a swift one. Out of the corner of one eye, I see Papa drop to one knee and the silver flash of his dagger as he beheads her. He keeps her body pinned to the flagstones while it twitches in its final throes.

My breath catches in my throat and one small sob escapes me. I fight to swallow the others.

Still kneeling, Papa lifts the lid of the thurible. Reaching into the various pouches hanging from his belt, he retrieves handfuls of aromatic herbs and casts them onto the coals. Fragrant smoke arises. Replacing the lid, he rises and takes the thurible from me, swinging it gracefully on its chain. With his other hand, he holds his staff aloft. Sunlight sparks from the crystal atop it.

"May God bless you, O Moon, you who are the blessed lady, fortunate, cold and moist, equitable and lovely," Papa intones. "You are the chief and the key of all the other planets, swift in your motion, having light that shines, lady of happiness and joy, of good words, good reputation, and fortunate realms."

I wait quietly as he continues the invocation, my hands clasped before me. I am grateful that Papa has not dismissed me. Overhead the sky lightens to blue, the pale blue of the embroidery hemming his robe. The day will be clear after the night's storm. Strange to see, the moon is visible in the morning sky, a ghostly white orb.

It is not quite full. I imagine that the Lady Moon turns her face away out of modesty, yet listens attentively to Papa's prayer.

I try to keep my gaze trained upon her. I pretend to myself that this is because it is the polite thing to do, but also it is because I do not want to look down. When I blink, at the bottom edge of my gaze I see whiteness below me; white feathers stirring in the light breeze. There will be red blood splattering the rain-washed paving stones, too.

"Camar, Luna, Mehe, Zamahyl, Cerim, Celez!" Papa calls to the moon. "By all thy names I invoke thee that you hear my petition!"

He kneels once more, swinging the thurible around himself in a circle, then rises and repeats the invocation.

My feet grow sore from standing on the flagstones. I shift my weight from one foot to the other.

I do not believe that it required so great a working of Papa's art to summon Oriana the first time, but then she is a mere beast, no matter how willful. A man is a reflection of God Himself, and that is another matter.

I *think* the wild boy is a man, or at least a boy. I cannot be wholly sure, for I have never seen him clearly. When he spies upon me from the garden wall outside my bed-chamber, he is clever about lurking in the dappled shadows. Still, I feel almost certain that he means me no harm. I cannot say that is always true of Oriana, who butts me with her bony head and the hard nubbins of her horns when she is in a foul mood.

The sun climbs overhead and the morning grows hot. I feel prickly with sweat and hollow with hunger.

Papa finishes a third recitation of his invocation, stands, and sets aside the thurible. Now he holds forth a new amulet strung around his neck on a chain. It is in the form of a silver cage wrought in a sphere, and there are strands of coarse black hair wrapped around the silver wires.

"By the strength of mine art and the very hairs of thine head, I summon thee!" Papa says in a commanding voice, thumping the metal-shod heel of his staff on the flagstones. "Come forth!"

We wait.

I had not reckoned on waiting so long; but of course, that is foolish, too. The wild boy might be near or far. He is free to roam the whole of the isle, and it is almost half a league from the palace to the seashore alone.

Papa stands tall and motionless, as though an eternity might pass without his noticing, his gaze fixed on the east. His hair, which is long and iron grey, spills over his shoulders. The faint breeze stirs his hair and his beard, which is also iron grey marked with two streaks that yet remain black.

I am thirsty, too.

Our shadows grow smaller as the sun climbs. The spirit trapped in the great pine lets out a wail, unexpected and plaintive. I jump at the sound of it, but Papa only glances at the tree. "Be at peace, gentle spirit," he murmurs. "It is my hope that this endeavor will one day bear fruit that may aid thee."

I am not sure what he means by it, but the spirit falls silent.

And still we wait, until it seems to me that I have never done aught else save stand in this courtyard beneath the hot sun, footsore and hungry and parched. I grow so terribly weary that even a glimpse of the still body of my poor sweet Bianca no longer moves me to tears. It is merely another object with no more or less value than any other object. Only a strong desire to make Papa proud keeps me from begging to be excused. I fear that were I to do so, it would be a year or more before he would trust me to attend him in the practice of his art.

At last, there is motion in the distance; a hunched figure approaches on the horizon.

The wild boy is coming.

THREE

All at once, my weariness vanishes in a rush of excitement; and a little bit of fear, too.

"Come forth!" Papa says again, and there is a note of triumph in his voice.

The wild boy draws nearer. His gait is slow and halting. He does not walk upright, striding firmly on two feet, but advances in a crouch, steadying himself against the earth with the knuckles of first one hand and then the other.

Step by creeping step, he comes. It is hard, still, to make out his face, which is hidden by a ragged shock of coarse black hair that falls across his features. I catch a glimmer of dark eyes peering beneath the curtain of hair, wide and shining and moon-mazed.

"Hold, and come no further," Papa says, extending one hand palm outward. The wild boy halts warily. I cannot tell if he understands or if it is simply that his very flesh is obedient to Papa's spell. His skin is dark with grime and the nails of his fingers and toes are ragged and black. Even standing several paces away, I can smell the rank odor of him.

His face, though; his face is human. I can see enough of it now to be sure. His features are broader than Papa's and mine and the thrust of his jaw is stronger, but he is a boy, not a beast.

"Avert your gaze, Miranda," Papa says quietly. "It is unseemly that you should look upon his nakedness."

I do not want to look away, but I do.

Mostly.

"Good lad," Papa says to the wild boy. "Bravely done." The wild boy says nothing. "Do you understand?" Papa asks him. "Do you speak?" The wild boy cocks his head and sits on his haunches, knuckles brushing the flagstones.

My wise and learned Papa repeats the question in the different scholarly tongues he speaks, but the wild boy gives no answer. I watch him from the corner of my eye and see his dark, shining gaze flick sidelong behind his thick hanks of hair, stealing glances back at me.

It feels as though the wild boy and I are exchanging secrets, which is a dangerous and thrilling thought.

I wonder if he is mute, though.

I do not wonder it for long. When the spirit in the pine lets out another unexpected groan, the wild boy leaps sideways and gives an angry bark. His tongue and the inside of his mouth are surprisingly red.

"So you *can* speak," Papa muses. "But it is language you lack. Well, we shall see about teaching you." The wild boy looks uncertainly at him, nostrils flaring. Papa lays one hand on his filthy head. "Peace," he says firmly. "Come with us. Shelter and food and drink shall be yours."

Closing his eyes, the wild boy leans his head against Papa's hand like Oriana when she wants the hair at the base of her horns scratched.

"Come," Papa says again, taking his hand away. Turning, he walks toward the palace gate. The wild boy follows him obediently. "Miranda, retrieve the hen and place her in the larder."

It seems cruel that I must be the one to gather up poor Bianca's body now that the spirits have no more use for her, but I do it, making a pouch of my robes. Her body is slack and heavy in death and her head, her dear little head . . . I do not want to think about it. Her blood stains my robes.

My terrible chore done, I hurry through the empty halls of the palace.

Papa has prepared a chamber for the wild boy, placing a pallet, a tray of food, a great basin of water, and a chamber-pot in it. He chose the chamber specially because it is one of very few that has a stout door with a working lock and key; also, there is a gallery on the upper level that looks down into the chamber. Papa says it was made thusly so that the Moorish sultan could keep his favorite wives safely hidden away, yet gaze down upon them at his leisure. The chamber possesses a courtyard with a garden, but Papa tasked the earth elementals with sealing the entrance with great stone blocks gathered from the eastern end of the palace, which is in the greatest disrepair. Only the tall windows on the upper story admit light.

So it is a cell from which the wild boy cannot escape, which is another thing that seems cruel to me. Papa says I misunderstand the nature of kindness, which sometimes requires a firm heart and a firm hand, and that it will be a kindness to provide the wild boy with a safe place in which he may become accustomed to his surroundings.

I climb the stairs to the upper story of the palace and make my way to the gallery where I might observe.

I imagine that the wild boy will be staring about in amazement at the ornate tiled walls and the honeycombed ceiling, but he is curiously unmoved by them. His attention is fixed on Papa, although when I enter the gallery and sit perched with my legs dangling between the posts of the balustrade, his dark gaze flicks my way once more, quick as a bird's.

From above, I can see that a ridge of bristling hair runs partway down the length of his spine. I should like to know what it feels like to stroke it.

Papa gestures around. "Here is your new home," he says. "Here you may eat and drink, sleep deeply and be refreshed. Here we shall begin the great work of civilization." The wild boy gazes at him uncomprehending, and Papa smiles in response. "I pray that understanding may be granted to you in time. Soon you shall sleep, and when you wake, your will shall be your own; save in one matter." He grasps the new amulet with one hand and raises his staff with the other. His voice takes on the stern tone of command. "By the grace and favor of the blessed Moon, by the strength of mine art and the very hairs of thine head, I bind thee! Never shalt thou do aught to harm me or mine daughter Miranda, lest thee suffer torments untold."

The power in Papa's voice makes the very walls of the palace tremble. The wild boy lets out a fearful whine and sinks deeper into his crouch, wrapping his skinny arms around his head as though to ward off a blow.

"Peace." Papa's voice has turned soothing again; and again, he lays a hand on the wild boy. "Sleep now."

I know well the manner of sleep that Papa's art induces: deep and sudden. The wild boy topples over onto the tiles as though struck a heavy blow. In sleep, his face softens and his cramped limbs loosen.

"Pfaugh!" Papa sniffs. "The lad reeks to the heavens." He leans his staff against the wall and wipes his hands on the white fabric of his robe with disdain. One of the talismans strung around his neck, a pendant set with a clear blue-green gem, lets out a spark as he summons water elementals from the basin. "Bathe him as best you may."

The undines swarm the wild boy's form like a shallow stream spilling over rocks, twisting and twining. He stirs in his sleep, but does not awaken. A tide of dirty water creeps across the tiled floor. The wild boy's skin begins to turn a lighter shade of brown, speckled with a scattering of darker moles.

"Miranda!" Papa cautions me for looking.

I look away.

The sound of splashing water continues, then abates. There is a scuffling sound and the sound of Papa's breath huffing slightly.

"The lad is made decent, child," he announces. "You may observe and learn."

I look back. The undines have returned to their element. The tiled floor and the wild boy's skin glisten with wetness. His chest remains bare, but there is a length of cloth knotted around his waist.

"Now let us see what we have here," Papa muses, and I see that there is a coffer containing implements from his sanctum in the cell. He arranges the wild boy on his back, straightening his limbs. "Ah. We behold there is no actual deformity to the spine, which suggests his bestial crouch is born of habit, not necessity." He examines the wild boy's hands. "The layers of calloused flesh on his knuckles and palms suggest it is a habit of long standing. Why, one wonders?" He is talking mostly to himself. "There are no apes or monkeys on this isle where he might have learned such a habit."

I think of the rocks on the distant shore over which I have seen the wild boy clambering, of the crumbling walls of the palace he has scaled. I would use my hands and feet, too.

Using a pair of calipers, Papa measures the wild boy's height, the length of his limbs, and the breadth of his skull and jaw. He notes these measurements in a diary with a quill and ink, by which I know he is gravely serious about this endeavor. Paper is in scant supply and precious to Papa.

I am a little envious of the wild boy. I do not think Papa would waste paper on my measurements. But mayhap I am being ungracious because I have not yet broken my fast today.

"By the height of the lad and allowing for the effect of deprivation on the natural process of maturation, I should gauge his age within the range of nine to twelve years." Papa measures the wild boy's arms and shoulders, his calves and thighs. "Although by the breadth of his skull, it may be that he suffers from a form of dwarfism, and we might reckon him older." He sets aside his calipers and rubs his bearded chin thoughtfully. "As for that, time will out. Eh, lass?"

"Forgive me, Papa." Dizzy with hunger and thirst, I have lost the thread of his musing. "What is it?"

Papa's brow darkens, then clears. When he is deep in his studies, he sometimes forgets the need for food or drink, subsisting on nothing but air. I see him remember I do not have his endurance. He slides his arms beneath the wild boy and lifts him. The wild boy's head and arms and legs dangle. He looks small in Papa's arms. Papa shifts him onto the pallet and straightens, retrieving his staff. "Come," he says kindly to me. "Let us take sustenance, you and I. Whatever secrets the lad holds will wait."

On his pallet, the wild boy stirs and draws in his limbs a little, then lies still, splayed on his back like a dead frog. I hope he does not awaken while we are gone, finding himself alone and fearful in a strange place. I know I should not like it.

In the kitchen garden, I draw a pail from the well and drink straight from the dipper. I do this three times before my thirst is slaked. There is an egg in the nest that was Bianca's this morning. I slip it carefully under Elisabetta, who is acting broody over a clutch of her own, which I leave undisturbed.

The smell of journey-cakes cooking over the fire makes my mouth water as I gather greens and milk Oriana. When everything is done, we eat journey-cakes and boiled greens with a dollop of tangy white cheese.

"How long will the wild boy sleep, Papa?" I ask.

"Some hours, I should think," he says. "I shall allow him to awaken as nature dictates."

I push boiled greens around my trencher, trying to scoop them up with a crumbling bit of journey-cake. Papa is in good spirits, so I dare a bigger question. "Where did he come from? Did the Moors leave him behind?"

"The Moors?" Papa's brows rise. "No, no. They abandoned this isle long before he was whelped." He hesitates, frowning. "'Tis true, I have my suspicions, child, but I should never have spoken of them in your presence. It is not speculation fit for one of your tender years, and they may yet prove unfounded. It is as likely that the boy is a simple peasant cast adrift by superstitious kin for his lack of wits and foul mien, washed up on this isle and finding a primordial penchant for survival."

"Then what has he to do with the spirit in the pine tree?" The question slips out before I have a chance to weigh the merits of asking it.

The look on Papa's face is like a door closing. "Enough," he says firmly. "Do not plague me with questions the true nature of which you cannot possibly understand." He fetches the slate and a lump of ochre and sets them before me. "I want to see a fair copy of the alphabet in your best hand ere I finish readying the hen for plucking."

I bow my head to the task. It is difficult to write out the alphabet without smudging.

While I make my letters, Papa fetches Bianca from the larder. He has left the cooking-pot hanging from the spit to boil. He throws

Bianca's head into the pail for the midden, stretches out her wings and examines her tail-feathers, plucking out several for ink-quills before grasping her legs and plunging her headless body into the boiling water. Her scaly feet stick over the edge of the pot, clawed nails curling.

I concentrate.

L, M, O . . . no, L, M, N, O . . .

I keep going. The heel of my hand smudges T. I wipe the slate carefully with the edge of my sleeve.

Papa hoists Bianca's body dripping from the pot by the feet. He shakes the hot water from her feathers and lays her limp, bedraggled form on the shelf.

X, Y, and Z.

I put down my ochre. Papa inspects my work and pronounces it good, then bids me to make tidy the kitchen and complete my chores. Today, that includes plucking Bianca. Since I do not wish to do it, I save it for last.

I should not be ungracious. There are a good many chores that Papa or I should have to do were there no household spirits at his command. Each serves in accordance with their element. The airy sylphs sweep away the ever-present dust and breathe life into embers burning low when Papa tends the fire. The watery undines make the fountains flow and fill the wells. The gnomish earth elementals empty chamber-pots and till the gardens with ordure to render them fertile.

But they cannot make journey-cakes of acorn meal. They cannot mash tubers or cook greens or fry fish in a pan. And they cannot pluck a hen.

It is a long chore. I sit on a three-legged stool beside the midden and pretend I am petting Bianca one last time.

When it is done, I return her body to the larder. In the midden-pail, her discarded head gazes at me, bright black eyes turned filmy.

Since I cannot bear it, I take Bianca's head into the garden, where I dig a hole and bury it deep beneath a fig tree where she loved to scratch the dirt and peck at insects.

I have just finished when I hear the howling begin. For a moment, I think it is the spirit in the pine, but no. This sound is different. It is mortal and scared and angry, and I think it can only mean one thing.

The wild boy is awake and he is very, very unhappy.

FOUR

I hurry through the palace, back to the gallery above the wild boy's cell. Papa is already there, his hands resting on the balustrade as he frowns at the spectacle below.

The wild boy is flinging himself around the cell in a fury. He claws at the stone blocks sealing the door to the garden, but they are too heavy for him to move and he howls in despair. He claws at the planks of the door and yanks in vain on the handle. He leaps high, higher than I would have thought possible, clinging to the tiled wall with ragged, filthy nails and seeking to reach the windows, but he cannot get enough purchase to climb and falls to the floor with another howl. He has overturned the water basin and trampled the food that Papa left for him.

It frightens me, yet I feel sympathy for him, too. I think mayhap the wild boy is more frightened than I am. He does not seem aware of our presence. I should like to call out to him, but I dare not.

"He is more savage than I reckoned," Papa murmurs.

"Can you not do something to soothe his fears, Papa?" I whisper.

Papa continues to frown. "Yes, of course, but there is much to be learned in observation. I had hoped to discern in him the faculty of reason. Thus far, I am not encouraged."

The wild boy pauses in his efforts. His attention turns to the cloth knotted around his waist. He tugs at it with a whine, then claws frantically at it, spinning in a circle as the breech-cloth shifts around his waist.

Papa sighs. "No, not encouraged at all."

I say nothing.

The wild boy sees us and lets out a hoarse bark. Behind the hair that hangs over his broad brow, his eyes are stretched wide enough to show the whites all around.

"I shall go to him," Papa says.

I watch from the gallery as Papa descends to the lower level of the palace. There is a moment when it is just the two of us watching each other; the wild boy below and me above. Squatting on his haunches and looking up at me, he pauses in his efforts and cocks his head.

I cock mine in reply. It seems to me that there is a glimmer of understanding in him; but then Papa turns the key in the lock and enters his cell. The wild boy leaps backward, his narrow shoulders hunching uncertainly.

"Peace," Papa says in a deep, calm voice, holding out one hand in a soothing gesture. "Be at ease, lad."

The wild boy hesitates, then bares his teeth and swats at Papa's outreached hand. It is not much of a blow, but it is enough to invoke the binding spell that Papa has laid upon him. Straightaway the wild boy falls writhing to the floor, howling in pain. I see the muscles twitch and jump beneath his skin of their own accord as they cramp in knots. The wild boy curls into a tight ball. Only his hands move of their own volition, fists beating against his thighs.

Papa shakes his head. "Ah, lad! Even a singed cur learns to fear the flame. I pray you may prove at least as wise."

I think that Papa will likely make the wild boy sleep again, but he doesn't. He simply leaves him there, and bids me descend from the gallery. The wild boy's howling fades to a low keening sound that follows us through the empty halls and colonnades of the palace.

That evening Papa and I dine on chicken stewed with tubers from the garden. Although it is rich and good, my portion is seasoned with tears.

In the days that follow, at first I am hopeful. Never again does the wild boy raise his hand against Papa when he enters his cell, but cringes warily, wrapping his arms around his head. When no torments are forthcoming, bit by bit, he eases from his defensive crouch and lowers his arms. Now Papa shows him nothing but kindness. He seeks to teach the wild boy by example, speaking all the while in a calm and soothing manner. He cups his hand and drinks water from the basin, saying the words *drink* and *water* over and over. He picks bits of journey-cake from the tray and mimes eating, saying the words *eat* and *food*. After a time, the wild boy learns to mimic Papa's actions; although when he eats, he shoves whole journey-cakes in his mouth and gobbles them down in great gulps, crumbs of meal spraying. And when he drinks, he shoves his face into the basin and laps at the water like a beast.

But alas, there his progress halts.

No matter how much Papa plies him with words, no matter how gently he coaxes, the wild boy does not repeat them, only barks or grunts.

And when left alone, he continues to howl and rage against his confinement.

The wild boy's fingers and toes grow bloody, his ragged nails ripped from their beds in his vain efforts to scale the tiled walls. His breech-cloth hangs from his waist in bloodstained shreds, and if he could undo the tight knot, he would doubtless discard it altogether. Disdaining the unfamiliar chamber-pot, he makes waste in the corners of his cell. Sometimes in his fury, he smears the walls with his own ordure.

Despite the efforts of the earth elementals, whom he regards incuriously, the cell begins to stink.

When the wild boy has exhausted himself, he crouches on the floor of his cell and rocks back and forth on his haunches, keening softly and biting at the knuckles of his hands. After the first day, he does not look in my direction when Papa allows me to observe from the gallery.

Torn between pity and disgust, I do not know what to feel.

"I fear that my endeavor has failed, Miranda," Papa says gravely to me over supper. Some twenty days have passed since he summoned the wild boy. "Either the lad is so far sunk into savagery that he is beyond the reach of civilization's influence, or there is naught of humanity in him to be reached."

I look up from my trencher. "Will you set him free, then?"

Papa hesitates. "'Tis that, or bind him tighter. It means relinquishing the hope that the lad might hold a key to a particular mystery, but he may yet be of service to us on a smaller scale. Although I must give the matter further study, I do believe that there are ways it may be done. It would deprive the lad of will and reason, but since the latter appears nonexistent, mayhap the former would be no loss worth mourning." He lets out a mirthless chuckle. "Should it prove a success, mayhap I'll work a similar charm on that troublesome goat of yours."

Outside, a hot summer wind has sprung up. It sighs through the archways of the palace and skirls about the kitchen. The embers in the fireplace stir and glow. In the courtyard, the spirit in the great pine tree gives a long, plaintive wail that sounds like *Ahhhhhhh!* The wild boy in his cell barks in angry response.

I gaze at Papa.

Why?

It is the question I want to ask him, a question that breaches the pent-up dam of a hundred other questions. Why, why, why? Why not grant the wild boy the freedom he craves? Why do I dream of a time before the isle? Where is the house with stone walls that I half-remember? Who were the ladies who put slippers on my feet in the morning and kissed my cheek and sang me to sleep in the evening? Where did we come from and why are we here? Where did the wild boy come from? Who do you suspect were his mother and father? Who was *my* mother? What is the spirit in the pine, and what has the wild boy to do with it?

Why do they matter to you, Papa? Do *I* matter to you? What is it you seek and why do you seek it?

Why do you tell me so very, very little?

I say none of this, because I do not wish to grieve him. I know that I am only a foolish child, and if Papa keeps things from me, it is for the best. Still, it is hard when the questions crash like waves inside my head.

The next morning, Papa does not give me a lesson after we break our fast, but goes straightaway to his sanctum, warning me not to disturb him.

I do not, of course; and yet, and yet. I am restless, plagued by a spirit of willfulness. Mayhap it is born of the many unanswered questions I have swallowed. When the midday's heat is at its worst, I climb the stairs to the upper story of the palace and venture into the gallery even though I do not have Papa's permission to do so.

Below me, the wild boy sleeps on his pallet. He lies on his side, knees drawn tight to his chest, hands fisted under his chin. He twitches and shivers in his sleep as though stung by biting flies.

I watch him.

I think about how he leaned his head against Papa's hand on the day he was summoned, as though there was a deep yearning for kindness and companionship in him. I think about how he glanced at me that first day, a glance like a shared secret. I wonder if mayhap we might yet understand one another, the wild boy and I. If we might yet be friends.

If Papa bespells him a second time, I shall never know.

My bare feet carry me down the stairs, along the colonnade that leads to the wild boy's cell. I gaze at the stout wooden door, the haft of the iron key protruding from the lock. It would be wrong for me to enter the wild boy's cell alone; and yet, Papa has never forbidden it, has he?

No, he has not. He has told me not to enter the gallery without permission, but he said naught of the cell itself. Like as not, it is because Papa never imagined I would dare such folly. But the wild boy cannot harm me. Papa's magic has made certain of it. And if I am swift, Papa will never know.

Reaching up, I grasp the haft of the key and turn it in its lock. There are clicking sounds, after which the wooden door gapes open a crack.

My heart thuds in my chest.

I push the door.

It opens with a creak and I slip inside, closing it behind me. The sound awakens the wild boy. He leaps from his pallet and lands in a crouch. Behind his thatch of coarse black hair, his eyes widen in surprise.

My heart continues to beat hard and fast. The wild boy's cell is hot and it stinks like a chamber-pot left to stand unemptied for days on end. Not a single whisper of air stirs in it.

"Hello," I say. My voice sounds high and strange to my ears and my chest feels tight. I draw a deeper breath of hot, stinking air and make another attempt. "Hello!" The wild boy stares uncomprehending at me. I cock my head at him, but he does not cock his in reply this time. Daring greatly, I take a step forward. The wild boy retreats a step, his knuckles brushing the tiled floor. I hold out my hands in a pleading gesture. "Don't be afraid! I won't harm you. No one will harm you. I only want to be your friend."

The wild boy's gaze darts uncertainly around the room. I think about the unlocked door behind me and fear takes root in me, my skin prickling. If the wild boy escapes, Papa will be in a fury.

But no, the wild boy makes no move toward the door. I think he must not know what a lock is.

"Friends," I say softly, clasping my hands together in an effort to show him the meaning of the word. "Can we not be friends, you and I? Surely you must be lonely." My voice trembles a little. "*I* am. I know you cannot understand the words I speak, but can you not *try* to understand? Because I should very much like to be your friend, and I do not know how else to ask."

The wild boy hunches his shoulders and lets out a hoarse bark.

And all at once, a wave of despair washes over me. It is too much, all of it. The blanketing heat, the enduring stench, the wild boy's unteachable savagery, Papa's endless absences, and my own unbearable loneliness.

Hot tears scald my eyes and I find myself sitting down hard on the floor. "I hate you!" I shout at the wild boy. "It's not fair! All I wanted was a friend! I hate that Bianca was killed to summon you! I *hate* you!"

The wild boy whines.

Burying my face in my hands, I cry harder. There is a release in giving in to tears; not the quiet and decorous tears I shed for Bianca's death, but great sobs of self-pity that wrack my whole body. Absorbed in my grief, I do not hear the wild boy's stealthy, creeping approach.

I know nothing of it until I feel his hand touch my foot.

I look up.

The wild boy is crouching before me. His dark eyes are bright and troubled. He makes a crooning sound deep in his throat and strokes the bare skin of my foot with his knuckles.

He is trying to comfort me.

I stare at him in wonder, self-pity forgotten. He croons encouragingly at me. There *is* understanding in him. "Miranda," I whisper. Tapping my chest, I say my name again, as slowly and carefully as I can. "*Mir-an-da.*"

The wild boy squats back on his haunches. The filthy remnants of his breech-cloth hang between his thighs. His throat works and his mouth opens and closes. I think mayhap he is trying to speak.

I shift to kneel on the floor, sitting on my heels. If he stood upright, he would be taller than me, but sitting thusly we are at a height. "Miranda." I touch my chest again, then point to him.

The wild boy's brow furrows and his right hand twitches as he raises it and scrabbles at his own chest. I nod. His mouth opens again, his red tongue touching his teeth as though searching for something. His breath comes in short huffs and his nostrils flare, his tongue questing.

I remain very still, at once scared and excited.

"Cal—" It is a word, or a portion of a word. For all the howling and barking he has done, his voice sounds rusty with disuse. His lips move in an exaggerated manner as he struggles to make human sounds. "Cal . . . Cal . . ." He gives his head a sideways shake, bares his teeth, and tries again. "Cal-i-ban."

"Cal-i-ban." I echo him softly. "Caliban. Is that you? Is that your name? Caliban?" I can see by his frown that the name, if that's truly what it is, is the only word he recognizes. Leaning forward, I dare myself to touch his arm with one fingertip. *"Caliban?"*

"Caliban." This time the word emerges in a sigh of agreement, then is repeated more surely with a tone of rising excitement. "Caliban!"

It is at this moment that Papa emerges unexpectedly from his sanctum on the upper story and enters the gallery. We catch sight of him at the same time, the wild boy and I. I scramble to my feet, dumbstruck with fear. Oh, Papa will be sorely grieved! The wild boy gives one of his great startled leaps, landing in a crouch and covering his head with his arms. Papa's hands grip the railing hard enough to whiten his knuckles and he scowls down at us, thunder written on his brow.

Terrified though I am, I find my voice. "He has a name, Papa!" I call up to him, hoping the news will offset his anger. "The wild boy has a name!"

"Oh, does he indeed?" Papa's voice is dangerously quiet. "And how might you have discovered it, lass?"

Trembling, I stand my ground. "He told it to me, Papa."

Papa is silent for a long moment. I cannot tell what he is thinking. "For all of our sakes, I pray it prove true, child," he says at last. "But if it is so, I would hear the lad speak it himself that I may know it is the truth, and not a flight of fancy your overly tender heart has accorded to some savage utterance or bestial grunt."

I go to the wild boy, squatting before him and ducking my head low to meet his gaze. "You must tell him," I whisper. Even though I know he does not understand my words, I will him to grasp my meaning. "You must say it aloud or he will bespell you again, and we shall never be friends." I touch my chest. "Miranda," I say once more, then point at him.

Beneath the shelter of his wiry arms, the wild boy peers back at me. "Caliban," he whispers.

Louder; it must be louder, else Papa will not hear him. I stand, tapping my chest. "Miranda." The wild boy whines. "Please!" I beg him, my voice rising in despair. "Oh, please!"

The wild boy's shoulders tighten, but then he lowers his arms and straightens slowly from his crouch, lifting his head to gaze toward Papa in the gallery. "Caliban." He brushes his chest with his knuckles in unmistakable meaning and repeats the name with exaggerated care. "*Cal-i-ban.*"

I feel triumphant and scared.

Papa strokes his beard and looks down at us. "So it seems that youth and innocence has prevailed over wisdom and experience in the matter of taming the savage breast," he murmurs to himself. "Curious, indeed. 'Tis a phenomenon that bears further study. Mayhap there is a correspondence of innocence and ignorance at work, the significance of which I had not fully reckoned."

I begin to hope that Papa is so pleased with this discovery that he will not punish me.

But no, his gaze sharpens and he reaches for the amulet that binds me to him, the one that bears a lock of *my* hair. I look down at the floor and make my hands into fists in anticipation of the pinprick stings of correction that will follow.

"Miranda." Papa waits until I look up again. His expression is grave and disappointed. "Even if I did not expressly forbid it, I daresay you are sensible enough to know that you defied my wishes in entering the wild boy's cell without permission. Is this not so?"

I cannot be untruthful. "Yes, Papa."

"Very well." He lets go of the amulet. I slacken with relief. "Because I do not wish to agitate the lad's sympathies and cause him to regress to a state of abject savagery, I shall spare you the immediate punishment that is merited for this transgression. Confine yourself to your chamber and meditate on the nature of your disobedience until I summon you. For a daughter to willfully disobey her father is to violate the divine order of nature itself," he says sternly. "God in His heaven weeps."

I look down, ashamed.

The wild boy whines, then makes his crooning sound.

"Go!" Papa orders me.

I hesitate. "Papa . . . you won't work a deeper binding spell on him just yet, will you?"

Papa folds his arms and glares. "Begone, lass! To your chamber!"

I obey.

FIVE

CALIBAN

Caliban, Caliban, Ca-ca-ca-caliban!
Caliban.
Miranda.
Master.
Yes. No. Food. Water. *Eat* food. *Drink* water. Please. Yes, eat food, please. Yes, drink water, please. Thank you. Food, please, Master. Thank you, Master.
I Caliban.
She Miranda.
He Master.
Sun. Moon.
Good, bad. Yes, good. No, bad.
Bad, bad, bad.

I *am* Caliban. Caliban *is* good. She *is* Miranda. Miranda *is* good. He *is* Master. Master *is* good.

Food is good. Water is good. Yes, please. Thank you, Master.

Sun is good.

Moon is good.

Yes, please. Eat food is good. Drink water is good. Master is good. Miranda is good. Thank you, Master.

I am Caliban.

Caliban is good.

No, bad. Bad, bad, bad.

Sorry.

Caliban is sorry.

Yes, Master. Please, Master. Thank you, Master.

SIX

MIRANDA

Teaching the wild boy—no, teaching *Caliban*—to speak is a lengthy business, but I do not mind. I am grateful that Papa allows me to play a role in it.

And I am very, very grateful that Papa chose to let Caliban keep his wits after all, judging that it would be a greater endeavor to continue attempting to civilize him than to tame him with magic. He says nothing of the spirit in the pine, though I am sure it too has something to do with his decision.

Papa casts the deeper binding spell he devised on Oriana instead. I am not permitted to attend, but at least casting this spell on a mere beast requires no sacrificial offering. Papa grumbles about wasting his art on a goat, but I think he wishes to know if it works.

It does. Oriana no longer tries to escape. She is different, though. All her mischief is gone and her lively gaze is dull. She takes no interest in the antics of the clutch of chicks that Elisabetta has hatched. She never tries to butt me when I milk her, but she takes no pleasure in it when I scratch her head.

Papa is pleased with the results.

Yes, I am very grateful that he chose not to further bespell Caliban.

I should like to say that Caliban is a good pupil, but it is only true sometimes. On good days he is eager to please. On bad days, he works himself into a fury at his captivity and howls and rages as wildly as ever. When that happens, Papa punishes him.

It grieves me to see Caliban fall writhing to the floor of his cell, his limbs twitching in pain.

He learns, though.

Bit by bit, day by day, the fight drains from him. He ceases to bloody the nails of his fingers and toes in an effort to escape, and no longer claws at his breech-cloth. Although he has not learned to use the chamber-pot, he no longer smears ordure on the walls of his cell, and the elemental spirits are better able to clean his messes. It still stinks, though.

On good days, Caliban regards Papa with worshipful awe. Those are the days on which he is most apt to master a new word or come to a new understanding of the way that words fit together to form a greater meaning.

On bad days, Caliban regards Papa with a mixture of suspicion and craven fear, and although his rages lessen, he is sullen and willful. I do my best to make him understand that if he only *obeys* Papa, there will be no punishment. On good days, it seems he understands this, but on bad days, he is beyond the reach of reason.

I think that if Papa would only allow Caliban a measure of freedom it might help, but Papa will not soften.

"The ability to reason is what separates us from beasts, child," he says to me when I suggest it over supper. "I'll grant you, the lad has evinced glimmerings of the faculty I feared we might never see, but a mere glimmering does not suffice. If he ever proves capable of demonstrating it consistently over time, remaining helpful and willing to learn and earn my trust, I will reckon him deserving of a chance to prove himself worthy of it outside his cell."

"How much time, Papa?" I ask humbly.

He considers the question. "A full month's time."

A month.

It seems like a very long time; but then, it was a full month's time before Papa decided I might be entrusted to give Caliban lessons on my own. I think mayhap Papa found the process more tiresome than he reckoned in comparison with his own studies, but I am grateful to occupy myself gainfully. I begin making marks on the walls of Caliban's cell with ochre chalk to count the good days, hoping I might use them to teach him.

It is not easy.

"One, two, three, four." I point at a series of Xs. "Good, good, good, good. See?" I hold up four fingers. "For four days Caliban was good." I point at an O. "Bad. Yesterday Caliban was bad." I erase the chalk markings with the heel of my hand, dusting it on the folds of my robe.

Caliban sets his jaw. "No!" Although he has not altogether lost the habit of crouching, he stands straighter now than he did when Papa first summoned him, and is a head taller than me.

"Yes," I say firmly. I draw an X. "Today Caliban was good. One day." I hold up one finger, then all ten fingers thrice over. "Master says that if you are good this many days, you may have sun."

He lets out a long, wistful sigh. "Sun!" It is one of the first words he learned, pointing to the sun when its bright rays streamed through the high windows on the upper story. I think it has come to stand for all that is good in the world outside his cell, all that is lost to him.

"Sun," I agree sadly. Surely it would be easier to teach him were he allowed to leave his cell, for there are only so many things I can name within its confines. But I dare not defy Papa.

"Sun is good," Caliban says. "Miranda is good." He touches a lock of my hair with unexpected gentleness. "Miranda is sun."

I laugh. "No!"

"Yes!" His dark eyes are intent with a desire to convey meaning. "Miranda is sun."

It is a compliment, I think; the highest one he knows how to give. I do not know what to do other than return it. "Caliban is sun, too."

"No." He shakes his head, a shadow crossing his face. "Caliban is bad."

"Do not say so!" I catch his rough-skinned hands in mine. "Yesterday, yes. But not today, and not tomorrow, not for a whole month of tomorrows! Oh, Caliban, you *have* to be good! If you're not, Papa will bespell you and you'll be like Oriana, not yourself at all, and I'll be alone again!" I know it is far too many words for him to understand, but I cannot stop myself any more than I can hold back the tears that fill my eyes and spill down my cheeks. "I don't want to be so alone!"

"No, Miranda, no!" Caliban makes his crooning sound and squats to pat my shoulders and my hair. His jaw hardens and his wide brow creases in a disapproving scowl. "*Master* is bad."

"What? No!" Alarmed, I cover his mouth with one hand. "Never say such a thing!"

Though he continues to scowl, he quiets under my touch.

I take my hand away.

"*Friend*," Caliban says. It is another word he has learned from me.

"Yes." I nod. "Friend."

It seems strange to me that I should know such words, and yet have no memory of learning them. Who taught *me* to speak? And why was it not such a difficult endeavor as it is with the wild boy?

When I lie abed at night, I try to remember. There is Papa, of course. When he speaks to me, he speaks to me at length. Sometimes I think that because Papa has no one else to speak to, he forgets I do not always understand what he is saying, even as I forget Caliban cannot understand the words I blurt out in a rush of feeling.

But what about before? Before the island?

Was there truly a *before*?

If there was, I understood the lullabies the ladies with their soft hands and soft cheeks sang to me. How?

I do not know.

And so I cease to cudgel my wits. I think about teaching Caliban to speak and be civilized as a very long walk that we are taking together, step by step by step. Sometimes we go backward, but mostly we go forward. I keep a tally of the good days on the wall of his cell. It stretches to ten days before a bad day comes and we must start the count anew, and then to seventeen days. It is hard to start over after seventeen days, but we do.

There are triumphs great and small along the way. Every new word mastered is a triumph.

But my greatest triumph is convincing Caliban to use the chamber-pot. In the early days, he is in the habit of squatting to relieve himself whenever the urge comes upon him with no more sense of modesty than Oriana or the hens. When he does so, I avert my gaze, point to the chamber-pot, and leave his cell. Because he does not like for me to leave so abruptly, in time he comes to understand that this is not something to be done in front of others.

The chamber-pot is another matter.

In fairness, there is no reason Caliban should have any inkling of its purpose or understand why I point at it when he relieves himself. If I were a boy, I think mayhap I would simply *show* him; but Papa has made it clear that a girl must never be immodest. At last I think to mime the action, sitting on the chamber-pot and using a pail of dirt clods from the garden and a wooden cup of water in place of urine and stools. I feel foolish doing it and I am not wholly sure that it is *not* immodest to do so, but after I go through the mime several times, I see Caliban's eyes widen in surprised comprehension. After that, he begs for the pail and the cup so that he might sit upon the chamber-pot and imitate me, as though it is a cunning new game I have devised for us.

In fact, it is not until the next day when Caliban leads me proudly to the chamber-pot to view his waste that I am certain he understood.

"I am good?" he asks hopefully.

"Very good," I assure him. Clapping my hands together, I make a song of it. "Caliban is good today, Caliban is good today! Today, yesterday, tomorrow, and every day, Caliban is good!"

He claps too, and jumps up and down.

"Miranda!" Papa's voice calls from the gallery, sharp and stern. Once again, he has emerged from his sanctum to appear above us unexpected and unnoticed. "What manner of nonsense is this?"

Chastened, I cease. "I was only praising him, Papa. He has learned to use the chamber-pot."

Caliban rests on his haunches and lifts his bright, hopeful gaze to the gallery.

Papa hesitates, then nods in approval. "Is it so? Well done, lad," he says in a kind voice. "'Twas time and more for that revelation, but I daresay we shall all breathe the easier for it."

Caliban basks in his praise.

I wish Papa would praise me, too, but he does not; only summons a gnome to empty the chamber-pot and returns to his studies.

Nonetheless, I am inspired by my success.

It seems to me that making a game of things is a key, and so I decide to make a game of cleanliness. First, I rub my arms with soil in the kitchen garden until my skin is dark with grime. Then I bring an additional basin of water and a little pot of soap into Caliban's cell. I show him my arms. "Dirty," I say, drawing one fingertip through the grime. "Dirty is bad." Then I unstopper the pot of soap and make a show of smelling it.

Caliban sniffs it, too. "Sun!"

I smile. "Soap." In a way he is right, though. Papa makes the soap from wood ash gathered from the kitchen hearth and olive oil pressed from the grove outside the palace, and when the jasmine is in bloom, he gathers its blossoms and steeps them in the mixture to perfume it. The scent is very like unto the gardens in summer sunlight. I plunge one arm into the basin, then take a dollop of soap and scrub away the grime. "Clean!" I rinse and show him. "Clean is good." Caliban is delighted by this new game, and we play it until I daresay he's cleaner than he's ever been in his life. I have to call a halt to it lest we use too much precious soap.

Papa is pleased, too; so pleased that he decides Caliban is ready for more civilized clothing. I am not as certain, but to my surprise, Caliban is proud to don a pair of Papa's breeches cut down to size. Papa even succeeds in teaching him to knot them around his waist.

"The lad's dexterity has improved," Papa says to me at supper that evening. "Note it well, child! As the higher functions of speech and reason grow stronger, so do the lesser faculties follow suit."

I nod.

"Miranda." Papa's voice is gentle. I look up at him. "You have made wonderful progress with our wild boy. *Wonderful* progress. Do not think I am unaware that it is your tender heart that first stirred sympathies in his savage breast, and that it is your diligent efforts that have borne fruit. I am tremendously impressed with your achievements, my daughter."

My cheeks flush and my heart swells with pride. "Thank you, Papa."

Mayhap it is pride that makes me careless. I conceive a new game, a counting game wherein Caliban and I promenade around his cell and count the tiles on the walls, chanting the count aloud.

I think it will be a good way to increase his understanding of numbers.

But I forget about the door.

No, I do not *forget*, exactly. I reckon it in our counting. Thirty-six, thirty-seven, thirty-eight, door—and then we begin our count anew. The first few times we play this game, Caliban simply echoes me. He understands the idea of the counting game, but he has not memorized the names of numbers beyond seven yet. That is all I am thinking about when he hesitates on the fourth or fifth time, his hand splayed on the weathered planks, and questions the notion of the word. "Door?"

"Yes." I knock on the wood. "Door."

"Door." Before I can think to stop him, Caliban gives the handle an experimental tug.

Both of us freeze when the door creaks ajar. For the space of a heartbeat, I curse my folly. In all the hours I've spent with Caliban, it has never occurred to him to try the door in my presence, never occurred to him that it might prove yielding. I put too much trust in his ignorance.

Caliban's eyes take on a wild shine. He yanks at the door, looking much like Oriana used to look when she'd slipped her tether and was preparing to bolt.

"No!" I catch his arm. "You mustn't!" He shakes me off, and I grab at him again with both hands. This time, he bares his teeth at me and shoves me away. I stumble backward and fall. With a sharp yelp of agony, Caliban falls too, his muscles twitching and cramping.

Papa's spell has been invoked.

"Bad!" Caliban moans, curling onto his side. "Bad, bad, bad! Caliban is bad! Caliban is sorry!"

"No, no!" My heart feels like it is beating in my throat. "It's not your fault! It's my fault!" I scramble to his side and tug at him, praying I can shift him enough to close the door before Papa hears, but he is too heavy for me to move. "Caliban is good! *Miranda* is bad."

"No!" He curls into a tighter ball.

"Yes!" Desperate, I manage to roll him out of the way and shove the door closed. I sit down hard beside him and stroke his flinching skin. "Miranda is sorry," I whisper. "I am sorry. I know you weren't trying to hurt me."

Caliban grits his teeth against the pain and hisses, but he doesn't howl. "Master is come?"

I look up toward the gallery. "No."

He shudders. "Good."

It is then that I realize Caliban is trying to protect me from Papa's anger, and I curse myself twice over for my carelessness, but there is nothing I can do save sit with him until the spasms cease, apologizing softly.

Although it feels like an act of disloyalty, I do not tell Papa what happened.

When I return to Caliban's cell the next day, I am careful to keep myself between him and the door, frightened that he will make another attempt, but he is listless and obedient that day and in the days that follow, taking little interest in our lessons. It seems that having had an unexpected hope snatched away has caused him to lose all semblance of hope, and I begin to worry about him.

Papa does, too.

"How does our wild boy's tally stand, child?" he asks me. "Has it been a full unbroken month of good behavior yet?"

I shake my head. "Twenty-four days."

He frowns in thought. "Does it seem to you that he has a melancholic aspect of late?"

"Yes, Papa."

"Well, it seems that the lad's applied himself assiduously to your lessons, and I'd not see him languish for lack of reward." Papa nods to himself. "Yes, I think it meet. Do you agree?"

I am unsure I hear him aright. "Do you mean to let him out of his cell? Truly, Papa?"

Papa smiles at me, one of those rare smiles that breaks over his face like dawn, transforming its sternness. "I do."

I imagine that Caliban will react to his first taste of freedom with wild leaps and bounds of joy, but I am wrong. He is fearful and uncertain, as though he is afraid this, too, will be taken from him as unexpectedly as it was granted.

Papa chose the cypress garden for our outing, as it is the only one with no gaps in the walls; although there is no gate at either end of it and I am quite sure Caliban could scale the rugged blocks as handily as a lizard if he wished.

He does not, though. He hunches and shuffles along the path between the tall green cypress trees, squinting his eyes tightly against the bright sunlight. It was always dim in the bottom of his cell where the sun's rays could not reach. I try to think how long it has been since Papa summoned him.

A long time.

"All is well, lad." Papa lays a soothing hand on Caliban's head. "There's no cause for fear."

Caliban sighs as if in grave doubt.

And yet, bit by bit, the fear begins to drain from him. His tightly hunched shoulders ease. His spine unbends. He lifts his head and begins to look about the garden, his nostrils twitching. There is a good deal to see and smell—the cypresses, the lemon and orange trees with tart fruit ripening on their branches, beds of myrtle and lavender, jasmine on the vine. Oh, and there are swallows darting overhead on swift wings in pursuit of small insects, and soft, murmuring calls from other birds roosting in the trees, and the sound of water splashing in a fountain.

"*Sun*." Caliban utters the word as though it were a prayer. There are tears in his eyes. "Thank you, Master."

Papa inclines his head. "You are welcome."

I *should* be glad—and yet I am not, not wholly.

It is as though there are two Mirandas sharing the same skin. One is proud and grateful that Caliban has learned so well that he does not even attempt to flee. The other wishes that he would.

It is a wicked thought, a disloyal, disobedient, and *sinful* thought; and yet it is there nonetheless.

Papa claps Caliban's shoulder. "Do you continue to earn my trust, lad, one day mayhap you shall be free to roam at will."

"Free." Caliban echoes him, and although I have not taught him the word, he seems to find meaning in it. "Free."

SEVEN

CALIBAN

Grass, sky, birds.

Grass is green. Sky is blue. Birds fly.

Birds fly in the blue sky.

Birds are free. Free is sun and sky and grass every day. Free is no walls. Yes, please. Yes, thank you.

Caliban is good.

Trees, flowers, bees. Bees buzz-bizz-buzz-bizz. Bees are free. Trees have leaves. Flowers have leaves.

Lizards.

Lizzzzzards.

Caliban counts trees. Miranda and Caliban count trees. Miranda and Caliban count trees and birds and bees.

One-two-three-four-five-six-seven . . .

Many, yes.

Many-many-many.

Miranda is glad.

Master is glad. Glad Master is good.

I am good. Caliban is good. I am Caliban. *I* am good every day. *I* am good on the green grass. *I* am good in the blue sky. *I* am good under the trees.

One-two-three-four-five-six-seven . . .

Caliban counts days.

EIGHT

MIRANDA

As the weeks pass, Caliban's disposition improves on the daily doses of freedom that Papa allots him.

Our lessons grow increasingly productive now that there is more of the world to explore. Under Papa's watchful eye, Caliban and I occupy ourselves gainfully, gathering nuts and firewood against the coming winter's chill.

And Caliban *is* good almost every day; good and obedient and helpful. He learns words such as *what* and *where* and *how* and *why*, and begins to ask questions. Papa encourages him in it, except for when he is tired and impatient, and does not wish to be plagued with questions, some of which have no sensible answers.

I think surely that Papa will relent any day and grant Caliban a greater measure of trust and allow him his freedom, but no. Every night, Caliban is locked in his cell, until I begin to wonder what further sign of obedience Papa is waiting for.

One morning, Papa tells me.

He commences by announcing that on this day, I have reached seven years of age, and marks the occasion with a gift—a silver casket containing sewing implements: needles and a pair of shears and precious hanks of colorful thread. "It is time you began learning arts suited to a young lady," he says to me.

It is the most beautiful thing I have ever seen. Overwhelmed, I clutch it to my chest. "Papa! Wherever did it come from?"

He smiles indulgently at me. "Oh, I've had it in my possession all along, child. I was merely waiting for the right time."

"I don't know how to use it," I say humbly.

"You'll learn," he says. "You know how to tie a knot, and I daresay I can manage to show you a simple stitch."

I beam at him. "Thank you, Papa!"

Papa inclines his head. "You are welcome." His tone grows serious. "There is another matter I wish to discuss with you, Miranda."

I set the casket aside and pay him close heed. "Yes, Papa?"

He hesitates. "The spirit in the pine tree . . . I believe it was confined therein by Caliban's mother."

I stare at him in disbelief. "Caliban's *mother*?"

Papa strokes his beard. "It is a difficult matter to discuss with one of your tender years and sensibilities, but if I am right, yes. Some dozen years past, I recall hearing tales of the witch Sycorax, who was banished from Algiers for practicing sorcery of the darkest nature. Sailors armed with the strongest of talismans against her charms brought her to a deserted isle and there abandoned her." He pauses. "It is said that she was with child at the time."

"Caliban?" I whisper. "But what happened to his mother, then? And who was his father?"

Papa hesitates again, then shakes his head. "If it was indeed she, and let us postulate that it is so, the witch Sycorax perished years ago, leaving her young son, our wild lad, to fend for himself. Hence, his reversion to a savage state. As to the latter, I will not sully your ears with crude and idle speculation." Seeing a question forming on my lips, he holds up one finger for silence. "She kept a journal of her workings written in a cypher. I have spent countless hours unlocking its secrets, including the means by which she bound the spirit Ariel."

"Ariel," I murmur to myself. So the spirit in the pine tree has a name. It is a pleasant-sounding name for a being whose wails and moans make my skin creep with fear.

"Unfortunately, there is a piece of the puzzle lacking," Papa continues. His mouth draws into a frown. "The witch Sycorax served a demonic and unholy master, and it is in *his* name that she bound the noble spirit. And that name, I fear, she dared not set down in writing, not even in cypher."

I follow his thoughts. "Do you think Caliban knows it, Papa?"

"I think it is possible," he says. "If I guess rightly, he would have had some four years of age when she passed. He knew his own name; I suspect he was possessed of language ere it was lost to him. And it is likely that his mother would have raised him to worship the same foul deity."

I shudder, but I am already thinking. "It will not be an easy question to pose him."

"Yes." Papa gives me a brief nod of approval. "It is a more complex notion than our wild boy can yet parse. But it is toward that end that I wish you to begin working. Therefore, today we will visit the great pine, and I will put the question to Caliban."

My brows knit in distress. "Forgive me, Papa, but I fear he will not understand it. Not yet."

"Did I just not say that very thing?" Papa's tone takes on an edge of impatience. "Pay heed, child. Your duty is to shape Caliban's lessons in such a way that he *does* come to understand the question; and understands, too, that the price of his freedom is the answer I seek. Do *you* understand?"

Lowering my gaze, I study the rough-hewn wood of the kitchen table. Who built it, I wonder? The long-ago Moors? The witch Sycorax? Or did Papa build it himself?

"Miranda."

An unexpected jolt of pain seizes my limbs. I draw in a sharp breath, blink back tears, and lift my gaze to meet Papa's. His hand is closed around the amulet that bears a lock of my hair. "Yes, Papa?"

His grip eases. "Do you understand?"

"Yes, Papa." I take a longer, slower breath. "I do, and I will do my best to make Caliban understand, too. Only . . . only why is it so important to free this spirit?" I shiver. "It frightens me."

"Ah." Papa's expression softens. "Be not afraid, lass. The spirit does but inveigh against its confinement, much as our wild lad did in the early days of his tenure here. But it is of a higher order of beings, as far above the humble elementals as the thrones and dominions are above the angels. Although it rebelled against Sycorax's base demands, I believe it will serve a godly master with grace and goodwill." He rises from the table. "Enough. Let us be about the business at hand."

I stow the sewing casket in my chamber. My joy at the unexpected gift is tempered by uneasiness. I thought Papa meant to reward Caliban with his freedom if he continued to behave gently, and I have all but promised him as much. What if Caliban doesn't *know* the answer?

It seems unfair, and I still do not understand why freeing this spirit, this Ariel, is so important. To serve Papa, yes; but to what end?

There is so much Papa does not tell me.

I remind myself that he wants only to protect me, and that it is churlish and disloyal to question him.

After all, what if *Papa* were to perish, leaving me to fend for myself? The mere thought of it makes my mouth go dry with fear. At least I would not be wholly alone, as poor Caliban was—oh, the thought of it makes my heart ache!—but what would the two of us do without Papa? I do not even know how to tend the fire in the hearth, and if it were to go out, I would not know how to ignite it anew. All the elemental spirits would desert us; no more gnomes to till the gardens, no more sylphs to drive eddies of dust from the palace floors, no more cavorting undines to fill our wells with cool, clear water and make the sparkling fountains flow.

It would not be long, I think, before I was well nigh as savage as Caliban, covered in filth and gnawing on raw fish.

Thinking such things, I am ashamed of myself and filled with gratitude for Papa and all that he does.

The great pine's bark is shaggy and rough, and its long needles are dark green. Massive branches reach out from its trunk. The flagstones surrounding the square of bare soil at its base are cracked and tilted at odd angles, lifted by the force of its roots—or mayhap by the spirit's struggle. There are fallen needles and pinecones scattered over the flagstones. Caliban has no more liking for this pine tree and its captive than I do, and we have not dared venture beneath the shadow of its limbs on our foraging forays. Whenever we have cause to pass through the gates into the front courtyard, we give it a wide berth, and Papa has never objected.

Today, though, he leads us straight to it.

The needles rustle at our approach and the spirit lets out a low moan. Caliban whines in response, hanging back. Papa gives him a stern look.

"All is well," I say in an encouraging tone, marching up to the verge of the tree's shadow. "See?"

"Caliban." Papa beckons to him. "Tell me, do you know this spirit?" He gestures to the tree. "This *Ariel*?"

The spirit lets out a shriek, and I flinch. Near the top of the tree, high overhead, a knotty seam mars the trunk, as though its wooden flesh was split asunder and scarred as it knitted.

"Ar-i-el." Caliban's upper lip curls. "Ar-i-el. *Ariel*. Yes, Master."

"Good." Papa nods. "Very good. Caliban . . . do you remember your mother?" He pauses. "*Sycorax*?" Caliban gazes at him without understanding, and he tries several other words. "*Mitera? Mana? Manoula?*"

Caliban responds to none of them.

"Curious." Papa frowns in thought. "The witch's cypher was based on Greek, which leads me to suspect that was her native tongue, but the lad recognizes none of the terms for mother. Still, if she was practicing her dark arts in Algiers for many years . . . perhaps the script in which she kept her journal was the only written language known to her. Perhaps it is not the tongue she was accustomed to speaking." He tries another word. "*Umm?*"

I do not know the word; but this time it seems Caliban does. He blinks rapidly several times, his mouth opening and closing. "Umm." He croons the word, then shivers and shakes himself. "Umm."

"It is the Moorish word for mother," Papa murmurs to me. "'Tis a pity I know little of their tongue, for I suspect I have guessed rightly."

I think so, too.

"Caliban." Papa stoops before him, going to one knee so that their gazes might be on a level. "Umm imprisoned Ariel in the tree. I wish to free him." He touches his chest. "Master free Ariel."

"No, Master." Caliban's expression has turned stubborn. "No!"

"I believe there is a word locked in your memory, lad." Papa touches Caliban's brow with one finger. "It is the name of the unholy deity that Umm worshipped and taught you to worship in turn. It is the name with which she bound the spirit Ariel into captivity. You have but to recollect the name and tell me, and you shall have your freedom." Straightening, he smiles and holds out his arms. "When Ariel is free, Caliban is free!"

The last part, Caliban understands. "Why?" he spits, glowering. "Why, Master? Ariel is *bad*."

The spirit groans.

I think about the sewing casket Papa gave me this morning. It seems to me that I remember the ladies with the soft hands and soft cheeks sewing in the chambers of the stone house where pictures hung on the walls, silver needles darting and flashing, intricate patterns of embroidery growing slowly in their wake. Papa said he could show me a simple stitch; mayhap he is right, and I could teach myself more. If he would permit me to study one of his robes with fine embroidery at the hem, mayhap I might determine how it was done.

Although that is a foolish dream; 'twould be better were I to learn how to use whatever fabric remains to us to cut and sew simple garments. I know only that I should like to have been given a day, one day, to enjoy my unexpected gift; to examine the hanks of colorful thread one by one, to test the edges of the shears and the sharpness of the needles.

It would have made a fine new lesson for Caliban, too. Instead, he is being set a task that may be impossible to accomplish.

". . . must learn to trust Master," Papa is saying sternly to him. Caliban wears a sullen look.

"Papa," I say when he has finished. "Is it not possible that the name you seek might be found in one of your books?" Although I have only caught an accidental glimpse, I know Papa has a great many books in his sanctum. One day when I am grown, he says I may be allowed to handle some of them.

"Do you imagine I have not scoured their pages, child?" Papa says, but his voice is mild. "Do you suppose I have not tried invoking the names of demonic spirits known to the magi of yore in my attempts to free the spirit?"

"No," I murmur.

"The witch guarded her secrets closely, most especially the name of whatever foul deity she served." Papa raps his knuckles lightly on Caliban's head, and there is a measure of affection in the gesture. "If it is to be found anywhere, it is within the confines of her son's thick skull."

Caliban grunts.

I sigh, thinking what a difficult chore it will be to make him understand what is being asked of him.

"Miranda." Papa's gaze is at once stern and bright, like the sun's rays breaking through clouds far out to sea. "Your assistance in this matter is vital. There is a reason for everything I do, and one day when you are older, I promise, I will reveal the full scope of all that my plans encompass. Today I merely ask that you have a measure of the faith in yourself that *I* have in you."

Once again, I am ashamed. "Yes, Papa."

He smiles at me. "Very well."

We retreat from the outer courtyard, abandoning the pine tree and its captive spirit—*Ariel.*

In a generous gesture, Papa determines that Caliban and I might be allowed to conduct our lessons outside his cell without supervision, so long as we do not leave the palace grounds.

At least it is something, I think.

And I set about the task of attempting to explain the notion of God to the witch's son.

NINE

CALIBAN

God is big.

God is in the sky.

God is bigger than Caliban and Master and Miranda; God is bigger than grass and trees. God is bigger than the sun and moon.

Please, God is to pray. Thank you, God is to pray.

What is God? God is Master's Master. God is Miranda's Master. God is everyone's Master.

Why is God? God makes everything.

Miranda and Caliban count chickens. One . . . two . . . three . . . four big hens, then one . . . two . . . three.

Now Nunzia is not. Nunzia is *dead*.

We eat Nunzia. Nunzia is good. Nunzia is in the sky with God.

We count little hens. One . . . two . . . three . . . four . . . five little hens. Elisabetta is the little hens' mother. Claudio is a rooster. Claudio is the little hens' father.

Big hens make eggs. Eggs make little hens. God makes everything.

Master is Miranda's father.

Umm is Caliban's mother.

Umm is not. Umm is *dead*.

(I know.)

Is Umm in the sky with God? No. Umm is bad. Umm makes Ariel not free in the tree. Umm does not pray to God. Umm says please and thank you to a bad name.

What is the name?

It is a bad name.

Why?

Because it is not God.

Why is God good?

Because God is God.

To know a thing from yesterday and yesterday and yesterday is to *remember*.

I remember yesterday.

I remember Umm. I remember Ariel. Umm is good and bad. Ariel is good and bad.

Bad, bad, bad.

Master says no, Ariel is good. Master is good and bad.

I am good. I find nuts. I find nuts and dates and olives. I find sticks for the fire and fishes to eat.

I remember yesterday and yesterday and yesterday.

(I find Umm. Umm is dead.)

Miranda is good. Miranda has white thread and black thread and red thread and green thread and blue thread and yellow thread.

Where is Miranda's mother?

Where is Caliban's father?

Miranda says, I do not know. Miranda says, what is the bad name?

I am bad.

I do not want to say.

I say, I do not know.

TEN

MIRANDA

Winter is long and dull and grey, and even though it never gets truly cold on the isle, there is a damp chill that never seems to go away. The kitchen with its cozy hearth is the only place to escape it. In the past, I would spend most of my waking hours there, doing such chores or lessons as Papa set me.

This winter is different. Despite its discomforts, it is the finest one I remember. Under Papa's tutelage, I graduate from forming the alphabet to writing entire words and then full sentences on my slate, feeling my mind stretch and grow in the process.

But most of all, it is good, oh, so very good, not to be alone and lonely! And now I am a teacher, too.

'Tis true that there are days when I despair of teaching Caliban to understand the notion of *God*—a notion I cannot remember not knowing and struggle to explain—but he makes great progress in other things. With every week that passes, it grows easier to converse with him.

It is strange to think that Caliban was a young child in this palace just as I was. I have known him only as a part of the isle's very landscape, as much as the rocks and trees and sea, and never imagined it had been otherwise. Now I understand why he did not marvel at the palace when first Papa summoned him. It was already familiar to him; indeed, like as not he was born in it. He learned to crawl in its empty halls and played in its gardens while his mother Sycorax practiced her dark arts in the very sanctum that now belongs to my father, recording the results in a cypher.

Why did he leave the palace, I wonder? Did he flee upon his mother's death? Or was it something else that caused him to leave its shelter? If it is true that Papa and I did not always live on the isle, I wonder, I wonder . . . could it be that he fled in the face of our arrival?

Where did he dwell for all that time? How did the witch Sycorax die? And how is it that Papa is so very certain that she perished years ago?

There are so many questions.

When Papa decides Nunzia is no longer laying well enough and must be sacrificed for our supper it grieves me, though not as deeply as the loss of my poor sweet Bianca. Papa praises me for the maturation of my sensibilities, and I use the sad occasion to speak to Caliban of death.

It seems to me that he understands; and understands, too, when I explain to him that his Umm is dead. This does not seem to surprise him—but after I tell him that Umm is not in the sky with God, he does not wish to speak further of her. Not of his mother, not of the spirit Ariel, not of the bad name.

If I press him, he becomes sullen. And so I press gently and with care, hoping to tease the name out of his memories without disturbing the peace of our household.

It is so hard to know how much Caliban remembers! I find myself wondering not only what he might tell me of his past when he is better able to do so, but if there is aught he might tell me of *my* past.

It is a dangerous and thrilling thought, but I dare not ask.

So instead we speak of God and trees and hens and nuts and fish and all manner of things beneath the sun.

Papa is patient throughout the long months of winter, content not to rush matters. I should like to think it is wholly due to kindness, but I suspect it is also true that the stars are not yet favorable for an endeavor such as freeing the spirit Ariel. Whatever the cause, Papa continues to be generous. He even grants Caliban and me permission to forage farther afield to gather firewood and fill our larder with whatever we might find when our stores begin to dwindle.

Airy sylphs attend us on our journeys, but they do nothing to trouble us. Those are my favorite times, when I need not cudgel my wits about God and memory, and Caliban is in fine spirits.

Outside the palace grounds, our roles are changed. Caliban knows all the best places to forage, and he is fast and deft and sure. We do not venture so far as the seashore, which Papa has forbidden, but Caliban scampers up the ridged trunks of date palms as quick as thought, throwing down handfuls of fruits, their flesh shriveled but still sweet. I laugh and fill the apron of my robe until it sags under the weight; and Caliban laughs too, eyes bright with pride. He climbs olive trees too, shaking their limbs until they discharge their overripe bounty.

Oh, and there are fish, too! Heedless of the chill waters, Caliban wades in the swift stream that descends from the mountains and catches fish with his bare hands, tossing them to the banks where they flop halfheartedly, sluggish with cold. I pick them up and put them in a pail, their silver scales shining.

When we bring home our spoils, Papa praises us. At night, he locks Caliban into his cell, but Caliban does not seem to mind so much. I think mayhap he is grateful for the shelter during these winter months.

On the days when the driving rain keeps us indoors, if there are no other chores to do, I practice sewing on scraps of fabric. I gloat over the rich colors of the thread, and Caliban gloats with me.

I wish winter would never end.

It does, though.

I do not know when I begin to suspect Caliban is not being wholly truthful with me. It does not come all at once, but creeps into my thoughts. As the days grow longer, he becomes restless; reluctant to return from our ventures, chafing at being confined to his cell at night. When we are afield, I sometimes think that if he did not fear Papa's magic, he would flee. I often find him glancing toward the rocky crags northwest of the palace, a yearning look on his features; but when at last I ask him what lies yonder, he shakes his head and does not answer.

"Is it your home?" I press him. "Is it where you lived before Papa summoned you to the palace? Is it where you slept and took shelter?"

He affects not to understand. "I do not know."

I do not wish to disbelieve him, and yet more and more, I do.

Caliban knows more than he is saying; and if that is true of one thing, I fear it may be true of others.

And I wish, oh, I wish that Papa would simply change his mind about freeing the spirit Ariel; that he might grant Caliban his freedom instead, and the three of us might live peacefully together as we did during the winter months.

But no, Papa will not hear of it. I dread the day he loses patience and asks after Caliban's progress.

Like spring, that, too comes nonetheless.

I do not wish to confess my suspicions to Papa, but in the end, I do. The guilt I feel at betraying Caliban is nothing to the guilt I would feel were I to deliberately deceive Papa.

Papa listens without comment until I have finished. "I fear that I have been too lenient," he muses. "I've given the lad too loose a rein, trusting that his fledgling sense of reason would prevail in this matter, but it seems a greater incentive is required." He lowers both hands onto the kitchen table with a decisive thump, and the weathered wood rattles. "Well and so. 'Tis time to tighten the reins."

My stomach clenches. "What do you mean to do, Papa?"

He gives me a grim smile. "You shall hear it on the morrow."

And so I do.

No matter what his mood the previous night, Caliban leaps up eagerly every morning when his cell is unlocked, ready to embrace the day's measure of sunlight and freedom. Today is no different; not at first, not until Papa extends one hand palm outward in a forbidding gesture.

"No," Papa says. His voice is far colder than winter's worst chill. Caliban halts and cocks his head in confusion, glancing at me. I look away. "You've been dishonest with us, lad. You *do* know the name I seek, do you not?"

When Caliban does not answer, I steal a glance at him and see a familiar sullen look settle over his features.

Papa will have none of it. "Enough with your sulks and grumbles!" He raises his voice to a roar, and Caliban flinches in fear. "Did I not bring you into our home? Have I not bathed and clothed you, fed and sheltered you? Have my daughter and I not taught you the rudiments of language? Have we not transformed you from a filthy, savage beast crawling on all fours to something that bears the semblance of a man, walking upright and capable of rational thought?"

"Please, Master!" Caliban cowers on the floor of his cell, hunkered low with arms wrapped around his head, understanding one word in ten. "Caliban is sorry!" he pleads. "Caliban is good!"

"I have no interest in cringing obsequiousness," Papa says coldly. "You have abused my generosity. You have abused the patience and tender heart of my daughter Miranda, who has shown you nothing but kindness. Is this how you reward her for it? With lies and deception?"

He awaits an answer, but none is forthcoming. Caliban rocks on his haunches and keens in fear, and my heart shrinks in my chest to see all his progress undone. "Caliban," I whisper. "Listen to Master! Please, listen."

Papa gives me a sharp glance. "I'll handle this, lass." He turns his attention back to Caliban. "You have three days to think on the matter." He holds up three fingers. "Three days in your cell. You shall have water, but no food. At the end of three days, I will ask you to tell me the name of the dark deity that your mother Umm worshipped. Do you understand?"

For a long moment, Caliban remains silent.

I am fairly quivering with the desire to put the question to him in simpler words, words I know he will understand, but Papa lays a firm hand on my shoulder and stills me.

At last, Caliban unwinds his arms from his head and nods without raising his gaze. "Master wants the bad name."

"Ah, so our wild lad does understand!" There is a note of grim satisfaction in Papa's tone. "You have three days." With that, Papa steers me out of Caliban's cell. He locks the door behind us and pockets the key. "You are to have no communication with him during this time, Miranda," he says sternly. "None. His cell and the gallery above it are forbidden to you. Do *you* understand?"

"Yes, Papa," I murmur.

"Good lass." He pats my head. "I know it seems harsh, but I promise you, it is a kindness. If this tendency toward surliness and deceit were to go unchecked, it would fester in him. Speech alone does not serve to make us civilized, nor clothing, nor courtesies; nay, not even reason. It is a matter of virtues—the virtues of honesty, of loyalty, of integrity, of obedience to a higher order. These are the qualities I yet hope to instill in Caliban, although I fear that hope dwindles."

It is a long three days.

I think about what Papa said. In truth, I am angry at Caliban. I am angry at him for lying to me. Did he think I would not suspect, when I have come to know him so well? Did he think of me at all?

Mayhap it is asking too much to wonder such a thing, for I doubt Caliban understands the nature of *lying*. It is not a thing we have discussed, and it is unfair to blame him for not knowing things that no one has taught him.

Still, I cannot help it. I am angry.

And I am lonely, all the more so for having known companionship these many months. Papa spends the days in his sanctum as always, immersed in his studies. I go about my chores, though I do not forage afield. Without Caliban's guidance, I do not know where to find the spring mushrooms that are beginning to sprout. I cannot climb trees. I cannot catch fish. I milk listless Oriana and gather eggs from the cote and greens from the garden.

Caliban in his cell is silent.

By the second day, my anger has given way to sympathy. He must be hungry, but he neither pleads nor complains nor rages.

I wonder what he is thinking.

And then I begin to wonder what Papa will do if Caliban refuses to tell him the name at the end of three days, and I begin to fear, because I am quite sure I know: Papa will work a deeper spell of binding on him.

At supper on the evening of the third day, Papa confirms it. "If it comes to it, mayhap it is for the best, child," he says gently to me. "I know you're fond of the lad, and he's made great strides under your tutelage, but I fear there may be a limit to how far he might progress. It is a surety that there is a limit to the amount of time I can wait on his willing obedience. The day is fast approaching when the stars will be favorable to make an attempt to free the spirit Ariel. Caliban would still be a useful servant," he adds. "There is no reason that should change."

I think of Oriana. "He would not be the same, though."

"No."

It seems cruel when I have worked so hard, and made progress that even Papa praises, to return to the very place we began. "But you won't do it if Caliban is good, will you?" I ask. "If Caliban tells you the name, you'll grant him his freedom?" Papa hesitates, and tears prick my eyes. "You promised!"

Papa's expression turns stern. "No, lass. The offer was made in the assumption that Caliban would obey gladly once he understood, not engage in deception and sullen evasion."

"*I* took it to be a promise," I whisper.

"Ah, Miranda!" All at once, Papa's expression softens into something more complicated, filled with sorrow and regret. "Sweet child, you are the very angel of my better nature, descended straight from the Empyrean. You should not have to plead for the companionship of this poor rough brute of a boy. You should have maids of your—" He halts and shakes his head. "No mind. What's done is done, and the time to remedy it lies far in the offing. Very well. If Caliban obeys on the morrow and divulges the name, I shall grant him his freedom." He raises one finger. "However, if he fails to obey, I shall be left with no choice."

"I understand, Papa." I dash at my tears. "Must it . . . must it ever be thus? Shall he forever be ruled by this threat?"

"I doubt that the threat of losing his reason is one our wild lad understands," Papa says dryly. "'Tis your tender heart begs an answer." I look down at the table and say nothing, feeling the weight of Papa's gaze upon me. "Does it truly mean so much to you, child?"

"It is only that I am weary of being fearful." I dare a swift upward glance. "And I have worked so very hard."

"Very well." Papa nods. "I shall make you this promise, Miranda. If tomorrow's proceedings result in my freeing the spirit Ariel at such a time when the heavens are propitious, I give you my word that Caliban's will—poor surly, grudging thing that it may be—shall henceforth remain his own."

A sense of gratitude fills me like sunlight. "Do you mean it?"

"I have said it, have I not?" Papa says, but his voice is mild. "I pray you do not doubt my word when I give it. Mind you, it does not mean that bad behavior will not be punished."

"No," I agree. "Of course not."

He lifts one finger again. "And it is contingent on the spirit Ariel gaining its freedom. Do I make my meaning clear?"

"Yes, Papa." I hate that wailing spirit in the pine tree. I wish Papa cared half as much for me as he does for this Ariel. "As clear as day."

As if to spite me, the spirit Ariel keeps up a terrible din that night. I lie awake with my hands pressed over my ears in an effort to shut it out. I think of Caliban alone in his cell, his belly gripped with hunger. I think about all that is at stake on the morrow.

Outside the moon climbs high overhead and bright moonlight spills into my chamber, inching across the tiled floor. Hour by hour, I watch it.

And even though I *am* a little angry still at Caliban, I cannot bear the thought of seeing him like Oriana. I cannot bear the thought of losing his companionship, I cannot bear the thought of being alone again. I cannot bear the thought of Papa's promise being squandered.

At last I rise from my sleepless pallet. The spring night is cool and the moonlit tiles are cold beneath my bare feet. Caliban's cell and the gallery above it are forbidden to me, so I steal into the garden outside my chamber and through the unlocked gate.

In daylight, I should have no trouble making my way across the palace grounds to Caliban's cell, but everything is strange and unfamiliar in the bright moonlight. All the sharp-edged shadows point the wrong direction. I get turned about in the cypress garden, and wander into the next garden with its maze of hedges by mistake.

For a moment I panic. My heartbeat quickens and I blunder into the unruly evergreen bushes, my robe snagging on their prickly branches. I begin to fear I shall have to wait until dawn to find my way out, and that Papa will know.

I shall be punished for it.

And Caliban . . . I fear he may suffer for my disobedience.

Closing my eyes, I offer a prayer to the moon. "May God bless you, O Blessed Lady Moon," I whisper. "Fortunate one, cold and lovely and shining, I beg you to guide my steps!"

The act of prayer calms me. The gracious Lady Moon helped Papa summon Caliban. Surely she will help guide me to him. When I open my eyes, the silvery light seems kinder and I remember that I have wandered this maze a hundred times, and it holds no mysteries for me. I have made a game of it to teach Caliban directions. I see moonlight glinting on the dome of the cunning little temple that lies at the heart of the maze, and I know where I am, only two turns within the northern entrance. I begin to count the turns to the southern exit: Left, left, right, left, left, left, right, left, right, right.

Even so, it is a relief when I stumble free of it at last and backtrack to my destination.

There is no gate into the little garden outside Caliban's cell, but there are gaps in the walls. I clamber over one of them, awkward in my robes, bruising my shins on the rough outcroppings of stone. I think ruefully of the days when I would catch glimpses of Caliban crouching on the walls of my own chamber-garden, and I wish I had his gift for leaping and climbing.

To be sure, Caliban will catch no such glimpse of me tonight. The entrance to his chamber remains blocked; but there are chinks between the great squares of stone that block it. I creep across the garden, holding the skirts of my robe so that they do not trail in the cold dew, and find such a chink.

You are to have no communication with him during this time, Miranda.

That is what Papa said.

I am disobeying him.

As Caliban would say, I am bad.

But mayhap . . . mayhap if it is only me that speaks, it cannot be considered true communication?

I put my lips to a narrow opening in the stone blocks and call out softly. "Caliban? Caliban, can you hear me?" I wait for a moment until I think I hear the faint sound of movement inside his cell. "Caliban, it's me, Miranda. Listen and say nothing." Thinking, I choose my words with care. "I am sorry, but you must tell Papa the bad name tomorrow, Caliban." My heart feels squeezed in my chest. "You must! For one way or another, he will have it from you. And if you do not tell him willingly . . ."

Oh, I wish I could see him, to judge how much he understands! I may have said too much already.

Inside there is only silence; but that is what I asked of him.

"Please, Caliban," I whisper into the dark chink between the stone. There are tears in my voice. "Please? If you will not do it for yourself, do it for me. Do it because I beg you. Just tell Papa—Master—the name."

Silence.

A part of me wants to shout to the heavens, wants to pound upon the stone with my fists. It wants to be certain that Caliban has been roused and has heard me; to hear him respond and know he understood. It is disobedient and brave, that part of me. But it is also the smaller part of me.

The greater part of me has dared as much as it might for one night.

Gathering up my robes, I steal back to my chamber where I lie sleepless and await the dawn.

ELEVEN

CALIBAN

What is a lie?

I think, I think . . . to lie is to say a thing that is not. Or to say a thing is when it is not.

To say, *I do not know,* when I do know.

That is a lie.

A lie is bad.

Caliban is bad.

But, but, but, but, but . . . why? *Why* is it bad? Because Master says it is bad? But it is a bad thing to say the name, too.

I do not want to say it.

But I want to be free. I want sun and sky and grass.

I want Miranda.

I do not want to be alone. I am *angry.* I do not want to be angry. Oh, but I am.

You shall have three days, Master says. You shall have water, but no food, Master says.

Ha!

Master lies.

There are lizards; lovely little lizzy-lizards, one, two, three. Lizards are green. Little green lizards on the walls, creepity, creepity, skritch, skritch, skritch. Lizards are fast but I am faster. I jump and climb and catch them. Blood goes squish, squish and little bones go crunch, crunch, crunch in my teeth.

But one day is long.

Two days is longer.

I make marks on the wall. One day, two days. Where is Miranda?

Three days.

No lizards today. Today I am hungry. Today my belly hurts. I drink water. Today is a very, very long time.

At night Miranda comes. I am sleeping, but I hear her voice and I wake. Miranda's voice comes from the rocks. I go to the rocks and put my hands and face against them. Miranda talks through the rocks and says, listen and say nothing.

I am good.

I say nothing.

Miranda says, I am sorry. Miranda says, you must tell Master the bad name tomorrow. I listen.

Miranda says, please. Her voice is afraid and sad. *Please, Caliban. Please.*

I listen.

Miranda goes away.

The moon is in the window. I look at it and think. The moon is high and round and bright.

The moon is good.

I am not angry. I am sad, too. Why? Because Miranda is sad.

Because my belly hurts. The name is like a stone in my belly. Ariel is in the pine tree. Ariel is not nice, but Ariel wants to be free. I want to be free, too. I do not want to be hungry. I do not want Miranda to be afraid and sad.

The moon goes away, and I am alone in the dark.

I do not sleep.

In the morning, Master comes and opens the door. Miranda is beside him. She is little and he is big. Miranda's eyes are red.

Well, Master says, using his deep voice. Have you something this time to something something?

I look at him.

He looks at me.

Is a name bad because Master says it is bad? Is God good because Master says God is good?

I do not know.

I am tired and hungry. Miranda is sad and afraid. The name that is like a stone in my belly is heavy.

Master waits.

I say the name: "Setebos."

TWELVE

MIRANDA

"Setebos." Papa echoes Caliban in a thoughtful tone. I do not like the sound of the word. There is a kind of darkness to it that gives me a feeling like reaching under a rotten log crawling with grubs. But Papa is pleased, and smiles at Caliban. "That wasn't so difficult, was it, lad?"

Caliban says nothing. His shoulders are hunched and his eyes are dark and watchful beneath the coarse hair that falls over them, and I cannot tell what he is thinking. It seems to me that something has changed in him, but I do not know what. There is a stillness to him that was not there before.

If it is so, Papa does not notice. His face has a faraway look, and I know that in his thoughts, he is already in his sanctum, poring over his books of magic. "Well done, lad," he says absently. "Miranda, see that he's fed."

"Yes, Papa," I say.

In the kitchen, Caliban sits at the table and eats journey-cakes and boiled eggs that I peel for him. There is a silence between us that feels strange, but I do not know how to breach it.

Does he understand that he lied to me?

Does he know that I betrayed him to Papa for doing so?

I do not know.

"What shall Caliban and Miranda do today?" I say at last, falling back on familiar ground. "Shall we gather mushrooms? Catch fish?"

"Mussshhrooms, yes." Caliban rolls the word around in his mouth as though he is taking pleasure in the taste of it. "Now is good for mussshhrooms."

It restores a measure of ease between us.

I fetch a cloth bag that I have sewn out of the remnants of robes that Papa cut down to size for me, with a long strap that I might sling over my shoulder, and Caliban and I set out to forage.

I think that we will go to the pine woods to the south where Caliban has found mushrooms flourishing in hidden places in the damp pine mast before, but he heads northwest toward the rocky crags above the palace. He sets a quick pace and I struggle to keep up.

Airy sylphs trail after us, drifting effortlessly on the spring breeze.

"Caliban?" I am half breathless. "Where are we going?"

He slows. "A place."

"Is it *your* place?"

When I asked before, he pretended not to understand, but today is different. He nods. "Yes."

It is a long, hard climb; not for Caliban, who clambers agilely over the rocks using hands and feet alike, but for me. The rocks are dark and jagged. Caliban pauses often to help me, tugging me by the hand. Near the top, there is a cave, tucked away on the leeside of the wind. It smells of old bones and rotting fruit, both of which are strewn about the floor of the cave. Toward the back, there is a nest of fabric grown so dark with filth that its pattern can no longer be seen.

"You lived here," I say.

Caliban nods.

Squatting on his haunches, he rummages in the folds of dirty fabric. He brings out tarnished metal objects studded with jewels: a cup, a plate, a thing with a handle that I do not recognize. It catches the light and reflects it.

"See?" Caliban angles it my way. "See?"

I see a strange face in its surface and catch my breath, scuttling backward crab-wise on my feet and buttocks and hands in startlement. "Oh!"

Caliban laughs and presses the object into my hand. "See *you*, Miranda!"

I peer at it.

A face peers back at me. *My* face? It is a thing I have only glimpsed in the dim, wavering reflections of streams and ponds, framed with golden hair. I scowl and the face in the surface scowls back at me.

I thrust out my tongue.

So does the face.

Caliban leans his head beside mine, and then there we are, both of us, fair and dark. His eyes are bright with mirth. Mine are blue, blinking and uncertain. Somewhere in the back of my thoughts, my mind forms the word *mirror*. Caliban and I press our heads close together, scowl and thrust out our tongues, both of us, and watch our faces do the same, then dissolve into a fit of giggles, falling against each other.

"These were Umm's things?" I ask.

"Yes. Before." Caliban's expression turns serious. "Now this is Miranda's."

"Oh, no!" I try to give the mirror back to him, but he will not take it. "Now it is *yours*, Caliban."

"No." There is a note at once stubborn and pleading in his voice. "Now it is Miranda's." He pauses, gathering his words. "I lie. I make Master angry. I make you sad. I am sorry."

So he *does* understand the notion of a lie. Mayhap Papa's stern method of teaching is more effective than my gentler one after all. I look down, then back up at him. "I am sorry, too. But why did you lie? Was it because you did not want Ariel to be free?"

He frowns in thought. "Yes. But not only." Bounding to his feet, he beckons to me. "Come."

I tuck the mirror away in my bag and follow him. There is a narrow path that leads to the top of the crag. Using hands and feet alike, I manage to make my way to the peak. The wind is strong and buffeting. Although we are high above it, we are near the seashore and far below, waves beat against the rocks.

Atop the crag, there is a monstrous *thing*. Immense jaws rear out of the very rock, cutting semicircles in the sky. The jaws stand twice again as high as I do, and are lined with jagged teeth, each one bigger than my hand.

I do not know what to make of it. It looks like a skull made of stone, brown and stained; but a skull of what? Something huge and terrifying.

"Setebos," Caliban says with reverence.

Fist-sized rocks flecked with mica glint in the hollows of its eyes. The grinning jaws gape as though to take a bite out of the sky. I find myself backing away from it. "Caliban . . . no. This is bad! Surely it must be!"

"Why?" His face is as innocent as the dawn. "Because Master says? But Master wants the name. I do not want to give it because it is *mine*." He strokes the bony rock. "Setebos watches."

I shudder. "Watches what?"

"You." Caliban squats with careless ease beneath the shadow of the great jaws and points out to sea. "You and Master. Setebos watches you come. I watch, too."

Curiosity pricks me hard, hard enough that I forget to be afraid of the monstrous skull. "What do you mean?"

"I watch you and Master come over the water." He mimes a floating motion with one hand.

"When?" The word comes out in a whisper.

Caliban shrugs. "I do not know. One, two, three . . . four springs ago? Five?"

"You are sure you saw us?"

"I *watch* you, Miranda." He sounds patient, the way I sound when I am trying to make him understand something especially difficult. "Yes."

It is true, then.

It should not shock me so to learn it. I have long wondered, have I not? I have dreamed of the stone house with pictures on the walls and the ladies with soft hands and soft cheeks who sang me to sleep. I have even wondered if Caliban remembered Papa's and my arrival on the island. And yet it *does* shock me. This should be a thing I learn from Papa's lips as he takes me into his full confidence at last, telling me who we are—or who we were—and how we came to be here. It should not be a thing I learn from Caliban atop a windswept crag, beneath the looming shadow of a monster's bones.

An unexpected sob catches in my throat.

"Miranda?" Caliban rises, his voice filled with concern. He furrows his brow. "I make you sad?"

"No." I swallow my tears and summon a smile for him. It is not his fault. "Thank you. Thank you for telling me." He nods and drops back to his haunches, busying himself with rearranging rocks and shells that are strewn on the rocky ground around the monstrous skull. With a creeping sense of horror, I realize that he must have gathered and placed them there in tribute over the years. "Caliban, do you remember anything else about when Papa and I came to the isle?"

He shakes his head, but I cannot tell if it means he cannot remember or doesn't want to say.

I have upset him without meaning to. "No mind," I say. "This place . . . did you live here before we came?"

"Some days," he says without looking up from his labor. "I find after Umm is dead. After I find her."

"After you—" I pause, the meaning of his words sinking in. I was so proud of myself for using the occasion of the hen Nunzia's fate to explain death, I never thought to question how readily Caliban accepted the fact that his mother was dead. My throat feels tight. "You found Umm? Dead?"

He nods. "After Ariel is in the tree. One day Umm does not come and does not come. The tomorrow day I look for her. I find her."

My heart aches for him. "Oh, Caliban! I'm sorry." Kneeling beside him, I hug him as I should like to be hugged, but he tenses and I release him, fearful that if he resists, Papa's spell shall be invoked. A terrible thought comes to me. "Caliban, where did you find Umm? In the palace?"

"Yes." He looks up. "In Master's big room where Caliban and Miranda may not go."

Papa's sanctum.

I shiver. "She's not . . . still there, is she?"

He shakes his head. "No."

"Do you know what happened to her body?" I ask. "Do you know where Umm is now?"

"Master put her in the ground," he says. "I watch." His gaze searches my face. "Is that why Umm is not in the sky with God, Miranda? Because Master put her in the ground?"

It feels as though this conversation has grown too big and adult and complicated for me. "No," I say to him. "No, it is not because of that. But is that why you hid from Papa and me and came to live here every day?" I ask gently. "Because you saw Papa put Umm in the ground? Is that why you hid for so long?"

"No." Caliban frowns down at his rocks and shells, his shoulders hunched. "I do not know."

I do not press him. It is enough, more than enough, to learn in one day. I want to be gone from this stony crag perched high above the sea and its strange and fearsome watcher.

"No mind," I say again, making my voice bright and cheerful. "Thank you for bringing me here, Caliban. But we should go find mushrooms before it grows too late in the day."

He places one last stone before rising, his haunted gaze meeting mine. "Will you tell Master?"

I should.

I should tell Papa all of it, and most especially I should tell him about this monstrous thing rearing out of the rock that Caliban has been worshipping in place of the Lord God Himself.

And what would Papa do?

I fear he might perceive in it a violation of the terms of the promise he made me and take it as some fresh reason to punish Caliban or deprive him of his reason. I do not want to grieve Papa and I am not wise enough to argue with him, but I cannot help but feel in my bones that that would be unfair. After all, Caliban knew no better. He knew only what his mother taught him; and that half remembered at best. Whatever deviltry Sycorax practiced, I cannot imagine it involved placing pretty pebbles and seashells around this terrible stone monster.

And there *is* goodness in Caliban; I know it. He is kind and cannot bear to see me sad. This day, the gift of the mirror, the sharing of his deepest secret . . . it is all by way of apologizing for grieving *me*.

If a person does good in the name of bad all unwitting, surely God in His greatness must understand and forgive it?

Caliban watches me hopefully.

"No," I say to him. "I will not tell Papa. Not . . . not unless there is some cause for it I do not see today."

He sighs with relief and gratitude. "Thank you."

We descend from the crag, and I am grateful to leave it and its watchful monster behind. We make our way to the pine woods, where Caliban with his sharp forager's gaze picks out the round heads of mushrooms just beginning to push their way through a covering of pine needles. We find enough to fill half my bag before it is time to return to the palace.

Papa emerges from his sanctum in good spirits and I am glad of it, even though guilt makes a knot in my belly and dampens my appetite.

From the beginning, it felt as though Caliban and I shared a secret.

Now it is true.

Belatedly, I think to pray that the airy sylphs that accompany us on our journeys tell no tales.

THIRTEEN

CALIBAN

Why?

Why-oh, why-oh, why, why, why?

Miranda says, is that why you hide from Papa and me? Is that why you hide for so long?

No.

It was before he put Umm in the ground.

Why? What did I think when I had no words to think thoughts?

I do not know.

Miranda says, do you remember anything else about when Papa and I came to the isle?

Yes . . . but. But, but, but . . . to say will make Miranda more sad, yes? I do not want to make Miranda more sad.

I do not lie, but I do not say.

But later I think.

Why?

I had no words to think thoughts when you and Master come here, Miranda, but I had eyes to see and now I have words to say. I remember I wake with a feeling like creepity ants on my skin. I remember after I wake I go to the high place where Setebos watches.

I watch, too.

I see a storm. I see waves and clouds and rain and lightning, and a thing coming over the water; a thing like a leaf on a stream, only big and made of wood, with things like bed-linens that hang from trees on it, and where it comes is a path where there is no waves. I see on it a man standing and holding a big stick with a shiny thing on top.

A man standing on water! Long hair comes from his chin. He holds his stick high and makes sounds, and the clouds go away and the waves lie down.

Now I know it was Master singing his magic words.

Then I did not know.

But I remember Master's sounds come more slow and more slow, and the wood thing like a big leaf on a stream comes more slow and more slow. There are cracks in it and the water is going higher around it, but it comes, it comes until it cannot come anymore through the water because there is ground under the water that makes it stop. I watch Master put down his stick and pick up a thing in cloth. He holds it close to his chest like it is the very best thing. He goes into the water that is high as his waist, and carries it to the shore.

You, Miranda.

He puts you on the ground and moves the cloth. I see your little face, your arms and legs and hands and feet. You are asleep. He goes onto his knees and puts his hands together. He looks at you and then he looks at the sky and talks to it for a long time.

Praying to God in the sky, yes?

Master is more strong after the words. Master puts his head down and puts his lips on your head. Master stands and goes back into the water to the thing like a leaf to get his big stick, then comes back to the shore.

Master lifts his voice like it is a heavy thing, plants his stick, and says words that calls the little spirits, the earth and air and water spirits.

They come.

And I think . . .

No, I did not *think,* then. But I see. I see a thing change in Master's face.

What?

I do not know what.

A thing that makes me remember Umm. Not Umm who is good and pets my hair and puts her lips on my face. Umm who is bad. Umm who hits. Umm who is hungry for a thing that is not food.

(What are you hungry for, Master?)

Master makes a circle around you in the sand with his branch, Miranda. You sleep and sleep. The little spirits bring things to shore, things like the chest in your chamber, only many. They do not go near you sleeping in the circle. Master watches and smiles, but it is not a good smile.

I am afraid.

Master points his stick at the path to the palace and the gnomes begin to carry things there, but Master does not follow yet. He looks at the sea and opens his arms and lifts his stick and says more magic words. The waves come up and swallow the wooden thing.

When it is gone, Master says another thing. I do not think it is magic words because nothing happens, but there is a hard sound in his voice, and it is the sound of Umm's voice when she is angry. Not hot and fast angry, but slow and cold angry. When Ariel is bad again and again and does not do what Umm says, she uses the hard voice that is slow and cold. And then she puts him in the tree.

Then Master picks you up in his arms, Miranda, and he carries you after the gnomes.

You are sleeping, still sleeping.

I run fast to the palace, faster than Master and the little spirits. I take Umm's things that are shiny.

I go to my place and hide.

Why?

Because I am afraid.

I do not know what Master says, but I do not think he was talking to the sea, Miranda. I think there is another place beyond the sea, so far away we cannot see it, a place you and Master come from. And I think there is someone else there, someone that Master is very, very angry at.

FOURTEEN

MIRANDA

Papa needs a hare.

It seems the sylphs told no tales, for Papa's thoughts are wholly occupied by the endeavor of freeing the spirit Ariel. He keeps his promise, and that evening for the first time, Caliban is not locked in his cell.

I imagine Caliban will be excited, but he has been quiet since we left the crag, and even the prospect of his freedom does not stir him. He only tests the door a few times as though to reassure himself that it is true before retiring with his supper, leaving the door ajar.

I had thought mayhap Papa would allow Caliban to join us at the table since he had proved his loyalty, but it seems not.

"You must not get in the habit of thinking the lad your equal in stature, Miranda," Papa chides me. "Nor allow him to think it. You are as far in stature above base-born Caliban as the noble spirit Ariel is above the simple nameless elementals that serve us."

"I know nothing of the spirit save his moans and wails," I murmur.

"No mind," Papa says dismissively. "You shall gain a greater understanding of my meaning when Ariel is freed. According to the witch's notes, it is a powerful and a most mercurial spirit, so we shall invoke Mercury's aid. I intend to undertake the effort in the first hour of Mercury's day three weeks hence, when the planets are in a favorable aspect. I shall need a hare for the ritual," he adds. "Can you guess why a hare?"

It has been a long time since Papa set me such a test. I try to remember the stories he has told me of the planets which are the seven governors, and the tales written in the stars about them.

At last I give up and shake my head.

"Mercury is named for that Roman god whom the Greeks named Hermes," Papa says.

Now I remember. "The messenger."

Pleased, Papa nods. "Fleet-footed Hermes, divine messenger, patron of thieves and tricksters, shepherd of souls. The ancient Greeks depicted him with winged sandals on his feet."

"So he was swift like a hare," I say. "And like draws like."

"Indeed." Papa accords me another nod. "Thus do the emanations of Mercury wield influence over those creatures which are fleet of foot; and thus do those self-same creatures, among others, draw Mercury's influence." He looks at me, his gaze shrewd and thoughtful. "You've a keen mind, child, though I fear I've neglected it these many months. Once I succeed in this endeavor, that will change, I promise you. And one day, you may even be of aid to me in my own studies."

I say nothing, thinking.

Fleet-footed Hermes—it is a pleasing phrase. But I am not so sure about thieves and tricksters. I try to imagine a god with winged sandals. It is a pleasing image. But is he *real*? And if so, what has the messenger god of some ancient Greek people to do with a celestial body moving in its sphere in a harmonious universe ordered by the Lord God Himself?

I want to ask Papa, but I am weary from the day's long sojourn and my thoughts are crowded by too many questions to give voice to them.

And Papa is still talking. ". . . attributes of Mercury are neither masculine nor feminine, for he is either one or the other; in conjunction with a masculine planet, he becomes masculine, but in conjunction with a feminine planet, he becomes feminine. Of his own nature, he is cold and dry, and melancholic in aspect—Miranda, are you paying heed?"

I give him a guilty glance. "Yes, Papa."

His expression softens. "The day grows late and you should be abed," he says kindly. "On the morrow, I shall give you a list of confluences that you may begin copying and memorizing."

I am grateful for his kindness. "Thank you, Papa."

I sleep and my dreams are uneasy, tinged by guilt and overshadowed by the memory of the monstrous grinning skull rearing out of the crag, muddled with images of hares and hens. I dream of the great spheres turning in the heavens above and around us, and atop one crystalline sphere there runs a god with winged sandals on his feet. It seems to me that his face changes from a man's to a woman's as he passes the other planets in their stately orbits, but it always wears a trickster's grin.

But the dreams fade in the bright light of day, and I find I am excited about the new task Papa has set me. He gives me a slate with a list of beasts and birds and things over which Mercury has rulership to copy and memorize, cautioning me that it is only the merest beginning drawn from diverse sources according to his own studies.

To Caliban he gives the task of catching a hare. "Do you think you can do it, lad?" he asks.

Caliban looks uncertain. "Hares are very fast, Master."

"True," Papa says. "But hares are not blessed with reason. You need not be swifter than a hare, only more clever. Now how do you suppose you might outwit a hare?"

Caliban considers, then brightens and mimes a throwing gesture. "Hit it with a rock, Master?"

"Well reasoned," Papa praises him. "But I require the hare alive and uninjured. What else might you do?"

I look up from my slate. "There is a meadow where we have seen hares, Papa. Might one not study their pathways and dig a hole and cover it with long grasses to trap one?"

He gives me a stern look. "I am asking Caliban, Miranda."

Feeling slighted, I return to my slate.

"Dig a hole like Miranda say, Master?" Caliban suggests tentatively.

"Yes, of course, one might set a trap." Papa hands him a worn length of braided leather cord. "How might you use *this* to do so, lad?"

Caliban turns it over and over, tugs it taut, ties a knot in it. 'Tis true that he's become ever so much more dexterous, but I can see he has no guess. When he steals a glance at me, I shake my head ever so slightly. I do not have a guess, either.

"Here." Papa takes the cord back from him and ties a different kind of knot, one that slides up and down the length of the cord and makes a loop of it. He returns it to Caliban. "If you're cleverer than a hare, you ought to be able to find a way to make use of this to catch one. Only mind that it doesn't choke ere you've a chance to release it." Caliban looks askance at the cord, and Papa makes a shooing gesture at him. "Well? Go forth!"

"Shall I help him?" I ask Papa, half-rising from the kitchen table.

"No." Papa taps my slate with one finger. "I've allowed Caliban's education to take precedence over yours for too long. There's food enough in the larder to last a few days. Copy this list in a fair hand fifty times over, Miranda, and come evening, I'll expect you to recite its contents from memory."

I bend to my task. "Yes, Papa."

Caliban hesitates until Papa makes another shooing motion. "Go, you! Come back with a hare."

"You won't punish him if he fails, will you?" I ask when Caliban has gone.

"Ah, lass!" Papa laughs. "Such a tender heart you have, and such a keen sense for injustice visited on those less fortunate! No, I'll not punish the lad for not knowing what no one has taught him." He lays a hand on my shoulder. "Primitive man's ability to devise and use tools is one of the first elements to separate us from mere beasts. I am curious to see what our wild boy will do with the challenge."

"Oh, I see."

He gives my shoulder a squeeze. "To your studies."

I write out my list of words diligently.

Hare, hart, fox, weasel, ass. Quicksilver, tin, marcasite. Emerald, topaz, red marble. Nightingale, blackbird, thrush. Hazel, marjoram, parsley, grain.

I chant the words softly to myself, sounding out the ones I do not know. Many of the unfamiliar words roll wonderfully from my tongue: marcasite, emerald, nightingale, marjoram.

I wonder what manner of things they might be.

It seems to me that the words are clustered in groups of like things. Silver and tin are metals and marble is a stone, so I might guess that marcasite and emerald are either metals or stones; and blackbirds and thrush are birds, so nightingale is either a stone or a bird. Hazel is a tree and parsley is a green, so marjoram is likely a plant. *Hart* is a word I know, but it falls amidst the beasts, so mayhap it no more represents that heart that beats within one's breast than *hare* represents the locks that grow atop one's head. And quicksilver . . . what does that mean?

I cannot fathom how can silver be *quick*. And to think that this is only the merest beginning!

The depth and breadth of Papa's knowledge fills me with awe. I write out my list and erase it with a fold of my robe and begin again, over and over, until my robes are filthy with dust and my piece of ochre chalk is worn to a sliver. By the time I have finished, I feel as though these words have become a part of me; and that I, in turn, have forged a connection with Mercury in his gentlest aspect by memorizing a handful of those things that are dear to him.

In my thoughts, the trickster's sly grin curls upward in approval.

And I understand better, if only a little bit, why Papa's studies consume him so. To understand how and why the world is ordered is a heady business. I only wish I knew for certain what each and every word meant.

Caliban returns empty-handed that day, flinching at the prospect of reporting his failure.

"No mind, lad," Papa says cheerfully. "Keep trying. You'll find a way to use that cord. Tomorrow's another day!"

As for me, once Caliban has been sent to his cell with his supper, I recite my list flawlessly. Papa is so pleased, I dare to ask him what the unfamiliar words mean, and he tells me of fabulous beasts like the hart, which is crowned with majestic antlers like branches rising from its head, and the ass, which labors on behalf of humans as diligently as our little earth spirits. He tells me which of my guesses are right and wrong, describing the hard green radiance of emeralds and the beauty of the nightingale's song. He chuckles when I ask him how silver can be quick.

"'Tis a most wondrous chymical element, child," he says to me. "A liquid metal of surpassing virtue, a veritable parent to lesser metals. It is Luna to sulfur's Sol in the sacred marriage of conjunction." He collects himself, remembering to whom he is speaking. "Some call it *living silver,* for it moves and flows like water; swifter than water, as does no other metal on earth. Can you guess its true name?" I shake my head, and he smiles, touching the side of his nose. "Mercury."

"Mercury," I echo. "Because it is swift."

"Indeed," Papa says. "But it is dangerous, too." His expression darkens, and he glances in the direction of his sanctum on the upper story of the palace, musing to himself. "I fear that many a practitioner of the spagyric art has perished handling it without due respect."

I do not know what the *spagyric art* means, but I can follow his gaze. "Do you speak of Caliban's mother, Papa?"

His grey gaze returns, stormy-eyed. "That is not a fit topic for a young girl to discuss, Miranda."

I shrink. "I'm sorry! It's just . . ." He waits. "I wondered how you were so very sure she perished, Papa," I say quietly. "Caliban knew it was so. He . . . he found her. After . . . after she died, but . . ." I find myself trembling and swallow hard, cutting my words short. *But before we came here,* I think.

Papa's eyebrows raise. "He told you this?"

I nod. "He said you put her in the ground."

"I saw her remains given a decent burial." His tone is curt. "Likely it is more than the witch Sycorax deserved."

I look at the table. "She was his mother."

"Miranda." Papa's voice is like a cord jerking my head upward. "I seek only to protect you," he says in a gentler tone. "You are too young and innocent to bear the brunt of the world's unpleasantness. I thought it would trouble your dreams to know that the witch perished beneath our very roof. And I had no way of knowing the lad had found his mother's body," he added. "Indeed, until it was confirmed,

I could not be certain of his parentage. The witch's notes mention the boy only in passing."

I am silent, wondering if Papa's notes make mention of *me*.

Papa frowns, but it is a thoughtful frown. "Since it has come to it, mayhap this is an opportune moment to impress upon you the volatile nature of such an element, and the danger of seeking to bend it to one's will. Based upon my reading of the witch's journal, yes, I believe that she perished from prolonged inhalation of mercury's vapors, which are poisonous during certain stages of the work."

"That couldn't happen to you, could it, Papa?" I ask in alarm.

"No," he says firmly. "Because I approach the work with due reverence, and heed every precaution advised by those wise practitioners who trod this path before me. Sycorax, I fear, did not."

"Why?" I ask him.

He shakes his head. "In truth, I cannot say. But in every walk of life, you will find there are those who think to find a shorter path to their goals, and suffer for it in the end." Reaching across the table, Papa pats my hand. "As in all things, Miranda, patience is a virtue. I bid you cultivate it."

"I will," I promise him.

But in my thoughts, the trickster's grin has turned sly again, and my dreams that night are restless once more.

FIFTEEN

CALIBAN

Hares, hares, hares; hippity hoppity hares!

But oh, how is Caliban to catch one? Yesterday I take the cord Master gives me and go to the place where the hares are. I lie in the long grass and do not move. I watch the hares come and go. There are trails in the long grass.

When there are no hares, I am alone under the blue sky. Free. I do not have to do what Master says. He is not here to see. He is not here to punish me. I think, what if I do not catch a hare?

What if I do not go back to the palace?

My heart goes hippity hoppity like a hare when I think it, but then there are two things, one-two things, I think. One thing is a thing Miranda tells me: If I run away, Master will use his magic to make me come back. Oh, and he will be *angry*!

The number two thing is: you, Miranda.

So I do not run.

I do not know what Master wants me to do with the cord so I tie it around my waist like the cord of my pants. I dig a hole in one of the hare trails and cover it with long grass. I watch and watch but no more hares come. I think maybe they are afraid because I am here, so I leave and go to the high place where Setebos watches the sea.

I squat in his shadow and watch, too. Setebos makes Miranda afraid. I do not know why. No, that is a lie. It is because Master says Setebos is *bad*. But I do not *understand* why.

Set-e-bos, Set-e-bos!

I remember Umm's voice singing the name, deep and strong like when Master makes his chants. I remember it in my bones like my own name. Setebos smiles at the sky above me.

I wait and wait and go back, but there is no hare in the hole. I think Master will be angry, but he is not.

Then I think maybe in the morning on the tomorrow day, there will be a hare in the hole, but now that day is today and there is no hare, there is only the hole and dead, dry grass that falls in the bottom.

So, so, so.

Maybe if I put sticks over the hole and grass over the sticks, the grass will not fall. But maybe a hare will not fall either.

Master wants me to use the cord. I untie it from my waist and squat in the long grass and think. The knot Master ties is different than the knot in my pants. It moves up and down and makes a circle that goes bigger and smaller. When it goes smaller, the long end goes longer. I put my arm in the circle and move the knot. The circle goes small around my arm. I pull the long end and the knot moves. The circle goes so small it bites my skin.

O-ho!

To understand a thing all at once is like when there is a storm at night and everything is black and I cannot see anything and then lightning comes and *waah*! White bright lightning and I can see everything, everything in its place.

Oh, but then it goes and there is dark again, and I cannot remember where everything is.

If you're cleverer than a hare, you ought to be able to find a way to make use of this to catch one, Master says. *Only mind that it doesn't* something *ere you've a chance to* something *it.*

I pull the long end of the cord harder and the little circle bites harder into my skin, making it wrinkly-crinkly. My thoughts make a line between Master's *something* and *something*. I am to use the circle to catch a hare, only the circle must not be so small the hare dies before I free it.

I wait until there is a hare. I creepity-creep through the long grass. The hare sits up and looks. I throw the circle at its head, but I do not catch it. The hare runs away, jumping, jumping on its long hind legs.

No more hares come today.

But Master is not angry yet. I think it is because Master can summon a hare if he wants; but he wants me to catch it.

I say what I do with the cord and he nods his head up and down. "You're on the right path, lad. Only think, how might you set the cord to catch a hare without your hand upon it?"

That is all he says.

At night I think and do not sleep. I go outside to think. Now I am alone under the night sky. There is wind and the moon is bright. I count clouds going over the moon, one, two, three, four, five.

I climb the wall of the garden outside Miranda's chamber. Inside Miranda is sleeping. I think about Miranda sleeping. The wind makes my hair move. How is hair like a hare? I do not understand why it is the same word. Miranda says it is made of different letters so it is not the same.

And Master says to use the cord to catch a hare without my hands.

How-oh-how-oh-how? I am not the wind to make things move without hands. A big wind comes like it is laughing, *ha-ha, no you are not, Caliban!* It makes the long branches of the tree beside me move. And I think . . . o-ho! I pull a branch down and let it go. It jumps like a hare, hoppity-hoppity into the sky. *That* is how you make the cord move with no hands—pull down a branch and tie the cord to it.

But how do I make the branch stay until a hare comes?

I will think about it tomorrow. Now I do not have to be more clever than a hare, only a branch.

I go inside and sleep.

SIXTEEN

MIRANDA

Caliban has caught a hare.

It was some days in the doing, but it seems he has succeeded in devising something Papa calls a snare, and Papa is ever so pleased with him. I am happy for Caliban, though I will own, I am a little bit envious of the praise that Papa heaps on him. But that is petty of me.

The hare is understandably displeased at having been caught, and Caliban bears a number of scratches from its strong hind legs. Nonetheless, he bears it no ill will and keeps it in his cell since we have nowhere else to contain it. I rather wish that it had taken Caliban longer to catch it, or that the stars aligned for Papa's endeavor sooner, for within a week's time, Caliban has become passing fond of the hare. Resigned to its captivity, it hops around his cell and comes to nibble greens from his hand.

I am quite taken with it, too; but I have not forgotten Bianca's fate. When Caliban asks if we should name the hare, I say no.

And then altogether too soon, the stars have aligned and Mercury's day is upon us.

We gather in the kitchen in the darkness before dawn. Papa carries his staff and the thurible and he wears a robe I have never seen before, striped with blue and grey in the light of the banked embers in the fireplace. I know from my studies that these are colors that Mercury favors.

The hare is panicking. Caliban put it into the bag I sewed from scraps, but it kicks and thrashes. The bag is torn to shreds and the hare is tangled in it, which makes it struggle all the harder, scratching Caliban's arms and chest anew as he clutches it to him. At last Papa takes pity on him and sends the hare to sleep with a touch and a word. It hangs limp in Caliban's arms as we venture out to the courtyard and the great pine tree, and I am grateful I do not have to carry it. Papa gives me the thurible hanging from its silver chain to carry instead. I am pleased to be trusted with it, even if I do not like this undertaking.

The pine tree stands tall and stark against the grey sky, its branches creaking a warning. The spirit inside it is silent. Holding his staff in one hand, Papa chants the music of the spheres. The air trembles in response as dawn's rays break in the east.

Now Papa wakes the hare with a touch. It struggles in Caliban's arms and makes a terrible high-pitched sound.

"Hold it still for the knife, lad," Papa says, pointing at the flagstones. "The quicker done the better."

Squatting, Caliban holds the hare in place, stretching out its neck and pressing down on its flanks. The hare's back legs kick as it screams and screams. Caliban's shoulders tense, but he does as he's bidden.

I think we should have found some other place to house the hare. Papa drops to one knee beside Caliban, his staff tucked under his arm. His knife flashes in the rising sun and the hare's screaming stops; but the spirit Ariel rouses to let out a long, wailing screech.

"Soon, gentle spirit," Papa murmurs. "Soon."

I do not like this. I would that it were over and done with. No, I would that it were not done at all.

Papa beckons for the thurible and I bring it to him. He lifts the lid and scatters incense over the coals. Fragrant smoke trickles from the thurible's holes, and I know from my studies that it comes from a gum resin that contains elements such as oil of orange and clove and spikenard, scents that are pleasing to Mercury.

Rising, Papa takes it from me and swings it in a graceful arc. "May God bless you, good Lord Mercury!" he calls. "You who are wise, perceptive, intelligent, and the sage and instructor of every kind of writing, computation, and the science of heaven and earth! You have concealed yourself by your subtlety so that no one can possibly know your nature or determine your effects!"

In the tree, Ariel groans.

Papa's face is gilded and bright with the dawn as he chants the invocation, his eyes keen and sure.

I glance at Caliban and find him looking at me. His chest is scored and streaked with blood and his expression is unhappy.

I wonder what he is thinking. This is how it began for us all those months ago; with Papa's magic at dawn.

I wonder if he is sorry.

I hope not.

I think . . . I think if Papa succeeds in freeing Ariel, everything will change, though I do not know how or why. But at least Papa has promised not to threaten to take Caliban's will away and leave me friendless.

"Hermes, Hotarit, Haruz, Tyr, Meda!" Papa calls, swinging the thurible in a circle around him. "I call upon you by all your names! I conjure you above all by the high Lord God who is the lord of the firmament and of the realm of the exalted and great! Good Lord Mercury, receive my petition, and pour out the powers of your spirit upon me!"

Three times the invocation is repeated, and each time, Papa's voice grows stronger and more resonant. At last he rises a final time and hands the thurible to me, holding his staff aloft.

The air feels like it does before lightning strikes.

The great pine shivers and creaks.

Papa says a word I do not know, so softly it is almost a whisper, except that there is power in it that rumbles like thunder. He stamps the heel of his staff against the flagstones and the crystal atop it flares; and then there *is* a flash of lightning and a crack of thunder, sudden and ear-shattering. It startles me, and I cry out without meaning to.

"Shh!" Caliban is beside me, attempting to shield me from the splinters of bark and wood that rain down upon us. When it stops, he pats my shoulders in a clumsy effort to comfort me, his dark eyes worried. "It is only Master's magic."

I shudder and lean against him. "I know."

The top of the pine has been split asunder, the two halves of its trunk gaping. A glowing red mist, like a cloud of sun-struck blood, fills the gap. The sight of it makes my skin prickle and puts an unpleasant taste in my mouth. It seems the spirit Ariel is not yet free, for it lets out a plaintive wail and then sighs, forming words for the first time in my memory. *Free me! Oh, free me!*"

"That I will do gladly," Papa says. "In exchange for thy service."

The spirit groans in anguish. "Thou bidst me exchange my prison for fetters," it says bitterly. "Is Ariel never to be free? I cry thee mercy, good magus!"

I feel a twinge of pity for the spirit Ariel, and beside me, Caliban lets out his breath in a huff.

Papa is unmoved. "I am a godly Christian man," he says. "Unlike the foul witch Sycorax who bound you in this knotty prison, I shall demand no deed of you that is offensive in the eyes of the Lord God most high. Gentle spirit, if you serve me loyally and without complaint, I shall grant thee thy freedom."

The spirit is silent for a moment. "What term of service dost thou demand, good magus?"

Papa frowns and glances at me. Why, I cannot begin to guess. "In good faith, I cannot set a number to it," he says. "Events will fall out as heaven ordains them, and I can glimpse the future but dimly at this juncture. I will make you no false promises. But I think no more than thrice three years, mayhap less. 'Tis less time than you've been imprisoned in this rude bark, howling your agony to the skies," he adds, his voice taking on a hint of impatience. "What sayest thou, gentle Ariel? Will you swear fealty to me and become my trusted servant?"

The spirit's words come grudgingly. "I will."

"Then do so in the name of the Lord God," Papa says in a stern tone, his staff planted firmly.

A gust of wind sighs through the branches of the sundered pine, making its needles tremble and quake. "In the name of the Lord God most high, I, Ariel, do swear my fealty to thee."

"So mote it be." Papa raises his staff aloft. The crystal flashes as more words of power spill from his tongue. The nameless hare's limp corpse lies at his feet, slow blood seeping from its slit throat and pooling on the flagstones. The sundered pine tree sways and shivers. "By the cursed name of Setebos, I release thee!" Papa cries, slamming his staff down once more.

There is a long, drawn-out shriek; whether from the spirit or the tree, I cannot say. The bloody mist roils and the flagstones in the courtyard heave and shudder underfoot. I stumble and nearly drop the thurible. Caliban reaches out a hand to steady me, and I am grateful for it.

Bright rays of sun pierce the red mist, turning it golden, then silver, then dissipating it altogether.

Papa smiles in quiet triumph.

A wind springs up from the very heart of the riven pine; springs up and takes shape, descending to touch lightly on the flagstones in front of Papa. The hare's blood is smeared beneath its bare, delicate feet.

Ariel.

The spirit is more substantial in appearance than the airy sylphs or the transparent undines, but less so than the earthy gnomes, and altogether more singular. It is fair to look upon, bearing the semblance of a slender youth with skin as white as the churning crests of waves, drifting hair as pale as fog, and eyes as changeable as the sea; one moment lucid and clear, the next dark and stormy with hidden depths. A filmy garment that appears to be woven of gossamer spider-thread and jasmine petals hangs from its shoulders and clings to its limbs, quivering in the breeze. I cannot help but stare at the spirit, for it is wondrous and lovely to behold.

It bows to Papa. "Well met, Master."

Papa inclines his head. "Well met, my servant Ariel."

Ariel's gaze shifts to me and Caliban. He—for I suppose it is a *he* after all—smiles faintly. It is a beautiful smile, but there is something cold and cutting in it. Caliban lets out a harsh barking cough and moves away from me, and the spirit's smile deepens, its lips curling. "Ah!" he says. "This pretty little lass must be thine own daughter, Master. And I see thou hast found the witch's unwholesome whelp. Dost think it wise to keep him so close?"

"Do not bait the lad, gentle spirit," Papa says in a mild tone. "I could not have freed you without his aid. Caliban's parentage is no fault of his own, and he has proved himself a good and loyal servant this day."

"Is it so?" The spirit Ariel's voice is light, but his eyes are dark and brooding. His pale hair stirs in the breeze, floating about his head like wisps of fog. "Well, I shall prove myself the better."

Papa smiles again. "Nothing would please me more."

SEVENTEEN

CALIBAN

Servant.

I do not know this word, and I do not like its sound in Ariel's mouth. I am happy when Master says for Ariel to find him this thing and that thing, herbs and flowers and stones, and Ariel goes, whooshity-whoosh, away like the wind.

Oh, I remember that Ariel, how he smiles like a knife and comes and goes like the wind.

I carry the dead hare by its hind legs. It is long and skinny and I am sad that it is dead. Fleas creepity-hop in its soft hair.

Hare hair.

Master says to hang it from a tree in the kitchen garden so its blood can come out. Before he goes to his big room to be alone, Master says to dig tubers and onions in the garden and we will have stew for supper. No studies for Miranda today, Master has too many things to do. Master is oh, so very, very happy today.

I am not.

Miranda is not.

But we dig onions to peel and tubers that we wash in water from the well and I ask Miranda, what is a *servant*?

Miranda thinks, and the skin on her little brow goes wrinkle-crinkle, then it goes smooth. "Why, it is someone who is good and helpful, isn't it?" She touches my arm with wet dirty fingers and smiles at me. There are no knives in Miranda's smile, only sunlight. "Like you, Caliban."

But, but, but . . . if that is true, why does it itch so? Oh, it is not an itch, not really, but it is a feeling I do not have a name for—an angry not-knowing feeling, a feeling that if I did understand the thing I do not understand, I *would* be angry. And that is a feeling like an itch.

Twisty words for twisty thoughts. I do not want to think them, but the itch makes me. Miranda says a servant is someone who is good and helpful, but I do not think that is what Master means.

Master means it is someone who does what Master says, what Master wants. And Ariel did not want to be a servant; Ariel wanted to be free.

Like me.

But I was not trapped in a tree. I *was* free before Master made me come to him. And I did not make a promise to the Lord God in the sky to do what Master says for years and years and years.

So why am *I* a servant?

I ask Miranda this.

"Oh, Caliban! Why does it matter?" Her brow goes wrinkle-crinkle again. She touches me again, puts her hand on mine. "You're my *friend*. Servant is only a word. Like Master."

I look at her hand on mine. It is little and pale. Even with dirt under them, her fingernails are like seashells. My hand is bigger and stronger and darker, and my fingernails are raggedy jaggedy. Not as much as before, but still.

Only a word.

Words fall through my thoughts like stones through water.

Servant.

Unwholesome. That is another word, a word Ariel said about me. I do not know it, and I do not like the sound of this one either; but it does not make as strong of an itch inside me, not yet. I let it fall. I will pick it up another time.

Master.

But *Master* is not a word in the same way as *servant* because it is his name, and one person's name is not the same as a word that is a name for every one of that thing, like boy or hare or tuber.

I say this to Miranda.

Her eyes go wide and her mouth opens and closes. "Oh! It's not . . . Caliban, did you think *Master* was Papa's name?"

"Yes." I feel my own brow crinkle. Could it be untrue? It is the name Master gave me to call him. "Is it not?"

She takes her hand away, puts her hands together in front of her and looks down. "No." Her voice is soft. "No, it's, um . . . I suppose you would call it a title. A term of respect."

I echo the word. "Respect?"

Miranda looks up and her eyes ask me silently to understand. "To show thanks and loyalty, yes. Just as I call him Papa because he is my father, and just as we say that God in His heaven is the Master of us all. Remember? I taught you as much."

I scrub dirt from a tuber and think a great many thoughts. Servant and Master; these words are knotted together. Ariel did not say the word until he says his promise, until Master frees him from the tree. Ariel knew. I did not know. It is like Master has told me a lie.

Did he?

I cannot remember all the words from when I had no words. I remember the first knowing and that is Miranda, knowing *she is Miranda* even if I did not have any words but her name yet; and then the second knowing that is like when lightning comes, and that is finding a thing that was lost from long, long ago when Umm was alive. Me. A word that is my name. Caliban. *I am Caliban.*

What did Master say? Did he say, "I am Master"? Did he say, "Call me Master"? Or did he only touch his chest and say, "Master"?

I look at Miranda. She is peeling onions now, her hands go peel, peel, peeling away the crinkly brown skin. If I ask about the word again, it will make her sad. Maybe it is true it does not matter, it is only a word. But there is magic in words.

There is magic in *knowing*.

And I did not know the meaning of this word, Master. Now I do. The itch grows stronger.

I am angry.

But I think . . . what if I am angry and bad? Master does not need me anymore. He has Ariel; Ariel with his smile like a knife, Ariel who whooshes away like the wind. Ariel who can fetch things from every corner of the island and the deepest depths of the sea around it.

Ariel who says, *Well, I shall prove myself the better.*

The better servant.

It is a thought that tastes bad to me, but, but, but . . . I look down at Miranda's bright golden head bent over the onions. And I think about the day that she and Master came to the island, oh, so long ago, and how little she was in his arms and lying asleep on the sand, and his cold, angry voice speaking to someone across the sea. I think how Master put his lips on her while she sleeps, and I think that he loves her, but I think maybe she is not the thing he loves best of all. I think maybe Master loves his anger more. And I think about the way Master looks at her today, and speaks of things to come.

(What things, Master?)

Oh, yes, there is a worse thing Master could do than call me his servant when I do not know what it means. He could send me away.

Away from you, Miranda.

I know in my bones that Master can do this, and I know in my bones that I do not want it.

It is why I stay.

So I put my anger aside, just like Master raking the coals in the hearth and covering them with ashes.

I will be a good servant.

I will smile and say the word *Master*.

EIGHTEEN

MIRANDA

Now that the spirit Ariel is free from the great pine and sworn to Papa's service, our lives are different.

In some ways, that is no bad thing. Ariel knows every nook and cranny, every crag and crevasse, every meadow and wood of the isle, and he can traverse it in a trice, as swift and blithe as the wind itself. Every herb and flowering plant that Papa bids him fetch that can be found, he brings. The little gnomes till the earth and tend the plantings industriously, and soon our kitchen garden doubles, then trebles in size. Papa sets me to memorizing the qualities and the correspondences of each new planting.

At Ariel's behest, the gnomes delve into the earth and bring forth metal-flecked ore and stones sparkling with quartz, and the undines plunge into the depths of the ocean and bring forth oysters with shimmering pearls nestled on their beds of soft briny flesh.

Save for the oysters, which are roasted and eaten, these things vanish into Papa's sanctum.

It is not only the natural bounty of the isle that Ariel provides. When he has accomplished all the tasks that Papa has given him, Ariel reveals knowledge of a hidden trove of pirates' treasure buried in a small cove along the shore.

"You scoundrel of a sprite!" Papa says, but he is too gladdened by the news to be truly grieved. "Did you not think to tell me sooner?"

Ariel gazes at him with blue-green eyes as clear and innocent as a calm sea. "Why, didst say naught of *treasure*, Master! Does it please thee?"

Papa smiles at him like dawn breaking. "Indeed, it does."

And so there is treasure, trunks of it brought forth from its resting place buried deep beneath the sands. There is jewelry set with precious stones, a round mirror in a gilded frame, a checkered game-board accompanied by cunning little figures wrought in silver and gold, a set of chased silver dishes, and an entire trunk filled with once-fine gowns and other garments encrusted with gold and silver embroidery and seed pearls, wrapped in coarse oiled sailcloth to protect them. Papa supposes that it was plundered from a ship bearing a noblewoman's dowry some years ago; after the Moors abandoned the isle, but before Caliban's mother Sycorax laid claim to it.

Some of the more delicate fabric has rotted beyond the point of salvage, but some of the sturdier stuff is merely spotted with mold and mildew. I yearn to see what I might make of it with my sewing casket, but it is not to be.

"Such garments are meant for a woman grown, Miranda," Papa says to me. "One day, such things and finer shall be yours, but not for many years yet."

Instead, he gives me the remnants of a handful of garments made for a babe or a small child on which to ply my fledgling skills. The rest of the fine attire, along with the jewelry, the game-board, and the mirror—an item which seems to please Papa more than all the rest, and makes me feel not a little guilty for failing to tell him about the mirror Caliban gave me—vanish into his sanctum.

Not the dishes, though. The silver dishes etched around the edges with scenes of what Papa says is a hunting party, complete with wondrous images of a hart crowned with antlers, replace our worn wooden trenchers.

I feel like a very fine young lady indeed dining on silver.

Those are the ways in which Ariel's presence in our midst has changed our lives for the better.

There are ways in which our lives have changed for the worse, too.

I do not *trust* Ariel.

Oh, he conducts himself well enough while Papa has him busy combing the isle, but once he is idle and Papa is immersed in his sanctum, it is another matter. I know that Ariel had no fondness for Caliban, but one pleasant afternoon, while Caliban and I are picking sour oranges in the walled orchard, I learn how deeply his hatred runs.

A gust of wind announces Ariel's presence.

"See how he climbs, agile as a monkey!" he exclaims as Caliban hangs from the branches and tosses oranges down to me. "Mayhap there is a measure of truth in the rumors. What thinkest thou, fair Miranda?"

"I know naught of rumors," I say, gathering oranges in the skirt of my robe; but it is a mistake even to reply.

"Naught of rumors!" Ariel sits cross-legged in midair on a cushion wrought of nothing save clouds, his filmy garments fluttering about him. "Why, I speak of the boy's father, of course. Hast thou not thought to wonder?" I say nothing and Caliban does not even glance at the spirit, but Ariel is undeterred. "The sailors who brought thy cursed witch of a mother to this isle, bound in chains and gravid with child, did gossip amongst themselves," he says conversationally to Caliban. "Some did claim that thy father was an imp from the pits of hell, and some did claim that he was the fiercest of Barbary pirates, black of hide and heart. But others . . . ah!" Ariel drops his voice to a whisper. "Others claimed that thy mother mated with a great ape, a dumb, hairy beast from the deepest, darkest jungles."

With a hoarse bark, Caliban drops from the branches, landing on his haunches. There is banked fury in his expression.

"Why must you be so cruel?" I ask Ariel indignantly. "Caliban has done nothing to you!"

"Has he not?" Ariel's eyes turn cold and wintry. "And yet it is because of him that Sycorax imprisoned me." He turns his pale gaze on Caliban. "Dost thou know what thy mother demanded of me? Dost thou know what demand I refused to earn such a punishment?"

Caliban's shoulders hunch. "No."

"She bade me to lie with her as a man lies with a woman," Ariel says, and there is disgust and loathing in his voice. "Dost thou know what that betokens? She beseeched me to get her with child. A child of light to replace the spawn of darkness that condemned her to exile from the presence of all decent, God-fearing folk. Thou."

Caliban snarls and hurls an orange at him. "You lie!"

Ariel's form dissolves in a flurry of mist and tendrils of fog, and the orange passes through the mist to land harmlessly on the grass; and then Ariel is there once more, hovering above the earth and smiling his cutting smile. "Do I?"

With an effort, Caliban turns his back on him.

"Go away!" I shout at the spirit, my hands fisting in the folds of my robe, heavy with the weight of gathered oranges. "Leave him alone! Leave *us* alone!"

"*Us.*" Ariel echoes the word and laughs. "So I shall, for now!"

And then he is gone.

Without a word, Caliban walks away, his shoulders still hunched and tight. "Wait!" I call after him, and he breaks into a loping run. "Caliban, don't go! Don't listen to him!" I give chase, the oranges spilling from the apron of my robe, but Caliban is too swift for me. Within minutes, he has scrambled over the wall and is out of sight.

And I am left alone to wonder.

There is so very much I do not understand.

By suppertime, Caliban has not returned and Papa is wroth with him. "If he thinks to shirk his duties without punishment, he shall find himself sorely mistaken on the morrow," he says in a grim tone. "He has gathered no kindling and the woodpile is all but empty."

I push a bit of fish around my silver platter; fish that Caliban caught for us that very morning. "Do not be too angry with him, Papa," I murmur. "Ariel goaded him cruelly today."

Papa makes a dismissive gesture. "'Tis a poor excuse. The spirit has a mercurial nature."

"He spoke of Caliban's father." I hesitate. "He said . . . he said mayhap his father was an ape, a great hairy beast."

Papa frowns. "That is no fit topic for a lass of your tender years. I shall have words with Ariel."

"But it's not true, is it?" I ask.

"No." Papa's voice is firm. "Such a thing is impossible, Miranda. What else did he say?"

Ariel's words come into my mind unbidden. *She bade me to lie with her as a man lies with a woman.* I do not know what this means, only that the words, and the manner in which Ariel spoke them, make me feel uncertain and unclean, and I do not want to repeat them for fear that Papa will chide me for listening to them. "Ariel said that the sailors who brought Sycorax to the isle gossiped," I say instead. "Some said Caliban's father was an ape, some said he was a fearsome pirate, and some said he was an imp from the pits of hell."

Papa is silent for a moment. "Such rumors should never have reached your ears," he says gently. "Yet I will say that while whatever deviltry Sycorax practiced may have affected Caliban ere his birth, having examined the lad at length, I am quite certain that his father was a mere mortal and human." His frown returns. "What *manner* of human, I cannot say; and indeed, we may never know. No one wholesome of character, of that you may be sure."

"But it is cruel and wrong of Ariel to goad him, is it not, Papa? And is it not right that Caliban is hurt and angered by it?" I ask, daring greatly. "I think . . . I think Ariel blames Caliban for what his mother did. And it's not *fair!*" I wish he would say, *No; no, of course it is not. I will make an end to it.* I wish I could make him understand the sheer malice and hatefulness of Ariel's taunting.

Instead Papa fixes me with a hard gaze. "As always, your tender heart is to your credit, but Caliban is responsible for his own actions," he says curtly. "I will deal with him on the morrow."

And so I am dismissed to my bed-chamber.

NINETEEN

CALIBAN

I watch the sun set over the sea. Behind me, Setebos laughs his sound-less laugh at the sky, his shadow long and black on the rocks.

My heart is hot and angry.

Master will be angry, too. If he does not summon me, I will go back in the morning; for you, Miranda. Always for you. I will say, oh, oh, I was bad, Master, I am sorry, Master.

But not yet.

The sky is gold. Drop by drop, my anger falls away, like drip-dropping blood falling from the hare's throat.

I do not hear Miranda come until she calls my name. "Caliban!"

My mouth falls open and I jump up quick as a hare. I look at her standing in the falling light of the sun, her little face scared. I am scared, too. "Oh, Miranda! You should not be here. It is late!"

And then she changes and she is not Miranda, no; it is Umm

standing there with gold light on her face, her back bent from many hours working over her books. She opens her arms. "Caliban, my son! Come to me!"

Oh, it has been so very, very long since I did see her! And I remember the hits and the bad words, but I remember she would put her arms around me, too, and put her lips on my face.

My feet move even though I do not tell them to, as though it was Master summoning me.

And then Umm laughs, and it is a sound like something breaking, and there is a whoosh of wind that goes in a circle, and *Umm* changes— and it is not Umm, no, or Miranda there atop the high place with me. It is Ariel, oh-so-pretty, sparkling like sea-foam and smiling like knives. "Ah, thou poor, sorry, unwholesome creature!" he says, laughing. "Thou pitiable monster! Didst truly think thy mother had returned from the dead? Didst truly think she yearned to *embrace* thee?"

All my anger comes back, hot and hurting. Water comes to my eyes like Miranda's when she is sad, and I *am* sad, but I am angry and hurting, too. I am hot and cold and shaking. I have a feeling I cannot name, a feeling of having been bad even though I have not, and it makes me more angry, because it is not right. I make my hands into fists. "*Why?*"

It is a word that comes out like a child's cry, all alone and lost and scared. I do not want it to but it does.

Ariel stops laughing. "I am here at our master's bidding." His voice is cold, but the knives have gone out of his smile. "He would fain have thee know that there is nowhere on this isle thou might hide where I cannot find thee, and nowhere from whence he cannot summon thee." He looks at me, and his face is like there is a bad smell in the air. "And yet with night a-falling, I see that thou art but a frightened little boy longing for his mother."

There is truth in his words and it hurts me. "I am old enough to wish Setebos would strike you dead!" I say, hoping my words will hurt him, too.

The knives did not go far. "Ah, Setebos!" Ariel says, smiling. "I rejoice to say that *his* reign o'er this fair isle, and that of thy foul witch of a mother, has come to an end." He bends at the waist and moves his arms to his sides, and bits of clouds dance around him, and the knives grow sharper, though I think they are not only meant for me this time. "Why, it has been replaced by that of the good Lord God and the master thou and I serve alike."

I say nothing.

The only promise I did make to serve Master, I did make to myself. I made it to me, Caliban.

For Miranda.

Ariel puts his head to one side and looks at me, his eyes dark and churning like storm-clouds. "A child, and harmless . . . for the nonce," he says. "But blood will out in time. Thou shouldst abjure the girl ere you harm her."

I show him my teeth. "I will not!"

There is only a little red sunlight on the far edge of the sea and the gold is going away from the sky, turning to violet.

Ariel sighs. "No," he says. "I suppose not."

TWENTY

MIRANDA

In the morning, Caliban is still missing.

I imagine that Papa will summon him as soon as he finishes chanting the music of the spheres at dawn, but I am mistaken. Instead we break our fast in the usual manner, though it is a good deal more work to gather firewood for the hearth without Caliban's aid. I manage to find enough fallen branches in the kitchen garden to cook our morning meal, but I shall have to venture alone into the forest if Caliban doesn't return soon.

I do not dare ask about Caliban for fear of rousing Papa's anger. Instead, I ask if he might not bid the spirit Ariel to fetch wood for us.

Papa frowns at my suggestion. "I would not set so noble a spirit to such a menial chore." I glance at my palms, dirty from gathering branches, and scrub at them, trying not to let him see. "To be sure, 'tis a pity the gnomes have no affinity for wood or I'd have set them that chore long ago," he muses. "But Ariel is of a higher order altogether . . . What are you doing, Miranda?"

"Naught." I hide my dirty hands beneath the table. "Forgive me, Papa."

"Oh, child!" Reaching across the table, he takes my hands in his. "No, 'tis I who begs your forgiveness." His face is grave. "Doubt not that such base labor is beneath you; and yet, we do what we must to endure."

I do not meet his gaze. "But not Ariel?"

Papa hesitates. "The spirit Ariel was imprisoned by Sycorax because he refused to honor such base demands," he says. "If he is to serve willingly, I must honor his nature in turn."

That is a lie, I think; but is it a lie Papa believes? Does he know the truth that Ariel imparted to Caliban and me? *She bade me to lie with her as a man lies with a woman. She beseeched me to get her with child.*

Or did Ariel lie?

There are lies and lies.

I do not know.

Papa squeezes my hands, then lets them go. "Never think I do not appreciate your labor, Miranda," he says. "One day . . ." He shakes his head. "No, no mind. That is for another time."

I peer at him. "When?"

"When you are a woman grown," he says and his voice takes on a stern note. "Not before."

"When will that be, Papa?" I dare to ask. "When I am ten?"

"Ten!" He laughs. "'Tis unlikely. Do not trouble your head about it, child. When the time comes, you'll know."

It seems careless and unkind of him to answer me thusly. *How?* How am I to know when I am a woman grown? Will it be in four years or five years or ten? Is there some manner of sign for which I might watch? I want to howl and storm and rage like Ariel in his tree or

Caliban in his cell. I think of the endless lists of properties and correspondences he bids me commit to memory when all I want to know are the most basic of truths: Who are we and where did we come from? Why are we here on this isle? And now this . . . how in the name of all that is good and holy will I know when I am a woman grown?

The questions swell inside me until I think I will surely burst, and I open my mouth to let them out.

It is at that moment that Caliban's shadow darkens the doorway that leads to the kitchen garden.

I swallow hard and close my mouth.

Papa rises to his feet, a thunderous expression on his face. "Get in here, boy!"

Caliban obeys him, his head hanging low. "I am sorry, Master."

"Not as sorry as you shall be, I daresay." Papa's hand closes around the amulet that contains Caliban's hair. "I entrust you with your freedom, and you repay the kindness by abandoning my daughter without a word, leaving all your chores undone and left to fall to her alone?"

Caliban flinches. "I am sorry, Master," he says again. "I was bad." He steals a glance at me, misery in his gaze. "I am sorry, Miranda."

My heart fills with pity, my own anger forgotten. "'Tis all right," I say gently to him. "You were angry."

"Enough!" Papa's hand tightens around the amulet and Caliban lets out a howl of agony, falling to the floor. His limbs draw tight to his body, his fists pressing into his belly, and his skin shudders and twitches as the muscles beneath cramp into knots. On and on it goes, Caliban writhing and groaning with pain, and I find myself standing with no memory of having risen, my own hands fisted at my sides in helpless sympathy.

At last Papa releases the amulet. Caliban lies unmoving on the floor, his breathing hoarse and ragged.

"I take no pleasure in punishing you, lad," Papa says, and his breath comes hard, too. "Do not make me do so again." Eyes closed tight, Caliban nods. "Very well." Papa adjusts the amulets that hang about his throat and smooths his robes until every fold is in place. "When you have recovered, you may replenish the woodpile. Miranda, I would have you attend to your studies today."

I nod my obedience, too.

When Papa has gone to his sanctum, I kneel beside Caliban, patting at him in a vain effort to soothe away the pain. "Oh, Caliban! I'm sorry."

Although he does not open his eyes, one rough-skinned hand covers both of mine and stills them. "Do not be. I was bad."

"You were angry," I say again. "I was angry for you!"

Caliban smiles a little bit, his lips curving upward. "I know." He opens his eyes and gazes at me. "Now I will go fetch wood."

I shake my head. "Rest. I will go."

"No." With an effort, Caliban pushes himself upright and clambers to his feet. He stands wavering and unsteady, taking a deep, long breath as though to test his ability to take air into his lungs. His dark eyes are very serious and intent. "Do your studies, Miranda. Master is angry, too. Do not make him more angry. I will go."

"All right," I whisper.

I watch him limp away. Somehow, I feel myself to blame for his pain.

Since I do not know what else to do, I ply myself to my studies as Papa bade me, sitting at the kitchen table with my head bent over my slate and a bit of ochre chalk in my hand, copying and memorizing the properties and correspondences of jade and other stones that are green in hue, none of which I have ever seen, nor ever hope to see within my lifetime.

"Oh, la!" a light voice says, and a light breeze brushes over me. "What art thou about?"

It gives me a start to see Ariel in our kitchen. With his moon-pale skin, sea-changing eyes, and fluttering white garments, the spirit looks out of place in such homely surroundings. "No business of yours," I say, rubbing my slate clean. It is an hour's worth of labor gone, but it gives me bitter satisfaction to deny him. "What do you want of me? Why are you here?"

Ariel's eyes widen, as clear and blue as a summer sky. "Why, I am here to tender my profound apology, milady!" He gives me a sweeping bow. "I heartily beg thy forgiveness for having offended thee."

I am unmoved. "Did Papa bid you to do so?"

The spirit's lips purse and his eyes darken a hue. "Thou hast my promise, milady, that never again shall words unfit for the tender ears of a child escape me in thy presence. Come, now, Miranda!" His voice takes on a wheedling tone. "Shall we not be friends, thee and I?"

"We are not friends," I say. "*Caliban* is my friend, and you were wickedly cruel to him."

"I did but speak the truth," Ariel says. "And betimes the truth is cruel. Ah, but that topic is forbidden to us now, milady. What other things might we discuss, I wonder?" He plucks an orange from a bowl on the table, tears away a bit of peel, and sucks at the underlying flesh, then makes a face and spits. "Pfaugh! 'Tis sour."

"'Tis a symbol of the sun and of gold," I say coldly. "Its oil may be used in an incense. And Papa says that even though these were grown solely for ornament, they are healthful to eat and serve to balance phlegmatic humors."

"Thou art a veritable scholar among maidens and wise beyond thy years!" Ariel says in admiration. "No wonder thy father has such grand plans for thee."

My heart quickens. "Of what plans do you speak?"

"Alack and alas!" Ariel raises both fair, shapely hands in dismay, one still holding the bitten orange. "That I am forbidden to say, milady. But surely thou knowest better than I, being privy to thy father's plans."

"No." I flush with a trace of my former anger. "He tells me naught."

"Naught!" The spirit's eyes widen again, turning the hue of rain-washed violets. He glances around and lowers his voice. "But at the very least, surely thou must know what wonders and horrors thy father's laboratorium contains?"

Realizing that Ariel is baiting me, I do not reply, but it is too late. I have already given myself away, and I cannot help but feel hurt that Papa has allowed the spirit into his very sanctum.

Ariel shakes his head in sorrow, his mist-colored hair floating. "'Tis a pity he does not trust his own daughter."

It is almost as though he has voiced my own thought. "I trust Papa!" I say in a fierce voice, willing it to be true. "In all that he does, he seeks only to protect me. And he is teaching me his arts!" I gesture at my piece of slate, forgetting that I have wiped it clean. "When I am a woman grown, Papa will tell me all his plans and allow me to assist him in his sanctum."

"'Tis a long time to dwell in ignorance, milady," Ariel observes.

"Is it?" I cannot help asking. "How long? How shall I know when I am woman grown?"

Ariel gives a careless, graceful shrug. "As to that, I cannot say."

I should like to scream. "You do but seek to plague me as surely as you plagued poor Caliban!"

"No, milady." Ariel's eyes darken ominously once more, black and roiling like the sea at night. "Forgive me. I do but chafe at the bonds of servitude that bind me. Upon my honor, I mean you no harm. But mayhap in the wisdom of thine innocence, thou art wise indeed to pay me no heed." He opens one hand and lets the orange fall to the floor, where it rolls under the table. "Still, were I thou, I should not sleep soundly without knowing what manner of dreams and nightmares thy beloved father concocts in his laboratorium," he adds in a thoughtful tone. "No, not at all."

With that, he is gone.

Trickster or not, the spirit has planted a seed inside me that grows at an unnatural pace throughout the day. I would that Ariel had kept his silence, but it is too late. Dreams and nightmares, indeed. Whatever does it mean?

That night my dreams are crowded with shapeless terrors, things that swarm out of the darkness. I awaken with screams caught in my throat, choked whimpers like a hare caught in one of Caliban's snares, only to find shadows pooling around my pallet, rising like dark waves, formless things in the depths reaching for me with open mouths filled with teeth; and then I scream and wake again with a whimpering jolt, knowing the first awakening to have been false.

Over and over, this happens.

And when I am awake, truly awake, lying alone and afraid in the darkness, I wonder. What *does* Papa's sanctum contain?

I know only that I cannot bear any more of this not-knowing.

When Papa's chant greets the first rays of dawn, I slip from beneath the linens. The tiles are cool beneath my bare feet, all the Moorish patterns on the walls faint in the dim grey light.

Clutching my robe about me, I climb the stairs to the upper story. There is no lock on the doors to Papa's sanctum, only a pair of heavy iron handles. Trusting to my obedience, Papa has never needed a lock.

I tell myself I will steal only the merest glance. One glance, just to confirm that there is nothing to fear, that Ariel does but seek to bait me as he baited Caliban. And then I will tell Papa what Ariel said to me, and he will bid the spirit to hold his tongue. Papa need never know I doubted him.

I turn one handle and the door creaks open a few inches. Outside, Papa chants the songs of the spheres.

Beyond the door, it is still. A waft of air emerges, carrying the scents I have smelled on Papa's robes; scents of herbs and oils, acrid scents of chymicals and heated metal that catch in my nose.

I push the door open.

Dreams, oh! Papa's sanctum contains such things as I never knew existed; fantastical instruments of gleaming metal with bits that spin and turn and fit together in intriguing ways. There are shelves and shelves; an entire shelf filled with books, shelves filled with animal skulls and seashells and coral, horns and hooves, rocks and feathers. There are jars of herbs and unguents, and strangely shaped glass vessels with tubes protruding from them. There are cases and cases of drawers, some labeled in Papa's neat hand, others labeled in unfamiliar hands and unfamiliar letters. The very walls are covered with strange drawings and symbols I cannot begin to decipher.

I stare, gaping.

There on a long counter, there is a brazier glowing brightly, so brightly the bars of the metal grate are red-hot. It makes a faint crackling sound. And I know, I *know,* I should close the door and go, but I do not.

I need to know what it is that burns so brightly within it.

My feet move soundlessly across the smooth tiles. Inside the brazier, there is a nest of fire; inside the nest, a salamander lies curled, and although I have never seen a fire elemental, I know it as such. It uncurls itself at my approach, lifting its head from its tail and stretching out its legs, unfurling its claws and opening eyes that blaze like I imagine rubies must do, its gaze on a level with mine.

"Oh!" I whisper in awe, for it is so very beautiful in the heart of the fire, all red and gold and shining.

The salamander's eyes blink. *"You mussst be the child,"* it says in a voice that crackles and hisses like embers.

I take a step backward. "You speak?"

A tongue like a tiny forked flame darts forth from its lipless mouth and retreats. *"Yesss."*

"Oh," I say again, feeling foolish.

The salamander regards me with red eyes faceted like jewels. *"Have you come to sssee it?"*

"It?" I echo.

"Her." The salamander amends its choice of words, its jeweled gaze slewing sideways. *"Her."*

I follow its gaze.

There is a glass jar atop the counter. It sits some foot and a half away from the brazier. It is filled with clear liquid, and there is a . . . thing . . . floating in it. A dead thing, I think at first; a skinned hare or some such thing that Papa has preserved here.

But it is not a hare.

And it is not dead.

The thing floating in the jar is a tiny misshapen person. Its skin is as white and sickly as the gills of a mushroom. Its features are un-formed blobs, but as I stare in sick fascination, its lids open to re-veal pale, milky blue eyes. Its mouth opens and closes, and its limbs stir.

"What—" My voice cracks. "What is it?"

The salamander laughs, a sound like a shower of sparks rising. *"Look clossser,"* it says. *"Look closer."*

I do not want to look closer. I want to run away, I want to turn back the sun and unmake this morning until I am safe in my cham-ber, all thoughts of disobedience abandoned and forgotten. I do not want to have seen this thing in Papa's sanctum, and I do not want to know what it is. And yet I find myself moving forward nonetheless, rising on tiptoes and putting my hands on the jar, inching it across the counter to draw it toward me for a better look.

It bobs as the liquid sloshes a bit. There is a thin braid of hair tied around one ankle like a tether, golden hair a shade darker than mine, the stray ends of strands floating in the liquid.

My throat feels thick, and my heart is thumping and thumping, faster than a hare's inside my breast.

Its milky gaze holds mine. Can it see, I wonder? I am not sure, but it seems so. Somehow there is sorrow in those sightless-looking eyes. Its pale bud of a mouth opens and closes, and I think it is trying to form words. The fingers of its tiny hands open like the petals of a flower, splaying to touch the glass.

"What?" I whisper. "Oh, what is it? What do you seek to tell me? What are you? *Who* are you?"

"Miranda!"

Papa's voice crashes over me like a wave. I jerk away, but I am scared and careless, and . . . oh, I can hardly bear it.

The jar topples over the edge of the counter and falls.

It smashes to bits on the tile floor, liquid splashing everywhere. And the thing . . . the thing . . .

It lies amid the shards, a pale, naked, misshapen thing, its mouth opening and closing, gasping like a fish. Bubbles rise from its lips. Its soft, narrow chest rises and falls; quickly at first, and then slower and slower.

I am shaking, shaking.

"Oh, you foolish child." Papa's voice is soft and deadly, filled with more fury than I have ever heard. He holds his staff in one hand, and the other rises to grasp one of the amulets strung about his neck; not Caliban's, but the one that contains a lock of my own hair. "You foolish, careless, *treacherous* child! Do you have any idea what you've done?"

Unable to speak, I back away, shaking my head in wordless denial, willing him to understand, to forgive.

Papa does neither. "You've killed your mother all over again,

Miranda," he says in that soft, terrible voice, and his fist tightens on the amulet.

There is no time for understanding before the pain comes, a great tearing shriek of pain, tying my entrails in knots and pounding within the confines of my skull. Like Caliban, I fall writhing to the ground, but I cannot even draw breath to cry out. My lungs heave in vain as surely as the poor misshapen thing in the broken jar dying on the floor beside me, sorrow fading from its milky eyes. The pain is too vast, encompassing the whole of my existence. I see only red and think my eyes must be filled with blood. I think my body will tear itself apart, and my skull split asunder.

I think I must be dying, too.

Somewhere Papa is still speaking words laced with anger and venom, but I cannot hear him above the pain.

Oh, merciful God! I would listen if I could; I would beg Papa's forgiveness if I could. But I can do nothing save endure his wrath.

Oh, merciful God, it hurts, it hurts! Something inside me is breaking.

And then . . .

. . . nothingness.

TWENTY-ONE

CALIBAN

Miranda has done a bad thing, but I do not know what it is.

I think . . . I think she goes into Master's room, the big room that was Umm's room, the room where we are not to go, never ever never. But I think it is a bigger thing, too, because Master is so very, very angry.

I find him taking Miranda down the stairs. She is asleep in his arms like when they came to the island and she was *so* little, but she is not so little now; not so little that her head and feet do not hang over Master's arms. Her golden hair hangs, too, and her face is very white. And he does not carry her like she is the very best thing now. He walks hard and angry and he carries her like she is nothing more than so many sticks to throw on the woodpile.

I am afraid.

"What?" I say. "Master . . . what?"

Master's face is like a thing made of stone. "It is no concern of yours, lad," he says. "Tend to your chores."

So I do, but it is not the same with Miranda asleep during the day. And I do not know why Miranda sleeps and sleeps, with her face so very white, lying without moving under her bed-linens where Master puts her.

(What did you do, Miranda?)

I look for that Ariel but he is nowhere. Then I see a thing that is new: Master leaves the palace with the sun high in the sky. He is carrying something again, something small wrapped in pretty blue cloth from the pirates' treasure.

I follow him, but not so close that he sees me. He goes to the far garden where he put Umm in the ground. I climb the wall and hide in a broken place in the corner to watch. Master summons one of the little gnomes to dig a hole. It paddles in the dirt with its strong hands, paddlity-paddle.

Soon it is a deep hole.

Master goes on his knees beside it. He moves the cloth away from the thing and puts his lips on it, but I cannot see what it is. Master puts the cloth back and puts the thing in the hole.

A wind comes behind me. "Thou skulking churl!" Ariel whispers, and I jump like a bee has stung me. "Hast thou no decency? Wouldst spy on a man laying his own dear wife to rest?"

I turn to him and put my teeth together hard. "Wife?"

"His beloved." The spirit shows *his* teeth and smiles knives at me. "Miranda's mother."

I shake my head. "No."

"Ah, well! Not *her*, not exactly. *She* died giving birth to Miranda." Ariel touches one finger to his lips. "But our dear master thought to use his arts to grow himself a homunculus to replace her. Poor deformed creature! It should never have been made. I reckon 'tis a piece of God's mercy that it perished, though I daresay the magus thinks otherwise." He shudders. "And poor Miranda!"

My thoughts are dark and muddy, and I do not understand the spirit's words. "What of her?"

Ariel looks at me sideways. "She caused its demise," he says. " 'Twas an accident, but . . ."

"No."

"Yes."

And now I do and do not understand. Not all the words, no, but enough. My heart hurts inside me.

Oh, Miranda!

In the garden, Master pushes dirt into the hole with his own hands, his head low and his shoulders going up and down. I think maybe he is crying tears. I am not sad for him, though.

"An accident," I say.

"It means she did not do it a-purpose," Ariel says.

"Yes," I say. "I know. I know what is an *accident*. But Master punishes her for it anyway and I think she is very hurt. She sleeps and sleeps and does not wake." I look at the spirit in his eyes, in his eyes that turn colors and change. "If you know everything, tell me this thing. Will Miranda die?"

Now Ariel shakes his head, all his white hair floating around his pretty face. He does not look back at me. "I know not," he says. "I do not know everything. Only God does and 'tis for Him to decide. All things are His to decide."

God.

I would like to spit on the ground. I do not like this God in the sky who decides everything.

I do not like this Ariel.

Most of all I do not like Master.

I do not want to see or hear anything more. I push past Ariel on the wall, only there is nothing to push when I do, only *whoosh* and he is gone, a feeling like wind and mist on my face.

I go to Miranda's garden and crouch on the wall and watch her sleep. She sleeps and sleeps. I creepity-creep to the window and say her name. Quiet, so quiet, like she says my name through the rocks that night long ago; then louder; then more louder, so loud I am afraid that Master will hear all the way in the far garden.

But Miranda does not wake.

What else to do?

I look at the sun in the sky and think it is high enough to go to my place and back before Master knows I am gone.

First I gather flowers and vines from the gardens; the little white ones like stars that smell so sweet, and some bigger ones that have flowers that are orange and red and shaped like a thing that makes a loud shout that Miranda says is called a trumpet, though she never did see one. I make them into a big circle as I go, tying them like a snare to catch a hare, but in my thoughts I am making what Miranda says is called a necklace. It is a special thing.

It is harder to climb to the most high place with my arms full, but at last there is Setebos laughing at the sky.

I put the circle of flowers and vines around his neck and it is oh, so pretty! Little white flowers and big orange-red flowers like flames side by side, and all the green leaves and vines, smelling so nice. I remember what Ariel says about Setebos, but I do not care. The spirit does not know everything.

Setebos watches over the isle and the sea, and Setebos watches over me since Umm is dead.

I am alive.

And Setebos is here.

So.

"Setebos." I reach to put my hands on his upturned face and say his name. The hard brown stone of him is warm from the sun. My eyes are hot and wet, and my hurting heart is afraid inside me. To pray is to say please and thank you, so I do. "Oh, please! Let her live. Let Miranda wake and live." I stretch tall and put my lips on his jaw. The circle of vines and flowers tickles against my skin, ticklety-tickle. "Please, Setebos! Thank you, Setebos!"

Little bits in the rocks in his eye-holes that I put there so he might see better sparkle in the sun.

I think he hears me.

"Please," I whisper again. "Thank you."

I go back.

Master is in the kitchen, moaning and groaning as he makes some bad-smelling thing on the hearth. Now that he is not so very, very angry, he thinks to be sad for Miranda who is hurt and not only himself, but I am still not sad for him. But now he is afraid, too, and that makes me more afraid. "Oh, oh!" he says. "Oh, Miranda, my poor, sweet child! You innocent fool! What have I done, what have I done?"

(*I* know what you have done, Master.)

He sees me. "There you are, lad!" There is white all around his eyes. He takes the pot from the fire and puts some cool water in it. "'Tis a tisane to reduce the fever and swelling of the brain," he says. "Willow-bark, yarrow, elderberry . . . come, I may require your assistance."

In Miranda's chamber where she lies sleeping, still sleeping, I watch as Master puts a spoon to her lips, but she does not swallow. Bad-smelling liquid dribble-drabbles away on both sides of her mouth.

Master takes out a thing that is like the shape of a trumpet-flower, only it is made of metal. "Hold her upright."

I do.

I am careful, oh, so very careful! I crouch beside her pallet and slide one arm beneath her back, lifting ever so very slow. I can smell the too-hotness of her skin. Miranda's head falls back and her hair tickles my arm.

Her mouth falls open, too.

Master puts the thin end of the metal trumpet-thing deep inside her mouth, puts it inside her throat. "There," he says. "Hold her fast, lad."

I hold Miranda and watch while Master pours spoon after spoon of liquid into the trumpet-thing. She does not wake, but her throat goes up and down as she chokes and coughs and swallows in her sleep, and some of the liquid goes into her even though she fights.

"Enough."

I lower her, ever so very slow.

Master stands. "I have done my best," he says. "'Tis in God's hands now."

I look at him.

He looks away.

And I wish, I wish . . . oh, I wish I had *all* the words I wanted, but I do not even have words to say how I feel.

Master says without looking at me to leave and I do, but I cannot sleep. When it is full dark I go back outside, back to Miranda's garden. There is a little oil-lamp burning in her chamber and Master sits in a chair beside her pallet and reads a book, his lips moving and his voice low like a buzzing bee. I cannot hear, not quite, but I think he must be praying to God in the sky; and I think oh, where were your prayers before, Master? Where were your prayers when you were putting the thing you should not have made in the ground?

But I say nothing.

All night I watch them like Setebos watches. I think I should hide myself when the dawn comes, but Master does not even see that I am there on the wall of Miranda's garden, watching, watching. He puts down his book and goes to make his chants, his strong voice rough today.

I creep through Miranda's window and look at her face. Her eyes open and my heart jumps like a hare, ready to be happy, hoppity-happy.

But then . . .

I see Miranda see me and I see her know me, but her mouth opens and no words come to her. I see her brow wrinkle, and then the fear of knowing and not-knowing and having no words comes in her eyes.

It is a fear I know.

Oh, Miranda!

"Caliban," I say to her, oh, so soft. "I am Caliban."

TWENTY-TWO

MIRANDA

Even looking backward from a distance of years, it is difficult to think about that time.

Caliban tells me that Papa was solicitous during the early days of my affliction, that he spent long hours beside my pallet while I slept, reading to me from the Bible, dosing me with tisanes and concoctions. That it was Papa who taught me anew how to bathe and dress myself.

I suppose it must be true, but I do not remember it. There are gaping holes in my memory.

Whatever broke inside me was slow to mend. My memories of those early days are little more than a haze of dread and guilt and confusion. Nothing seemed to work properly; my vision was blurred and my hands plucked uselessly at the bed-linens, seeking to restore some measure of order to my world. My limbs would not obey me, and my very wits were dim and befuddled.

For a long time, I had no memory of the incident itself. That returned to me in bits and pieces, each one more unwelcome than the last.

The crackling voice of the salamander . . .

Breaking glass . . .

The pale, misshapen thing gasping on the floor . . .

But I did not speak of those fragments of memories or what they might betoken. Indeed, I spoke very little in the early days of my affliction. My tongue was thick and clumsy and words were like familiar objects that had been placed just out of reach, frustrating me to no end.

Caliban understood. Oh, how well he understood! Caliban was the very soul of patience. It is *his* dear face I first remember seeing clearly when my blurred vision settled at last, not Papa's.

Papa.

I should so like to believe that he cared for me and prayed for me and tended to me in the most dire hours of my affliction, and yet as my memory begins to return, I remember *too* much. Words I would feign not grasp return unwanted and unwelcome and seep into my thoughts, words spoken in a soft, terrible voice, each one nonetheless as sharp and cutting as a shard of broken glass.

You've killed your mother all over again, Miranda.

And so it seems fitting to me that Papa is cool and withdrawn by the time I am well enough to begin my convalescence.

It is a lengthy process, but at every step of the way, Caliban is beside me. It is his arm on which I remember leaning when I take my first uncertain steps. It is his steady gaze that waits patiently while I search for the right words to come, and it is he who supplies them to the best of his ability when they do not.

Together, we become student and teacher alike as we learn and relearn the art of speech.

As for Ariel, the spirit makes himself scarce from my presence, and I am grateful for it.

When I have regained enough of my wits to understand what has befallen me, Papa tells me that he believes that I have suffered a seizure that caused bleeding in my brain, which governs and affects all aspects of the corpus. He says that because I am young and strong and healthy, he expects that with diligence and hard work, I shall make a full recovery.

He does not say why it happened and I do not ask. I wonder if the guilt that Papa feels for punishing me so harshly weighs as greatly on him as the guilt I feel for my profound disobedience.

Beyond that we do not speak of the incident in his sanctum, though it lies between us in all its mute horror.

Caliban does not speak of it either, but it seems to me that there is a different quality to his silence; a careful, waiting quality. It makes me fearful of what he might say if I question him about it, so I keep my counsel during the long months of my convalescence. I make progress in fits and starts, but slowly, slowly, all the broken parts of me heal.

I come to delight in ever so many things I took for granted before the incident: the quickness of my wits; the words that fall tripping from my tongue; the strength of my limbs; the dexterity of my hands and fingers. And Caliban . . . in all the goodness of his heart, Caliban delights with me.

It is an unseasonably warm day in the late autumn when I dare at last to break my silence on the matter.

We are sitting side by side in the kitchen garden with a large mound of acorns that Caliban has gathered. With his strong hands and coarse nails, he tackles the difficult chore of cracking and peeling them, while I grind their meal into flour in a mortar. It is tiresome work and the flour will need to be soaked many times over to leach out the bitterness, but the sun's warmth is congenial and I am glad of Caliban's company.

With my hands occupied and my gaze on the mass of acorn meal in my mortar, I find the courage to speak of it. "Caliban," I say to him. "That day . . ." My voice betrays me and quivers. I will it to firmness. "The day when I was . . . stricken." Out of the corner of my eye, I see his own hands go still.

"Yes?"

I clear my throat. "You know what happened, don't you? You know . . . you know what I did?"

He bows his head over the acorn he is shelling, his hair hiding his eyes. "I know you did go into Master's room." His voice turns grim. "And I know Master did punish you for it and hurt you."

"There was a *thing*." I do not know what else to call it, but it is at once a painful and vast relief to speak of it at last. I lower the pestle and my hands trace a shape in the air. "A *thing* in a jar. Oh, Caliban! It was so pale and it looked so very sad. I think it was trying to speak to me. And I . . ."

"I know," he murmurs.

"I caused it to fall!" The pent-up words flood from my mouth. "I broke it! There was glass, glass everywhere, and it . . . it *died*, Caliban! Right there on the floor! And Papa . . . Papa said . . ."

And then I am crying too hard to get the words out, great heaving sobs that wrack my body.

Caliban abandons his acorns and comes to stroke my hair, strands catching on his calloused skin. "I know," he whispers to me. "I know, Miranda. Do not cry."

At last the storm of my grief passes, leaving me limp and exhausted. I lean against Caliban, grateful for the solid warmth of his presence. "Papa said, 'You've killed your mother all over again,'" I say in a dull voice. "But I do not know what he meant by it. Do you?"

He is silent for a moment. "The spirit had a name for the thing. He called it a . . ." He trips over the word. "A homunculus."

"Ariel did?" I say.

Behind me, Caliban nods. "He said it was a thing that should never have been made. And that it was a mercy that it died." He hesitates, lowering his voice. "I watched Master put it in the ground."

"But why would Papa say what he did?" I say. "Why would he say I killed my *mother*?"

Caliban shifts away from me, his shoulders hunching. "I do not know what it is, this homunculus. I think it is something to do with your mother but it is nothing I understand." His tone is careful. "But that Ariel, he did say another thing about your mother that day."

I press him. "What?"

He looks at me, reluctance in his gaze. "The spirit did say that she died giving birth to you."

There is a part of me that thinks it should not hurt as much as it does to hear these words; and yet it does.

I had a mother.

She is dead; and I am to blame. Fresh tears sting my eyes. My mother died giving birth to me. And I do not even understand how such a thing can be. I have seen many a newborn chick hatching from their shells, and no hen ever took harm from it.

"How?" I say to Caliban, at a loss for words. *"Why?"*

"I do not know." Shaking his head, he takes up the stone he has been using to crack acorns. "I do not know!" He strikes another nut with a vicious blow, striking his thumb in the process and letting out a surprised bark of pain.

"Oh!" Reaching out, I take his hand in mine and kiss his bruised thumb. "I'm sorry, Caliban."

He pulls his hand back and cradles it, gazing at the purpling flesh around his nail-bed. His expression is soft and curious. "What is it called, Miranda?" he asks me. "To put your lips on a person so?"

I smile at him through tears. "A kiss."

He smiles back at me. "Thank you."

With that, Caliban and I resume our labors and do not speak further of the incident; but I do not forget what he said. The following day, when Caliban is out gathering wood, I seek Ariel.

As I soon discover and should well have imagined, it is a vain and foolish quest. Ariel might be anywhere on the isle and he might take any form; a passing breeze, a cloud floating overhead. I search the palace ground for what must surely be an hour on the sundial before I give up my quest and simply prevail upon whatever goodwill the mercurial spirit possesses.

"Ariel!" I cry aloud. "Ariel, please! If you can hear me, I would speak to you!"

At first there is no answer, and I feel all the more foolish. I am not my father to command the spirit with his art. Why should Ariel come at my beck and call? And then a telltale gust of wind swirls into the orchard, where sour oranges hanging from the trees put me in mind of the night that Ariel baited me, and he is there.

"Yes, milady?" There is a studied tone to the spirit's voice and his changeable eyes are light and crystalline, almost colorless. "Thou didst wish to speak to me?"

It is the first time in the long months since my affliction that I have been in Ariel's presence, and I find I am angry, so angry that I am trembling with it. "I want to know about my mother," I say to him.

A look that might almost be regret crosses Ariel's finely wrought features. "Of that, I am forbidden to speak, milady."

"You spoke of it to Caliban!" I shout at him.

"I spoke in thoughtless haste," Ariel says coolly. "'Twas an error on my part to do so."

"What of the . . . thing?" I ask. "The homunculus?" The spirit says nothing. "Are you forbidden to speak of that, too?"

"Shall we speak of the weather, milady?" Ariel makes a graceful gesture all around him with one arm, his white sleeve fluttering like a pennant. "'Tis passing fine for the time of year, though I fear a storm is brewing in the west some leagues from here. Shall we speak of speckled trout in the streams or late berries yet on the vine?"

"Why did you heed my call if you'll do naught but prattle at me of trout and berries?" I ask bitterly. "You told Caliban my mother died in giving birth to me. I do not understand how such a thing can even be. No hen ever died of a chick hatching."

"Oh, milady!" The spirit catches his breath as though I have struck him an unexpected blow. It is a sound that is not quite a laugh. His eyes darken to the hue of twilight and a mixture of involuntary pity and mockery fills his voice. "Thou poor innocent. Dost thou know nothing of the way of the world, and men and women in it? Dost suppose thou wast hatched like a veritable chick, scrabbling forth from the shell of an egg into the bright light of day?"

Misliking his tone, I do not answer.

Ariel sighs and casts his gaze skyward. "Oh, la! But of that, too, I am forbidden to speak lest I sully thy tender ears and render myself foresworn. Nature must be allowed to run its course. Master, Master, methinks thou art a fool," he says to the empty sky. "'Tis the fine edge of a blade that divides innocence from ignorance, and methinks it a blade that will turn in thy hand and cut thee one day."

"I don't understand," I say stiffly.

"No." Ariel lowers his gaze to meet mine. "Surely thou dost not. But I fear 'tis not my place to enlighten thee, milady."

I scowl at him. "Why did you come, then? Why did you answer my call?" Ariel's gossamer garments stir uneasily around him, and I realize he is fearful. "You baited me a-purpose," I say. "You *wanted* me to defy Papa. But he doesn't know, does he? And you're afraid that I'll tell him. That's why you came, isn't it?"

Ariel hesitates. "I did not intend thee harm, milady," he says with surprising gentleness. "Truly, I am sorry for thy suffering. But if thou hast questions unanswered, thou must ask thy father."

"But—"

He is gone.

And so that night at the supper table I ask Papa about my mother.

Papa stiffens. "If you value this peace we have forged between us, do not speak to me of your mother."

I look down at my platter. "I just—"

Papa slams his hand onto the table, making our fine silver platters jump and rattle. "I said, *do not speak of her!*"

So I do not. I do not speak of my mother or the incident.

I bury the memory of it as surely as Papa buried Caliban's mother and . . . whatever the thing was. The thing I killed in Papa's sanctum. The homunculus, the pale floating thing that is somehow tethered to my mother, who died in giving birth to me, tethered by an anklet of dark-gold hair, tethered by Papa's art.

The thing that should not have been made, the thing that died gasping amid shards of broken glass, sorrow fading in its milky eyes.

I do not think of it.

I am diligent.

I work hard.

Days turn into weeks, weeks turn into months. The sun sinks ever lower in the shrinking evenings, and autumn turns to winter.

Papa praises my progress and gauges it sufficient that I might resume my studies. This I am glad to do. The alphabet returns to me; I memorize lists and lists of correspondences, tracing them painstakingly on my slate. As time passes, I begin to learn about the powerful and arcane images that influence the seven governors and the three faces of each of the twelve signs of the Zodiac. Papa attempts to impart to me the rudiments of charting the paths of the planets throughout the spheres of heaven and the astrological signs and houses, but this is a complex mathematical endeavor I find impossibly difficult, and in time he decides that it is not worth his while and abandons his efforts.

I should have been terribly dismayed at disappointing Papa so, had I not discovered within myself a talent for illustration. There is a kind of magic in bringing images to life with mere lines of chalk on a slate, and I am content to spend hours immersed in the process of doing so. Papa is pleased by it and encourages me to develop my gift. I take to carrying a bit of chalk with me everywhere I go that I might sketch the flora and fauna I encounter on whatever surface I find that allows it, adorning smooth rocks and the trunks of trees with chalk drawings of birds and flowers and beetles that linger until the next rainfall washes them away.

There are long stretches of days wherein I do not think of the incident at all, wherein it seems it was naught but an unpleasant dream, half forgotten by the dawn.

It is better not to remember.

Had I not been so grievously afflicted, mayhap I would have felt otherwise, my natural sense of curiosity prevailing; but as the seasons pass and months turn into years, I am increasingly content to let matters rest.

One year passes much like the other, and the next and the next, all of us on the isle existing in a tenuous accord.

Papa has his secrets, Ariel has his mysteries, and the three of us share an unspoken guilt, with Caliban in his innocence at the center of it all, growing taller and stronger with each passing year. Although his limbs do not grow straight and true, they are powerful and sturdy, and as his shoulders broaden and his voice deepens, his kindness to me is unfailing.

I come to think nothing would change.

I am wrong.

TWENTY-THREE

Blood.

It begins with blood.

As I near fourteen years of age, I am not insensible of the changes to my body. Like Caliban, I have grown; not so tall or strong as he, but taller. My robes fall only to my shins and I think with covetous envy of the gowns from the pirate's loot that Papa has hidden away, though I do not dare to say so. Hair has begun to sprout in unexpected places, dusting my shins and growing wiry in the soft pits beneath my arms and at the juncture of my thighs. Tender buds of breasts grow on my chest, and I wonder if it means I am a woman grown at last, but Papa says no.

He is waiting for something, but I do not know what.

The passing years have touched Papa, too. There is more white than grey in his hair, and the dark streaks in his beard have faded.

Only Ariel remains unchanged.

In all the years that pass, I never do tell Papa that it was the spirit's taunting words that tempted me to an act of such profound disobedience. I am not at all certain that it would have tempered Papa's wrath; and, too, it pleases me to know that it is a prospect Ariel fears. Although the spirit conducts himself gently enough in my presence, I am quite sure that he continues to bedevil Caliban, who does not care to speak of it. But there are times when he returns from chores ranging far afield in a surly mood, and I know Ariel has been at him. Although I mislike the unfairness of it all, if Caliban prefers to endure it in silence, I respect his wishes. Still, it is a comfort to know there is a threat I can wield against the meddlesome spirit.

Otherwise I put the past behind me. If betimes my sleep is plagued by nightmares, I set them aside with the rising of the sun.

On the day that I awaken out of sorts, my small breasts sore and a dull ache low in my belly, I think little of it. The memory of my affliction will never grow so distant that I am not grateful to be alive and hale. I imagine this is but a touch of indigestion, and although I remember no troubling dreams on that particular morning, like as not I slept poorly for the griping of my belly, tossing and turning and bruising my flesh a trifle in the process. I cannot think what else it might be.

And so I ignore my discomfort, which after all is not so great that I cannot bear it without complaint. I am sure that my stomach will settle once I've broken my fast. I eat plain journey-cakes, unadorned by aught that might render my belly more bilious; and yet come noon, I feel no better.

Indeed, I feel rather worse. The dull, heavy pain expands to encompass my lower back and fitful cramps grip my belly. It is not wholly unlike a time some years ago when I took ill from eating unripe figs, and yet I suffer from neither nausea nor a flux of the bowels. It is a strange kind of pain, and I feel irritable and lumpish and almost weepy with it.

As the day wears on I begin to suspect it is not indigestion at all, but an imbalance of the humors. It is probable that I am suffering from an excess of black bile, rendering me melancholic. The realization is a relief, and I resolve to speak to Papa about it when he emerges from his sanctum in the evening. Doubtless he knows a purgative that will restore my humors to the proper balance, and mayhap he will even be proud of me for diagnosing my own ailment.

Melancholia, I think to myself, is ruled by Saturn, whose attributes are cold and dry. Plants and herbs that accord to Saturn include aloe, myrrh, onions, cumin, rue, and all plants that have thick leaves. These things I know by rote, though I do not understand their applications.

Although Papa has not yet entrusted me with a glimpse into his books of wisdom, he has described to me at length the various images the sages of yore claim one might wreak to draw Saturn's influence. With great care, I limn one of those selfsame images, which is that of a standing man holding a fish above his head and a large lizard resting beneath his feet, upon my slate. It is my favorite among all the images of Saturn because fish and lizards are creatures I have seen with my own eyes, and I have practiced drawing them enough times on my sojourns that I can render them with considerable accuracy. The standing man resembles Papa. It is a good likeness, and for a few moments, I am passing pleased with it.

My belly cramps in a sickly manner.

Oh, and now I am not sure at all that I should be seeking Saturn's favor to dispel this excess! Mayhap it is quite the contrary, and I should seek the favor of one of the seven governors such as Jupiter or Venus, whose attributes are hot and moist and sanguine, to balance my humors.

I erase my slate with the heel of my hand, brushing ochre dust on the skirts of my robe. I am dabbling in ignorance; and as Ariel said to me long ago, it is the fine edge of a blade that divides innocence from ignorance.

I am weary of both, and my low belly hurts with a dull, persistent ache that grows surprisingly difficult to ignore.

In the late afternoon, Caliban returns from foraging with a pail full of fish. I rise to assist him. I have been sitting for so long, my thighs feel wet and sticky. When I turn from opening the larder door, Caliban has a peculiar look on his face.

"Miranda," he says in a cautious tone. "You are bleeding."

"How so?" I look blankly at him, sure that I have sustained no injury. Nonetheless, his expression alarms me. "Where?"

He answers reluctantly. "On your bottom."

"How can it be?" I turn to look behind me, tugging at the worn blue fabric of the robe I am wearing. Caliban is right. I can see the edge of a dark bloodstain spreading on the thin cloth and my throat tightens with fear. "Oh, no!"

"Are you hurt?" Caliban sets down the pail. "I will look."

"No!" I back away from him in horror. For all that he has been a dear and constant companion for years, to let him see my privy parts is unthinkable. Having suffered grievously for disobeying Papa in the past, I am all the more mindful of his dictums. "No, Caliban, you mustn't! Papa says I must *never* be immodest!"

Caliban scowls. "Master says many things. If you will not let me look, I will get him."

I shake my head. "And disturb him at his studies? No, you mustn't do that, either."

His scowl deepens. "You are *bleeding*."

I spread one hand over my belly. "I'm sure it's naught but a flux brought on by something I ate." My voice is shaking; I do not believe my own words. "Oh, I'm sorry! How very embarrassing."

"Miranda—" Caliban takes a step toward me.

I retreat farther, filled with fear and mortification. "Leave me be, Caliban!" When he hesitates, I flee.

In my chamber, I place my wash-basin on the tiled floor and fill it with water from the ewer. I strip off my robe and crouch over the basin, examining myself. My thighs are smeared with blood. I splash water on myself with a cupped hand. Thin strands of crimson swirl in the clear water in the basin.

"Miranda!" It is Caliban's voice, Caliban's face at the window. In my haste, I have forgotten to close the shutters, which I am accustomed to leave open in all manner of clement weather.

"Caliban!" My voice is high and shrill. I cover my breasts with one arm, reaching for my soiled robe to cover my nether region. I am naked and terrified and furious, crouching like a beast and bleeding. Humiliated tears stream down my face. My nose runs, and I can taste a sickening salty slick on my lips. *"Go away!"*

At last he obeys and vanishes from sight.

Clutching the robe to me, I fling myself across the chamber and yank the shutters closed. The wood is old and cracked and the intricate latticework would do little more to keep out a prying gaze than it does a chill wind, but the garden is empty.

I return to crouch over the basin, my back to the windows. The blood on my thighs is gone, but when I touch the place between them, my fingers come away bloody. With a scrap of cloth, I scrub furiously until the water in the basin is pink and there is no more blood on the cloth. I pray that that is the last of it. I cannot think why my body should bleed thusly, unless it means that the very organs within me are dissolving.

Mayhap what broke inside me years ago never truly healed after all. I do not know.

My blue robe is in a sorry state. Its threadbare fabric already bears a myriad of faded stains amidst the years' worth of wear and grime that washing will no longer remove, but there is something deeply shameful about this one. It is blood, only blood, but it seems as shameful to me as though I have soiled myself.

Kneeling naked on the tile floor, I scrub and scrub at the stain with a dollop of Papa's soap. It lightens, but it is clear it will not go away.

I am weeping as I scrub.

My belly cramps, and I feel a fresh hot trickle of blood on the inside of my left thigh.

I weep harder.

"Miranda!" It is not Caliban's voice at the door of my chamber, but Papa's, deep and firm. He knocks, but does not enter unbidden. "Calm yourself, child. I would speak with you."

"Oh, Papa!" I struggle to suppress my tears, but my voice is ragged. "I fear there's something terribly wrong with me."

"I promise you there is not." Now Papa's voice is gentle, more gentle than I recall hearing in years. "May I enter?"

I pluck a clean brown robe from my chest and don it in haste, then stand very straight, mindful of the slow blood seeping from the juncture of my thighs. "Yes, Papa. Of course."

If I had a hundred years to guess, I do not think I would have guessed that Papa would enter my chamber smiling that day, a bundle of something tucked beneath one arm; and yet he does.

"Congratulations, my dearest daughter," Papa says to me. Cupping my face in his free hand, he leans down to kiss my brow. The amulets around his neck rattle faintly and his long grey beard tickles my nose and chin. "Today at last you are a woman grown."

I have never felt like aught less.

"I do not understand." My voice sounds small. "Papa . . . I am bleeding from inside."

He nods gravely. "Yes, I know. Caliban told me his concerns. Your woman's courses are upon you."

I stare at him in confusion. "I'm not ill?"

"Far from it," Papa says. "Did you not hear me? You have flowered, Miranda. The day for which you have long yearned has arrived at last."

"This?" I gesture at the blameless walls of my chamber, at the closed shutters, at the basin full of bloody pink water, at the sodden mass of my stained blue robe lying on the floor. Suddenly, I am outraged at the thought that this mess and discomfort is the harbinger of womanhood for which I've waited so long. *"This?"*

"It is a sign that your body is ready to bring new life into the world," Papa says. "Your womb, which is the vessel of life within you, does but shed an excess of sanguine humor to make room for the possibility of a child."

"A *child*?" I say in wonder and dismay.

Now Papa shakes his head, raising his hand to forestall me. "I speak only of the possibility, Miranda. Of course, you shall remain a virgin until you are wed in the eyes of God."

I do not know what that means.

Do I?

A memory of Ariel's voice whispers in the far recesses of my thoughts. *She bade me to lie with her as a man lies with a woman . . . Dost thou know nothing of the ways of the world, and men and women in it?*

I do not.

And yet . . .

Papa is still speaking. ". . . the first great mystery of womanhood. The second shall be revealed to you on your wedding night, and you shall suffer no man's touch until your husband claims his rights."

"My husband!" A startled laugh escapes me; it has never occurred to me to think on such a prospect. "Who am I to wed, Papa? Caliban?"

A thunderous look crosses Papa's face. "Hold your tongue, child!

Heaven forfend. Do you think I would see my only daughter, my own flesh and blood, wed to a monstrosity?"

"Well, *I* don't think him monstrous at all," I say defiantly. "Caliban is kind and good. And if I am to take a husband, I'd sooner wed him than Ariel."

"Ariel!" Papa takes a sharp breath. "Miranda, you must not even think such thoughts."

I temper my defiance with humility. "What *am* I to think, Papa?"

He lays one hand on my shoulder. "I do but ask your trust, child. One day, when my plans come to a head, all shall be revealed." *You keep saying that,* I think to myself, but I do not say it aloud. "I promise, the man you wed will be neither a tame savage nor a spirit such as Ariel. But today—" Papa untucks the bundle he carries under his arm and shows me its contents: a number of muslin pouches, a clay jar with a lid, and a lengthy parti-colored sash pieced together from various fabrics. "This is a serious business, Miranda. The menstruum of a virgin possesses powerful magical properties. You must manage it with care."

I swallow, reminded anew of the vile trickle making its way down my thigh. "How?"

Papa holds up one of the pouches. "Dried sphagnum moss. While your woman's courses are upon you, you will place one of these pouches beneath your privy parts as necessary to capture the flow, binding it in place with the sash."

He sounds proud of himself, as though this is some difficult problem he has solved. "Yes, Papa."

"When a pouch will absorb no more of the menstruum, place it in the jar and notify me," he continues. "You may knock upon the door of my sanctum, leave the jar in the hallway, and depart. I will take custody of the jar and its contents and return it to you. Is that clear enough, child?"

I nod. "Yes, Papa."

"Tonight is the first night of the waning moon, which is to the good," Papa muses. "It means your womb reaches fullness in accordance with Luna herself, and your menstruum shall be all the more powerful for it. And if your cycle remains constant and true, as I hope it does, you shall know that your courses will commence each month when Luna begins to wane."

I find a faint ray of hope in his words. "Then I shan't *always* bleed henceforth, Papa?"

"Always?" He chuckles. "No, of course not. Your courses will come upon you once a month and last for several days, mayhap a week. You must notify me if they last longer."

"Yes, Papa," I say.

Papa smiles at me. "Very good. And when your courses have concluded *this* month, we will speak of your assisting me in my sanctum." He pauses, waiting for me to respond. I look at the floor and do not say anything. Although I once yearned for it above all else, now the thought of entering Papa's sanctum fills me with quiet dread. His smile fades. "Understand that you must never enter without permission, and not at all when your courses are upon you. Never. At such a time, your very gaze could pollute the delicate working of my art." He pauses again. "Miranda, may I trust that I have impressed upon you how vital it is that you observe these strictures with the utmost scruple?"

I choke back a bitter bark of laughter.

I should like to say, *Yes, Papa, you may be sure of it, for I have no desire to invoke your wrath. I do not wish to return to the helplessness of childhood and spend another year of my life learning to walk and talk anew.*

"Yes," I murmur instead. "Of course." And yet I cannot keep my peace, not wholly. I steal a glance at him. "Papa, if you knew this day would come, why did you not tell me?"

He furrows his brow. "But we have spoken of it often, Miranda."

"No." I shake my head. "You told me often that one day I would be a woman grown. You told me I would *know*. You did not tell me I should know it by the sign of pain and blood." My voice rises, taking on a shrill note once more. "How was I to know? Why did you not tell me it would be *this*?"

Papa's expression turns stern and his hand rises to take hold of my amulet. "Calm yourself, child!"

I fall silent, my body stiffening in terror and my bladder threatening to void itself in a hot gush.

"It was not always thus for womankind," Papa says. "In the Garden of Eden, our foremother Eve knew no such travail." His voice deepens as he lets go the amulet and quotes from the Holy Bible. *"And they were both naked, the man and his wife, and were not ashamed.* But what transpired?"

I look away. "Eve disobeyed God. She ate the fruit of the tree of knowledge of good and evil, and Adam did, too."

Papa nods. "Indeed. And as God cast them forth from Eden for their disobedience, he said unto Eve, *I will greatly multiply thy sorrow and thy conception; in sorrow thou shalt bring forth children, and thy desire shall be unto thy husband, and he shall rule over thee.* It is Eve's punishment you endure, child."

"But I am not guilty of Eve's sin," I protest in a low whisper; yet even as the words leave my mouth, I know that they are untrue. I succumbed to Ariel's temptation even as Eve succumbed to that of the serpent in the garden. I disobeyed Papa as surely as Eve disobeyed God.

I have been punished for it.

Years later, I am still being punished for it.

"All of humankind bears the cost of Eve's sin, Miranda," Papa says dryly. "Women are weak in body and will. I suggest you use this time to contemplate the price of disobedience."

I say nothing.

Papa glances at the pinkish water in my wash-basin. "If you bathe yourself when your courses are upon you, you must dispose of the leavings thusly. Empty the basin on barren ground facing east and rinse it clean in running water; water from the stream, not water drawn from the well or a fountain where traces of the menstruum may linger and taint the elemental spirits. Do you understand?"

"Yes, Papa."

"Very well." He sets down his bundle. "Then I shall leave you to attend to the business of womankind, daughter."

Now I want nothing more than for him to go and leave me alone with my shame and uncleanliness; and yet there is one last fear niggling at me. "Papa?"

He pauses. "Yes?"

"You're not angry at Caliban for disturbing you, are you?" I ask him. "It's only that he was afraid for me."

"Angry?" Papa frowns. "No. Our wild lad's concern was misplaced, but I do not blame him for it."

I sigh with relief. "I am glad."

TWENTY-FOUR

CALIBAN

Oh, Setebos!

I have seen a thing I should not have seen.

I do not think this the very first thing when it happens, no; I do not think it at all. I think only that Miranda is hurt and scared, and I have not seen her so since she woke oh, so many years ago after Master did punish her and she almost did die. Only then I did know how to help, how to help Miranda walk and grow strong and find the words she has lost, how to help Miranda be Miranda again, and she did understand and let me.

Today is different.

Today there is blood and Miranda is scared and angry and shouts, Miranda runs and hides from me.

Today Miranda is not Miranda.

And so I go, I go to fetch Master, and at first he is angry, but I tell him that Miranda is bleeding and Master laughs, ha-ha, like I have told him a good thing, his face all bright and happy. "Oh ho!" he says. "Miranda is not hurt."

I think mayhap Master does not understand. "But she is bleeding."

"Yes, yes." Master pats my shoulder. "It is all very natural and part of God's plan. Do not be alarmed. Go about your business, lad. I will go to her and explain."

But I do not go. My shoulders go tight with anger. I do not understand how Miranda can be bleeding without being hurt. "Explain *what?*"

Master's face changes. "It is no concern of yours," he says in his cold, hard voice. "Now or ever. Believe me when I say that she is unharmed and leave her be. You're not to lay a finger on her."

I do not show him my teeth, but my lip curls even though I do not mean it to. "I would *never* hurt her!"

"No, of course not. I've made certain of it." Master touches one of the amulets that hang from his neck, acting as if it was *me* that almost killed you, Miranda, and not him. "I'm bidding you not to touch her."

Why?

I open my mouth to say the word, but then I see in my memory the thing I should not have seen, and it is as though I am seeing it for the first time.

Miranda.

Miranda naked.

Oh, oh, oh!

I lower my head so that Master cannot see what I am seeing behind my eyes. I did not tell him I saw Miranda in her chamber, only in the kitchen.

"Good lad." Master's voice is kind again. "Now begone with you and do not fret. I promise you, Miranda is healthy and well."

I go.

I leave the palace and run far and fast and hard to the high crag where Setebos awaits me, I run with my legs going pumpity-pump and my heart going thumpity-thump until my blood pounds in my ears like waves breaking on the shore. I climb the sharp rocks with hands and feet, not caring that the rocks cut me. I am trying to run away from the memory of what I have seen, but I cannot run from a thing I carry inside me. Atop the crag, I throw myself to the ground beneath Setebos's shadow.

Miranda.

I'm bidding you not to touch her.

Oh, but Miranda's skin where the sun has not kissed it is soft and white, as white as milk.

And I have seen it.

I have seen the curve of her little breasts hanging above the wash-basin with their tender pink tips. I have seen her slender, pale thighs and the little thicket of dark golden hair where they join together.

Oh, Setebos!

I cannot unsee it.

There is an ache deep inside me, an ache in my chest that such beauty should exist in the world.

There is another ache, too.

It is a different ache, an animal ache. The rod of flesh at my groin swells and stiffens with it, rising to stand upright beneath the rough canvas of my breeches. The twin sacks that hang under it rise and tighten, too. It is a thing that happens sometimes that I do not speak of. I do not want Miranda to know my flesh is unruly and immodest. I would not tell her any more than I would make water in front of her; but before today, it seemed like a thing with no harm in it, no more shame in it than making water.

Oh, but now it is different, everything is different. It is because I saw Miranda naked that my rod rises, and there is a wanting in me like in dreams where there is a secret pleasure that comes hard and fast, and in the morning there is a mess.

But this is not a dream and there is shame in it.

Setebos laughs at the sky.

It aches, it aches so very badly! It has never ached so before. I crouch on my feet and untie the drawstring of my breeches, then take my swollen rod in my hand. I think if I try to make water, mayhap it will not ache so badly.

(That is a lie, Caliban.)

My rod pulses to the touch, blood beating hard in my veins. The head of it has come all the way out from beneath its hood of skin, and it is hot and swollen and weeping. I feel like weeping, too.

I am ashamed.

Oh, but it feels so good to hold it! And I think, I think . . . no, I will *not* think of it, but I do. Miranda's tender little breasts naked, their pink tips hanging. I think of touching them. My aching rod twitches like a fish in my hand, my hand slides on it, the loose skin slides under my hand, and it feels so good, so very good. I let my hand keep sliding, sliding, up and down, and my sacks rise higher and tighter, and I cannot stop. The pleasure is coming like a stream bursting its banks.

Closing my eyes, I try not to think of Miranda.

I think of Miranda.

"Ungh!"

It is a deep groan, an animal groan, that I give as a gush of milky-white fluid spurts into the air.

And then it is like a storm that has passed. The ache is gone. My sacks feel empty and my rod softens and droops, hiding its head once more.

I sigh.

"If thy bestial nature were in doubt, I should say 'tis now heartily disproved," says a light, mocking voice.

Ariel.

Hot with shame and anger, I rise and pull my breeches over my privy parts, tying the drawstring. "You! What do you want?"

Sitting cross-legged on a cloud, the spirit ignores my question. "Thou hast committed Onan's sin and spilled thy seed on the ground," he observes. "Though I think that the Lord High God would surely rather it found no purchase, and will not smite thee for it." He smiles his thin, cruel smile. "Shall I guess what has stirred thy passion, monster? Blood is the harbinger that tells the tale. Eve's curse has come to fruition in the magus's daughter."

"A curse!" Now I am alarmed, too. "Master said nothing of a curse. Master said Miranda is healthy and well!"

"And so she is, as well as any lass blossoming into womanhood," Ariel says, unconcerned. "Eve's curse is the burden of all womankind; aye, and the burden of mankind, too." He looks at my face and laughs. "Oh la, poor monster! Wilst thy dullard's wits not allow thee to compass the truth that thy lustful loins would fain shout to the heavens?" He leans forward. "Surely thou hast seen goats at rut in the mountainside in autumn, and give birth to gamboling kids come spring's warm breath. Miranda's womb has become fallow ground. The lass is ripe for breeding."

Rut.

I do not know this word, and yet I fear I do. What the spirit says is true. I have seen he-goats climb atop she-goats, humping and pumping with their stiff rods; yes, and wild dogs in the empty fishing village at the shore, too. I did not understand their game. Now understanding comes upon me and it is like a dark tide in my blood, an understanding I do not want.

"No," I say, shaking my head. "Do not speak so of Miranda! Master would punish you for it!"

"Oh aye, so he would, my fine fellow servant. The magus wouldst punish me most grievously." Ariel makes his cloud go away with one wave of his arm, dropping lightly to the earth on his white feet. "Though not, I think, so harshly as he wouldst punish *thee* did I tell him what I caught thee at this day. Didst think of the lass whilst thou pleasured thyself?"

I bare my teeth at him. "Do not speak of her so!"

He laughs, but there is sorrow in it. "Oh, poor monster! Thou hast a tenderness for her."

"How should I not?" I say through my teeth. "Miranda is my friend!"

"Ah, but now that thou knowest there is more to dream, thou wilt dare to dream it," Ariel says softly, as softly as the wind. "Thou shouldst not, for there is only pain in it for thee. Methinks the magus in his sanctum has already chosen a bridegroom for his daughter. Who shall it be? A prince? A potentate? A pharaoh?"

I should know better than to let Ariel bait me into responding; oh, I *do* know better! But, but, but . . . how can such a thing even be true? If Miranda is only this day a woman, how can Master think to see her wed, when yesterday she was a child? "That cannot be," I say. "Who? There is no one!"

Ariel holds up one slender hand. "I, a humble servant, do but speculate. Who am I to know what the great magus dost see in his mirror? Who am I to know what the great magus wilst call forth with his art or when that day shall come? But of this I am sure. The bridegroom will be well formed and pleasing to behold." The spirit's appearance changes, and of a sudden it is a young man who stands before me, tall and fair-skinned, dressed in fine attire. "He shall be hale of limb and handsome of face," the spirit continues in a deeper voice. "Eloquence shall grace his tongue. He shall be possessed of all the qualities to charm and delight a girlish heart." He pauses. "Shall I tell thee what he most assuredly shall *not* be?"

"No," I say. "I would hear no more!"

But Ariel does not listen. "He shall not be swart and stooped, with hunched shoulders and bowed legs," he says, and his appearance shifts. "Nor shall he have a villain's low brow and out-thrust jaw."

I recognize myself take shape before me.

"He'll not have hair as coarse as a pony's mane, nor sullen eyes that glower beneath it," Ariel continues, and now his voice is as rough and harsh as my own. A sprinkling of darker moles emerges to dot the brown skin of his face and throat and shoulders. "He'll not be speckled like a toad."

I see myself.

I am ugly and misshapen.

It is a thing which Ariel has told me before, but today he has *shown* me. Now I understand it truly in my bones, an understanding that sinks into me like a heavy stone into those dark tides.

Beside Miranda, I am a monster.

And then I am running again, running like a poor dumb wounded beast, running and falling and scrambling on bleeding hands and feet down the crag, my chest hurting and my breath coming hard in my throat, picking myself up and running, running, running with nowhere to go from a knowing I cannot run away from, and all the while Ariel's laughter follows me, sharp and bright as knives.

TWENTY-FIVE

MIRANDA

Day by day, I accustom myself to the unpleasant business of womanhood. I cannot help but feel betrayed by it, as though I were promised a wondrous gift and given something loathsome in its place.

I suppose that is unfair, for Papa never promised me that it would be wondrous to be a woman grown. No, that is a fantasy I created for myself, daring to hope that it would be a glorious day on which Papa entrusted me with all of his secrets at last, and I would know who I was and from whence I came.

I see now that that was a vain hope. Contemplating the price of disobedience as Papa bade me, I come to see that the trust that I lost when I disobeyed him can never be regained, no more than Adam and Eve can hope to regain the lost paradise of Eden after disobeying God. Like Eve, I sought knowledge forbidden to me; and like Eve, I have only myself to blame for my sin. I should be grateful that Papa yet speaks of allowing me to assist him in his sanctum.

If the prospect fills me with creeping dread, well, I have only myself to blame for that, too.

Still, there is a small resentful part of me, the faint spark of rebellion not extinguished by my punishment and ensuing affliction, that cannot help but think that Papa *might* have warned me about the burden of Eve's curse.

After all, it is an alarming amount of blood that I lose, and it is no easy task to bind the moss-filled muslin pouches in place with the sash to capture it. Although I pass the sash between my thighs and knot it firmly around my waist, the pouches are prone to shifting nonetheless. In order not to dislodge them, I am forced to walk with a careful, spraddle-legged, shuffling gait, ever heedful of the bulky pouch of dried sphagnum that is wedged between my thighs and growing sodden and distasteful as it absorbs the blood that continuously seeps from me. I find it necessary to place the jar outside Papa's sanctum and knock upon the door at least three times a day. Of course, the shifting of the pouches causes blood to soak the sash, too, in patches that dry and crust and chafe my thighs. Given that Papa regards this blood—this *menstruum,* as he calls it—as such a valuable and dangerous substance, I am not sure what I am to do about it.

When I ask Papa, he frowns. "I should have thought the arrangement sufficient," he says. "Can you not manage these matters more carefully, Miranda?"

I look down. "Forgive me, Papa. I am doing my best."

"Ah, child!" A rueful note enters Papa's voice. "I would that . . . no mind. I am doing my best, too."

In the end, he bids me wash the sash in running water and gives me a generous length of the canvas that Ariel has purloined from somewhere—a wrecked ship within some leagues of the isle, I suspect—that I might make additional sashes from it.

Grateful, I use the canvas to fashion a garment that girdles my waist with a wider sash affixed to the rear of it that passes between my thighs and knots in the front. Although the canvas is coarse against my skin, the garment I devise serves better to hold the pouches in place. It works well enough that I fashion a second and a third such garment that I might always have a clean, dry sash at hand. By the third day, the sickly pain that grips my belly goes away. I empty my wash-basin on barren ground where no gnomes delve, rinsing the basin and my befouled sashes in a swift-running portion of the stream where no undines frolic. Such are the small victories of my messy and burdensome introduction to womanhood.

And yet along with the unexpected inconvenience of the business of womanhood comes a slow-dawning sense of wonder.

In the innocence of childhood, I had supposed that to become a woman grown was a simple matter of reaching a certain age; ten years, mayhap. It seemed likely enough to me that passing from one to two digits of age marked a threshold before Papa disabused me of the notion. He said that I would know when the day came, and I suppose there is a certain truth to it since I most assuredly took note of the day's arrival.

But it is better not to think of that and fan the spark of resentment. Instead, as the days pass, my thoughts turn from contemplation of disobedience to the words that Papa spoke on the day my courses began.

It is a sign that your body is ready to bring new life into the world. Your womb, which is the vessel of life within you, does but shed an excess of sanguine humor to make room for the possibility of a child.

A *child*!

I marvel at the notion. To think that a child might grow inside me! There is a great deal I do not yet understand about it, and I know it is a thing that cannot come to pass ere I am wed—and how that might transpire on our lonely isle if I am to wed neither Caliban nor Ariel is an almighty mystery—but the mere prospect of it is a wonderment.

'Tis no wonder, then, that there is power in the blood I shed, for it is blood shed in the service of life.

I should like to know how this whole business works. I have not forgotten Ariel's condescending pity when he learned I imagined that human babies were hatched much in the manner of chicks, nor have I forgotten that it is a business fraught with danger if 'tis true that my own mother died of it. *In sorrow thou shalt bring forth children* . . .

Sorrow or death.

Yes, I should very much like to know.

But when I raise the topic with Papa—carefully, oh, so tentatively— he says only that I need not trouble myself with such knowledge yet and cautions me against pursuing it.

"It is no fit topic for an unwed virgin," he says in a stern tone.

Having learned the price of disobedience all too well, I let the matter lie, though it does not stop me from wondering.

And I wonder . . . I wonder what Caliban knows. When Papa did first summon him, it seemed to me that I should be the wild boy's teacher in all things always, for he was almost wholly savage and I knew ever so much more than him. In a sense the latter remains true as Caliban can neither read nor write, and knows naught of the multitude of correspondences and imagery that Papa has bade me memorize. As pleased as Papa was with Caliban's success in mastering language, he gauged it not worth the time and effort it would require to teach him any higher skills.

Yet our roles changed during the long months of my recovery, and they have remained changed.

Is there a sign such as the onset of a woman's courses that marks a boy's transition into manhood, I wonder? If so, Caliban has never spoken of it.

Over the years, Papa has taken regular measurements of the growth of Caliban's limbs and skull and corpus, and refined his initial reckoning of his age, placing it at ten years when he was summoned, which means that Caliban is some four years my elder. At seventeen, surely he must be considered a young man.

I think there must not be a sign or he would have told me so . . . but mayhap I am wrong. He does not tell me when Ariel torments him, and I suspect the mercurial spirit speaks to Caliban of things he is forbidden to say to me.

And, too, Caliban is angry at me.

On the day my courses begin, he vanishes and returns at dusk empty-handed, covered in scrapes and bruises, and Papa is forced to punish him. I do not blame Caliban for his anger, for I shouted most unkindly at him when he was but trying to help. I tender him a sincere apology for it the next day, imagining he will accept it and we shall be friends again.

Instead, he is strange.

"You should not apologize," he mumbles without looking at me. "I should not have done what I did."

"No," I agree. "You should not." Of course, I did not tell Papa that Caliban came to my window. "But you were only trying to help, and I should not have shouted as I did. Will you not forgive me for it?"

He shrugs, his shoulders hunched and tight.

I lay a hand on his arm. "Caliban?"

To my surprise, he jerks away as though my touch has scalded him and gives me a swift, fierce glare. "Do not touch me!"

Bewildered, I seek to apologize anew, but Caliban turns his back on me and stalks away. Nor does he forgive me in the days that follow, but remains sullen and withdrawn, refusing to meet my gaze. When I enter a room, he leaves it. He vanishes for hours on end, and reappears to stomp about the palace and grounds, tending to his chores with ill grace, doing just enough that Papa reprimands him without punishing him.

I do not know what I have done to grieve him so. I think it must be the uncleanliness of my woman's courses that offends him and makes him recoil from my presence.

'Tis a hurtful thought, but there is naught that I can do about it.

On the fourth day, my courses slow to a mere trickle and on the fifth day there is no more blood.

I tell Papa.

Papa is pleased. "On the morrow, you shall assist me in my sanctum," he says to me.

I make myself smile at him. "Thank you, Papa."

That night in my dreams I see *it*. The pale misshapen thing floating in its jar, tiny hands like starfish pressing against the glass walls, its milky eyes and its bud-shaped mouth opening and closing.

Shattered glass.

Its mouth gaping, gasping for air.

Oh, but when I awaken with a gasp of my own, the dream fades. I have learned well how to put it behind me. And now there is sunlight and the sound of Papa's chanting. There is a fine gown of whisper-soft blue fabric draped over the chest in my chamber. With a quick glance to be certain that the shutters of my window are closed, I don it with alacrity. It is a bit too large for me and it smells faintly of an incense Papa must have used to suffumigate it, with an underlying hint of mold, but it seems to me the most wondrous thing in the world, so wondrous I burst into tears.

This is the kind of gift for which I have yearned for so long. Now I truly feel like a woman grown.

I open my chest and take the mirror that Caliban gave me from its hiding place beneath my ragged robes. It is too small to show me the whole of my image, but when I hold it at different angles and turn this way and that, I see myself in pieces. More of the skin of my chest shows than I am accustomed to seeing and the gown gapes in the front to reveal the faint shadow of the valley between my breasts, but it reaches all the way to the floor so that I am no longer bare-legged below the knees.

Holding my skirts so that they do not drag upon the floor, I hurry to the kitchen so that I might begin my chores.

Caliban is tending to the fire in the hearth, a task with which Papa entrusted him some years ago. I am so glad, I forget that he is wroth with me.

"Oh, Caliban!" I twirl, letting my blue skirt flare out around me. "Look! Isn't it beautiful?"

I think he forgets for a moment too, for his mouth curls into a smile as he looks up from the hearth, warm and kind and familiar; and for the space of a few heartbeats, it seems to me that everything might be as it was long ago, happy and peaceful. But then a different expression crosses Caliban's face as swiftly as a shooting star across the night sky, a mingled look of sorrow and regret and anger . . . and then it is gone.

Turning back to the fire, he mutters something under his breath.

Weary of trying to decipher his moods, I choose to ignore him and go into the garden to fetch the morning's bounty, feeling gently beneath the sitting hens and placing their warm, fresh eggs in the apron of my long blue skirt. When I return, Papa is seated at the table. I set the eggs on the sideboard with care, and then, heedless of decorum, I fling my arms around him in an impetuous embrace. "Papa! Thank you ever so much."

Papa chuckles. "You've earned the right, child. Or, dare I say, young lady? Come, let me behold you in your finery."

Taking a step back, I make a deep curtsy, the hem of my skirt puddling around my bare feet.

Papa smiles at me, the creases around his mouth deepening with pride. "You are the very picture of a fine young lady."

At the hearth, Caliban breaks a stout branch over his knee with a sharp, defiant *crrrack,* shoves both halves into the fire, and stomps out of the kitchen, taking the milk-pail with him. I watch him go with dismay, feeling my brow furrow.

"In the name of all that is holy, what ails the lad?" Papa complains. "He's been sulking for days."

"I do not know," I murmur. "He will not speak of it."

Papa waves one hand in dismissal. "Then let us pay him no heed. He does but seek attention."

I do not think that is true. Something is troubling Caliban; something greater than my own burst of fear and temper, and something other than the uncleanliness of my woman's courses, since they have passed for now. But I do not know what it is, and I cannot force Caliban to confide in me. I can only hope that he will choose to do so in his own time.

Papa and I break our fast together. My heart is beating too quickly in my chest. At first I wish that the meal would never end, then I wish it were over so that I might confront my fear of entering Papa's sanctum and be done with it. I gobble my food in unseemly haste and must sit and wait while Papa eats.

"Come," he says when at last he has finished. "You may tidy the dishes later. Today, you are to assist me."

I follow him through the palace and up the stairway, down the long hallway to the door of Papa's sanctum. My chest feels tight, my heart continuing to flutter like a trapped butterfly inside it. There are spots behind my eyes and the walls seem to pulse in my vision, the Moorish writing etched on them wriggling. I tell myself that I am being foolish. I have walked this very hallway several times a day during the past five days, carrying my jar of menstruum. I have knocked upon this very door.

But there was no question of entering the sanctum itself.

Papa reaches for the handle of the door and pauses. "Your face is so very white, child," he says. "Why?"

I swallow. "I am afraid."

"You are here today with my blessing," he says gently. "And I promise you, there is naught to fear."

He opens the door.

For a moment, I am paralyzed once more, bolts of pain shrieking in my skull; but no, there is no pain, only the memory of it.

I peer past Papa.

It is as I remember, and yet it is different, too. There are the gleaming instruments, there are the shelves of books, there are the cases filled with curiosities and the strange glass vessels, the neatly labeled jars and drawers. There is the glowing brazier with the red-gold salamander lying curled in its nest of flame; but its gemlike eyes are closed. There is no glass jar of clear liquid with a pale, floating *thing* in it.

I let out my breath slowly and follow Papa into his sanctum. There are no strange drawings or symbols on the walls. The walls are clean and white with a fresh coating of lime.

A breeze blows through the open windows and a pair of sylphs chase each other through its eddies. One of the earth elementals squats expectantly before a table that contains various stone pots and clay bottles and implements, rubbing his spade-shaped hands together, a broad grin on his rough-hewn face.

Papa gestures toward the table. "That is for you, Miranda."

I approach it, and the little gnome scampers out of my way. With tentative hands, I open the lidded pots. The pots; oh, the pots contain colors! Pigments such as I never dreamed existed—a blue as deep and vibrant as the distant sea under an August sky, a green as rich and verdant as palm leaves, a yellow as bright and sunny as a fresh egg yolk, a red as crimson as blood. There is black as black as a moonless night and white as pure as a cloud.

My mouth waters to behold such colors.

There is an array of long-handled brushes, finely hewn spindles of wood to which goat's hair has been cunningly affixed; some in pointed tufts, some in broad fans. I examine them one by one.

"You have a gift for illustration, Miranda," Papa says. "One that surpasses my own."

There is a tall book-stand beside the table, a book open upon it. I peek at it. I cannot read the language in which it is written, but there are colorful drawings inked upon its pages.

"That is the *Picatrix*," Papa says in a reverent voice. "That book which Moorish sages of ere named the *Ghāyat al-Ḥakīm*, or the Goal of the Wise. It is an illustrated Latin translation and it is worth far, far more than its weight in gold. You are not to lay hands upon it."

"I won't," I murmur, gazing spellbound at the image of a dark-faced man in white clothing, a rope tied about his waist. The dark-faced man's expression is fierce and ruthless, haughty and command-ing. He holds an axe upraised in one hand and his red eyes glower from the page.

"Do you know the image?" Papa inquires.

I glance over my shoulder at him and nod. "It is the first face of Aries, is it not?"

He bestows a proud smile upon me. "Indeed."

No mistake, it is a powerful image. I look back at it. The thought of re-creating it, of bringing the image of this man to life, writ large upon the white-washed walls of Papa's sanctum in vivid hues, fills me with a strange eagerness. My fingers twitch at my sides, itching to take up one of the long-handled brushes and begin limning the outline of the dark-faced man's figure. I clasp my hands behind my back to be safe. "Do you wish me to render it for you, Papa?"

"In time. I have prayed long on this matter, Miranda." Papa puts his hands on my shoulders and turns me to face him. "You are the flesh of my flesh and blood of my blood. It is my belief that the Lord God has given you this gift for the purpose of aiding me in my arts." A wondrous light suffuses his face. "You shall be my right hand, my *soror mystica*, in our great working." Unexpectedly, he gives me a little shake and his expression turns stern. "But within these walls, you must never, ever seek to render any image save those I have explicitly bidden you to execute; nor at any time save that I have specified. To do so without understanding the conjunctions of the stars and planets is to jeopardize the working itself. Do you understand?"

"Yes, Papa."

"Very well." He gives my shoulders a meaningful squeeze, hard enough that his fingertips dig into my flesh, then releases me. "You may begin."

The unfamiliar materials and the vast expanse of white-washed wall should intimidate me; and yet they do not. I study the image in the book, memorizing the lines of the figure. I choose a brush of middling size, the cleverly bound goat's hair tapering to a point.

Papa watches me.

I dip the brush into the pot of oily black pigment. There is a stepping stool placed against the wall and I understand without being told that it is there for my use, that I might render the image on a scale larger than life itself. I climb the steps of the stool with care, heedful of my trailing skirts. Hidden from view, my bare toes curl to grip the edge of the top step. The brush's handle feels good and right in my hand and the brush droops under the weight of the pigment, black as night and shining with infinite possibilities. The white-washed wall beckons me in all its emptiness. Holding the image of the first face of Aries in my mind, I put the brush to the wall.

A heady sense of power fills me. I shall be like the Lord God Himself, dividing light from the darkness.

With one fearless stroke, I begin.

TWENTY-SIX

CALIBAN

Miranda is alone with Master in his big room today.

It is a thought that follows me as I go far, far away from the palace, away from Miranda in the blue gown that shows all her throat and the curves of the tops of her little breasts, down to the seashore.

I know, because I did hear him say it yesterday when he did not know I was listening around a corner. Tomorrow, Master did say. *On the morrow, you shall assist me in my sanctum.*

That is where it happened.

Where he punished her.

I shake my head hard to shake away the thoughts, thoughts of Miranda that are all mixed together; Miranda naked, Miranda in the blue gown . . . oh, you were so happy this morning, Miranda! But then there is Miranda still and pale and not moving, Miranda almost dead, Miranda waking scared and unknowing, Miranda learning slowly, so slowly, all over again.

The tide is low and the air smells of salt and briny things that live in the sea. Undines play in the waves beyond where the tide is breaking, but the shoreline is empty. I climb over the rocks with my pail and gather mussels. There are many, many, many of them on the rocks where the sea has gone out, olive-black shells closed tight with hairy little beards. I twist them loose and drop them in the pail filled with seawater one by one, plinkety-plink-plink. It is a thing that should be pleasing to me, a sound that makes singsong sounds echo in my thoughts, but today it is not. This work is suited to my hands, my monster's hands, rough and ugly with half-healed scrapes on the knuckles and sharp, ragged nails good for prying loose stubborn shells.

These are not hands that should touch anything so fine as Miranda's skin, I think to myself; no, Caliban, they are not.

Oh, but, but, but . . .

She did kiss the thumb of this rough right hand once, kissed it so tender when I hurt it. Yes, she did.

I tear more mussels from the rocks.

It was the day she did speak to me at last of what happened in Master's big room, Master's *sanctum*. She cried and cried, and I did stroke her hair, her soft golden hair, with these very hands.

Master almost killed her, and she is with him there now.

I do not know what to do.

The more I think upon it, the more my heart becomes angry and hurting inside me. I swing my pail, roaring and shouting, and I splash and stomp through the shallow pools the tide has left, crushing harmless, soft little sea-creatures under my splayed monster's feet, squelchity-squelch. I think that Ariel will come to mock me, but he is nowhere.

At last I look toward the high crags behind me. "Oh, Setebos!" I cry. "What am I to do?"

There is no answer in words, but a quietness comes inside me, and I remember I did make a promise beneath Setebos's very shadow—long, long years before the sight of Miranda naked, even before Master did hurt her so badly that she almost died—that I would always return for her.

So I do.

In the palace, I place the pail full of mussels in the larder and creep up the stairs, creep down the hallway.

Outside Master's door, I listen.

I hear nothing.

I raise my hand to rap upon the door, then lower it. Today is not like the day when Miranda began to bleed. Today I have no reason to disturb Master at his studies; no, nor Miranda with him.

Master will be angry, and my flesh flinches at the thought of the punishment he will inflict upon me. I only want to know, to be sure that Miranda has taken no harm. She was frightened to return to this room where she did almost die, where the *thing* her father called her mother, the thing that Ariel named a homunculus, did die at her careless hand. I know she was.

And yet I cannot make myself knock upon the door. Angry at my own fearfulness, I retreat.

Oh, but there are ways and ways.

Outside, I circle the palace, gazing upward. There is a balcony on the upper story that looks into Master's big room, his *sanctum*. A gleaming metal tube sits atop it, pointed at the sky.

It is not meant to be a place that anyone could reach save from inside Master's sanctum itself, but I am not anyone. I am Caliban, a misshapen monster with strong bent legs and hunched shoulders meant for climbing, and hard-nailed fingers and toes that can wedge deep into the smallest of cracks, like those between the crumbling old stones of the palace.

I scale the wall like a lizard, trying not to think about the drop below me, and haul myself onto the balcony on my belly, hiding as best I might beneath the shadow of the bright metal sky-pointing tube. Lifting my head, I peer over the lintel.

"Oh, la!" an idle voice remarks behind me. "How very intrepid thou art!"

Ariel.

I turn my head to glare at him. "Hush!"

The spirit is half shape, half cloud, drifting wisps coming together and falling apart in endless churning motion. A keen-featured face emerges, a hand touches one finger to its lips. "I am the soul of discretion," he breathes in a whisper. "Why, when it comes down to the nub of the matter, are we not in this together, thee and I, my fellow servant?"

I ignore him.

Mayhap I was a fool to have worried, for it is a peaceable scene. Master's grey head is bent over his books. He mutters to himself and makes notes on a slate close at hand, sometimes rising to pace the room, clutching at the amulets around his neck. When he does, I duck low and plaster my belly to the balcony.

Miranda . . .

Miranda stands atop something and draws upon the wall with strong colors, making the image of a fierce man's face with red eyes that glare out at the world. Her face . . . her face is like the face of a girl in a dream, in the best dream.

I watch her.

Girl, yes; and woman, too, and the both of them gone to a place where I cannot follow. My heart and my rod ache alike, the latter stirring beneath my loins against the hard stone of the balcony. A slanting ray of sunlight catches a mirror against the back wall of

Master's sanctum, the round mirror from the pirates' treasure, now etched all around its outside with letters and symbols. The mirror winks as though it would speak to me, but it is in no language I know.

There is nothing for me here.

Retreating, I clamber over the balcony. Down is harder than up, and I must reach wide to find hand- and foot-holds, my weight hanging from my left side while I seek purchase with my right.

Ariel drifts beside me as I make the careful climb downward. "Dost thou think to *protect* the lass from him?" he asks in a curious tone. "Her own father?"

I put my teeth together hard. *Clench,* that is the word. I know oh, so many words now, and none of them do me a bit of good. "I had to be sure. He did very nearly kill her in that room."

"Oh, aye, for disobedience," Ariel says as though it is nothing. "But the lass has long since learned her lesson, and she is there at her father's bidding." He waits for me to drop the last few feet onto the dusty rocks. "The magus has brought her into his laboratorium," he muses. "Into the very working of his arts. Yet methinks he has not taken her into his confidence. What thinkest thou, fellow servant?"

"What do you care what I think?" I ask him bitterly. "I am only the poor dumb monster who loves her!"

"Love!" Ariel's shifting features go still in astonishment, his eyes flaring crystal-bright. "Thou dost use the word?"

I stomp away from him across the palace grounds toward the kitchen. "Leave me alone."

He follows me nonetheless. "Thou art a fool, tender-hearted monster. Dost think to deny thy baser nature?"

"I am not ruled by it!" I say in defiance. "No more than any man! No more than Master himself!"

"Master!" Ariel laughs, but this time the sharp edge of his laughter is not meant for me. "Oh, la!"

I make my eyes go narrow. "What do you mean?"

Ariel shrugs his shoulders. "Not all base desires stem from the root of thy manhood," he says dismissively. "To what end dost thou suppose the magus works?"

I am weary of his taunting. "Why do you ask me when you know the answer and will not share it?"

"Why?" Ariel echoes the word. "Why not? Should I pretend to understand mine own whys and wherefores? Indeed, my monstrous friend, I do not." His hands dance in the air, weaving back and forth, breezes streaming from his fingertips. "While I remain at our master's beck and call, my whim and will is as the wind, blown hither and thither and yon; no more am I free to say. Wilst tell me thou hast not wondered at our master's purpose?"

A monster he has named me and a monster he has shown me to myself, so it is a monster I will be. Opening the larder, I thrust my hand into the pail full of mussels and seawater. Plucking out a mussel, I pry it open with my nails and tear loose the morsel of orange flesh. I pop it into my mouth, poppity-pop, and chew it raw with savage pleasure. I fish out a second mussel, but it is closed hard and tight and will not open, so I thrust it whole into my mouth and crack its shell with my strong back teeth. Sharp shards cut my mouth, but I do not care that it hurts. I chew it anyway, chomp-chomp-chomp, tasting brine and blood. "I wish the wind would blow you away for-ever!" I say fiercely, spraying bits of shell and bloody seawater.

Ariel's eyes have gone cold and dark with no light in them. "There is a storm in the offing, and where it will blow the lot of us, not even I can say. Thou hast wits and will not use them. Methinks thou art a greater fool than I had reckoned."

I spit out a mouthful of shards. "I care naught for what you think!"

"As thou wilt." Ariel bends at the waist, sweeping one arm behind him; Miranda taught me long ago that is a thing called a *bow*. It is a thing a man does to show honor and respect to someone, and there is a thing that a girl or a woman does that is called a *curtsy,* and she showed me that, too. It was a thing I had seen her do to Master many times, but I did not know what it was called. Oh, we did bow and curtsy to each other all one long day, Miranda and I, laughing and laughing.

But that was many years ago, and there is no honor in Ariel's bow, only mockery. He goes away and I am alone.

My mouth is cut and hurting, and there is a taste in it like ashes from the mussel shell. I spit out the last of the shards and think to myself, oh Caliban, you are a foolish monster indeed.

There is a storm in the offing.

That Ariel is a tricksy spirit and I do not trust him, no, not for one heartbeat; but he has no love for Master. It may be that in his own tricksy way he was trying to tell me something.

Or it may be that the spirit only sought a new way to make mock of me.

But, but, but . . .

I think of that day, oh, so long ago, when Master did arrive on the isle with you, Miranda. There was a storm that day, too. I think of Master's voice and the cold, hard, angry words he did speak across the sea while you were sleeping, sleeping on the sand. I wish I could remember what words Master did say, but that was from before, when words were lost to me.

I think Ariel did speak truly. Another storm is coming, and I do not know what it will bring.

Oh, I *would* protect you, Miranda! You are like sunlight to me. I would protect you from aught that might harm you; yes, and from your own father who seeks to use you for his own ends, whatever they may be.

If only I could bear to look you in the face.

TWENTY-SEVEN

MIRANDA

Papa's sanctum is a wondrous place.

I have not forgotten what befell me there, but the more time I spend in his private chamber, the more faint and distant the memory grows; and the more ashamed I feel of the fear it instilled in me.

I am oh, so enamored of this process of *painting*! It is quite simply magical. With every stroke of the brush, I learn more and more of what I am about and to what I aspire. When I sleep, I dream of figures passing over me as the spheres of heaven rotate above me, and I seek to memorize the lines and planes of them, and every aspect of their visages that I might render them truly.

Under Papa's tutelage, I learn to care for my brushes, cleaning them in the pungent turpentine he has distilled from pine sap and wiping them dry on rags. I learn about the bright pigments which the little gnomes have delved from the deepest and most remote places on the isle and ground to a fine powder: lead white, red cinnabar, azurite blue, yellow ochre, green malachite, brown umber, and carbon black. For each of these elements, there are correspondences; some logical and some unexpected. Cinnabar, for example, from which the vermilion pigment is ground, is also the element from which quicksilver, the living metal itself, is extracted.

Who could have imagined such a thing? Truly, this isle is filled with magic.

Papa is generous with praise for my efforts, and I drink it in like a thirsty plant.

I am careful, always, to touch nothing without permission, but Papa takes pleasure in showing me some of the wondrous apparatuses that aid him in his working. He allows me to peer through the mighty telescope on the balcony that lets him see great distances across the isle, and into, he tells me, the very heavens themselves when the skies are benighted. It seems to me a very work of divinity, but Papa assures me that it is all a matter of lenses and mathematics.

To be sure, I cannot fathom it.

A great deal of Papa's art involves charting the heavens. There is the brass astrolabe with its moving plates that calculates time and distance and oh, ever so much! There is its near cousin the cosmolabe that Papa uses to calculate the angles between heavenly bodies and cast his charts. Many of Papa's calculations regarding the planets, he records in tables he calls ephemerides. There are pages and pages of these tables, so that he can determine the position of the planets and the aspects of the stars on any given date and time.

I confess, my mind fair boggles at the complexity of the work that Papa's art requires.

And yet I feel the power of it in my bones. When I paint upon the walls of Papa's sanctum, it seems as though I am at the very center of existence, with the spheres of heaven rotating far above and all around me while the images I render draw down the influences of the seven governors and the crystalline sphere of fixed stars in the firmament beyond them; and beyond that, the Lord God Himself in the Empyrean where nine orders of angels sing His praises. Hours pass without my notice while I am engaged in the process of painting, until I realize my arms are aching from being raised so long and my fingers have become stiff and crabbed.

Papa says that I am filled with the *Spiritus Mundi* when I paint, the mystical energy that suffuses the whole of creation.

I believe it is true.

Always, I paint at his bidding; and I am content to do so, humbled by the realization that the calculations Papa employs are so very far beyond my ken.

As the weeks pass, additional figures slowly take place alongside the glowering, crimson-eyed form of the first face of Aries. The first face of Virgo is a young girl holding a curious red globe of fruit called a pomegranate. Papa is in good humor and tells me a tale from the myths of the ancient Greeks about a maiden named Persephone who was abducted by Hades, the god of the underworld, who sought to make her his bride. After wandering the earth in despair, her mother Demeter learned of her abduction and begged Zeus, the king of the gods, to rescue her and restore her, but because Persephone ate six seeds of a pomegranate fruit, she was bound to spend six months of every year in the underworld with Hades.

It seems to me that the gods are cruel to women who eat fruit, but that is a thought I keep to myself.

Thinking to use my own face as a model for Virgo, I seek to steal a glimpse of it in the round mirror which Papa obtained from the hoard of pirates' treasure that now hangs upon one wall. It is greatly altered as Papa has etched a series of concentric circles of arcane names and symbols upon its bright surface, but there is room enough between them that I can make out my own features.

Papa rebukes me sharply for it. "Miranda! Leave it be."

Stung, I turn away from the mirror. "I was but looking! I did not touch it, Papa, I promise."

"'Tis dangerous merely to look." Finding a length of ragged cloth, he drapes it over the mirror. "But 'tis not your fault," he adds in a gentler tone. "Of course a young woman such as yourself would be hard-pressed to resist the lure of vanity, and I did not think to forbid you until this moment."

Across the chamber, the salamander in its nest of fire opens its jewel-red eyes to regard me. In all this time, it has not spoken once, and I have begun to think I imagined it years ago.

Still, there is something unnerving in its stare.

Papa forgives me my unwitting trespass. He does not work with chymicals in my presence, but applies himself to his multitude of charts and follows my progress with a keen eye. I paint the initial lineaments of Virgo's face from memory. Alone in my chamber the next morning, I peek at the hand-mirror that was Caliban's gift that I might better bequeath Virgo with the likeness of an actual living maiden. Papa praises my work, but if he notes the resemblance, he does not comment on it. I wonder if it is true that it is vanity rather than pragmatism that compelled me to render my own features, and resolve not to do so again. It seems the safer course, even if I must call upon my imagination to render the illustrations in Papa's book writ large. Although they are finely wrought, they are too small to afford a great deal of detail.

I should have to do so in any case with the next image that Papa bids me to render, which is the second face of Gemini and an image of which I can barely make sense. Papa translates the description and reads it aloud to me. "It is a man whose face is like an eagle, clad in a coat of leaden mail," he says. "A linen cloth covers his head, and an iron helm with a silk crown upon it."

At his side, I clasp my hands beneath my back and stare at the incomprehensible illustration of a man with a bird's fierce beaked head crowned with metal and silk. "Is an eagle somewhat like an angry chicken, Papa?"

"An angry chicken?" Papa laughs, a hearty, full-throated sound such as I have seldom heard from him. "I suppose it is at that, though it is a far nobler bird. It is a bird of prey, akin to the hawks that hunt mice and rabbits in the meadows, Miranda. Surely you have seen those, albeit at a distance." He returns to the book. "Now, he holds in his hand a bow and arrows. This is a face of oppression, evils—"

His voice stops and I glance up at him.

"That is all," Papa says, and the laughter is gone from his voice.

A chill trickles down my back like rainwater and although I do not wish to grieve Papa, I cannot let the matter pass unremarked. Never had I imagined that there was aught unwholesome in the images that Papa bade me render.

But then there was the pale thing, floating in its jar . . .

"Oppression and evils?" I whisper without looking up from the illustration. "I do not understand."

Papa is silent long enough that I peek to see if he is angry. He is frowning, but it is in thought, not anger. "There is no evil in this image, nor in any such image," he says at last. "That I promise you. 'Tis true that they may be used for evil by an unscrupulous magus; and 'tis true, also, that a careless magus may wreak great harm using these images if, let us suppose, he does not take care that the planet which is lord of that astrological house is not conjunct with either of the infortune planets, or cadent at the time of the working, or that the working itself is compromised by an eclipse of the sun or moon." He raises one finger. "That is why I bid you render no image save at my command."

"What of those I have sketched up on my slate?" I ask in alarm. "I've drawn many that you described to me, Papa, and not always at your bidding!"

He smiles into his beard. "There is no harm in such impermanent scribbles. Outside the walls of my sanctum, you are free to practice at will and continue to hone your skills. It is only here in this place of power, wherein enduring images are wrought with purpose on a mighty scale, that there is danger."

I dare to look up at him. "And yet I know naught of our purpose, Papa."

"Nor need you," he says sternly. "Not yet. This is a delicate business we are about, and any intention you bring to it might taint the working. Your innocence of the nature of our working is required to ensure it will be a pure expression of *my* intention. You need only to trust me. Do you?"

I nod.

I am not sure if it is true, but I am sure it is the only answer that I am unafraid to give him.

"That is well," Papa says. "Know that there is no evil in our purpose, Miranda. If I bid you render an image of one of the faces of a sign, or an aspect of one of the seven governors, that rules over cruelty or injustice or misery, it is not because drawing down such unsavory elements is our purpose." He pauses, lost in thought again for a moment and gazing into the distance. "It is because those elements bear influence on our purpose, and I seek the favor of the stars and planets to influence them in turn. Does that suffice to ease your fears?"

I nod again. "Yes, Papa."

It is a lie.

It *suffices* to fan the spark of resentment and rebellion that yet lingers in me, and for the first time in many years, I should like to shout and rage to the heavens, to ask Papa *what* and *how* and *why*?

But I do not.

I have grown circumspect. Quietly, I excuse myself to venture afield where I might seek to study the visage of a hawk.

It is the sort of quest in which Caliban would have delighted to accompany me not so very long ago, but when I attempt to entice him into joining me, he declines in an ungracious manner. Since I began assisting Papa with his work, Caliban's sullenness toward me has continued unabated, and I am none the wiser as to the cause of it.

"Why are you being so churlish?" I cry. "Have I not apologized many times over for my bad behavior?"

Caliban hunches his shoulders, looks away, and mutters, "It is no fault of yours, Miranda."

"Then *why*?" I grasp his arm and tug it, trying to make him turn to face me. "Tell me! Will you not even look at me?"

He shakes off my grip with unexpected force, then doubles over in pain as Papa's binding takes effect.

Filled with remorse, I crouch beside him. "Oh, Caliban! I'm sorry."

Caliban staggers away from me with a grunt of pain, bracing his hands on his bent knees. "It is no fault of yours, Miranda!" he says again, and then he straightens and lopes for the doorway, one arm pressed against his belly. I watch him go, tears of frustration stinging my eyes.

When I am not immersed in the wonder of painting, this divide between us troubles me more than I can say.

We had grown so very close, Caliban and I. During the seemingly endless months when I was recovering from my affliction, he showed me such tenderness and patience. As I healed and we grew and learned together in those months, and indeed the years that followed, it seemed almost that we were two parts of a whole, each of us reflecting the other's strengths and weaknesses. We were two souls who found each other in our times of need, providing companionship and solace. So long as the distance between us persists, there is an emptiness inside me.

For the first time in long years, I remember what it is to be lonely.

TWENTY-EIGHT

CALIBAN

Oh, Miranda!

I do not wish to be unkind to you; never. Never in the everest ever!

But it is best that I am, because you are good and innocent and everything that I am not.

One day you will understand.

One day you will hate me for what I am, as I have learned to hate myself for it.

TWENTY-NINE

MIRANDA

To my dismay, I am unable to finish the image of the second face of Gemini before Luna, the Lady Moon herself, waxes full and bright in the night sky, and I feel the heaviness and the dull ache that I now know portend the start of my woman's courses. Papa is pleased that my flow arrives in a timely manner, but of course I am banished from his sanctum until it ends.

The anniversary of my birth arrives and Papa entrusts me with his Bible that I might read it for myself now that I am fourteen years of age and a woman grown, which is a mercy; still, it is a hardship to be forbidden the labor I have come to love, and all the more so for Caliban's strange and enduring coldness toward me.

"Is it because I have been spending so many hours aiding Papa in his sanctum?" I ask him, still seeking to make sense of his behavior. "So many hours painting? Are you angry at me for it?"

"No."

I press him. "Are you quite certain?"

Caliban gives a sharp bark of laughter in response. He glances at me, a quick, furtive, and darting glance, and there is a misery I do not understand in his dark eyes. "Yes, Miranda."

He leaves.

He has grown skilled at leaving, grown skilled at ensuring that our paths cross as little as possible.

I only would that I knew *why*.

I think of the monstrous thing he showed me with such pride so long ago, the great bony brown rock of a skull that perches atop the high crag with its maw agape as if to devour the sky, that thing that he called Setebos. Since first Caliban showed it to me, I have never returned, but I suspect he takes refuge there often. It has been the only point of contention between us in the years since my affliction, for I have no love for the gruesome thing, and yet Caliban clings stubbornly to a belief that it is a manifestation of the foul spirit his mother worshipped; and moreover, that it is his prayers to Setebos that restored me to wakefulness.

I have said naught of this to Papa, for he is quick to anger where Caliban is concerned and I have no wish to rouse his wrath, but when I think on it, worry gnaws at me like a maggot in an acorn. I have long excused this fancy of Caliban's, supposing it is a mere holdover from his savage, abandoned childhood that causes him to hold fast to this belief and take comfort in the monstrous figure he imagines to be Setebos.

What if I am wrong? Caliban said more than once that his cruelty was no fault of mine. What if there *is* power in the hideous formation, and it exerts a subtle, malign influence over Caliban, rendering his once tender and gentle heart dark and hateful toward me?

Such are the matters that occupy my mind as I go about the lonely business of tending to my courses. I am grateful to have Papa's Bible to distract me, though I will own that there are many passages in it I do not understand, and others that stir a queer yearning inside me.

There is one such that is called the Song of Solomon, which I read over and over. Though it makes me feel unsettled and strange to myself, for it is about the love between a man and a woman, I cannot help but return to it.

It is a glad day when my menstruum ceases to flow and I am able to rejoin Papa in his sanctum. Although I was unsuccessful in catching a glimpse of a hawk at close range, I saw a number of them from afar—and too, I spent a good deal of time in the garden sketching our chickens—and I am eager to resume work on the second face of Gemini, but Papa informs me the time is no longer opportune. He laughs to see me disappointed anew, though not unkindly.

"There will be time aplenty to complete it when the stars realign," he says to me. "'Tis a far grander image I bid you render now."

Papa speaks more truly than I reckoned for it is an image of the Sun—Sol, the Lord Sun himself—that he wishes me to create.

It will be the first time I have painted one of the seven governors, and I am apprehensive about undertaking such an important task. The illustration in Papa's book depicts a man with a noble face and a fiery crown upon his head. His right hand is raised as though in greeting, and in his left he holds a round mirror. Beneath his feet is a curious creature bescaled like a serpent with twisting coils and veined wings, which Papa tells me is called a dragon. Its jaws are open wide and curling flames of crimson and gold come forth from its throat.

"As you may recall, there are those sages who hold that the image is that of a man in a chariot drawn by four horses," Papa says. "But this is the one that speaks the loudest to me." He strokes the edge of the page with one finger, grazing it with a touch as light and fleeting as a butterfly's wing. "Now that you behold it, does it speak to you, Miranda?"

I glance involuntarily at the salamander, curled sleeping in its glowing brazier. "Yes, Papa. It does."

He smiles. "I am pleased to hear it."

I ready my paints and stare at the blank wall. The image of the Sun is to take pride of place upon it.

The wall taunts me with its empty whiteness.

I do not know how to begin.

I think of Papa chanting the music of the spheres each and every morning, calling down their influence. I should like to do the same, but it is not a part of his art that he has taught me, saying only that my girlish voice lacks the proper resonance for it.

Still . . .

I recall the night long ago I slipped from my chamber to beseech Caliban to obey Papa and betray the name of Setebos; how I lost my way in the maze of hedges and prayed to the Lady Moon to guide my steps; how she answered my prayers and helped calm my spirits that I might find my way free of the maze. And it seems to me now that I must ask the Lord Sun for his blessing in this undertaking. Papa thinks it is a fine idea and gives me leave to go.

At first I think it is a thing that should be best done outdoors beneath the open skies, in the courtyard where Papa performs his chants; and yet once I am there, with the ominous shadow of the riven pine that once held Ariel captive stretching over the flagstones, I do not feel the rightness of it. No, it is height that I crave; closeness to the sky, as close as I can come to the Sun. And so it is the winding stair of the watchtower that I climb, all the way to its high chamber with windows open to the four quarters of the winds.

It is a clear morning and the Sun shines merrily in the east, rising above the horizon degree by degree with the steady turning of its sphere.

I kneel before the eastern window and clasp my hands in prayer, closing my eyes. The Sun's light is warm upon my face and I see red and gold as vivid as dragon's fire behind my eyelids.

"May God bless you, O blessed Lord Sun," I murmur. "Lord Sun, whose eye illumes all the sky, all-seeing, fiery and hot and dry, bearer of fruit and seed, almighty Lord of brightness and all that is good and holy, I beg you to guide my hand that I might render your image most truly."

The crimson brightness behind my eyes blooms and the Sun's warmth on my face feels like a blessing given. My heart expands within my breast as though the very Sun has ignited a divine spark within it.

Opening my eyes, I rise.

I am ready—oh, so ready!—to begin, and yet I find my feet hesitating and my gaze turning westward. Once upon a time, I sought to catch glimpses of Caliban from this very vantage.

I find myself seeking him now.

I do not spot him, but I see the parted jaws of Setebos arching toward the sky atop his crag, rendered small by the distance. I had seen them from this very tower as a child many times, taking them for naught more than spires of rock. Now I know better and a shiver runs over my skin as though a shadow has passed above me, dispelling some of the Sun's warmth. Holding fast to the memory of brightness, I return to Papa's sanctum and commence.

For many hours, I lose myself in the work of outlining the figure on a vast expanse of blank wall, concentrating on imbuing it with the Sun's bright majesty. It is only when I reach the complicated form of the dragon that my hand falters and I realize the extent of my weariness.

With Papa's permission, I approach the salamander in its brazier and study it closely. It shares a correspondence with a dragon, for I believe that they are reptiles in kind with an affinity for fire. But the salamander, which wakes to gaze at me with unblinking eyes, is not much bigger than the length of my hand, and it lacks the dragon's twisting coils and bat-veined wings. And although it is a creature of fire, flames do not issue forth from its mouth. Indeed, its mouth remains closed, a delicate curve at the hinge of its jaw suggesting a smile in the flickering firelight.

"Are you kin to a dragon, I wonder?" I murmur to it. "Why do you not speak?"

Across the chamber, Papa raises his head from a chart he is studying. "What's that, child?"

I do not like to remind him of my trespass. "I was just wondering, Papa, if the salamander is kin to a dragon."

"Yes, indeed," he says. "Though on a small and insignificant scale." He frowns a little. "Surely you're not thinking to use it as a model? A dragon is a far grander thing, Miranda."

"Yes, but I have no dragon—" I pause, thinking once again of Setebos's gaping maw. Mayhap there is a reason I glimpsed it from afar this morning, for it is not at all unlike the jaws of the dragon in the illustration. "Papa? Could a dragon be turned to stone?"

His frown deepens. "How so?"

I hesitate. "There is a thing that Caliban showed me once. He . . ." I swallow against the lump of betrayal in my throat, and whisper my next words. "He believes it to be Setebos incarnate."

Now I have Papa's full attention. "Tell me."

I do.

It is at once a relief and an agony. Had Caliban not been so strange toward me in the past weeks, I do not think I would have revealed his secret; and yet there is a great release in divulging it and confessing my fears regarding it.

Papa's face is stern as he listens. "You should have told me this long ago, Miranda."

I look down. "I know."

"This thing you describe . . . I am quite certain it is naught but the bones of a great whale caught in an event of volcanic upheaval some centuries past, preserved in basalt at the moment of its demise," Papa says, and his tone is dismissive. "'Twould be of considerable interest to study were I not caught up in more pressing matters, but I assure you, 'tis neither a dragon nor a demonic spirit made manifest. It is only Caliban's fancy that accords it agency." He shakes his head with rue and regret. "I fear that for all the civilizing influence that we have afforded him, your wild lad retains a savage's love of superstition."

I sigh.

Bones; only bones.

Of course, 'twas folly to imagine it was aught otherwise, and I feel foolish for having let Caliban's ill-founded belief color my thinking. But Papa does not mock me for it, only assures me that if the whale's jaws will serve as a model for the dragon's, I should use them. This I do, although I pay no second visit to the great skull, but render its terrifying jaws from memory abetted by the distant glimpse of the watchtower.

Mayhap I cannot help but retain a touch of Caliban's superstition.

I do study the mummified corpse of a bat which is among the many curious objects that adorn the shelves of the cabinets in Papa's sanctum. With Papa's bemused but approving indulgence, I gently stretch out one brittle, leathery wing that I might observe the fine veins, the armature of its bones, and the manner in which its joints are articulated.

Accompanied by a trio of drifting sylphs, I spend a sunlit morning hunting along the banks of a stream where Caliban and I have in the past encountered harmless grass snakes that lurk in the reeds and prey on small frogs and lizards there. When I find one, I follow its winding progress, marveling at the way it propels itself effortlessly through water and over land alike with the sinuous motion of its endlessly coiling and uncoiling length. It moves far too swiftly for me to capture its undulating lines in chalk, but I commit them to memory.

It is a thing I have seen before, of course, but now I see it through new and different eyes, and I am filled with wonder at the richness and complexity of the vast whole of the Lord God's creation.

To paint, I think, is to give praise to the Creator.

"Shouldst thou not have a care, daughter of Eve?" a breezy voice says behind me. "Thou art a member of the fairer sex, and thus heir to a troubled history with serpents, my lady."

Ariel.

The snake vanishes among the reeds, its lashing body following the probing wedge of its head.

I turn to face the mercurial spirit. "Yes, and the Lord God did curse the serpent to crawl upon its belly for its sins," I say in a grim tone. "Mayhap this isle is no Eden, but here as there, when temptation approached me, it walked upright like a man, and I have paid the price for heeding it."

Ariel raises his hands in a peaceable gesture, the insubstantial sleeves of his garment fluttering around his slender white arms. "I mean no harm. Thou art about thy father's business, Miranda, and the sooner it is brought to a head, the sooner I am freed from servitude."

I eye him. "And is it my father's business that *you're* about today? Or is there some other reason that you come to plague me?"

He blinks at me, blue-eyed and ingenuous. "Is it not conceivable that I merely desire the pleasure of thy company?"

"It is unlikely." Although I am eager to return to Papa's sanctum and begin painting while the fluid lines of the snake's coils are fresh in my mind, I find myself hesitating. If there is anyone who would know what troubles Caliban, it is Ariel; though it is equally true that that is because if there is anyone who is the cause of Caliban's troubles, it is the vexsome spirit himself. "Gentle spirit, if I ask you a question, will you answer me honestly?"

He purses his lips. "As to that, I cannot say without hearing the question, my lady. Thou knowest well that there are matters on which thy father has forbidden me to speak, and I am bound by mine oath."

"Will you answer honestly if you may?" I press him.

"I will."

"For a month and more, Caliban has been angry at me," I say. "Do you know why?"

Ariel's eyes darken. "He is not angry at thee, my lady."

To my chagrin, I feel the prick of tears in my own eyes. "Then why does he treat me so unkindly?"

"O la!" The spirit's expression changes to one of dismay. "Do not weep, my lady." He sighs, the sound like a wind in the trees. "But as to thy question, it is one I may not answer."

I wipe my eyes with the sleeve of my gown. "Did you do or say aught to set him against me?"

"I?" Ariel touches his breast. "I tell thee again, Caliban is not set against thee. He is set against himself, and thou art the cause of it."

"How so?"

The spirit shakes his head. "That, too, I may not answer."

I realize that Ariel has evaded my prior question. "Do you deny that you had aught to do with it?"

He is silent a moment. "Thou thinkest that I have no fondness for Sycorax's spawn, and I will not gainsay it. Her loathsome blood and the darkness that is attendant on it runs in his veins. And yet, the witch's whelp has a tender heart and mine is not unmoved to pity. Am I cruel to him? Aye, betimes I have been; and betimes it has been for no greater cause than a whim born of tedium or lingering spite. But in this matter, there is kindness in my cruelty, Miranda, and cruelty in thy kindness."

I gaze at him. "I do not understand."

"Nor can I make thee," Ariel says with unwonted gentleness. "But thou didst beseech me to speak honestly, and thus I shall say this: Leave him be, my lady. Allow him his brooding and sullen anger and do not seek to assuage it; for if thou dost not, both of thee will suffer for it."

"For kindness?" I say. "For *love*?"

There is a terrible sympathy in Ariel's gaze. "Thou art the shoals on which Caliban wilt dash his heart to pieces."

I shake my head in vehement denial. "No! Caliban is my only and dearest friend! I would never hurt him!"

Ariel casts his sea-shifting gaze skyward as though to beseech the Lord God in His heaven for patience, then lowers it to meet mine. His trickster's smile is tinged with regret and the shadow of knowledge unspoken. "I wish thee the courage of thy convictions, Miranda, but I grow weary of thine ignorance."

"'Tis not—" I begin indignantly.

A breeze springs up, and he is gone in a swirl of mist.

The sylphs that have accompanied me cavort without a care. Despite their presence, I feel so very alone.

Even so, I have attained that which I sought, and it is a thought that cheers me. I turn back toward the palace and thrust the memory of Ariel's unwanted intrusion and his harsh implications aside, concentrating my thoughts instead on the movement of the serpent's coils and the intricate patterns of its smooth, overlapping scales, envisioning them writ large on the walls of Papa's sanctum and adorned with clawed feet and mighty wings, curls of flame spewing from its gaping jaws.

Bit by bit, the dragon takes shape in my mind and my hands itch to take up a brush and bring it to life.

By the time I return to Papa's sanctum, I have nearly managed to forget the entire encounter.

THIRTY

CALIBAN

I do not mean to go back to the balcony outside Master's sanctum, but after weeks pass . . . I do. At first I do because I am lonely and I miss Miranda, and even if it is dangerous to be there, I can watch her and she does not know. But then it is not only Miranda, but it is the pictures she makes.

You have magic in your hands, Miranda.

Those are the words I think to myself. I do not dare say them out loud and be found, no, but I think them to myself.

Magic.

And I think it is a finer magic than Master's, for what is his magic good for? It is good for making servants and punishing them; yes, and for punishing his own daughter, too, punishing her almost to death. It is good for freeing Ariel, and that is good for no one but Ariel and Master, and Ariel is still angry at being a servant anyway. But

Miranda's magic, oh! Such colors! Such men! Such women! Such creatures!

I did like it when Miranda did draw bugs and birds and flowers on her slate before, but those are things I have seen and know, and these pictures are so big and grand; and they are things I have never seen and I do not know how Miranda can see them in her head. What is the great coiled thing like a winged serpent beneath the bright-faced man's feet? I do not know, and yet I know pieces of it: snake, bat, lizard. How does it become a whole?

To watch her make a picture is like listening to a story, like the stories Miranda did tell me sometimes about the pictures that the stars in the sky make at night, stories that Master did tell her.

They are beautiful.

She is beautiful.

I would watch her every moment of every day, but the longer I stay, the more it may be that Master will see me and punish me; and there are chores to be done, hey-ho, for Caliban is a servant, the poor dumb monster. So I fetch wood and figs and fish like a good servant, I gather acorns and honey and sour oranges, I obey and I am quiet and good, oh so good, that Master does not think about me.

Miranda . . .

Oh, oh, oh.

It is hard, so hard, to be cold when I am not. The hurt on her face makes my heart hurt inside me.

I do not like for her to look at me, not anymore; and it is not safe for me to look at her. Only when Miranda does not know I am there and looking, only when she is making magic pictures on the walls of Master's sanctum and her face is pure and dreaming and holy, and I do not think about Miranda naked with her tender little breasts with their pink tips hanging down above the wash-basin.

Oh, Setebos! I am bad.

But I am not only the badness within me that yearns and thinks of *rutting* like a goat or a dog; no. I have made a promise to myself.

When the moon goes all the way round then begins to go small, and Miranda's blood begins to flow, Master sends her away and does not allow her into his sanctum. The first time that it happens, I keep watch over her from far away so that it is safe; yes, and the second and third time, too.

As the days grow short and winter comes, I am thinking still, oh, I will protect you, Miranda. Yes, yes, I will protect you from the storm that is coming, this storm that will bring trouble to the isle as a storm once brought you and Master to these shores.

But foolish Caliban, you do not *know* what this trouble is.

Tricksy Ariel knows, but he is forbidden to say; and even *he* with his oh-so-sharp smiles and his sharp cutting words does not know what will happen when it comes.

Thou hast wits and will not use them, Ariel did say to me. *Methinks thou art a greater fool than I had reckoned.*

The spirit's words are true. Since Ariel did show me to myself, I have been too angry and heart-aching to think. I have been what he did show me; only the poor dumb monster, not that Caliban that Miranda did call a friend, not that Caliban that did teach her words all over again when she was hurt.

So I think, thinkety-think-think, and what I think is: How does Ariel know that a troublesome storm is coming? Oh ho, indeed! How does Ariel know what Master plots and plans?

It comes to me that there are three ways, and the first is that only Ariel is a clever spirit and knows many secret things; and if that is the way, then oh, it is too bad for poor Caliban, he cannot find a secret that is locked inside Ariel's tricksy head.

The second way is that Master did tell Ariel his plans, because he did need for the spirit to know them to help him; and if it is that way, then it is too bad again for poor Caliban, Master will not tell *him*, the savage brute. No, he will not, never ever.

Oh, but the third way . . . the third way is that Ariel is guilty of many, many things that he says are true of me, of cruel and cutting words like *skulking* and *lurking* and *spying*, and it seems that these things are a bad thing when you are ugly Caliban hiding belly-down on a balcony or crouching hidden around a corner, but not when you are oh-so-pretty Ariel floating like a cloud or blowing like a whoosh-ity breeze.

Ha!

And if it is *that* way, if Ariel did learn what he knows by spying, then it may be that I can learn it, too.

(What do you do when you are alone in your sanctum, Master?)

So I do not keep watch over Miranda on her blood-days, which is a thing that does not truly need doing; it is only a thing that made me feel as though I was caring for her from afar. Oh, I watch enough to be sure she is at her studies in the warm kitchen or at least nowhere where she might see me scaling the palace walls to lurk on the balcony outside Master's sanctum. I do my chores, always, always, so that the woodpile is stacked high and embers glow on the hearth, and there are acorns gathered and blanched and ground into flour, and there are always fish or mussels in the larder ready for the cooking.

And then I spy.

It is not a nice thing to do, no; not with the chilly winds of winter blowing. With my bare belly pressed to the marble floor of the balcony, I shiver and watch while Master does his work.

Sometimes it is only what I have seen before, Master looking at his charts and books, talking to himself and making notes. He talks louder to himself when he is alone than he does when Miranda is there, and when the wind is not whooshing so hard I cannot hear, I listen and try to make sense of it; but it is all words I do not know and nonsense to me.

Oh, but other times, there are other things Master does. He takes the cloth from his mirror and says magic words, and then *waah!* There are *faces* that show in it! Not Master's own face, no, but the faces of other men like him, old men with beards, and their lips move as though they are talking to each other. I stare and stare to be sure I am seeing true, and Master stares and stares as though their faces make him hungry, and his lips move too, as though he is whispering their words to himself.

I wish I could creep closer to see and hear better, but I do not dare.

And then there is the clay jar that Miranda leaves outside his door during her blood-days. I do not know what is in it, but then I see Master take a thing from it with long tongs, a thing like a little stuffed sack, only it is soaked with blood, and the first time I see it, I make a sound so loud that Master puts down his tongs and comes to the door of the balcony to look, and I almost do not get away in time, leaping for the wall and climbing so fast, fast, fast to hide under the balcony.

There I crouch and cling to the stones of the wall, my arms and legs shaking, shakity-quakity, my heart going pound, pound, pound like a hare's, my breath going in and out of my throat so loud, and I am scared because I think Master will hear; and I am scared because it is *your* blood that Master gathers, Miranda, the blood that comes from you after the moon is round since you are a woman.

I am sure of it.

"O la!" the wind whispers in my ear. "Careless, careless! Our master will catch thee a-spying!"

Of course, that Ariel must come trouble me at the worst time. I want to shout at him to go away, but then Master *will* catch me. I clench my teeth together hard and say nothing, trying not to fall; and Ariel only laughs and goes on his whooshity way. And I think to myself, oh *ho*! I am right and Ariel spies, too—and he does not want Master to catch him, either.

I am using my wits.

Now I want to run away, but I do not. I climb back and watch, quiet as a mouse. Master puts the sack in a funny-shaped bottle with a bit of water until the water is red and bloody, then he takes the sack out with his tongs and puts it in a different jar. Then he puts the bottle on the metal thing that is like a little hearth, and the little salamander glows and glows, oh, so bright, and the bloody water boils and boils until it is gone, and then Master adds something like grains of sand to the bottle and there is a sharp smell that gets into my nose.

When it is done, Master takes a long spoon and scrapes the bottom of the bottle and there is a dark red powder and this he puts in a little pot.

Why, oh why?

I cannot guess, but I do not like it.

Master boils other bad-smelling things on his hearth, too; but it does not trouble me like Miranda's blood.

One month when Miranda's blood-days come, it is very cold, more cold than I ever do remember, and I do not spy on Master. The wind is so cold on my bare skin, I am shaking like a leaf on a tree when I bring the wood that I have gathered for the hearth inside.

Miranda sees this and sews a shirt for me out of the same coarse cloth as my breeches.

She gives it to me in the kitchen the very next day. "I know you no longer reckon me a friend," she says without looking at me. Her voice is soft, so very soft, and there is oh so much hurting in it. "But I hope you will accept this nonetheless. 'Tis uncommonly cold and I should hate for you to suffer a chill and fall ill for it."

My throat goes tight.

I take the shirt. "You are my friend, Miranda," I say to her. "You will *always* be my friend."

Miranda does look at me, then.

Her eyes are wide and blue and shining with hope. "Can we not be as we were, Caliban?"

I want to say yes, yes, oh, yes; I want to go back to the days of sharing lessons and chores, sitting side by side. Oh, but we are not children anymore, and there is no innocence in me, only wanting things that are forbidden. Miranda's pink lips are parted; I would like to put mine on them.

I would like to . . .

Behind my eyes, I see Ariel's mocking face; I hear his knife-sharp laughter ringing in my ears.

My rod stiffens.

Rut.

"No." I back away from Miranda. I pull the shirt over my head, my rough-skinned hands fumbling to find their way into the unaccustomed sleeves. "No, not that, Miranda. Not ever."

She takes a step toward me. *"Caliban—"*

I run.

THIRTY-ONE

The shirt is stiff and it scratches, but I wear it all winter because Miranda made it for me, made it with her own hands.

I do not spy on Miranda that month.

But when her blood-days come next, I return to Master's balcony; and when spring is coming at last I see a new thing.

Oh ho!

Master spies, too; spies in his mirror on the faraway strange men, and now he sees a thing that he likes, a thing that makes him laugh and shout, oh yes, and more. Master leaps and jumps around in his sanctum, kicking up his legs under his robes. All his magic charms go chinkety-chink-chink hanging from his throat and tangle in his beard. It is such a thing I never did think to see that from my hiding place on the balcony I am staring at him with my mouth open wide.

"A most excellent decision, my liege!" Master says. "Oh yes, most wise!" He bows toward the mirror, a mocking bow like Ariel's bows. "No doubt the wedding shall be a fine spectacle with your beloved son and all your most trusted courtiers in attendance." Master rubs his hands together like there is a great feast before him and his voice goes low and cold and hard, only just loud enough for me to hear it still. "Oh, my liege! Oh, my brother! You shall reap as you sowed, gentlemen, and after lo, these many long years, the day and hour of your harvest shall soon be upon you."

He summons a pair of the little gnomes and bids them to cover the walls with a fresh layer of limestone, to cover all of Miranda's pictures. I think it will sadden her heart, for she has worked so very hard on making them just right, but I do not have time to worry because then Master covers his mirror and leaves his sanctum, leaves it empty in the very middle of the day.

I think . . . do I dare?

For Miranda, yes.

And so I get off my belly and creep into Master's big room. My skin is twitchety with knowing that Master might come back at any moment and punish me. I take the cloth from Master's mirror and look into it.

I see nothing but my own face, low-browed and thick-jawed, coarse hair hanging over my eyes.

"Didst thou expect otherwise?" a light voice inquires. "Thou art no magus, witch's whelp or not."

I turn to face Ariel. "What did Master see in the mirror?" I ask him. "You go everywhere, you see everything. What was it?"

Ariel shrugs. "And I am oath-bound not to speak of it. Even were I not, why shouldst I tell thee?"

"I do not know," I say truthfully. "Spirit, I do not know why you do anything you do. And if you have told me true, neither do you." Always I am running away from him, but today, no; today, I take a step closer. "Do you?"

The line of Ariel's mouth twists. It is not a true smile, for there are none of his knives in it; but I think it is a true face, for there is a deep and honest sadness in it. "No," he whispers, then; "Yes."

I take another step. "Which is it?"

Ariel laughs and his eyes blaze, blaze; as bright as the mica-flecked rocks I set in the empty hollows of Setebos's eyes long ago blaze in the sunlight. "Both, thou fool!" He shakes his head, hair flying like foam around his head, his mouth twisting harder as though it fights to flee his face. "I am set against myself as surely as thou art. Aye, I chafe at the yoke of my captivity under our master Prospero, and it sits ill with me that a man should use his daughter thusly to gain his own ends, use the skill of her hands and aye, the very blood of her womb; and yet my goal is mine own freedom and I cannot attain it save that his plans come to fruition. Those are the horns of the dilemma on which I am hooked." Now his mouth is hard and not smiling, not at all. "Mayhap I have learned not to hate thee, but thou shouldst not trust me, monster."

"I do not," I assure him. "*Prospero?*"

Oh, but the handle of the door is turning, and like that, whoosh, Ariel is gone and I am alone.

Spying.

I throw the cloth over the mirror, run for the balcony, and dive over it, clinging to the walls of the palace like a lizard and scrambling downward.

That evening Master orders me to kill a hen, and I do it. That evening we have a feast, for Master is gladsome and merry and bids me to join them in the kitchen and make merry, too.

That evening I speak to Miranda.

THIRTY-TWO

MIRANDA

Papa will not say what has come to pass that has him in such high spirits, only that his great work is progressing in accordance with his hopes, but it is a welcome change. In an expansive gesture of generosity, he even bids Caliban to join us for a grand meal; and somewhat to my surprise, Caliban does so with a modicum of good grace. Although he is quiet and withdrawn throughout the meal, I begin to nurture a spark of hope he has softened toward me.

After we dine on a rare meal of stewed chicken, Papa retires to his sanctum to survey the night sky; and miracle of miracles, for the first time in long months, Caliban does not flee my presence, but asks if he might speak to me, fanning the faint spark within my breast.

I smile at him, or at least in his direction, since he remains loath to meet my eye. "I would like that."

Alas, I have spoken too swiftly.

Without once looking at me, Caliban tells me how he has been spending his days and what he has observed.

I listen without comment and a growing sense of hurt and anger. In truth, I do not know what to think. Mayhap I should be grateful that Caliban has softened at all, that he cares for me still; and yet I feel betrayed. Betrayed by his spying, yes, and his unexpected collusion with the spirit Ariel, but most of all by the fact that Caliban prefaces his tale by telling me that he *saw* Papa and me arrive on the isle all those many years ago.

Yes, that is the most painful.

It is quiet in the kitchen. The banked embers in the hearth crackle every now and then, their orange glow shifting beneath their blanket of grey ash. A clay lamp filled with oil pressed from last year's olives flickers on the table between us and the night breeze carries the scent of pine pollen.

"*Why*, Caliban?" I say to him at last, and the words come out with an injured passion I cannot suppress. "Why did you never tell me that you saw Papa and me come to the isle?"

It startles him enough that he lifts his head to glance at me, dark eyes glimmering in the hearth-glow. "Miranda . . ." He looks confused. "I *did* tell you. Do you not remember?"

"No," I say and it is true; but now a memory surfaces, a memory of Caliban's voice divulging a momentous truth beneath the jaws of Setebos casting long shadows over the high crag. "Oh, Caliban! You knew I forgot so many things when I was . . . afflicted. Why did you not remind me?"

His shoulders rise and tighten. "After Master did hurt you, after you did heal and learn to be Miranda again, we did not speak of *before* things. But . . . but I do not think that is the very most important thing I am telling you tonight."

I raise my voice. "It is to me, Caliban! All I have *ever* wanted to know is where I came from!"

He looks away. "You were sleeping. That is all I know, Miranda. All the time, you were asleep. I do not know where you and Master came from or how or why. Only that you did."

I am weary.

The bulky pouch of moss strapped between my thighs feels wet and sodden. Soon it will begin to leak and stain my gown if I do not attend to it. I shall have to change it for a fresh pouch before I may take to my bed; change it and place it in a jar, a jar I must deposit outside the door to Papa's sanctum.

"Let it be," I say tiredly to Caliban. "Whatever end Papa works toward, I must accept it is for the best."

He shakes his head, and the line of his jaw is stubborn. "No. He hurt you. I prayed to Setebos—"

"Setebos!" A jagged laugh escapes me. "Oh, Caliban! Do you know what your Setebos is?" I stand and dash tears from my eyes with the back of my hand. "It is the remains of a whale, Caliban; a great fish trapped in a volcanic eruption and turned to stone long before you or I was born. Nothing more."

It is a cruel manner in which to deliver such news. Caliban flinches as though I have struck him, yet he persists. "I think they are coming, Miranda. Coming to the isle, whether they want to or not. Not tomorrow, but soon, very soon. The men in Master's mirror, the men that he is so angry at. *My liege,* he did say today; and *my brother.* They are coming. And I do not know what will happen when they do."

"I don't care," I whisper, although it is a lie. "Let them come! Mayhap it is for the best."

Caliban meets my eyes. "What if it is not? What is it that Master does with your blood, Miranda?"

What, indeed?

I should like to know; as I should like to know a great many things. But not now, not tonight; mayhap not ever. I do not have the heart for it. I have paid a great price for the desire to know, and my curiosity is not what it once was. Tonight, I wish only for the solace of a warm pallet and a dry pouch between my thighs. I take the oil-lamp from the table. "Ariel goads you," I say to Caliban with as much gentleness as I can muster. "The spirit is ruled by Mercury and 'tis in his nature to stir trouble. Pay him no heed, or you will suffer for his mischief as I did."

I think that shall be the last word on the matter and turn to go, but Caliban surprises me again. "I know," he says. "That Ariel even did say I should not trust him, and I do not, not even when he is kind and not cruel. But he did say one other thing, too. I think it is a true thing. I think . . . I think he said Master's name."

I pause. "What is it?"

"Prospero."

Prospero.

Why, in all my years, did I never think to wonder what Papa's given name was? I cannot say, yet I did not, not even when I realized that Caliban mistook the word *Master* for Papa's name. It is a piece of knowledge that settles into me, filling a gap I had not realized existed until this very moment.

And yet, does it matter?

No.

Of all the knowledge that Papa has withheld from me, that is a thing for which I cannot blame him, for it never occurred to me to ask.

"Thank you," I say to Caliban. "I am . . . I am grateful for your concern. And I wish we had spoken of the matter of your memory of our arrival on the isle sooner."

Caliban stands with his head bowed, ragged forelock obscuring his eyes. "I am sorry, Miranda," he murmurs. "I did not know."

I fight the urge to reach for his hand, my throat tightening. "Oh, Caliban! Of course you didn't. You meant it as a kindness, and I am sorry to have thought otherwise. But you say we are friends still and always; if it is true, there should be no secrets between us." A bitter note creeps into my voice. "The Lord God in His heaven knows there are enough secrets in our lives! You and I, we should be different, as we have always been to each other. But you must promise me that you'll not spy on Papa again. It's not worth the risk." He says nothing, but his shoulders hunch again. "Caliban, *please*! Will you not promise me? I should be heartsick if Papa were to catch you and punish you for it, to hurt you as badly as he hurt me. You are dearer than a friend, as dear as a brother to me. Is it so great a boon to ask?" Still his silence continues, and at once I am hurt and angry again. "Do you love me so little that you will not grant me this one small kindness?"

"So little!" Caliban utters a bark of laughter, a harsh grating sound. "No, Miranda. Too much."

I stare at him. "Then why—"

He interrupts me. "Is it truly what you wish?"

I swallow, only just beginning to understand what he has said to me. "I . . . yes. Caliban, it's too dangerous, and you're no match for Papa's magic. But—"

"Then I will do as you wish." He backs away from me, avoiding my gaze. "Good night, Miranda."

I am left alone in the kitchen.

I make my way to my bed-chamber, then tend to the business of my woman's courses. The Moorish writing on the walls of the palace wavers in the flickering light of my oil-lamp as I creep upstairs to deposit the clay jar with the latest blood-sodden pouch outside the door of Papa's sanctum, then return to my bed-chamber. Although I lie on my pallet, my thoughts are reeling. The solace and the promise of sleep that I had craved only a short time ago now seems as distant and unattainable as the moon.

Caliban's declaration has cracked open the wall of weariness with which I sought to protect myself, and now the evening's revelations cascade through my thoughts.

Prospero.

Papa's name is Prospero, and Ariel has known it all along. Caliban saw Papa and me arrive on the isle and surmised that Papa has enemies somewhere across the wide sea, and he has known it all along; and oh, I cannot help but feel a sting of betrayal in it still.

And yet Caliban has only ever sought to protect me. It is not his fault that he did not realize the memory was lost to me.

Caliban loves me.

Too much, he said; and I do not think he meant as a dear friend, as a sister. No, this is different. It is a thought that makes my heart feel wild and tender and strange, and yet it frightens me, too.

Oh, but Papa! My thoughts circle back to him. Can it be true that his great working is an undertaking of vengeance? Against whom? *My liege, my brother,* Caliban said.

My brother.

If it is true, Papa has a brother; a brother who betrayed him. Somewhere, I have an uncle.

My liege.

Somewhere, I have a king; a king who also wronged us.

If it is true.

I think of the various images that Papa has bidden me to render; of the second face of Gemini; the image of the eagle-headed man that is to be invoked in matters of oppression and evil, the image I was only just given permission to finish a month ago.

Oppression.

Evil.

I think of one I have only just finished, one I was proud to complete before the onset of my courses; the first face of Libra, an image of a man with a lance in one hand holding a bird dangling by its feet, an image which Papa deigned to tell me ruled over matters of justice.

I think Caliban is right. As more bits and pieces of knowledge settle into place inside me alongside Papa's name—Prospero!—it is like painting the outline of an image. I begin to see the picture that they form. The dim remnants of my memories are true. Papa and I came from elsewhere, a place where the kind ladies with gentle hands who sang me to sleep dwelled; and yet somehow we were betrayed and cast out.

Mayhap, like Caliban's mother, Sycorax, we were exiled to this isle because of Papa's magic. Can it be?

My mind shies away from the thought. No, I will not think it. Papa worships the good Lord God in His heaven, and the influence that he draws down from the celestial spheres originates in the very Empyrean where God dwells. I have felt the sacred power of the *Spiritus Mundi* flow through me when I paint at Papa's bidding, and I cannot believe it is anything but holy. No, there can be no comparison between Papa's art and the dark sorcery practiced by Caliban's mother in the name of a demonic spirit. Even the spirit Ariel, as much as he loathes the servitude to which Papa has bound him, has never suggested such a thing.

Ariel . . .

It comes to me now that Ariel knew of Caliban's feelings. *He is set against himself,* Ariel told me, *and thou art the cause of it.*

Too much.

But what does it mean to love too much? How can there be such a thing as too much love?

All my life I have yearned for nothing more. I think of the profound ache of loneliness that filled my childhood days before Papa summoned Caliban; and oh, I do love Caliban! I love him fiercely. I should not have been so angry at the notion that he kept a secret from me did I not love him so.

How can it be too much?

And yet another memory slides through my thoughts, one I have sought to suppress; glass shattered on the tile floor, the pale thing gasping amidst the bright, broken shards, and Papa's voice, soft and terrible. *You've killed your mother all over again, Miranda.*

The homunculus.

It was a thing that should never have been made, Ariel said; so Caliban told me. But Papa did make it. I think of the braided circlet of dark gold hair tied around its ankle like a tether.

My mother's hair?

Is that why Papa made the homunculus? Because he loved my mother too much to let her go, so much so that he sought to restore her in defiance of the Lord God's divine order? If that is so, then I cannot be sure that whatever great working Papa undertakes now is truly in the service of all that is good and holy.

Although it is not cold, I shiver under my bed-linens, my skin prickling with apprehension. I cannot bear to think these thoughts any longer. Too much—yes, it is altogether too much indeed. In the harsh light of so many possible revelations, I feel as fragile and exposed as a newly hatched chick. I pull the linens over my head, curling my body around the dull ache in my lower belly that accompanies the flow of my woman's courses, and pray for the merciful comfort of sleep. It comes in time, although it does not come swiftly nor does it come without a final worrisome thought, one that chases me down the well of oblivion to haunt my dreams.

Caliban spoke truly when he said I failed to grasp the most important thing he told me this evening.

If he is right, Papa's enemies, whomever they may be—brother, uncle, king—are coming to the isle.

And they are coming soon.

THIRTY-THREE

CALIBAN

I go to my high place.

It is dark, but there are no clouds and the moon is only a few days past its full roundness. It is enough light to see if I am careful and slow. I do not like to leave Miranda alone after what I did tell her about Master's plans, but whatever thing is going to happen, it is not going to happen tonight.

And there is the other thing I did tell her.

I need to think about it.

Atop the crag, Setebos laughs at the night sky. I see the shape of his big head and jaws as darkness against the stars. The faraway stars look so little, like they are little silvery fish for Setebos to swallow, gulpity-gulp-gulp.

In his sanctum in the palace, Master is looking at those very stars through the shining tube on the balcony—the balcony where

I did promise I would not hide and spy—and making notes on his charts.

(What do you see in the stars, Master? Not fish.)

Miranda says Setebos is a fish, a great fish turned to stone. She did say it because she was angry, but I think she believes it is true. Maybe it is true. But why can it not be Setebos, too? If Miranda's painting of the bright-faced man standing on a winged serpent is the sun, maybe my Setebos-the-fish is also Setebos in the same way.

I do not know, only that Setebos watches over the isle, watches over me. I prayed to him and Miranda did wake.

I sit on my haunches with Setebos behind me and look out at the sea. The water is black under the night sky, starlight and moonlight making silver sparkles that dance on the little waves that ripple, ripple, ripple. Far below the crag, the waves make soft splashing sounds on the rocks. There are no fish jumping, no undines playing, no birds flying in the moonlight.

All is calm.

There is a storm in the offing.

I do not trust Ariel, no, but in this I do believe him. It was a storm that brought Master—no. No, I will not call him that anymore, not in the thoughts I think. If I dare not say it aloud, I will call him by his name in my thoughts. For all his magic, he is only a man, and I swore no oath to serve him. Prospero. *Prosssspero.* I roll the word over, hearing it inside my head. Yes, it was a storm that brought *Prospero* and Miranda to the isle.

Now I am afraid it is a storm that will take them away.

Not him; her.

You, Miranda.

I wrap my arms around my knees and rock back and forth. I did not know I should have told her what I saw. I did not know she had forgotten.

How is it that I hurt her when it is the most veriest thing I never, ever wanted to do? Poor, dumb, clumsy monster. No wonder that Miranda thinks I do not love her.

But I did tell her tonight.

Yes, I did.

I think of her face when I did say what I did, of her pink lips open in surprise and her smooth brow going wrinkle-crinkle as she does try to understand; oh, and I wish that was all I think of, but it is the first time I have been so close to Miranda in oh, so many days, and I think of the light of the oil-lamp showing the curve of her breasts under her gown, warm golden light like honey on her skin, and I remember Miranda naked over the wash-basin and my rod stiffens and rises in my breeches, the head pushing out from its hood, and in my thoughts I say, no, no, I will not do it. Not thinking of Miranda, no. I pray to Setebos to take the wanting away, but Setebos only laughs at the stars, laughs and laughs as though to say, no, this is what you are, Caliban, not even I can change it.

Then it is too late and I am already untying my breeches and reaching for my aching rod, my hand sliding up and down, up and down, the poor dumb monster hunched over his swollen flesh.

Oh, it feels so good; and oh, it is cruel that a thing that is bad should feel so good.

Miranda, I am sorry.

Afterward I lie on my back and look at the stars like silver fishes between Setebos's laughing jaws.

Is this badness inside me because Umm was bad, I wonder? It is the thing she did try to make Ariel do, I understand it now. To lie with her the way I want to lie with Miranda.

It is a thought that makes my belly feel sick, as though I have eaten fish that did spoil in the sun, but it makes my rod stiffen, too.

Why?

Maybe my father was a poor dumb monster, too.

I wish I did not have this badness inside me. I wish I could be a man like that Ariel did show me, handsome-faced and straight-legged, who would look at Miranda and think only good holy thoughts, and not want oh, so much to touch her little breasts, to feel the curve of them in the palm of his hand.

But I cannot.

I cannot, Miranda.

I will keep my promise to you. I will not spy; I will only be the good servant. I will go back to the palace at dawn so Master—*Prospero*— does not punish me and make your heart sore. I will wait and watch like Setebos for the storm that is coming, and I will put myself between you and anything that would harm you.

Always.

It is only that I did never believe one of those things could be me, because I do love you so much; and I am glad I said it to you, because it cut me like knives to think you did not know it.

But I am glad you do not understand it yet.

I do not want you to see the badness inside me.

THIRTY-FOUR

MIRANDA

Having declared that his fondness for me does, in fact, endure in a most pressing manner, Caliban proceeds to demonstrate it by continuing to avoid me. Given that he fled my presence after having done so, I cannot confess myself surprised; and yet I am hurt all over again. Now more than ever, more than any time since my affliction, I need my dearest friend by my side.

I begin to think I will never understand him.

Even if I were clever enough to think of a way to ask Papa about Caliban's revelations without betraying the cause of my curiosity, I do not think I would be brave enough to do so.

Not anymore.

And so I bide my time, waiting for my woman's courses to pass and thinking mayhap that when I return to Papa's sanctum and resume my painting, I may find some pretext to make ever-so-subtle inquiries—but when I enter the chamber, all such thoughts go clean out of my head.

The walls are empty and white.

It shocks me to the core of my being. One hand flies to cover my mouth and I hear myself utter a muffled cry of dismay. "Oh, Papa! What happened?"

Papa gives me a careless glance. "What's that, lass?"

I point at the walls, my finger trembling. "The first face of Aries . . . Virgo . . . Libra . . . oh, the *Sun*, Papa! What happened to them?"

"Ah." He places a marker in the book he is studying and closes it. "Do not concern yourself, for there is naught amiss. I bade the gnomes cover them that you might begin anew."

The unexpected loss of the paintings over which I labored so long and with such love fills me with anguish. "Oh, but—"

"Did you think such images were meant to endure, Miranda?" Papa shakes his head. "Even as the heavens revolve around us, that which will serve the needs of our working changes from day to day, week to week, and month to month; both with the movement of the spheres and those changing events that transpire on earth to which we beseech the seven governors and their various aspects to lend their influence." A faint note of reproach enters his voice and his face creases in a frown. "I thought you understood as much. Was I mistaken?"

"No, but—" I catch myself short and cast my gaze downward, realizing his comments have afforded me an opening for inquiry. "Forgive me, Papa. It caught me by surprise. Has something of note transpired?"

Papa is silent a moment. I steal a glance toward the mirror, but it is covered. I feel Papa's stern gaze upon me, as heavy as a touch. "All shall be revealed in the fullness of time, child," he says. "But although it is drawing near, that time is not yet upon us. Did I not make myself clear in this matter? If you are to serve as my *soror mystica* in this endeavor, I require your innocence. I require you to act in perfect trust and perfect faith that the working may not be tainted." He pauses, knitting his brows. "Has your trust in me faltered, Miranda?"

Yes, I whisper in my thoughts. *I fear it faltered a long time ago, Papa; when I found the* thing *you called my mother.*

Oh, but the habit of obedience is deeply engrained in me, and I shake my own head, no, no. "Of course not, Papa." I hesitate. "It is only that Ariel once said to me that it is the fine edge of a blade that divides innocence from ignorance, and I should hate to do harm all unwitting."

"Ariel!" Papa's frown deepens. "Meddlesome sprite."

I say nothing.

Papa strokes his beard. "I shall have a word with him. Meanwhile, I should like you to commence an image of Venus."

On its stand, the book *Picatrix* is open to the corresponding page. I study the image of Venus, a woman standing with a red fruit in one hand and a comb in the other. She wears a pale green gown and long tresses of golden hair flow over her shoulders. Despite everything, the chance to paint another one of the seven governors makes my fingers itch to pick up a brush.

"Do not fear that you may err out of ignorance," Papa says to me in a voice so kind I almost wish it was not a falsehood I told him. "So long as you work at my behest, I promise you that will never come to pass. And do not mourn the loss of your journeyman efforts, Miranda. God has given you a gift, but as with any skill, practice will hone it. You will do better work."

I cannot deny the truth of it, for I myself could see that my work had improved with each image I rendered over the long winter months. The first face of Aries was looking distinctly lumpish to my eyes. Still, it pains me that it is all simply *gone,* gone without warning. "Thank you, Papa."

He lays a hand on my shoulder. "I shall summon Ariel while this business is fresh in my mind and return anon."

"Yes, Papa."

It is not the first time that Papa has left me alone in his sanctum, but it is the first time I have been tempted to disobedience; a thing I never should have imagined would happen again. Had I not been so stricken by the unexpected loss of my paintings—indeed, had Papa but thought to warn me—mayhap it would have been different. I do not know, only that today the cloth-covered mirror beckons me as irresistibly as the lamp-flame beckons the moth. It is a piece of folly; oh, I know it is, for like Caliban I have gazed at the mirror and seen naught but my own face, but if there is a chance I might see these strange men of whom Caliban spoke—these men that Papa named *my liege* and *my brother*—for myself, I must attempt it.

I creep toward the mirror and reach for a corner of the ragged piece of cloth that is draped over it.

"Foolisssh girl," a crackling voice behind me says. *"It will avail you naught without the ssspell."*

I very nearly leap out of my skin, my heart pounding.

Across the chamber, the fiery salamander in the brazier regards me with its bejeweled eyes.

"You *do* speak!" I breathe.

It blinks.

I cross the chamber and kneel before the brazier. "Will you teach this spell to me?" I beseech the salamander.

"And ssee you sssuffer for it?" In its nest of bright embers, the salamander flexes delicate claws tipped with nails of molten gold. *"No."*

I sit back on my heels. "How is it that you alone among the elementals speak?" I whisper.

It laughs, that sound like a burst of sparks rising. *"I lisssten,"* it says. *"And fire has a thousand tongues."*

"Has Papa spoken of his plans in your presence?" I ask the salamander. It seems my curiosity has not deserted me after all, for now that I have allowed myself to give voice to it, the questions flood forth from my lips. "Do you know what he intends? Can you tell me what it is that he sees in the mirror? Is it his brother? His king? Do you know how we came to this isle and from whence?" I hesitate. "Do you know what he means to do with my blood?"

"Shall I *ssspeak and sssuffer for it?"* The salamander flicks its tail in a gesture of refusal. *"No."*

I am unaccountably disappointed. "And yet you *do* speak to me," I say. "Why?"

The salamander is silent for a long moment, so long I begin to wonder if I have lost my wits and imagined the entire business. Patterns of light and shadow shift beneath its glowing skin. *"I do not know the whole of your father's plan,"* it says. *"Only pieces. But grant me a promissse and I will anssswer one question that you have asssked of me."*

"What promise?" I ask it.

"A promissse that you will not leave the isle without ssseeing me freed from thiss iron prison," it says in a voice as dry and crackling as kindling.

"Leave the isle?" I echo in startlement. "Why, however in the world should that come to pass?"

The salamander blinks its jeweled eyes. *"Promissse."*

Once, when Papa was in good spirits, I dared to ask him why he did not bind another fire elemental to serve in our kitchen hearth and spare us—or at least poor Caliban—the endless labor of gathering firewood; his reply was that the salamanders were the most dangerous and difficult to control of the elementals, and that our humble hearth was safer without one. I am not sure I should trust this one. It has spoken to me twice, and both times when I was in disobedience of Papa's orders.

And yet it is a piece of cruelty that the salamander has been imprisoned in the brazier for these many long years, while the other elementals that serve Papa enjoy their freedom when they are not about his bidding.

I am ashamed that I did not think it before.

The notion that I might one day leave the isle seems a possibility as remote as the very stars and planets in their distant spheres, but if such a thing were to happen, surely it would be a simple act of kindness to ensure that the salamander—and indeed, all the elementals—were freed from whatever magic bound them.

"You'll not burn me to cinders by way of thanks for setting you free?" I ask the salamander. I have grown more suspicious than the trusting child I was.

It laughs a hissing shower of sparks, and yet somehow there is a note of bitterness in the sound. *"No."*

I take a deep breath. "Then yes, I promise it."

The salamander's eyes wink and sparkle like rubies. *"Which quessstion will you asssk?"* it says. *"Choose wisely."*

Oh, it is so difficult to know! I think about the questions I posed, turning them over in my thoughts like rare shells to examine them, and it seems to me that some of my questions have already been answered in part. If I believe Caliban—and in my heart, I fear that I do—then I know what Papa saw in the mirror. I have an inkling of what is coming. And it seems to me, too, that the salamander sought to warn me; it knows only pieces of what Papa's intentions are.

I should dearly like to ask the salamander if it knows how we came to the isle and from whence, but what if the answer is no? I would have made a bad bargain in exchange for my promise, then.

I hear Papa's footsteps approaching in the hallway.

The flames surrounding the salamander in its brazier flare into urgent brightness. *"Choose!"*

Had I more time to consider, I might have chosen otherwise, but there is only one question to which I have not the slightest portion of an answer, and I ask it now in a hurried rush. "Oh, salamander! What magical working is it that Papa seeks to accomplish with the blood of my woman's courses?"

It gives me another slow, deliberate blink; in approval? In disappointment? I cannot tell.

"A love ssspell," the salamander says. *"To ensssnare a king's ssson."*

THIRTY-FIVE

In the earliest days of my affliction, I was dumbstruck. I had no under-standing of what had befallen me, only the terrified realization that something was very wrong and my world had changed forever.

Thus do I feel today. The salamander's revelation is one too many for my wits to encompass. Once again, my world has changed and I no longer comprehend my place in it.

A brother.

A king.

A king's son and a love spell.

How is it that such things might come to be here on our lonely isle? I cannot fathom it. And yet 'twas ever true that there was a secret goal toward which Papa plied his arts.

It is why he summoned Caliban, that he might learn the name by which Sycorax imprisoned Ariel.

It is why he freed Ariel from the great pine and bound him to his service.

It is why he charts the skies, why he encouraged my budding talent for illustration, why I paint at his bidding. And today he bade me render an image of the Lady Venus herself, Venus who is the very Queen of Love among the seven governors.

I do my best to comply, but my thoughts are as scattered as a handful of petals tossed to the wind, blown hither and thither and yon. My hands shake and refuse to obey me as though I have been afflicted anew, and my brushstrokes, that had grown so sure and joyful, become clumsy and crude.

Why a love spell?

Even in the privacy of my own thoughts, I fear to speculate.

The initial lineaments of my Venus depict a poor, botched thing lacking all semblance of grace and beauty. Mercifully, Papa attributes my failure to the shock of finding all my prior work vanished beneath a thick coating of fresh white-wash.

"Forgive me, child," he says at the end of the day. "I should have known you would take it amiss and thought to forewarn you." He gives me a kind smile. "I'll not be remiss the next time."

I clasp my hands before me to hide their trembling. "Thank you, Papa. With your permission, I'll take time to gather my thoughts and offer prayers to Lady Venus ere I begin tomorrow."

Papa casts a wry glance at my ungainly strokes on the wall. "I think that would be wise."

Papa.

Prospero.

It is as though he has become a stranger to me. Although my knowledge is far from complete, I now know secrets that he did not divulge to me; did not wish divulged to me. If 'tis true that any knowledge of his purpose on my part will taint our working, well, then, the damage is done, and I do not know if that should be a source of abiding shame or relief to me.

Both, mayhap.

One thing I *do* know, and that is that I have an urgent desire to speak to Caliban. When I first awakened from my affliction, it was his dear face I saw; my first memory is of Caliban seeing my confusion and reminding me of his name, oh, so gently.

Now I regret that I was short with him the other night, but it was a great deal to take in.

I did not want to believe.

But I do.

On the morrow, I manage to catch Caliban before he succeeds in evading me, and ask him nicely if he might procure fresh river trout for our supper. This he agrees to do with a curt nod, taking the pail with him as he leaves.

When Papa adjourns to his sanctum, I do not engage myself in contemplation and prayers to the Lady Venus. No, instead, I set out to find Caliban.

It is a beautiful spring morning on the isle, balmy and clear, the promise of afternoon's coming heat alleviated by the lingering freshness of the night's dew. The jacaranda trees are in bloom, great clouds of violet blossoms clinging to their limbs, and the tall rhododendrons offer up pink and white and purple clusters, such hues as make me long for my paints. In the courtyard where the sour orange trees grow, buzzing honeybees are already at work gathering the pollen of their delicate white blossoms that they might transmute it into golden sweetness. Papa says that bees are nature's alchemists, and that as proof, honey is the only food that never spoils but retains the goodness of its essence in perpetuity.

The reminder of Papa gives me a pang of guilt, but I persevere, leaving the palace grounds behind me. The flowers that blossom in the wild are less spectacular, but no less lovely for it—myrtle shrubs with their pungent leaves, fields of scrubby yellow broom bright beneath the sun. A great fondness for the isle's beauty fills me, and my heart aches to imagine that I should ever leave it.

There are two places where Caliban is wont to catch fish and I know them both, for I accompanied him thence on excursions many times in happier days. The first is a bend in the stream where the current slows as it rounds the reed-covered banks. In high summer or midwinter, the level of the water is no higher than the calves of his legs, but today the stream is swollen with snowmelt from the distant mountain peaks to the east.

It is at the second place, a place where the stream runs swiftly, but great rocks lying just below the surface break up its current and create eddying pools in which the speckled trout bask, that I find Caliban. He crouches low on one of the boulders, water running in a torrent over his feet. Translucent undines frolic in the stream around him, but he ignores them, crouching to gaze intently into the water, hands poised at the ready. The pail is perched precariously on another boulder nearby.

Not so very long ago, I would have been holding the pail for him and shouting encouragement from the banks, both of us laughing for the sheer joy of being young and alive.

With the advent of spring, Caliban has abandoned the coarse shirt I made for him and is clad only in worn and tattered sailcloth breeches. His bare skin gleams like polished wood in the sunlight. The muscles of his bent back fan like wings, reaching for his shoulders. Below the pointed ridge of black hair that descends from the nape of his neck, I can see the knobs of bone running down his spine.

I should like to touch them.

I should like to understand how a man is made.

It is a curious thought, and I am not sure if it is a thought of

Miranda-the-painter who would stretch out the wing of a mummified bat to see how its tendons conjoin to the bone or . . . something else.

And then Caliban plunges his hands into the stream and catches a fish, its scales glistening silvery green as it thrashes in his grip.

"Oh, well done!" I cry, clapping my hands together like the child I had been; I cannot help myself.

"Miranda!" Caliban's head comes up. He tosses the fish into the pail and glowers at me, straightening from his crouch. "Why are you here? You should not be here."

"Forgive me," I say to him. "But I would speak further to you of what you told me the other evening."

"No." Caliban lowers his head and shakes it like a goat balking at the rope. "You told me to let it be."

I take a step toward the bank. "You caught me unawares."

"There is nothing we can do," Caliban says. "You did say it; I am no match for Master's—for *Prospero's*—magic."

"We can seek to allay our own ignorance, Caliban!" I say. "Are you not weary of it?" I think I have him cornered on the rocks and he must stay and answer me, but I have underestimated both his agility and his determination to avoid my presence, for he abandons the pail and turns his back on me, leaping from boulder to boulder across the rushing stream.

Well, he has underestimated *my* determination, too. I am done with letting him flee my presence without ever once telling me what in the name of all that is holy troubles him so.

"Caliban!" I call after him, hoisting the skirts of my gown to my ankles. I step onto the first boulder. "I will follow you day and night until you stop and talk to me!"

Midstream, he pauses and turns to face me, his gaze filled with alarm. "Miranda, no! It's too dangerous."

The rocks are slippery, but Caliban is looking at me, truly looking at me without flinching away. True, 'tis with fear and concern, but for the first time in long months, I feel as though he is seeing *me* and not whatever it is I have become in his eyes that he cannot abide the sight of. It is a big step to the next boulder. I let go my skirts and flail my arms for balance, toes clinging to the surface of the slick rock beneath the shining rush of water. "Will you stay and talk to me, then? Else I *will* follow."

He hesitates.

It will require a short jump to reach the next boulder, which protrudes from the surface of the stream. The water is colder than I reckoned, and I am not so hardy as Caliban; nor even so hardy as I was before I began spending my days assisting Papa in his sanctum. My feet are growing numb and the hem of my gown is sodden and heavy, tangling around my ankles. On the far bank, shimmering dragonflies hover above the reeds. Some distance upstream, the water elementals cease their antics and watch with idle interest.

If I do not make the attempt, I shall lose my nerve and my threat shall be proven a vain one. Gathering my skirts and my courage, I leap. For a moment, I think I have gained the boulder safely and begin to smile in triumph, but then one foot slips, and suddenly I am falling.

"Miranda!"

Caliban's cry is the last thing I hear before the rush of the stream stops my ears. The shock of the cold water drives the breath from my lungs; cold, colder than I reckoned, and deeper, too. When I open my mouth, it fills with water and it is all I can do not to inhale it. The weight of my gown drags me down into the depths of the stream and the current takes me. I thrash against it to no avail.

I cannot breathe.

Oh, good Lord God, I cannot breathe! The water is cold, so cold, and the current is so strong that I cannot tell up from down.

My lungs burn.

Papa will be so angry at me for dying thusly, I think foolishly.

And then a hand clamps my wrist, pulling so hard that my shoulder aches in its socket. My head breaks the surface, and I gasp and sputter. Caliban gets his hands under my arms and hauls me from the stream to the safety of the near bank, where I lie curled and trembling with the cold, my teeth a-chatter.

"Miranda!" He pats at me with anxious hands, his worried face inches from mine. "Are you hurt?"

"N-n-nuh!" I force the words out between my chattering teeth. "Cold!"

Caliban bounds away to fetch an armload of broom, returning to scrub vigorously at me with the coarse stalks. Although it is a strange course of treatment, it causes the blood to rise to my skin and warms my limbs until I am no longer trembling. "Is that better?"

"Yes, thank you." I manage to sit upright. "Forgive me, Caliban. That was unwise."

He backs away from me and averts his gaze. "Yes."

I should like to weep in sheer frustration. "Oh, Caliban! What has come between us? Why will you not look at me?"

"I cannot," he murmurs. "You are too beautiful, Miranda."

"Beautiful!" A wild laugh escapes me. I am a mess, soaked from head to toe. My hair is dripping and I am covered in bright yellow broom blossoms, their ragged petals clinging to my wet gown. I stare at him. "Do you jest?"

Caliban's shoulders tense. "Do not look at me. You should not look at me."

"*Why?*"

He steals one quick, darting glance at me. "Because you are beautiful," he says again. "And I am a monster."

The words are like a blow to my heart. "How can you say such a thing?"

"Because it is true!" There is a savage note of anguish in Caliban's voice. "I am a swart, stooped thing with hunched shoulders and bowed legs, and . . . and a villain's brow, and sullen eyes, speckled like a toad!"

Each word is a fresh new blow, cruel and vicious, cracking open my ignorant, selfish heart and driving understanding into it. Caliban loves me not as a friend, not with the innocence of childhood, but as a man loves a woman; loves me and believes himself unworthy.

Love is strong as death, says the Song of Solomon; *jealousy is cruel as the grave.*

I should like to laugh and rant like a madwoman at the blindness of my own folly; I should like to weep an ocean of salt tears for Caliban's pain. He does not seek to flee my presence, only squats quietly on his haunches, his head hanging low, breathing like some hunted beast that can run no farther.

He is set against himself, Ariel said to me, *and thou art the cause of it.* Ariel.

The words Caliban spoke are not his own, I am sure of it. Only the mercurial spirit would be so cruel.

Gathering myself, I go to Caliban. When I touch his shoulder, he flinches. "Did Ariel say as much to you?"

"It does not matter," Caliban mutters. "It is true."

"No." I flatten my palm against his warm skin. "It is a lie. You are dear to me, and beautiful in my eyes, Caliban. Every part of you. You could never be otherwise."

Caliban shakes his head. "Do not say so."

"Should I not love you because your skin shines like polished wood in the sunlight?" Kneeling before him, I stroke his upper arms, feeling the corded muscles tense beneath my hands. "Should I not love you for the strength of these limbs that have saved my life this very day?" My heart quickening in my breast, I touch his averted face, stroke the hair from his brow. "Should I not love this face that is so dear to me? It is the first thing I saw when I emerged from a sleep like death. And your gaze . . . since we have been friends, your gaze has always been sweet toward me, has it not?" One by one, I touch the scattered moles on his face. "Should I not love you because you wear a constellation of stars upon your skin?"

"Miranda!" he groans. "Do not do this."

Oh, but I have gained understanding; an understanding that is fragile and precious, and yet there is power in it.

"A constellation of stars," I whisper again, touching his throat, his shoulders, the broad expanse of his bare chest, making a pattern with my fingertips. His skin is warm, so warm! At the base of my own throat, my pulse flutters like a dragonfly's wings. "Will you not look at me, Caliban?"

The sun climbs higher into the sky and the stream sings a fast, burbling song to itself as it rushes over the rocks.

The scent of bruised flowers hangs in the air.

Somewhere, a bird is singing.

Caliban raises his head and looks at me with dark, dark eyes filled with longing and misery and desperate hope.

Now he touches *my* face, and though his hands are rough, his touch is oh, so gentle. He kisses me, his lips soft on mine.

Now I am trembling.

Let him kiss me with the kisses of his mouth: for thy love is better than wine.

The understanding I have gained unfolds and unfolds and unfolds, growing vaster and deeper.

I am a woman.

Caliban is a man.

Behold, thou art fair, my beloved, yea, pleasant: also our bed is green.

He kisses me and kisses me, and I kiss him and kiss him in turn, both of us trading kisses back and forth like presents we demand and exchange in a game of rewards in which every player wins, and although I do not know what *wine* is, I think it must be a heady thing, for it seems my head is spinning with pleasure, and I find that I am no longer kneeling but lying on the green bank of the stream, the green bed of Solomon's song, Caliban's weight pinning me to the sweet earth.

I hear my bodice tear.

A bundle of myrrh is my well-beloved unto me; he shall lie all night betwixt my breasts.

Caliban's mouth is at my breasts. My nipples are yet hard and tight from the coldness of the stream, exposed in the morning air. I sink my fingers into his thick, coarse hair and guide one into his mouth and moan when he suckles it, drawing hard on my taut flesh.

I welcome it.

There is a hardness that presses at the juncture of my thighs where Caliban lies between them and I understand that this is the immodest thing, the part of a man that I am forbidden to see; and yet I feel no wrongness in this moment. My hips lift of their own urgent accord to push against the hardness.

Later I shall wonder if there was a moment when Eve first ate of the apple and gained forbidden knowledge that she reckoned it worth the price.

Mayhap.

Mayhap not.

"Oh, vilest of wretches!" Papa's voice breaks like thunder over the isle, deep and resonant with fury. "I'll flay your muscles from the bone!"

I do not see him stride across the field of yellow broom to grasp the hair at the nape of Caliban's neck and haul him off me; I know only that Caliban's weight is gone. I clamber to my feet in horror, grasping the edges of the torn bodice of my gown.

Caliban staggers and Papa stalks after him, amulet clutched in one hand as he calls down all manner of torment upon him. "Knave! Villain! Did I not forbid you to lay so much as a finger on my daughter?" he asks grimly. "And instead you attack her and seek to *violate* her innocence?"

"Papa, *no*!" I cry. "It's not his fault!"

Papa ignores me. His hand clutches the amulet so hard I think he will crush it. With a groan of agony, Caliban falls to his knees, and then to his side. His body twitches and convulses. The skin that I have just touched writhes unnaturally as his muscles cramp and twist beneath it. The hands that have just touched me with such tenderness scrabble at the earth, pulling up stalks of broom.

"Piece of filth!" Papa's face is purple with rage. "Oh, ungrateful beast! Would you flee the scene of your vile deed? Would you flee the righteousness of a father's wrath? Then crawl on your belly like the worm that you are!"

"Papa!"

"Crawl, I say!"

Caliban attempts to crawl on limbs that do not obey him. It is a piteous sight.

"Shall I let you flee? No, I think not." Papa plants one foot on the back of Caliban's neck, shoving his face into the grassy bank. He lifts the amulet high. "Indeed, I can think of no reason to suffer you to live."

There is murder in his voice, and the sound of it makes my blood run cold with terror.

Letting go my torn bodice, I catch Papa's arm in both hands. *"No!"* He looks at me in disbelief, but I do not relinquish my grip. "Caliban did not attack me," I say to him. "How could he? Caliban cannot raise a hand against me in harm. Your own magic precludes it."

I see myself reflected in Papa's gaze; bare-breasted, wet-haired, and bedraggled in my torn, soaked gown with grass and petals clinging to it, my skin still flushed with desire. I see him take in the truth of my words, and understand the meaning of them. A look of profound disgust suffuses his features.

Although I am ashamed, I do not let go his arm. No matter what punishment I suffer for it, I will stay his hand.

In the grass, Caliban groans.

"So be it." Papa jerks his arm from my grasp, lowering the amulet. He takes his foot from Caliban's neck. Breathing hard, he lowers his voice. "The lad lives. I'll not shed innocent blood."

"Thank you, Papa," I whisper.

Papa shudders and looks away from me. "Begone from my sight, Miranda," he says. "I do not trust myself to mete out a fitting punishment to you. Until such time as I send for you, confine yourself to your chamber."

I clasp my torn bodice and curtsy. "Yes, Papa."

"*Go!*"

When I turn to depart, I see Ariel. In the shock of the moment, I had not thought to wonder how Papa knew to find Caliban and me, but of course it was Ariel. The spirit's eyes are dark and I cannot fathom his expression.

He bows his head and lets me pass.

THIRTY-SIX

CALIBAN

Oh, Miranda!

Mirandamirandamiranda.

I hurt.

I hurt so very badly.

But I see your face behind my eyes when I close them and there is love in it. You did see the badness in me and make it beautiful with kisses. You with yellow flowers on your blue gown, and your skin like milk.

I did touch you.

I did tear your gown.

And you did not run, no; you put your breast that was still cold from the stream to my mouth, and I did suck and suck on your pink nipple, and that was the sweetest thing in the everest ever.

You in the sunlight.
You on the grass.
You with the yellow flowers.

THIRTY-SEVEN

MIRANDA

It is three full days before Papa can bring himself to speak to me, and I spend them in a state of suspended terror, awaiting his judgment. I do not stir from my chamber, not even to venture into my garden. Although I have no food to eat, there is water in my wash-basin that I might drink.

One of the silent little gnomes comes every morning to empty my chamber-pot and for once, I am glad they do not speak.

Still, it is a long time to be alone with my thoughts.

I mend my torn bodice, which I am forced to do with red thread that is all that is left in the sewing casket Papa gave me so long ago. Although I try to make my stitches as small as possible, when I have finished a ragged red line of mending meanders down the front of my bodice.

Caliban.

Oh, dear Lord God, how could I have done such a wanton, immodest thing?

Betimes the shame of it flushes my entire body until I feel hot and sick and feverish, my empty stomach heaving in a vain effort to expel the food it does not contain, only the bitter taste of bile in my mouth.

But betimes I think of the longing and hope in Caliban's eyes; I think of the kisses we traded back and forth like gifts, I think of his mouth on my breast, and it seems to me that there is a curious innocence in it.

A bird sang.

Did a bird sing in the Garden of Eden when Adam and Eve first discovered what it was to love as man and woman, naked and unashamed together beneath the blue skies of heaven?

I do not know.

I do not know.

On the evening of the third day, Papa comes to my bed-chamber. I sit on the edge of my pallet, head bowed, hands clasped before me in a pose of supplication. My body tenses in anticipation of the long-awaited punishment; and yet I think I shall be glad to have done with it. Although I am light-headed with hunger, I am grateful that Papa chose to wait rather than act in anger.

"I have considered," Papa says without looking at me. It is a cruel irony that now that Caliban can bear the sight of me, Papa cannot. "And I shall not punish you further, child."

My breath catches in my throat; I am not sure whether it is due to relief or fresh apprehension, for I do not even for a single heartbeat's worth of time imagine that Papa has forgiven me.

Papa gives me a sideways glinting glance, nostrils flaring with distaste. His grey eyes are stormy and beneath his beard, the line of his jaw is set and hard. "Women are weak, perfidious creatures," he says. "Even the best of them may fall victim to their lesser natures. Your mother had the appearance of a virtuous woman during our lives together, Miranda, but after . . ." He pauses for a moment, scowling at his own dark thoughts. "Would you know why I sought to create a homunculus endowed with her very soul's memories?"

It is the first time he has spoken of my mother since the incident. "If you would have me know, Papa," I whisper.

"Suffice it that you understand it is because there came a day when I was given cause to doubt the loyalty and trustworthiness of everyone I knew." Papa begins pacing the room with such vigor that the amulets strung around his neck rustle and clink. "Some were proven to be traitors indeed; some proven faithful, yet powerless. But your mother . . . your mother's true nature, I could not know, for she died in the bearing of you. I could not ask her if she was a faithful and true wife, or if she pinned a cuckold's horns upon me. Did I have cause to suspect her?" He shakes his head. "No. And yet, I suspected naught of those who took everything from me until the very moment that it came to pass. How could I not suspect her in turn?"

I fix my gaze on my clasped hands and say nothing.

"'Twas not a thought that came to me at the outset," Papa muses, and I realize he is talking more to himself than to me, as he was wont to do when I was a child. "And yet, here on the isle, betimes I came to wonder: *Were* you in truth the daughter of my blood and the fruit of my loins, Miranda? Or did your mother betray me, too?"

I glance up with a sharp gasp. "Oh, Papa! Do not say so!"

"Hold your tongue!" he reprimands me, one hand rising to grasp my amulet. I obey. "I made the homunculus with my own seed and a lock of your mother's hair that I might ask her from beyond the grave if she was a faithful wife and you were, in truth, my daughter."

He falls silent.

I think of the pale thing floating in its jar, its lips moving as though to speak. In the world beyond my windows, dusk is descending. I can hear swallows twittering in concert and the faint splash of a fountain. In my bed-chamber, the silence stretches until it grows unbearable.

"Am I?" I ask at last.

"You are," Papa says in a tone that makes it clear he takes no pleasure in the fact; not today, mayhap never again. "Appearances did not lie; your mother *was* a virtuous woman, Miranda. Virtuous and true. And I tell you, you have shamed her memory most grievously."

Hot tears seep from my eyes, trickle down my cheeks.

"I should not have doubted," he continues. "Those who betrayed me took everything from me but you. Had you not been mine, they surely would have taken you, too. You were precious to me, once, and what I did in my hunger for certainty was wrong. It was a violation of the Lord God's order. I knew it in my heart, and yet I pursued it. I thought her death and your affliction was my punishment for it, but I think now that I was too hasty to presume that I in my finite wisdom understood God's intention."

You were precious to me, once. I bow my head, tears falling to spatter the backs of my hands.

"What you did—" Papa pauses again, breathing hard through his nose. "It was perverse and unnatural. To cast aside all modesty, to lie brazen beneath the open skies with a misshapen brute of a creature, a witch's spawn, an illiterate, half-tamed *savage,* and suffer his touch willingly—"

I think of the profound gentleness with which Caliban touched me, and weep harder.

For myself?

For him?

I am not sure.

Papa cannot bear to continue in the same vein. "It was a violation of God's order as surely as was my own trespass," he says firmly. "And as such, I believe that your transgression is the just penance I have reaped for my own. It is for that reason that I have chosen not to punish you further."

I lift my head and gaze at him through my tears, and there is a bitter edge to my voice. "Shall I thank you for it?"

Papa frowns. "You should give thanks to the good Lord God in His mercy and wisdom that His servant Ariel alerted me before your honor was wholly despoiled," he says in a curt voice. "If you would give thanks to me, I will take it in the form of your unquestioning obedience."

"Yes, Papa." What else am I to say? My empty belly gripes with hunger. "May I have something to eat now?"

"You may spend this last night in fasting and prayer," Papa says. "On the morrow, you may break your fast and resume your labors."

So I am to be allowed to continue. A month ago, I should have been nothing but grateful to hear it. Now I merely wonder that Papa does not reckon my innocence so despoiled that I will taint his great working.

Oh, but for all that he has hinted at its very purpose tonight, he reckons me too ignorant to grasp it. He does not imagine the breadth of the illicit knowledge I have gained.

My brother, my liege.

A love spell to ensnare a king's son, the salamander said.

Papa seeks vengeance on those who betrayed him, and I . . . I am nothing more than the bait in his snare. Lowering my head once more, I let my hair fall to curtain the sides of my face.

"*Miranda,*" Papa says in a harsh tone, and I jerk my head upward in response, feeling faint at the sudden movement. Oh, dear Lord God, I am so very hungry. Papa's gaze pins me to the pallet where I sit. "You are to have no further communication with . . ." The hard line of his lips twists in disgust, as though the name he will utter tastes foul and rotten in his mouth. "*Caliban.* And if you fail to obey me . . ."

One by one, he touches the amulets that hang from his neck, selecting Caliban's and closing his fingers around it with deliberate menace. "I will not punish you, no. The witch's whelp will pay the price for both of you. Do you understand?"

Understand? Oh, I am fairly well sick with understanding. But at least his threat means Caliban yet lives.

I nod. "Yes, Papa."

He nods back at me. "Very well."

THIRTY-EIGHT

CALIBAN

Yes, Master. No, Master.

I will not touch Miranda, no, not with the littlest finger of my hand, never ever never again.

I will not speak to Miranda.

I will not look at Miranda.

Yes, Master, I will do my chores. I will fetch wood for the hearth, I will bring food for the larder.

No, Master, I will not go to the high place; I will not say prayers to Setebos, which is nothing but a whale's skull, because you have forbidden it.

(Oh, Setebos!)

Yes, Master, you are merciful.

Yes, Master, you are wise.

These are the things I say, but they are only noises I make with my mouth. Inside my head, I am thinking how I might kill you.

Oh, it is a bad thought, a very bad thought, the worstest of thoughts, but I cannot help it.

You would have killed me if Miranda did not stop you, Master. *Prospero.* You very nearly did. You very nearly did kill Miranda, too.

But I cannot raise my hand against you, no. Even to think it makes me shake with my skin all a-creeping, and all the hurting you did give me hurts like it is new. And so I look at the chains around your neck and the charms that do hang from them and sparkle in the sunlight, silver and gold, bits of hair and blood, and oh, there is Miranda's charm and there is Caliban's charm, and if it were not there, you could not tell me to come and go and hurt me so.

You could not punish Miranda so.

They do not look so very strong, those chains. I could break them with my hands. Oh, but that is another thought that makes my skin creepity-creep and a sick feeling come into my belly.

Too bad for the poor dumb monster, poor dumb Caliban. He will have to use his dull wits and not his strong hands.

I gather mussels and think.

I gather wood and think.

And I think to myself, oh ho! *I* cannot raise my hand to Master, not even to pull the charms from his neck, but Miranda can. Her little hands are not strong enough to break the chains, but they are quick and clever enough to find the clasps that hold them closed and undo them.

And then—

I raise a big branch high over my head and bring it down hard over a fallen log; hard, so hard it *crrracks*! Even though it makes my body ache, it feels good to do it.

"I would that was your head, *Master*," I whisper.

"Oh, la!" a hated voice says behind me. "Thou shouldst not say such things."

My shoulders go tight and rise toward my ears. I have not seen the spirit since . . . that day. "I will say what I like!" I say without turning around. "Or will you betray me for this, too?"

Ariel comes around before me, all foamy-white and a-flutter in the breeze, stepping oh, so lightly over the bits and pieces of scattered wood under his feet. "I do but serve our master."

I look at him. "*You* would be free if he were dead, too."

The spirit's eyes blaze unexpectedly. "Free? Say rather that I shouldst be damned for all eternity!"

"So?" I pull back my lips and show him my teeth. "Miranda does love me, and I would suffer any hurt for her!"

"Thou speakest of things thou knowest not," Ariel says with pity. "Dost suppose the tenderness of her maiden's heart shouldst survive thy cruel dispatch of her own father?" He shakes his head, wisps of fog stirring. "Set aside these murderous thoughts."

"Thoughts are not deeds," I say in defiance. "You cannot tell me what I may or may not *think*!"

Now the spirit's eyes go clear and cold, as cold as the stream in winter. "Thoughts give birth to deeds, and thine run red with blood. I tell thee, if thou hast an ounce of wisdom lodged within the dense bone of thy skull, set them aside."

I laugh a hard laugh. "Will you carry tales to *Master* if I do not?"

"The more fool thou if thou thinkest Prospero takes thee for aught but a villain," Ariel says with the cutting knives in his voice. "Thou didst seek to defile his own daughter!"

(Oh, Miranda!)

"I'd do it again, too!" I spit at him.

"Aye, thou wouldst," Ariel says as though the words taste bad in his mouth. "But thou shalt have no second chance; no, nor to plot bloody vengeance either, for I am bidden to keep watch over thee and make certain thou cause no further mischief until our master's work is done."

I look at wispety Ariel and laugh again. "You? What will you do other than fetch Master?"

Ariel smiles, a smile like the edge of a blade. "Thou thinkest me a harmless sprite?" He does open his arms wide. "Ah, but I have other guises."

A wind comes, not a whooshity little breeze but a great rushing wind that roars and roars, and that Ariel does grow and grow up into the sky, bigger than a man, yes, taller than trees, and his hair like white wisps of foam and fog goes dark and spreads like storm-clouds across the sky. He says something like thunder and lightning flashes in his eyes, then rain is coming down and I am on my belly in the dirt with fear shaking my aching bones, my hands over my head and my eyes squeezed tight shut, poor dumb monster, the rain hitting hard like little stones on my back and making the dirt to mud.

There is another *crrrack* sound so very near and I see red flash behind the lids of my eyes and smell wood burning, and sounds that are not words come out of my mouth.

Then there is only rain, then nothing.

I open my eyes and pull myself out of the mud.

Ariel is the Ariel I know again. I stare at him and wish I were Umm to put him in the pine tree.

"Now thou knowest," he says. "Take heed and think to do no harm. I will be watching."

Whooshity-whoosh.

Smoke is coming from an oak tree where lightning split its bark, but only a little bit. The wood is wet and I do not think it will keep burning. All the wood I did gather is wet, too.

Oh, I do hurt.

I limp to a new place and begin to gather dry wood. There is rage in my heart and it is hot and angry.

I try to make it go cold.

I must be cold and angry to think; to plan like Master did begin to plan all those years ago.

By and by, I think that Ariel did tell me a true thing. Miranda's heart is tender; tender and true.

I cannot kill her father. Not with my own hands, no.

Oh, but what if it is true that there are other hands coming? Hands that belong to men who are already Master's enemies.

I do not say the thought aloud, because that Ariel might be any-where, lurking and spying; but I smile and now it is my smile that has knives in it. And then I think it may be dangerous even to smile such a smile, so I unsmile it. I bend my back and gather wood like a good servant, and I think the thought very very quietly to myself.

I will find a way to use their hands against you, Master.

THIRTY-NINE

MIRANDA

When morning comes and I am allowed at last to break my fast, it is difficult to contain my hunger. Famished as I am, I am hard-pressed not to gobble my food with unseemly haste; but Papa's scowling face across the table reminds me that I have only just been paroled for my most unseemly behavior.

The thought of it makes me flush all over again with shame, and I must duck my head to conceal it.

Of Caliban, I catch but a glimpse when he comes to rake the coals in the hearth. Although I am careful not to look directly at him, out of the corner of my eye I see that he is moving stiffly.

I can tell that he is careful not to look in my direction, too. Were I not wrung dry of tears, I should like to weep anew for both of us poor innocent sinners.

Once we have finished and I have wiped the silver platters clean,

Papa bids me accompany him to his sanctum. There I see that he has completed the painting of the Lady Venus on his own while I was confined to my chamber.

The sight fills me with dismay. She is a crude caricature, her gown a triangle of grassy green that lacks any suggestion of folds. The red fruit she holds in one hand—an apple, the same fruit that tempted Eve in the Garden of Eden—is a vague, round blob. The golden tresses that are meant to spill over her shoulders are rendered in stark yellow squiggles. Her eyes are mismatched, one narrow and squinting, and the crimson smear of her mouth leers out at the world.

The Queen of Love has been ill served by Papa. Although I say naught, he follows my gaze and divines my thoughts.

"I had no choice but to render her myself," he says in a curt tone. "It was necessary that the image be finished while the stars were yet favorable."

"Of course, Papa," I say. "What do you require of me?"

It transpires that there are two images Papa wishes painted in quick succession ere the stars shift to an unfavorable alignment, and these are the first and third faces of Cancer. I do not know what influences they govern, and he does not deign to tell me; wishing, I suppose, to preserve what ignorance is left to me.

It is less than he imagines, a thought that reminds me I never did tell Caliban about the secret the salamander revealed to me. Nor shall I ever if I remain obedient to Papa's will, for he has forbidden me all communication with Caliban. And if I disobey him, it is Caliban who will bear the cost of it.

If there is any course of action save obeying Papa that lies before me, I cannot see it.

I study the images of the first and third faces of Cancer. The first face is the trickiest, for it combines elements of man and beast into a single creature, a four-legged being with the face of a man and the body of a horse. It wears a blanket of fig leaves, and has queer, attenuated fingers. Of course, I have never seen a horse, but gazing at the illustration, it seems to me that its body is not so different from that of a goat, which is a form I know well.

There are a good many horses in the Bible. A line from the Song of Solomon comes to me unbidden.

I have compared thee, O my love, to a company of horses in Pharaoh's chariots.

Once again, I flush, remembering the sound of birdsong, the smell of grass, and Caliban's mouth on my breast. I glance at the crude image of red-lipped Venus on the wall and she leers at me.

I shudder and return my gaze to the first face of Cancer, forming an image in my thoughts.

The little gnomes have replenished my pots of paint during my confinement. I take up the pot of shining black pigment and climb atop my stepping stool. I dip my brush, and with one sweeping stroke, I outline the curve of the horse's neck. Another line from the Bible comes to me as I do so.

Hast thou given the horse strength? hast thou clothed his neck with thunder?

It is from the Book of Job, which is a terrible tale and one I do not wholly understand. Papa should like me to have the same faith in him, I think, that Job had in the Lord God. Job was rewarded for his suffering in the end, though I cannot help but wonder if he continued to mourn for the children that were lost to him. I hope so. I should hate to lose everything that was dear to me; and yet I fear I may.

I feel as insubstantial as a leaf borne on the rushing stream of Papa's formidable will. All the bits of knowledge that I have gathered or that have been thrust upon me matter naught.

The lineaments of the first face of Cancer emerge beneath my brush. Were I made otherwise, mayhap I should not seek to make such a good job of it; and yet I cannot. It seems the last measure of joy left to me. After some hours, I climb down from my stool, step back, and admire my work—the proud arch of the horse's neck, the bunched muscles of its haunches, the unlikely human face.

Why, I wonder, is one thing gauged noble and beautiful and another hideous and unlovely when it is all part of God's creation?

Why is a horse more noble than a goat?

Why is a hawk more noble than a toad?

I am a monster, Caliban said to me, and though it be a sinful act I would undo if I could, there is a secret part of me that is glad I showed him he could never be monstrous in my eyes.

I wish Papa could see Caliban as I do; see the goodness and kindness in him, but I fear that is a thing that will never come to pass.

I clean my brush with sharp-smelling turpentine, then shake out my arms which are numb and aching from having been raised for so long, opening and closing my hands until my blood is flowing freely in my veins once more. I dip my brush into the pot of green pigment. The malachite from which it is ground corresponds with Venus. I do not use the pigment straight from the pot, but mix it on a piece of slate with other colors, brown umber and yellow ochre, until I have attained a more subtle leaflike hue.

I wish that I had been able to paint the image of the Lady Venus. I've learned ever so much more than when I first began. I would have made her dress the pale green hue of the sea below the white curl of a breaking wave when the sun shines on it. I would have made the golden locks of her hair graceful and flowing. Oh, I would have made her face so beautiful and kind.

But mayhap love is not always kind.

Ariel said as much to me once; and as much as the spirit meddles, I do not believe he lies.

There is kindness in my cruelty, he said, *and cruelty in thy kindness.*

Is it an unkindness I dealt Caliban after all? And yet I *do* love him dearly. And yet, and yet . . .

Oh, Lord God, I wish I could undo what I did.

I climb onto the stepping stool and begin painting fig leaves.

FORTY

CALIBAN

Miranda paints and paints.

I know it is true because she is gone to Master's sanctum every day, and at night there are colors on the skin of her hands and fingers, but I do not spy because it is a promise I did make to her.

It is hard, oh, so very hard, not to look at her!

I want to look.

I want to speak.

I want to touch.

But I do not; only the littlest little bit when Master—*Prospero*—is not looking. We look, then; only look. Quick looks, as quick as little fishes in the stream.

It is like it was in the beginning.

Oh, I did love you from the beginning, Miranda.

In the beginning when I had no words, even before Master did summon me, I remember I did try to speak to you with my eyes and my hands; my eyes that did watch you from the walls of your garden, my hands that did bring you gifts.

Now there are only looks like whispers.

Are you?

Yes.

Do you?

Yes.

I love you, I say with my eyes.

I love you, I say with my rough hands that do gather wood, gather greens and tubers in the garden, gather eggs from the hens, gather milk from the goat's teats, gather fishes from the stream and mussels from the rocks. *I love you, I love you.*

I gather flowers from the gardens and the fields, and put them on Miranda's window-ledge when she is not there.

I love you, the flowers say.

Ariel, that Ariel, does frown at the flowers, but Master has said nothing to him of flowers.

So I leave flowers; spring flowers, then summer flowers. I gather the red and orange and yellow trumpet flowers, for a trumpet is a thing that makes a loud noise like a shout, and I tie their vines together and leave them to shout *I love you* in a row from Miranda's window-ledge.

Soon, I think.

Soon.

FORTY-ONE

MIRANDA

Papa is consumed by his labors.

He pores over his charts, then paces his sanctum, muttering to himself. He concocts incenses and vanishes to perform private suffumigations upon himself, returning with his robes smelling of resins and herbs and acrid things. Betimes he banishes me from his sanctum that he might invoke the mirror's magic and gaze into it. He eats little and sleeps less, up at all hours of the night.

He grows thin, the bones of his face becoming prominent and angular as his flesh dwindles, the joints of his hands and wrists emerging like knobs beneath his skin. The last of the grey vanishes from his hair and beard, leaving it as white as Ariel's.

I paint at his bidding and obey him in every particular, because I am afraid to do otherwise.

The salamander in its brazier remains silent, watching me with its glittering ruby eyes.

The moon waxes and wanes; my woman's courses come and go.

Papa bids Caliban to procure a white he-goat from amongst the wild goats that roam the isle. When Caliban succeeds, the goat is tethered in an abandoned garden where it bleats in protest all day long, until Papa is sufficiently irritated to silence it with a charm. It continues to bleat noiselessly, opening its muzzle to expose its curiously even and childlike teeth, its pink tongue protruding. Its amber eyes with their inhuman vertical pupils beg the empty skies for an answer.

I do not give the goat a name. Those days have long since passed. I have not named a hen since Bianca's sacrifice, and I did not name Oriana's replacement when she grew too old to give milk and was slaughtered and rendered into stew meat.

I fear for Papa's health and wonder if he has begun to lose his wits. In the secret part of me where I think dreadful thoughts to which I dare not give voice, I wonder if it would not be so terrible if Papa were to perish with his great work undone. It is a vile thought unworthy of my filial loyalty and I am ashamed to think it; and yet, I do.

Once, I should have feared for my own survival were aught to befall Papa, but those days, too, are behind me. Caliban provides for most of our needs now, and he would be more than capable of providing for our survival if we were bereft of Papa's presence. The elementals would not obey us; there would be no gnomes to till the gardens, no undines to fill the wells and make the fountains flow, but we could till the earth ourselves and fetch water from the stream.

We could make the isle our own Eden, Caliban and I.

Betimes it is a pleasant thought; betimes, a terrifying one. I have an inkling, now, of what it means for a woman to lie with a man as bride and bridegroom, and that I do not fear. Rather, I welcome it. And yet, what do I know of bearing children? Only that my own mother died of my birth, and that I suspect that like my woman's courses, it is a bloody, messy business. I have not forgotten the Lord God's injunction to Eve.

I will greatly multiply thy sorrow and thy conception; in sorrow thou shalt bring forth children . . .

And so I put the disloyal thought aside and continue to paint at Papa's bidding, peopling the walls of his sanctum with images of all of the seven governors, including an image of the Sun even more splendid than the first, and many of the various faces of the twelve signs of the Zodiac, until such a morning when Papa greets me with his grey eyes wide and shining, gladness radiating from him as though the very marrow of his bones is alight with it.

"Miranda," he says in a deep, hushed voice, and I could weep at the suggestion of affection in it, the affection he has not shown me since the day he found me with Caliban on the grassy banks of the stream. "The hour is nigh. I have prayed and prayed upon the matter, and God has spoken to me."

My throat tightens. "Yes, Papa?"

Papa nods with great solemnity. "If I am to succeed in this working, a great sacrifice is required of me."

"Is it the he-goat, Papa?" I say.

"Oh, the goat, aye; but it is merely an offering." Papa shakes his head, white hair stirring. "No, if I succeed on the morrow, I have pledged to the Lord God Himself that I will renounce my magic."

I gaze at him.

Papa smiles a tranquil smile at me and places his hands on my shoulders. "Your rightful destiny awaits you, Miranda; yours and mine alike. And I shall procure it for the both of us. Once it is done, there shall be but one last image for you to render."

If I am to succeed on the morrow . . .

There is no more time left.

I swallow hard against the taste of fear in my mouth.

FORTY-TWO

CALIBAN

It is still dark when I wake with a feeling like creepity ants crawling on my skin, summer-dark and warm, but oh, my skin is creepity-crawling, and I have felt this before. It is a warning from Setebos who watches.

Something is coming.

Across the sea, someone is coming.

I want to go to the high place to see even though Master has forbidden it, but no, there is Master himself, there is *Prospero,* banging on the door of my chamber with his staff and shouting, *"Awaken, awaken, make haste and fetch the white he-goat to the courtyard, you lazy villain!"*

Fetch it yourself, I think; but I do not say it. He would only punish me, or worse, make Miranda do it.

So I fetch the goat. It does not want to come and fights the rope, its mouth opening and closing without any noise, but I am stronger than the goat is. "I am sorry," I whisper as I drag it to the courtyard. "I am sorry."

"Cease your muttering," Prospero says to me, and I do. He is in fine robes I have never seen before, all yellow-gold and shimmering, and there is a circle of gold around his hair.

I look sideways at Miranda and see that she is in a fine new yellow gown, too, although this I did see in the pirates' treasure so many years ago. Oh, and there are gold necklaces with sparkling stones around her neck, too; but she looks sideways at me, quick, quick, and I see her face is pale in the faint light.

She is afraid.

I am afraid, too. The creepity feeling grows stronger and stronger; biting ants, now. But I am angry, too.

The sun does rise in the east and Prospero says his dawn chant, the deep, magic words rolling from his mouth. The air feels shivery, and Miranda shivers although it is warm, and the lid on the smoke-trickling metal bowl that hangs from a chain she holds shivers, too. The goat tugs at the rope, its mouth opening and closing, opening and closing.

Master—*Prospero*—takes out his knife. "Hold it fast, lad," he says to me, and I do. I hold the goat by its curling horns, lifting its head toward the sky and holding it in place to show its throat. Its tongue sticks out.

Prospero goes to one side of the goat, and *flash*, waah! He cuts its throat open. Blood comes out hard and fast, one, two, three, then slower. The goat's legs go crumplety-crumple under it and it sags heavy, its horns sliding in my hands. I catch it and lower it gently to the stones. Some of its blood gets on my hands. The fear goes out of its eyes, and they are empty like glass.

Now Master wipes his knife on the goat's rough white hair, leaving smears of red. He puts away the knife and lifts the lid of the smoking bowl, puts herbs and things on the coals. He takes the chain from Miranda and begins to swing the bowl around, leaving trails of strong-smelling smoke like streaks of clouds in the air, and begins to make his long prayer.

This is the part I remember from when he did free Ariel that is so very long, only it is the sun that Master prays to this time, and it is all, oh, Lord Sun who is so wonderful, oh, Lord Sun who is called this thing and that thing and another thing, oh, Lord Sun who is the light of the world, I ask you this, I ask you that, oh, Lord Sun, hear me, hear me, hear me.

All the while the creepity feeling is shouting at me to go, go, go, go to the high place and look!

But even if I did dare, I would not leave Miranda. It is the longest time I have been near her since that day. Master is not looking at us, he is looking toward the sun, waving his staff and his bowl around, making his prayer.

Behind his back, Miranda and I look sideways at each other again. She is so near, I could touch her hand; only mine are bloody.

I love you, I say to her with my eyes.

She gives me a scared little nod. *I love you, too,* her eyes say.

On and on Master's prayer goes until at last it is over, and I wait for something to happen.

Nothing does.

"Ariel!" Master calls. "Come, brave spirit!" And there is Ariel, whooshity-whoosh, coming all white and fluttering, like he has been waiting for this very moment for all of his life. "The hour is upon us, good Ariel!" Master says to him. "Do you recall all that I require of you? Are you prepared to do as I bade you?"

Ariel does bow. "I do and I am, Master."

Master lifts up his staff. "Then fly, brave spirit; wreak my will, and earn your freedom in the bargain!"

Ariel laughs a high, wild laugh and leaps into the air, wind gathering beneath him. "I go, Master!"

My skin creeps and creeps.

Master watches him go, then gives me a dark look. "You have no further part to play in the events of the day. Hang the goat's carcass in the garden outside the kitchen that its blood might drain, then be about your chores."

I would like to cut *his* throat open. "Yes, Master."

"Come," he says to Miranda, giving her the smoke-trickling bowl on its chain to carry. "We are bound for the watchtower."

Leave the goat and *go, go, go,* says the creepity feeling; but Miranda looks one last look behind her at me, and Master looks, too.

So I pick up the dead he-goat, which is very heavy, much heavier than a hare, and put it over my shoulders, holding it in place by its front and back legs. Its head hangs down and bounces when I walk and more blood comes from its white throat that is cut open in a wet red smile, getting on the skin of my arm and my chest. More blood gets on me in the garden when I tie its back legs together and hang it from the strong branch of an oak tree, hauling on the rope to lift it and tying knots in a hurry.

At last the dead goat hangs upside down, its tongue sticking out of its mouth. Its eyes are like balls of yellow-black glass and slow drops of blood fall from its cut throat onto the dust.

"Poor dumb monster," I whisper to it; I do not know why. It is only a goat. "I am sorry."

The upside-down goat with its stiff dead tongue says nothing. The wind is beginning to rise, strong enough to make the goat sway on its rope.

Setebos is calling me.

Go, go, go!

I run.

FORTY-THREE

MIRANDA

In the watchtower, Papa lowers the spyglass from his eye. "There!" he says in triumph, pointing. "Will you see?"

"If you would have me do so," I murmur. He passes the spyglass to me. I transfer the chain of the thurible to my left hand and raise the spyglass to my own eye, following the line of his pointing finger.

Far out at sea, there is a ship. Unlike the poor faltering vessel which Caliban described when he told me of witnessing Papa's and my arrival on the isle—a ship of which I have no memory—it is a beautiful thing, proud and graceful, riding the waves with majestic white sails bellied out with wind. Tiny figures swarm over the surface of it. For the first time, I well and truly understand that whatever Papa plans, there are human lives at stake, and dread grips my heart.

"What do you mean to do, Papa?" I whisper, lowering the spyglass.

"Watch and you shall see," he says sternly. "But as you love your life, Miranda, disturb me not, for this working requires the whole of my attention."

I nod in obedience. "Yes, Papa."

Papa spreads his arms wide, his staff in his right hand. *"Barchia!"* he cries. *"Bethel almoda, Hamar benabis, Zobaa marrach, Fide arrach, Samores maymon, Aczabi!"* Although I have heard Papa chant the secret names of the seven governors many times, these are words unknown to me.

A wind springs up in answer, and I realize that Papa is summoning it. At first it is a light breeze and harmless-seeming, but as Papa continues to chant, the wind grows in intensity. It comes from every direction, swirling through every window of the watchtower.

The pale blue sky begins to darken as clouds gather.

The wind rises and rises.

The sea begins to turn angry, darkening in turn beneath the darkening sky. Gentle rolling swells are churned into peaks crested with white foam.

"Barchia, Bethel almoda, Hamar benabis, Zobaa marrach, Fide arrach, Samores maymon, Aczabi!"

Wind blows in buffeting gusts, the sound of it rising to a roar.

The sea is roiling and my stomach roils, too. Although I am hard-pressed to keep my feet in the gale, I manage to put the spyglass to my eye. The ship that was sailing so gracefully only moments ago is now pitching violently up and down as it climbs the peaks of waves which grow ever steeper and plunges into troughs that grow ever deeper. The tiny figures are scrambling in a frantic attempt to lower the sails. Overhead, lightning flickers in the depths of the dark, towering thunderheads; flickers and then strikes with a furious suddenness, jagged blue-white veins reaching for the churning sea. I stagger backward, dropping the chain of the thurible. The clang of the bowl's falling is inaudible beneath the howling of the wind. The lid comes loose and coals scatter across the floor of the watchtower.

There is a crack of thunder so loud it seems my ears must burst to hear it. All my childhood terror of storms returns to me tenfold, and I should like nothing better than to run to my chamber and hide under my bed-linens.

But oh, dear Lord God, the *ship* and its poor inhabitants!

Papa's tone shifts, and the wind shifts with it, gathering in the west in accordance to his will.

Lightning flashes and thunder booms. The heavens unloose a pelting rain that comes sideways through the west window of the watchtower. I wipe my face with the sleeve of my gown and look through the spyglass. Enwreathed in strange flames, the ship is being driven by the wind, driven straight for the isle; straight for its rocky shoals. When that happens, I think every man aboard the ship will perish.

This is the great working to which I have contributed.

I cannot bear it.

"Papa, please!" I catch his arm. Tears streak my face, erased by the rain. "Please, do not do this!"

He turns his face toward me and his expression is terrible. Rain plasters his hair to his head; wind lashes his beard into tatters. "Did I not bid you not to disturb me?" He grasps my amulet in his left hand and gestures in my direction as though to swat a fly. "Leave be, Miranda!"

My muscles seize in response to his admonition and pain assails every part of me.

My legs give way beneath me and I fall to the floor of the watchtower, the spyglass tumbling from my hand. A lone coal from the thurible, miraculously unextinguished by the rain, burns through my yellow gown to sear the flesh of my hip. It is the least of my hurts.

Ignoring me, Papa resumes his chant.

The storm rages on.

FORTY-FOUR

CALIBAN

Oh, oh, oh! Master has raised such a storm!

I try to reach the high place before it comes, but it is too far; I am fast, but not fast enough to outrun a storm. I am only beginning to climb when the rain comes.

It is bad, but it is not *so* very bad. The rain makes the rocks slippity-slidey under my fingers and toes, but then I am very good at climbing and the rocks keep away the worstest of the wind that blows so hard from the west.

I do not care about the thunder and lightning. Setebos will protect me, and this storm is not meant for me, not like when that Ariel did make himself a storm above my head.

No, this storm is for the men who are coming.

It is dark, though; so dark it does not seem like day anymore. The sun has answered Master's prayers by hiding his face away. I have never seen such clouds! Lightning flashes when I reach the high place and I see Setebos laughing against the sky, ha-*ha*!

Now the wind is so strong it is hard to walk. I creepity-creep on my feet and hands like when I was little.

I am breathing hard, so I rest for a moment under Setebos's jaws. Here the wind and the rain cannot reach me so much; oh, but there are voices in the howling wind, and I must see. And so I leave Setebos and creep in the very face of the wind to the edge of the cliff and lay myself flat to look over it.

Waah!

There is a ship and it is close, so close! The sea is boiling like water in a pot and the ship is tossed all about.

Lightning does strike it and it burns with blue-white flames; burns on the tall poles, burns in the ropes and sails. Men run about here and there, and their voices are like tiny gnat voices crying in the storm.

Does Master—that is *Prospero*—mean to kill them all, I wonder? If it is so, my plan is lost.

Thunder sounds like rocks breaking. The rain puts my wet hair in my eyes so I cannot see.

I push it back.

Big waves, the biggest waves, crash and crash on the jaggedy rocks below me. On the ship the blue-white fire leaps from place to place, joining itself to itself like ropes of cracklety lightning.

But lightning does not burn so, and I think to myself: Ariel.

Ariel is in the storm.

"All is lost!" says a voice from the ship. *"Mercy on us! We are wrecked! Save yourselves!"*

Oh, that is no human voice that could make itself heard in such a storm, no. Only Ariel. What game is this?

"Do not listen to him!" I shout into the wind. "Do not trust him!"

Oh, but I am far away, poor dumb monster; I almost cannot hear my own voice. Little figures like ants jump from the ship, jump into the boiling sea, one; one, two, three, four; one, two.

I think they will drown, but no, there is Ariel, a great whooshity darkness sweeping down like wings out of the storm. One he carries away, whoosh-whoosh; and then the four, whooshity-whoosh, he carries them away far away to different places on the isle where I cannot see.

The ship does not crash on the rocks, but spins in a circle. There is no more blue-white fire on it.

Little gnat voices cry.

The wind shifts and whoosh, there is Ariel again, a great looming thing of storm-clouds, taller than trees, raising the waves and carrying the ship, the whole ship, away to the south.

I am holding my breath.

I let it out.

The rain stops.

The wind stops.

I push my wet hair out of my eyes and look over the cliff. There are still two men in the water. One is swimming, swimming strong toward the shore. One is holding on to a wooden thing that floats and kicking his feet.

I did think to seek out Master's enemies, but now I think those are the men that Ariel did save his own self; and he will be watching over them. I do not know why, but these two in the water do not matter to him. If these are men Ariel does not care to save, that *Prospero* has not bidden him to save, these are the men I need to do what my own hands cannot.

I go to find them.

FORTY-FIVE

MIRANDA

When the storm dies at last, it is like a long-sought blessing. Still, I cannot stop weeping. I sit with my back pressed against the wall of the watchtower and my knees drawn up beneath my rain-soaked yellow gown. Silent tears slide down my face. My body aches, my burned hip hurts, and I cannot summon the will to stand.

Papa lowers his staff, retrieves the fallen spyglass, and surveys the sea. "The greater part of the deed is done," he says in a voice grown hoarse from long chanting. "Though it is no thanks to you my working did not fail."

"I trust there are no survivors," I say, and I am surprised at the depth of bitterness in my own voice.

Papa stares at me, his face haggard. "No survivors? What manner of man do you take me for?"

I look away. "I do not know."

"Oh, Miranda!" Now a note of sorrowful reproach enters his voice. "Could you not, just *once,* have done as I bade you? Could you not have trusted me as I have begged you so many times? If Ariel has carried out the fullness of my bidding as I believe he has done, he has spirited them all to safety, and not a man aboard the ship did perish."

So they are not dead.

I am not complicit in killing an entire shipful of men.

My breath hitches in my throat, and I take in a gulp of air. I do not know whether to laugh or scream. I let my head fall back against the stones of the tower and gaze at Papa. "Well, if it is so, I am surpassingly glad to hear it. But could you have not, just once, entrusted *me* with the whole truth?"

He frowns at me. "Child, you know full well that it was imperative that the working be untainted—"

"If knowledge be a taint, the working *was* tainted!" I shout at him. Papa falls silent in astonishment at my interruption, looking at me with lips parted. I press the heels of my hands against my stinging eyes, then lower them. "I know you seek vengeance against your brother and the king, Papa," I say wearily. "I know you seek to ensnare the king's son with a love potion."

Papa takes a deep breath, the spyglass in his hand trembling. "How did you come by this knowledge?"

I rock my head back and forth against the hard stone. "Oh, Papa! It matters naught. What matters is the truth, and the truth is that the working *didn't* require perfect ignorance on my part."

I should like him to acknowledge the truth of my words; I should like him to apologize.

He does neither.

Papa, I think, does not like to be wrong. I do not think he understands how a world can exist in which he is wrong and I am right.

At least he does not punish me for my disrespect. I suspect he is too exhausted to do so.

I am tired, too.

I do not want to quarrel.

Neither, it seems, does Papa. He slumps to sit heavily on the ledge of the window across from me, bracing himself with his staff. "Do you remember a time before the isle, Miranda?"

"I think so." I keep my voice low. "I remember a house with pictures—paintings, they were paintings—on the walls. Betimes it seems as though I must have dreamed it. And yet I remember women with soft hands and gentle voices, who combed my hair and put ribbons in it, who sang me to sleep at night."

Papa nods. "'Tis true. There were several women who attended you. Do you remember how we came to the isle?"

I hesitate, then shake my head. Although I know what Caliban has told me, I have no memory of it. "No, Papa."

He gazes out the window opposite him. "Would you hear a piece of irony, child? It is in this very hour, with the greatest part of my working done, that I meant to divulge the truth of our origins to you."

I do not know whether to believe him.

His gaze returns to me. "Twelve years gone by, I held the title of Duke of Milan, ruler of a great city and a mighty duchy, and you, my only child, were not yet three years of age. But I cared naught for the trappings of power, only for my studies. I entrusted the affairs of state to my brother Antonio, your uncle." He grimaces. "I should have seen the ambition growing in him like a canker. But being absorbed with celestial matters, I paid too little heed to worldly ones. He suborned the loyalty of my courtiers with bribes, favors, and promotions; and at last, he struck a vile bargain with the king of Naples, offering him fealty and tribute in exchange for the title of Duke of Milan."

Papa's voice cracks at the telling of this, and despite everything I am ashamed of my disloyalty. "A vile betrayal indeed," I murmur.

"Under cover of night, my brother opened the gates of Milan to the king's troops," he continues. "We were abducted, child; abducted and set adrift at sea on the rotten carcass of a ship lacking sails or rigging."

I cannot help but shudder, thinking of the storm I just witnessed. "Why did he not kill us outright?"

"He dared not," Papa says simply. "Although Antonio had turned the court against me, the commonfolk yet revered me for my hard-won reputation for fairness and wisdom. And then there was you, Miranda, innocent as the dawn. My brother and the king dared not besmirch their hands with our blood, but trusted the sea to do it for them."

"How did we survive?" I whisper. "By your arts?"

"By my arts, by God's grace, and by the kindness of one of the noblemen entrusted to carry out the deed," Papa says in a grim tone. "Lacking the heart to condemn us outright, he saw to it that the ship was outfitted with a measure of food and water, clothing and linens, many of my books and instruments, and my staff. Without those things, we surely would have perished."

So there it is, the truth at last.

I am the daughter of a duke, although I do not fully fathom what that means. My memories are true.

I take a slow, shaking breath. "What do you mean—"

A gusting breeze announces Ariel's presence, swirling through the westernmost window of the tower.

"Greetings, Master!" The mercurial spirit manifests with a bow. "I come to report that I have carried out thy will to the letter. I put such a terror in them, all save the sailors did jump into the sea."

Papa stands, fresh vigor infusing his features. "All are safe?"

"Aye, Master. Two made landfall on their own; the others, I have deposited about the isle as thou bade me." Ariel gives a little shiver of distaste and holds out his hand. "Here are hairs plucked from the very heads of thy brother and liege and their courtiers."

I remember solving the riddle of Caliban's hair trapped in honey. How very long ago that seems to me.

"Bravely done!" Papa tucks the spyglass into the sash of his robe and takes the hairs from Ariel's hand. "And the king's son?"

"The prince mourns, supposing his father drowned and lost," Ariel says soberly. " 'Tis a sight to stir the hardest of hearts. The king mourns, supposing his son met the self-same fate." He purses his delicate lips in disapproval. "Master, thou shouldst know that the king's own brother and thine plot against him, thinking to make much of this opportunity thou hast afforded them."

"Suffer no harm to come to him," Papa commands Ariel. "*I* shall determine the king's fate; yes, and my brother's, too."

Ariel inclines his head.

My own head is spinning, seeking to encompass the events and revelations of the day. For once, I am grateful to be ignored.

"What of the ship and its sailors?" Papa asks.

The spirit makes a graceful gesture toward the south. "I have borne them to the pirates' cove as you bade me."

"Noble spirit!" Papa says. "Go forth, and heed my words. Keep the king from harm; yet lead the king's son to our doorstep."

Ariel's eyes darken and churn like the depths of the sea. "And my freedom, Master?"

Papa scowls at him. "Have you forgotten the torment from which I freed you? The torment unto which Sycorax bound you? I could visit the same upon you."

Ariel's gaze slides sideways to meet mine, and I look away. I have no sympathy left for him, not after all his games and the way he betrayed Caliban and me. "No, Master. I have not forgotten."

"If the fullness of my working is accomplished by the day's end, you shall have your freedom, ungrateful sprite. Until that hour arrives, do not trouble me with your impudence." Papa flicks one hand at him. "Begone!"

Ariel departs to carry out his bidding.

I am left alone with my father, the erstwhile Duke of Milan; a title that means naught to me. It is true, all true. There are strange men roaming the isle and its shores, scores of them. I find myself trembling. I would that Caliban were here that he might help me make sense of it all.

Staff in one hand, plucked hairs in the other, Papa considers me. "Get up, Miranda. I've work to do. Did I not gift you with gowns and finery for this very day? Go forth to change your attire and make yourself presentable."

I drag myself to my feet, clinging to the wall. "What do you mean to do to them, Papa? Your brother and the king?"

He hesitates. "As to that, I've yet to decide. We shall see if there is any penitence in their hearts."

"And if there is not?" I say.

Papa does not answer. "Go, and do as I bade you."

FORTY-SIX

CALIBAN

I scramble down the crag, but I cannot go as quick-quick as I would like. Although the rain has stopped, it is still slippity-slidey and going down is more dangerous than up. When I reach the shore, the men already did find each other.

I look for Ariel, but I do not see him. I hope it is because he is about doing Master's bidding, and not because he is hiding in the wind.

The wooden floating thing—it is round in the middle and flat on the ends—did crash on the rocks. There is a raggedy-jaggedy hole in it and the men are splashing in the water to drag it ashore.

I think it must be a great treasure for them to work so hard; but no, there is only red water spilling out of it. When the men do drag it onto the stony shore, they fall to their knees and take turns putting their hands in the hole, drinking the red water from their hands like it is fresh cold water and they are so very thirsty.

Although I go slow so I will not make them afraid, the men are afraid when they see me anyway.

"The prince spoke truly!" one says, his eyes so very wide there is white all around them. "Hell has lost its devils, and here's one come to claim us!"

The other picks up a big rock.

"Do not be afraid," I say to them. "I will not hurt you."

"It speaks!" the white-eyed one says to the other; and then to me, "What manner of devil are you?"

"No devil." I open my hands so they can see they are empty. "Only a friend."

"A friend!" The other laughs, only it is a laugh like a great sob. He puts down the rock. "Then I pray you, friend, tell us we are not the sole survivors of this wreck. Did you see any others gain the shore safely?"

"No," I say truthfully, for I did not see where Ariel put the men he did save. I think it is best if these two believe they are alone on the isle. "Only you."

The men weep and curse, dipping their hands into the wooden thing.

"To His Majesty King Alonso!" one says, and drinks from his hands, red dripping from them like blood. "To His Highness Prince Ferdinand!" the other says, and he drinks, too.

I begin to think this will be harder than I did know. "I can show you where there is fresh water."

The men stare at me. "Shall we drown our sorrows in mere water when there is sweet red claret at hand?" one says. He beckons to me. "If you call yourself a friend, come, and toast to the memory of our dear, drowned sovereign and his only son and heir."

I hesitate.

"Drink or be damned!" the other cries. "If you be not a devil, what manner of creature be you?"

I join them. "Only a monster," I say soft and low. "A poor dumb monster."

They laugh and laugh as though it is the best of jests I have made.

I put my hands through the hole in the wooden thing and fill them with red water that is called claret. I drink it down, slurpity-slurp, and it burns in my mouth and in my belly.

The men laugh and sob and laugh and drink and sob and laugh, red dripping, dripping. "To Alonso! To Ferdinand! Drink, friend monster!"

I drink and the world spins. I cannot think how to make them do as I want. Yes, this will be harder than I did know.

"What is this place, monster?" one says to me. There is no longer white around his eyes; they are tired and heavy. "Where is it that we find ourselves fetched and wrecked and forsaken?"

I do not drink any more of the sweet red claret. "It is an isle; if it has a name, I do not know it."

They drink.

"How came you here?" the other asks me. "Who else abides here?"

Oh ho!

I dip my hands and make a show of drinking, letting the sweet red claret spill through my fingers. "A great magus rules here," I say. "He is powerful and cruel. But he has a daughter."

One of the men sits upright, his eyes no longer so sleepy. "A daughter, you say! Is she beautiful?"

Oh, Miranda!

I put my hands through the wooden hole again, and this time I do drink, and now the sweet red claret is singing in my mouth, singing in my throat, singing all the way down to my belly. "Yes," I whisper. "She is beautiful in every way, as good and bright and beautiful as the sun."

One of the men nudges the other. "Tell us more!"

I do.

I see hunger grow in them, especially the white-eyed one who was most afraid at first; I see him think yes, yes, I could wed the beautiful maiden and be king here, and then I know what he does want to hear. I tell him I will be his faithful servant, he will live in the palace and I will call him Master, I will bring him nuts and honey and fish every day, I will gather wood and tend the fire; everything, everything if only he will kill the cruel magus. Oh, Master, oh, Prospero, you did teach me very well what things men do want to hear! But the day grows long and I am afraid you may summon me, and I will not have a chance to use these men's hands anymore.

"It must be done soon," I say to them. "Quick quick! In the warm afternoon when he does take his sleep."

It is not true, but I cannot think how else to make them go.

One yawns, sleepy-eyed again. They have been drinking sweet red claret all the while. "Sleep's a fine notion. On the morrow, monster. Leave us this day to mourn in peace."

Oh, stupid Caliban, dumb brute!

"To mourn, yes," I say, and I hear knives in my own voice. "Who do you think did raise the storm that did kill your king and your prince?"

The men stare at me.

I have them now.

I point in the direction of the palace. "It was my master. He did drown them. He did drown them *all*."

Now they are on their feet and the fuddlement of the sweet red claret goes out of their eyes.

One picks up a big rock. "For King Alonso!"

"For Prince Ferdinand!" The other picks up a long piece of wood, heavy and wet from the sea, and slaps it against the palm of his hand. "Lead on, friend monster," he says. "Lead on."

FORTY-SEVEN

MIRANDA

In a waking daze, I do as Papa bade me, exchanging my rain-soaked finery for another fine gown, this one white and silver. The bodice is embroidered with seed pearls like the kidskin slippers that for so long were the only proof of my memories of a time before the isle.

Now I know; still, I have no slippers for my bare feet.

I comb out my tangled and wind-whipped hair. Once, I had ladies to perform such a task for me.

I am the daughter of the Duke of Milan.

I am Miranda.

Who is Miranda?

I am a stranger to myself.

Oh, Caliban! Where are you? I need you to touch my hand; the merest of touches, a fleeting touch with all the gentleness of which I know you are capable, to remind me who I am.

But you are not here. There are only trumpet flowers withering on my window-ledge.

Outside, I hear singing.

It is a high, clear voice, inhuman in its purity; inhuman, too, in the careless cruelty of the ditty it sings.

Full fathom five thy father lies; of his bones are coral made . . .

I think of the stranded prince, and although he is unknown to me, my heart aches to think of the grief this poor, innocent soul must endure, believing his father dead and drowned at the bottom of the ocean. Even Ariel reckoned it a piteous thing to behold, though not so piteous that the spirit does not seize the chance to torment him anew.

Although I suspect Papa should not like me to seek out the prince, he has not forbidden it, either.

So I leave my chamber to follow the sound of Ariel's song and find a young man staggering up the path toward the courtyard.

Even though I anticipated it, the sight is nonetheless a profound shock. Did I speak of strangers? He is a stranger in the veriest of truths, here on this isle where no mortal foot save mine, Papa's, and Caliban's has trod within my lifetime. I find myself dumbstruck, my tongue rooted to the floor of my mouth. The prince's wet hair clings to his head and face in tendrils like seaweed; his eyes, as brown as acorns, are wide and wild and staring. His mouth is agape. His eyes widen further at the sight of me in my finery.

"Help!" he says, and the word is a croak in his throat. He holds out his empty hands in a pleading gesture. "My father . . . please!"

"You should go," I whisper. "Leave this place!"

"My father . . ." The prince swallows, the apple of his throat rising up and down. "What is this place? How came I here?"

I do not know what to say, so I say nothing.

"There was a voice, I followed a voice . . . it sang a terrible song." He looks around him. "Was it you?"

I shake my head. "No."

He looks back at me. "The ship . . . it foundered on the rocks. I fear my father and all hands aboard it are lost. Are there no men here to help me search for survivors?" He swallows again. "Or at least seek to retrieve my father's body? If I can do naught else, I would give him an honest burial on dry land."

Do I dare tell him his father lives? It seems cruel to make him suffer in ignorance; oh, but I hesitate too long.

"Hail fortune!" Papa's voice says behind me, fulsome with amazement. "Can it be that you've survived the wreck, lad? You must be a hardy soul indeed to weather such a tempest."

"I was in the water, and then . . ." The prince's voice trails off; he has no inkling of how he found himself ashore. "Oh, but you saw? Good sir, I pray you, were there others? What of my father?"

"As to that I cannot say, but you've endured a terrible hardship," Papa says, and gestures toward the palace. "Come, warm yourself at our hearth and dry your clothing."

The prince follows Papa obediently, his wet boots making squelching sounds on the paving stones of the courtyard. Despite the warmth of the day, he is shivering.

I follow behind him.

It is strange, so strange, to see him in our kitchen. He sits in a chair beside the hearth, steam rising from his sodden attire. He is young, younger than I expected. Above the beginnings of a beard, his mouth looks tender.

"My father—" he says.

"Hush." Papa stirs the contents of a kettle hanging in the hearth with a ladle. "How are you called, lad?"

He laughs a dreadful laugh. "Called? Why, if my father is dead, I am called Naples."

Papa glances at him. "Your father is the king of Naples?"

"Aye." The prince buries his face in his hands, knuckles whitening as he clutches at his flesh. He lowers his hands and lifts his stricken face. "Good sir, I must go. Dead or alive, I must seek him."

"Hush," Papa says again. He ladles steaming liquid into a silver goblet. "First drink this tisane, and be restored."

No.

No.

The word—a mere syllable—burgeons in my mouth, and I think I will utter it; I think I *must* utter it. I think I will rise from my own seat, dash the chalice from the prince's tender lips.

Oh, but Papa looks at me, and his gaze is colder than the coldest days of winter; cold and hate-filled.

I am afraid.

I say nothing.

The prince drinks.

I watch the apple of his throat bob up and down as he swallows. He drinks deep, the prince does; deep and trusting.

Of course, it is no harmless tisane of herbs and bark he drinks, but a love potion wrought from my menstruum, the blood of my woman's courses which Papa has collected, reduced, and refined by his arts.

The snare has been sprung. Behind my eyes, I see the image of Venus leering forth from the wall of Papa's sanctum.

"Oh!" The prince lowers the goblet. A look of soft wonder settles over his features, smoothing away every trace of his grief and confusion. He gazes at me, sitting at our humble kitchen table, my hands clenched in my lap. "You . . ." he says, and I think he has quite forgotten his poor drowned father. "Oh, *you*! Fair one, fairest of the fair, tell me true, be you goddess or maiden?"

A wail of frustration rises to my throat and dies there. The thing is done, and I have done nothing to prevent it.

Papa smiles.

FORTY-EIGHT

CALIBAN

Oh, Setebos! The palace is so far away and the men are so *slow*!

The rocks are too steep for them to climb, so we must go down the shore to the gentle path that slopes down to the sea. At first anger and the sweet red claret burns hot in them, but the farther we do go, the slower and slower they do go.

The men are tired, I know; they did have to swim a long way to shore. I want to shout at them, to say, go, go, go like the voice that shouts inside my head, but I do not. I say oh, good masters, brave masters, only a little farther, masters.

And then they are thirsty, and say, oh, friend monster, you did promise to take us to good fresh water.

I am thirsty, too. My mouth is dry like I did swallow sand and I think oh, Caliban, stupid Caliban, why did you not think to tell them sooner that Prospero did kill their king and their prince?

Why did you not think of *vengeance?* They are men like him, and I think vengeance is all he ever did want.

Is it what *I* want?

I do not think so, no. Even though I am angry and I hate him so very much, I do not think it is the same.

It is only that I want him to be gone, so he cannot punish me anymore, so he can never in the everest ever punish Miranda again.

So I can look at her.

So I can touch her.

So Master cannot take her away from the isle and away from me forever, because I am afraid it is what he means to do.

Even though I am thirsty too, I do not want to take time to drink, but the men moan and groan and I think they will not go any farther, so I lead them to a little spring that trickles from the rocks. Now the men dip their hands into the spring and drink and drink cold clear water, and it drips from their hands.

I drink one mouthful thinking, hurry, hurry, hurry!

A little spirit of air dances in the breeze above the spring, going in dizzy circles. One of the men says, oh, oh, what is it I see?

In the distance, I hear Ariel's voice singing; and the other says, oh, oh, what is it I hear?

The breeze dies and the spirit drifts away. Slow, we are going too slow; and my belly is sick with fear at it.

"Do not be afraid," I say to the men. "The isle is full of wonders; spirits that will dance in midair and the splashing fountains, sing oh, such very sweet songs for you, and give you such dreams that you will weep to awaken and long to sleep once more. And when Prospero, my old master, is gone, all the spirits of the isle will serve you. But we must hurry, we must go now to catch Master before *he* wakes."

One of the men frowns. "Why do you not do the deed yourself and claim the isle, monster?"

I show him my teeth clenched in a smile. "It should be mine, for it was my mother's before me. But my master has laid such a charm on me that I cannot harm him."

"What's to keep him from laying such a charm on us?" the other says.

"Nothing, if we do not surprise him," I say through my smiling teeth. "That is why we must hurry."

The men look at each other and nod.

Onward.

FORTY-NINE

MIRANDA

The prince's name is Ferdinand.

I can scarce bear the way he gazes at me, besotted and unwitting. I should pity him, for 'tis not his fault; and yet there is no pity in my heart in this moment. I loathe him for being drawn into Papa's snare and setting aside the burden of his grief so lightly; I loathe myself for letting it happen.

I loathe Papa for doing it, although this I admit to myself only in the secret place inside me.

"Is your daughter wed?" the prince says to Papa. "Tell me she's not, for I'll make her queen of Naples!"

Papa laughs. "You must prove your worth, lad."

The prince's eyes shine. "What task will you set me, good sir? Name it, and I'll prove its equal!"

"Can you butcher a goat?" Papa inquires.

"I can dress a slain deer a-hunting in the field," the prince says.

Papa claps a hand on his shoulder. "Well, then, you can butcher a goat. You'll find one hanging in the garden and a knife on the sideboard. Make it ready for the spit, and see that the hearth is smoldering hot and the rack of firewood filled."

The prince rises from his chair beside the hearth and bounds forth to do Papa's bidding.

It is a relief to have him gone.

Papa and I regard each other. He wears a clean blue robe trimmed with silver, and I see that beneath his long white beard, there are new amulets hanging about his neck. "So you would see me made queen of Naples?" I ask quietly.

He plants his hands on the table, leaning over it, looming over me. The amulets sway and tangle in his beard. "Everything I have done, I have done for you, Miranda!" he says in a low, fierce voice. "For *us*!"

I look away, my eyes stinging. "The king's son might have come to love me in his own right."

Papa laughs again; this time it is a harsh sound. "Love! What do you know of love?"

Caliban.

I know Caliban in his constancy; I know Caliban in the depth of profound misery in his dark eyes, believing himself monstrous and unworthy of me. I know Caliban with his tense, hunched shoulders, the hard-muscled blades of his back spreading like wings as he crouches on the rocks above the stream to catch fish for our supper. I know Caliban who knows *me;* Caliban who knows Miranda.

Caliban, who leaves flowers on my window-ledge.

I do not know this prince.

He does not know me.

"I know love is cruel," I say at last. "Whether it is more cruel when it is true or false, I cannot say."

"You shall have your birthright and more restored to you," Papa says. "No more toiling for your supper; no more gathering greens and tubers and eggs; no more journey-cakes of bitter acorn meal; no more going about unshod in ill-fitting attire. Your meals shall be prepared by the finest cooks in the land, and you shall dine on good white bread, rack of lamb, roasted venison adorned with sauces of surpassing piquancy, pies and savories and sweetmeats. You shall have gowns and slippers for every occasion, you'll have maids to attend to your needs and ladies-in-waiting to befriend you and while away the hours in pleasant pastimes and conversation. You shall see such sights and splendors as you never dared dream, Miranda. And you shall learn, in time, to love the prince."

It is a dazzling picture that Papa sketches for me, and I should like to say I care naught for any of it, but it would be a lie. "Should I be allowed to continue painting?" I hear myself ask.

"You shall have pigments of the finest quality." Papa sounds weary. "And the doting prince shall indulge your every foible."

"Why could you not—"

Tell me, I mean to ask; but Papa divines the familiar plaint and interrupts me ere I can give voice to it. "I'd no wish to raise your hopes if it were in vain, Miranda," he says to me. "To bring the events of this day to pass, to influence matters from afar so that the king's vessel did pass near enough to the isle . . . it has been the undertaking of a lifetime."

"I know, Papa," I murmur.

He studies me. "Tell me, would you have been content on the isle these long years had I dangled the possibility of such a prize before you?"

I meet his gaze squarely. "As to that, we shall never know, shall we? No more than I'll ever know if the prince might have come to love me for myself."

Papa lifts one hand from the table and turns it palm upward as though to cede me the point. "Forgive me, child," he says in a quiet voice. "There was too much at stake, and I dared leave nothing to chance." His wrinkled eyes flicker. "Does that mean you intend to abide by my will in this matter with good grace, child?"

Although I am grateful for the semblance of an apology, I do not fail to note Papa's phrasing; one way or another, I *will* abide by his will. Whether or not to do it with grace is my choice. "What of Caliban?" I ask him. "What is to become of him?"

"*Caliban?*" Papa looks blankly at me. "I suppose some menial position might be found for him." He pauses to reconsider, stroking his beard in thought. "Although I might make better use of our wild lad. As a savage who learned speech, he would serve as the subject for many an interesting discourse."

Oh, Caliban! My heart aches at the prospect; but then here is Ariel, returned from his latest errand.

"Master!" the spirit announces, eyes sparkling like the sunlit sea. With every hour that passes, every piece of Papa's plan that falls into place, his freedom grows closer in reach. "The king and his retinue draw nigh!"

"Well done, gentle spirit!" Papa praises him. "Lead them to the innermost courtyard of the palace, bypassing our presence here, and there address them as I bade you."

Ariel bows. "In a trice!"

Papa turns to me. "I've pressing business at hand. Do I have your word that you'll make yourself pleasant and helpful to the young prince, or need I threaten punishment for the lack of courtesy?"

I have no cause to begrudge the prince my courtesy. "No, Papa. I will be as pleasant as I may."

"If all goes well, I shall send for both of you." Papa glances out into the kitchen garden where Prince Ferdinand is industriously skinning the sacrificial he-goat. He frowns to himself, and summons a pair of gnomes who come trotting obediently in answer. "They will tend to the spit, for it is metal and of their element," he says. "See to it that the prince is rendered presentable after his labors."

I incline my head. "Yes, Papa."

"I pray there's firewood to suffice," he says fretfully, and glances around again. "Where is that villain Caliban?"

I would that I knew. "I know not, Papa."

In another part of the palace, there are indistinct voices; men's deep voices, and then Ariel's voice.

"I must go," Papa says.

I venture into the kitchen garden to make myself pleasant. The silent gnomes trot after me, carrying the great spit from the hearth between them.

The goat's carcass lies on the dusty ground, headless and skinned. Kneeling on one knee, the prince slits its belly and removes the glistening offal, piling it neatly on the raw hide.

His hair has dried; it is brown with threads of bronze that glint in the sun. It looks soft to the touch.

"Such rude labor is no more fit for your delicate gaze than it is for a prince's stature, my lady!" he exclaims when he sees me; then he catches sight of the pair of gnomes and stares. "What new wonder is this?"

"Only simple earth elementals bound to Papa's service," I say. "They will tend to the goat's cooking."

"Such marvelous creatures!" he says as the gnomes set about spitting the goat.

"Are there no spirits to assist with the chores of the household from whence you come?" I ask.

Prince Ferdinand laughs. "No, to be sure! But you will find willing mortal hands a-plenty, my lady." I draw a bucket of water from the well to sluice the dust from the goat's flesh, and he takes it from me with alacrity. "Your father set me this task, my lady! You must allow me to complete it. Only . . ." He pauses. "Might I beseech the boon of your name as my reward?"

My name.

It seems to me there is a power in names. It was the gift of my name that allowed Caliban to remember his own, the first step on the road to regaining human speech. When I first awoke from my affliction, uncomprehending and terror-stricken, Caliban returned the gift to me, and thus began the long road of restoring me to myself.

If Caliban had not surrendered the name of Setebos to Papa, Ariel would still be howling in his pine tree.

Papa calls upon the arcane and numerous names of the seven governors to draw down their influence each and every day, and today, he summoned the raging wind by calling its secret names.

I am not sure I wish to give the prince my name.

Oh, but that is foolish, for he will learn it sooner or later; and since I am in large part responsible for his ensorcellment, mayhap 'tis only meet I should offer it to him as a gift.

"Miranda," I say. "I am Miranda."

Something in my heart twinges at the words.

Prince Ferdinand only smiles at me. "Miranda," he says. "It is a name as beautiful as its bearer."

I find myself loathing him a measure less, but oh, dear Lord God, I wish he was not bespelled.

Elsewhere in the palace—in the innermost courtyard, I trust—Ariel's voice has fallen silent. I can hear only piteous moans and low utterances muffled by distance and the crumbling walls. There the fate of dukes and kings and nations is being decided; and I have not the slightest say in the matter, nor even the chance to bear witness to it.

Outside, the sun is shining as though the storm never was.

It shines upon me.

It shines upon the prince.

Somewhere it shines upon Caliban, but I do not know to whence he has fled. I am alone in the garden with the dead goat and the live prince, two grinning gnomes shouldering the spit, a handful of chickens pecking and scratching in the dust, and in the far corner, the nameless nanny-goat scratching her ear with one hind foot, careless of the fate of one of her kind.

FIFTY

CALIBAN

The palace is in sight.

One two three four five six seven eight, I count my steps. Miranda did teach me to count, oh, so long ago.

The men's steps stumble and drag. They are tired, so tired! Still, one clutches his rock; the other his heavy stick.

The sun is hot.

My skin itches, blood and rain and mud salt-spray dried on it. I scratch at it with my ragged nails.

The men complain; the men wish they had a flask of the sweet red claret to carry with them.

I lie.

I tell them there are fountains of sweet red claret playing in every courtyard of the palace. I promise them everything that they do want; everything, everything.

They are cheered and pick up their feet a little faster.

There are footprints in the packed sand and scattered little pebbles of the path; footprints of men wearing boots. Other men have come this way. I hope that they are Master's enemies.

I do not hear Ariel's voice singing anymore.

Bees are buzz-buzzing in the wild lavender. I could follow them, I think; leave these men and follow the bees to find where their honey is hid, gather it and fetch it for Miranda.

I wish it were yesterday.

I wish it were a thousand yesterdays ago, long before I ever did see Miranda naked at her wash-basin.

But it is not; and there is hatred in my heart. I will not follow the buzzing bees. Even if it is too late, I will not turn back.

No, I will do whatever I can.

I count my steps and think of you.

Miranda.

FIFTY-ONE

MIRANDA

The goat is roasting in the hearth, and the rack is filled with fire-wood. The gnomes turn the spit, and fat and juices drip down to sizzle in the embers.

I fetch my wooden comb and little pot of soap from my chamber and draw water from the well so that the prince may wash away the gore and grime of his labors. He scrubs his hands and his arms to the elbow, splashes his face with cool, clean water, rakes the sea-tangles from his hair with my comb. I reckon that's as presentable as I can make him without fresh attire, and that I do not have.

Shadows creep across the dusty ground.

At last Ariel comes to summon us; and the spirit's presence is a new marvel over which the prince must exclaim, for he caught no glimpse of his ethereal rescuer amidst the storm's fury.

I am weary of marvels. "What transpires in the courtyard?" I ask

Ariel. He hesitates, and I beg him in despair. "Spirit, have pity on me."

Ariel beckons me some distance away from the prince. "This hour past, the king and his retinue have stood amazed in a spell of thy father's devising, my lady," he murmurs. "They behold a vision of their past sins from which there is no escape, and they shed endless tears of remorse at it; all save one who is that noble lord that did aid thy father and thee, and has no cause to repent of it."

"Does it move my father's heart to mercy?" I ask.

"It would move mine were I mortal," Ariel says soberly. "I should think thy father's heart made of stone if it is unmoved. But come, quickly."

He leads us through the fretted, crumbling halls of the palace to one of the enclosed gardens where myrtle grows in profusion, jasmine perfumes the air, and undines cavort in the splashing fountain.

The garden contains a latticed arbor covered in vines. The arbor has always been empty, but today there is a table and a pair of chairs, and atop the table sits the game-board from the pirates' treasure, the cunning figures of silver and gold arrayed in lines on either side of it.

"Sit and pass the while," Ariel bids us.

So we are to wait again. "How long?" I ask bitterly.

The spirit's eyes darken at my tone. "Until thy father decides whether to administer mercy or justice."

Prince Ferdinand gazes after Ariel as the spirit takes his leave, a slight frown creasing his brow. "What grave matter is it that your father does adjudicate this day?" he asks me.

How am I to answer?

Your father lives, I might say to him, *though I fear mine might yet dispatch him for his sins.*

What would he do?

What would *I* do?

I sit and bow my head, letting my hair curtain my face while my thoughts chase themselves fruitlessly. I touch one of the smallest figures on the game-board. Above the arbor, swallows dart and twitter on the wing.

"Forgive me, but I am not privy to my father's business." I glance up at the prince. "Do you know how to play this game, my lord?"

"Ferdinand." He smiles at me. "Call me by my name, for I think it should never sound so sweet as it might upon your lips, my lady. Have you never played chess?"

I shake my head. "No, never."

He sits opposite me. "Here, Miranda. Allow me the privilege of being your tutor."

I watch the prince touch each figure on the board and name them, committing each to memory. I have an excellent memory, for the studies to which Papa set me demanded nothing less. The prince's hands are strong, fair, and shapely. I listen to him describe the manner in which each piece is permitted to move, each player moving a piece in turns in accordance with his strategy. His voice is warm and pleasing.

You shall learn, in time, to love the prince.

Papa, I think, sees the entire world as a game-board; and all of us lesser beings merely pieces upon it.

Oh, how I wish Caliban were here.

But Caliban is elsewhere; and so I suffer the prince to teach me the rules of the game of chess, our heads bowed over the checkered board beneath the green shadows of the arbor.

I do not think about what is happening in the innermost courtyard.

I do not think about Caliban.

Only this moment; piece by piece, square by square. It is an orderly world, the world of this game-board. One might spend a lifetime mastering its intricacy, I think, but it holds no hidden secrets. I immerse myself in it, listening to the prince's murmuring voice, the twittering swallows, the splashing fountain. I ignore the faint sound of footsteps on the paving stones.

"Behold," Papa's voice says softly, and I ignore it, too.

"Oh, my son!" another man's voice cries, cracking under the weight of a hope too great to endure. "Ferdinand! Pray, tell me you're flesh and blood, and not a vision!"

"Father?" The prince rises, his eyes bright and incredulous. "Can it be true? Oh, the good Lord God be praised!"

So Papa has chosen mercy, and I can no longer abide in the pleasant fiction that none of this is happening. The prince and his father the king embrace, both of them laughing and weeping in their joy.

I try to imagine Papa weeping for joy on my behalf, and cannot. He wears a look of solemn pride, as though he were not the very cause of so much grief allayed. There are three other men; one is weeping, too, and I think he must be that noble lord to whom Papa and I owe our survival.

So many strange men! I feel overwhelmed by the sheer number of them, and I should like to flee.

But now the king's gaze falls upon me. "Who is this fair maiden?" he asks his son.

The prince comes and takes my hand, and I do not resist as he leads me to meet his father. "She is the good duke's daughter, sir," he says, "and by the grace of God, my own betrothed."

I curtsy to the king. "I am Miranda, my lord."

The king smiles at me through his tears. "Why then, I have gained a daughter as well as my son this day!"

FIFTY-TWO

CALIBAN

Toolatetoolatetoolate.

Words sound in my head with every footstep, thumpity-thump. Too late, Caliban; poor dumb monster.

Bad.

Badbadbad.

You did choose to do a bad thing; you did choose the wrong men to do it. You did *everything* wrong.

The men are angry there are no fountains of sweet red claret. They hear voices somewhere in the palace, other men's voices, and they are angry.

You did say there was no one here but the magus and his daughter, they say to me. You lied to us, monster.

I say I did not know.

The men follow the voices; now I follow the men. Now it is my footsteps that drag through the halls of the palace. The voices are not angry and shouting; the voices are saying please and thank you to God. It seems that Master's vengeance is not the thing I thought it would be.

Run.

Runrunrun!

The men go into the garden and I do not follow them. Thump; I hear a rock fall to the ground; thump, I hear a stick fall.

Oh, oh, my liege, the men say; oh, oh, my prince! Alive, all alive! Praise be to God! Forgive us, good duke! The monster did lie to us!

RUN.

I turn to run and there is Ariel, his eyes shining and terrible. "Fool!" he says to me. "I did warn thee."

FIFTY-THREE

MIRANDA

On the heels of the king's warm words, two of his courtiers stumble into the garden with crude weapons in their hands and a wild tale of deception on their lips, one that I pray is untrue.

Caliban. Oh, *Caliban*!

Papa's face is grim. "Ariel, my brave spirit!" he calls, his hand closing around Caliban's amulet. "Fetch forth the villain."

There is a great clap of thunder in the offing and a wind springs up along the colonnade that encloses the garden. It swirls down the hall and spills through the arched doorway, a maelstrom of wind and fog from which Caliban tumbles, landing sprawling on the paving stones. Ariel's figure resolves itself from the maelstrom, though it is Ariel as I have never seen him, taller and more fearsome. His white sleeves flutter behind him and now it seems to me that they are not sleeves at all, but wings; and I wonder if I have ever beheld the mercurial spirit's true form.

As for Caliban, he collects himself to sit crouched on his haunches, the knuckles of one hand braced on the ground, his head hanging low.

"What manner of strange brute is this?" the prince whispers to me, and for a moment, I cannot help but see Caliban through his eyes; a crouching, bestial thing smeared with filth and gore, half naked in ragged trousers, coarse and rough and repugnant in every aspect.

Monstrous.

I never believed I would see him thusly and I do not answer the prince, for I am ashamed.

Then Caliban lifts his head and gazes at me, and there is such love and misery and heartbreak in his dark eyes, I feel as though my own heart is shattering into pieces within me. My hand is yet clasped in Prince Ferdinand's. I withdraw it quietly, but Caliban has already seen.

He looks away, his shoulders hunching as though to absorb a blow.

"So, villain," Papa says to him in a voice as hard as stone. "Though I have shown you every kindness, taken you under my roof, fed and clothed you and seen that you were taught language when you had none, you stand accused by these good men of plotting my murder. Will you confess it?"

Caliban utters a harsh bark of laughter and stares at Papa. "Every kindness? I was free and you did make a servant of me!"

"I sought to civilize you!" Papa shouts at him. "An ill-advised effort, and one which you've sought to repay with murder! Have you aught to say for yourself?"

I wish that Caliban would deny it; I wish it were untrue. I wish . . . ah, dear Lord God, I do not know what I wish. When in my life have my wishes ever mattered?

"Yes," Caliban says in a low, savage voice, so low that all must strain to hear his words. "I only wish I did succeed, *Prospero*."

Papa's hand tightens on the amulet. Caliban flinches in anticipation of the agony to follow, and I flinch in involuntary sympathy. Out of the corner of my eye, I see the prince give me a bemused glance.

He does not know what Papa is capable of.

None of them do.

Nor will they learn it today, for Papa stays his hand and does not inflict a punishment upon Caliban for them to behold. I do not think it is mercy that dissuades him, but rather the presence of an audience before whom he wishes to preserve the semblance of magnanimity.

"I'll decide your fate on the morrow," he says instead. "Gentle Ariel! Take the ungrateful wretch to his chamber. Lock the door and bring me the key, and bid the little gnomes seal him within it as they did long ago."

Ariel bows. "It shall be done, Master."

Caliban accompanies him without protest, nor does he glance in my direction as he goes.

I am trembling.

"Are you frightened?" the prince asks me gently, touching my arm. "Do not be afraid, my lady. I promise you, whatever the sullen brute has done, he cannot harm you."

I think of the trumpet flowers withering on my window-ledge and very nearly burst into hysterical laughter.

Caliban.

Oh, *Caliban*!

Why, I should like to scream at him, *why?*

But in the secret place inside me where I once contemplated the possibility of Papa's demise, I know why.

There is a feast that evening. It takes place in the great dining hall that Papa and I never use, for it is far too vast a space for our modest stores of oil-lamps and beeswax candles to light.

But tonight, Papa is profligate; profligate with our stores, profligate with his magic, profligate with his magnanimity. Air elementals have driven the dust from the tiled floor, water elementals have washed it clean. The earth elementals have scoured the fixtures, and never-before-used sconces gleam beneath candlelight; the platters and chalices of the pirates' treasure gleam atop the long, moldering trestle table that stretches the length of the hall.

Papa has dispatched Ariel to bear the good tidings of the survival of the king and his retinue to the sailors in the pirates' cove; and to return with a barrel of wine from the ship's stores that all might celebrate on this joyous occasion of reunion, forgiveness, and reconciliation.

The barrel is tapped, wine is poured.

"To the betrothal of Ferdinand and Miranda!" the king proclaims, hoisting his chalice.

Everyone follows suit and drinks.

Let him kiss me with the kisses of his mouth: for thy love is better than wine.

I try not to choke.

Papa's cold gaze rests on me. I sip my wine, smile and blush, and hold my tongue lest I say aught to spoil the moment.

Ferdinand raises my hand to his lips and kisses it chastely, regarding me over the rim of his chalice with his besotted gaze.

There are things, so many things, I should like to say.

Do you not think it passing strange that you should love me so, when you scarce know me?

My liege, do you not think it strange?

My lords, do you not think it strange? This storm that sprang out of nowhere, do you not think it passing strange?

But I say nothing. There are too many men; their presence stifles me, their voices crash over me like the waves of the ocean. Dear God, how shall I endure on a ship filled with dozens of such men in close quarters? How shall I endure in a *city* filled with hundreds or even thousands? I fear I shall go mad.

The goat is carved; our platters are heaped high with slabs of roasted meat. I poke listlessly at mine.

The men eat their fill, belch into their beards, stretch their booted legs out beneath the long table, and compare tales of the storm.

I learn that the purpose of their journey was to see the king of Naples's daughter wed to the king of Tunis, and that this was accomplished ere the storm separated them from the royal fleet and drove them hence.

I understand that these are the specific set of circumstances Papa has sought to influence with my aid, the work of long years of intrigue and negotiations.

I learn that the king—Alonso is his name—and Papa's brother, who is called Antonio, repented of their wickedness and wept in the innermost courtyard; the former promising to restore Papa's title as Duke of Milan, the latter vowing to relinquish all claim to it.

I do not care.

Do I?

"Surely God is good to bring us together, Miranda!" the prince says fervently to me, squeezing my hand.

His heart, I think, is kind.

I am not sure mine is.

The men speak of Caliban and *his* wickedness. It is a wickedness, it seems, distinct from their own sins. It is a wickedness owing to savagery and ingratitude; a wickedness beyond redemption. The men speak at first of hanging Caliban for the crime to which he has confessed, and then of clapping him in chains and putting him on display when we return to the mainland so that all the world might mock him and jeer at him.

I am heartsick at the prospects, and yet how can I plead for clemency? Caliban is guilty, and he has shown himself lacking in all remorse. I should have known; I should have guessed what darkness was in his heart and dissuaded him from attempting such a mad, wicked thing.

But how was I to do so when Papa forbade all communication between us?

Oh, dear Lord God, if only I had not sought out Caliban at the stream that day, if only I had not insisted on following him, if only I had not lost my footing and fallen . . . if only so many things had gone differently.

If only Papa had fed Caliban a few more miserly crumbs of kindness; if only I had heeded Ariel's advice and understood that there was a measure of cruelty in my own kindness to him.

Ariel.

The night is late and the candles are burning low when the spirit enters the hall unbidden, the deceptively gentle breeze that accompanies him causing the guttering candles to flicker.

The men fall silent upon his entrance.

Ariel bows. "Master."

At the head of the table, Papa fixes him with a lopsided squint. "What are you about, sprite?"

"The moon rises high in the sky and the hours of the day are all but counted, Master," Ariel says. "Have I failed thee in any particular?"

"You have not," Papa says.

"Thou didst promise me my freedom," Ariel says, and although his voice is soft and low, there is the promise of thunder in it.

Papa hesitates. I am quite certain that he should like to refuse Ariel. I wonder if he will dare to do so, and I wonder what Ariel will do if Papa does so. But again, there is an audience present; an audience of men before whom Papa does not wish to appear aught less than a man of his word.

"So I did." Papa clambers to his feet, leaning on his staff. "So I did." He sways a little, makes a magnanimous gesture with his other hand. "Your oath is fulfilled to the letter, gentle spirit," he pronounces. "In the name of the good Lord God, go, and be free of it!"

There is no great thunderclap this time, no great rush of wind; only a sound like a sigh, and then Ariel is gone.

I cannot decipher the expression on Papa's face.

"Truly the Lord's blessing is on this day," he says. "But the spirit speaks the truth, for it draws to a close, and thus do I declare this night's revel to be finished. Sleep, gentlefolk, and awaken to a new dawn."

There is no bedding to spare, but the king and his men are content to stretch their length on the floor of the hall.

It is a relief beyond telling to be dismissed to the privacy of my chamber, though the prospect of sleep eludes me. I cannot help but picture Caliban; Caliban hanging from a gallows, his eyes bulging in the throes of death; Caliban in chains, his shoulders hunched, enduring the jeers and taunts of a hateful, mocking crowd.

I cannot bear it.

And so in the deep stillness of the night, I rise from my pallet and begin knotting my bed-linens together.

FIFTY-FOUR

CALIBAN

I tear and bloody the nails of my fingers and toes trying to climb the walls of my chamber to reach the high windows, but it is no good. There are no gaps between the tiles like on the stone walls outside.

I pull and pull on the handle of the door, but the lock holds.

Then I do push against the stone blocks that those little gnomes did pile in my door until the skin is scraped from my hands and arms and shoulders and my legs are shaking and sore, but that is no good, either.

Caliban is a prisoner, the poor dumb monster. Just like in the beginning, only everything is different.

Oh, Miranda!

I am sorry I am sorry I am sorry so very sorry so very sorry, oh Setebos, I think you must hate me.

If only I could see you.

If only I could tell you with the words that you did teach me that I am sorry, so sorry, that I could not help that hatred for Master did grow in my heart until it was red and hot and sick.

It is still sick.

I am sick.

He held his hand in yours and you did let him.

I am sick.

Outside the high windows I cannot reach, the sun sets and the light goes away. For a time it is dark, and then the moon rises and there is a little silvery light that comes through the high windows.

In the morning the sun will rise.

I wonder what Master will do. Prospero; oh, I did call him *Prospero* to his face, and I am not sorry for it. No, not for that. Only for the other thing I said, and only because you did hear it, Miranda.

But I think he will kill me for what I did try to do. He did want to kill me before. Yes, I think I will die in the morning. It is a strange thing to think of not being, but I sit in the moonlight and think it to myself.

I am Caliban.

Caliban is; but tomorrow, Caliban will not be.

How can I not be?

This thought is like a heavy stone falling and falling through my thoughts and I follow it down but it only keeps falling and falling like it is falling in a well that has no bottom and the more I think it the more heavy it is until my head is heavy with it, and my head falls forward to touch my knees, and it is heavy so heavy—

"Caliban."

Thunk.

I think it is the stone hitting the bottom at last, but no, there is no stone and no well, only my head coming up hard.

I was asleep; I did dream.

"Caliban!"

Then oh, oh, oh! I am awake and it is *Miranda's* voice I hear, Miranda's voice that calls in a soft, scared whisper from the gallery above my cell where she did watch me when we were little. Quick, so quick, I am on my feet. I lift my face to find her. She is there, the moonlight a shimmer on her hair. My heart sings inside me like a bird. If I had wings, I would fly to her.

There is a slithering sound and something long and white comes out of the darkness. It is a rope that Miranda has made from her bed-linens. One end hangs in front of my face. I take it in my hand and tug. It does not move. The other end is knotted around the railing of the balcony.

"Can you climb it?" Miranda whispers to me.

Laughter rises in me like a bubble from the deep sea. "Yes," I whisper to her. "Oh, yes!"

The cloth of the bed-linens is soft under my rough hurting hands and it smells of Miranda's own self. I pull myself up. The cloth is worn thin and frayed with age, but Miranda did tie strong knots in it. I climb them quick-quick, scrambling up the rope like I have wings on my hands and feet.

I climb over the balcony.

My heart is beating in my chest like a bird, like a bird's wings fluttering.

Can it be?

Can it be that Miranda loves me yet?

I hold out one hand to her; it is trembling. "Oh, Miranda!"

Her face is pale against the darkness, oh, so very pale. And she is trembling, too. "No." Miranda takes a step backward, a step away from me, her eyes shadow-holes in her pale face. "No."

FIFTY-FIVE

MIRANDA

I watch the rising tide of hope ebb from Caliban's face, confusion and bewilderment replacing it.

"What—" he begins, then halts, his gaze searching mine. "Miranda, why—"

I wrap my arms around myself, trying to stop myself from shivering. "Caliban, you must go. Leave me!"

He shakes his stubborn head. "No. No!"

Ah, dear God! I do love him, I cannot help it. Not enough to forgive him the attempt on Papa's life, but far too much to see him hanged, far too much to see him suffer in captivity.

"You *must*," I say, low and fierce. "At worst, Papa and the king's men mean to see you hanged to your death; at best, they will see you clapped in chains and made a thing of coarse mockery for all the days of your life, and that I cannot bear, Caliban."

Caliban gives one short bark of despair. "Where could I go on the isle that Ariel cannot find me, Miranda?"

"Papa has freed Ariel from his service," I say.

The news startles him. "Truly?"

"Truly."

His expression changes. "Prospero means to take you away," he says in a dark tone. "And you mean to go; to go with him, to go with that prince who did hold your hand and whisper in your ear."

"What else would you have me do, Caliban?" I ask him wearily. "The thing is done. I daresay my fate was sealed from the beginning, and you set the seal on your own when you sought my father's life."

"Oh, Miranda!" A note of anguish enters Caliban's voice. "I am sorry, I am so very sorry! I will do anything, I will be your father's servant for always and ever and never complain, only do not send me away from you!"

My eyes burn with tears. "Don't you understand? It's *too late*!"

"No." He shakes his head again. "Anyway, Prospero does not need Ariel! If I go, he will only summon me."

"I won't let him," I say.

Caliban stares at me. "How?"

I swallow hard. "I shall bargain with him," I say. "Papa has sworn to renounce his magic if this working succeeds. I shall offer my willing consent to his plans in exchange for your freedom."

"No." Caliban sets his jaw. "Do *you* not understand, Miranda? I would rather die than leave you."

Dear Lord God, why must he be *so* stubborn? "Then I should have your death on my conscience." My voice is shaking, and I rub my burning eyes with the heel of one hand. "Would you be that cruel to me, Caliban?"

He hesitates.

A wild notion seizes me. "I will send for you," I say recklessly to him. "The prince . . ." I swallow again. "'Tis a love spell that compels him, Caliban; a potion wrought from the blood of my woman's courses. Papa said himself that the prince will indulge my every foible. One day . . . one day when Papa is no longer there to forbid it, I will explain to the prince that you are my dearest friend, that I could not have endured on the isle without you. I will tell him how tenderly and patiently you cared for me when I was afflicted, how you nursed me back to strength and health. I will tell him that you are owed mercy for seeking to commit the self-same crime his own father committed in veritable truth. And I will beg him to send for you, beg him until he accedes."

The yearning in Caliban's gaze is terrible to behold. "Do you promise it?"

"I do," I whisper.

"Then I will go," he says simply.

Dizzy with relief, I coil my makeshift rope and lead Caliban down the stairs, through the darkened halls of the palace. The king and his men are snoring in the great dining hall, but they have drunk deep of the king's wine and do not awaken; nor does Papa in his chamber.

It is late; soon the sky will begin to turn grey in the east.

In the garden outside the kitchen where we spent so many hours together, Caliban touches my face with his rough fingertips; oh, ever so gently. "Miranda," he murmurs. "I do love you, and I will wait for you always."

I lay my hand over his. "I know."

And then there is nothing left to say. I lift my hand; Caliban takes his away. We gaze at each other in the fading moonlight. Caliban opens his mouth to speak; I shake my head at him.

No, there is nothing left to say.

He nods in understanding and goes, vanishing into the darkness.

I watch him go and return to my chamber, where I painstakingly untie the knots in my bed-linens, doing my best to smooth out the creases until the linens lie flat on my pallet where I lie sleepless and await the dawn, wondering what I have done.

FIFTY-SIX

"Miranda!"

It seems I slept after all, for I awaken to the thunder of Papa's voice in full fury and find him looming over my pallet.

"What," he says in a precise tone, "have you done?"

"Of what am I accused?" I ask.

He grimaces. "Caliban is missing."

I blink at him. "Oh?"

Papa reaches for the amulets that hang about his neck. "Do not play the innocent with me, child! He couldn't have escaped his cell without assistance, and no one but you would have aided him. Your wild lad sought to incite my murder. Do you imagine I'll not summon him back to stand the punishment for his crime?"

I push myself upright. "I do."

"How so?" Papa asks in a deep, deceptively gentle voice.

I should be afraid of him, and yet, I am not. I have gone somewhere beyond fear. In the secret place inside me, my heart is as cold and hard as steel.

"I will tell you exactly how, Papa," I say to him. "Would you have me play the doting bride? I will do so. Would you have me say naught of your great working, of the cause of the storm from which the king and his men are so grateful to be saved? I will say naught. Would you have me keep my silence in the matter of a certain homunculus that lies buried in one of the gardens? Of the punishment you inflicted upon me for discovering it? I will keep it, Papa. All that you ask of me, I will do. I ask only one thing in return."

"Caliban," he says with distaste.

"Caliban," I agree. "You did promise to relinquish your magic, Papa. Will you be forsworn?"

Papa lets go of his amulets and raises one hand as though to strike me, his fist trembling in midair. Never, ever has he struck me thusly.

I brace myself for the blow.

It does not fall.

"Our guests are hungry," he says, lowering his fist to his side. "Empty the larder and feed them as best you might, then attend to me in my sanctum."

I lower my gaze so that no hint of triumph shows in my eyes. "Yes, Papa."

There is not much in the larder—a few journey-cakes, a pot of soft cheese, and some early figs—but I set it on the long table in the great hall. Prince Ferdinand pronounces me a very angel of goodness. By their conversation, it seems that the king and his men have no idea yet that Caliban has fled.

I wonder what the prince would think of me if he knew what I have done.

In his sanctum, Papa is dismantling his instruments and packing them into trunks that have stood empty for years. The diligent little gnomes aid him in the task. Many of the shelves have already been stripped of their books and oddments, but the book *Picatrix* is open on its stand, and I remember that Papa said there would be one last image for me to render. Was that only yesterday? It seems as though an eternity has passed in the course of a single day.

"What would you have me paint, Papa?" I inquire, careful to keep my tone respectful.

"The third face of Capricorn." He comes over to point at an illustration depicting a man holding an open book in one hand, and in the other, a fish by its tail. " 'Tis an image to erase the influence of all images that preceded it."

I peer at it. "Will it not undo your working, Papa?"

"No, child." He shakes his head. "What is done is done; there is no more need for such influences. I do but fulfill my pledge to the Lord God in His heaven as you reminded me. With this final rendering, I surrender my arts and such influence as they have afforded me."

I pray that it is true, though I am not entirely sure that I believe Papa.

"Work swiftly," he adds. "The image must be finished in a matter of hours, for we set sail this very day."

My belly clenches at the thought, but I say nothing. I have won a great victory this morning; I dare not press him further.

A man, a book, a fish. It is a simple enough image, and I am familiar with all the components of it. The man I paint has Papa's likeness; Papa as I wish to see him, wise and noble and grave.

Papa, I think, is flattered by the likeness.

I paint the *Picatrix* laying open in the palm of his hand, and if I had more time, I should like to have painted an image in miniature on its pages of the very illustration I am rendering. Across the chamber, the salamander watches me from the glowing brazier, its bejeweled eyes reminding me of the promise I made it in exchange for a secret I learned to no avail.

Oh, dear Lord God, I do not want to think about promises.

I paint the fish that dangles from the man's other hand, using subtle curves to suggest that the fish is yet alive and wriggling in his grasp. I take more time than I ought rendering its fins and gills and scales in exacting detail, for I do not want this moment to end.

When it does, my life as I have known it will be over.

"Miranda." Papa's voice summons me from my trance. " 'Tis done, and done well. Your work is finished."

I step down from my stool, set down my brush and pigments. Flexing my cramped fingers, I begin cleaning my brushes.

"There is no need for that, child," Papa says.

"Oh, but—"

"Leave them," he says. "You'll have finer in Naples."

Save for the pantheon of figures gazing down from the walls and the laden trunks, Papa's sanctum is empty. Even the *Picatrix* has been packed away while I finished painting the fish. The little gnomes grin silently and await Papa's orders. The brazier glows, flames hissing softly. At their heart, the salamander regards me.

I take a deep breath. "Will you give the elementals their freedom as you did Ariel, Papa?"

He smiles and pats one of the gnomes on its stony head. "To be sure, once they've carried our belongings to the ship."

"What of the salamander?" I ask.

"Ah." Papa glances at it. "For the fire spirit, I have one final task." With ceremony, he removes the amulets from around his neck one chain at a time, untangling each carefully. Cunningly wrought charms of silver and gold entwined with hair glint in the light of the brazier; my hair, Caliban's hair, the nameless nanny-goat's hair, the hair of the king and his men.

I hold my breath.

One by one, Papa consigns them to the fire. The flames burn brighter and there is a smell of burnt hair and hot metal. Gold and silver melt, puddling beneath the salamander's delicate claws and its pulsing belly. One, two, three . . . All of them? I am not sure, not entirely sure. It seems to me I caught a glimpse of something shining vanishing up Papa's sleeve.

I do not trust my father.

And yet . . . do I trust the king, this Alonso who sought our lives? Do I trust my treacherous uncle the usurper? Do I trust their squabbling courtiers? Do I trust this kind prince with the tender mouth whose affection for me is compelled solely by the artifice of Papa's magic?

No.

There is only one person on the isle whom I trust, and I sent him away.

I wish Caliban were here.

And yet I am grateful he is not; grateful that I succeeded in bargaining for his freedom.

Papa dusts his hands together. "It is done."

"And the salamander?" I say.

He spares it another careless glance and a gesture, speaks a word in an unfamiliar tongue.

Fire roars through the grate of the brazier, roars up to scorch the walls of Papa's sanctum. Papa flings a protective arm around me, bearing us both to the floor. A circle of flame races around the chamber, and the figures I have rendered with such care are darkened to soot. Flames stream through the window of the balcony, dispersing and vanishing beneath the sky. The finality of the destruction is sudden and shocking, and yet it seems fitting, too. It is as though God in His heaven has spoken through the salamander, unleashing a purging fire.

For the first time, I find myself well and truly understanding that this is happening, that I can no more stop it than I can hold back the tide. My life already has changed forever.

Papa helps me to my feet. "I confess, I did not foresee this last working manifesting in so literal a manner," he says dryly, brushing at the sleeves of his robe. "But you may pack your possessions, Miranda, and I shall notify the king that we're prepared to take our leave of the isle."

Other than the finery from the pirates' treasure that Papa bestowed upon me, my possessions are few. There are the kidskin slippers I wore as a small girl, the sewing casket, and the little hand-mirror that once belonged to Caliban's mother. I gaze at my face in it, and it seems I am looking at a stranger. I remember Caliban and me putting our heads together, thrusting out our tongues at our reflections and laughing like the children we were.

I could weep at the memory of such innocence.

I glance toward the garden, half-imagining that I might catch a glimpse of Caliban watching from the walls, but it is empty. The only sign of Caliban's existence is a handful of limp trumpet flowers strewn on my window-ledge.

Unpacking my chest, I place one of the trumpet flowers in the bottom of it, then repack my things; all save the mirror.

I place the mirror on the window-ledge.

Do you promise it?

I do.

Caliban's absence is discovered. The king and his men are indignant; they offer to delay our departure, to scour the isle that the monstrous villain might be found and brought to justice.

"No, leave him," Papa says in a decisive manner. "Let him pine away his days in lonely misery. I daresay it is as fitting a punishment as any."

Dear Lord God, I fear Papa is right.

The ship awaits us in the harbor, where the king's crew have sailed it from the pirates' cove. We make the long trek to meet it. Little gnomes trot alongside us carrying Papa's trunks, my humble chest. Sylphs gambol around us in the jasmine-scented breezes. It is a fine, clear afternoon.

The prince is solicitous. He exclaims with horror when he realizes I have no shoes, and offers to carry me to spare my poor, delicate feet. I thank him and manage not to laugh.

He holds my hand.

I let him, because it is easier than explaining my refusal. And it is not so unpleasant, after all.

There is no sign of Caliban, but I do not doubt that he is somewhere near, watching. He knows every inch of the isle and all its secret places.

Thou art the shoals on which Caliban wilt dash his heart to pieces.

It is true.

Oh God help me, it is true.

In the harbor, a rowing-boat has been sent ashore to carry us to the ship. More men accompany it, sailors who rejoice in loud voices to be reunited with King Alonso and his men. The sailors marvel at the gnomes and the sylphs, at Papa's presence, and most especially at mine. They call me "my lady" and treat me with reverent courtesy, escorting me aboard the boat.

I wonder where Ariel is.

I pray he will not be unduly cruel to Caliban in my absence, until such a day comes that I may fulfill my promise and send for him.

I pray such a day *will* come, because there is a canker of fear within my heart that warns me it may not. It warns me that the urgency of my promise will fade in this brave new world toward which I venture; a world in which Caliban could never be seen as aught but monstrous.

I think of the glimpse of Caliban I saw through the prince's eyes and shudder.

I will not let that happen.

I will not.

Once the last of Papa's trunks is stowed on the rowing-boat, he dismisses the elementals. The sailors bend their backs over the oars and row, chanting in their loud voices.

So many, many men.

When we reach the ship, the prince climbs the rope ladder to board it before me so that he might extend a hand when I follow. The worn, sun-warmed planks of the ship are smooth beneath my bare feet.

Standing at the railing, I gaze across the sea at the isle that is the only home that I have ever known.

Orders are shouted; trunks are stowed. The rowing-boat is hauled aboard, the sea-anchor is lifted.

Ropes sing; sheets of canvas belly and snap.

The ship sets sail.

As the ship's prow slides westward through the rippling waves, I see the twin curved arcs of Setebos's jaws silhouetted against the sky. That is where Caliban will be, watching atop his high crag.

I raise my hand in farewell.

A warm hand comes to rest in the small of my back; it is Prince Ferdinand's. He smiles at me, slanting afternoon sunlight brightening his brown eyes. "Whom do you salute, my lady?" he asks me.

One day I will tell him the truth, I will; but not today.

"No one," I say to him. "No one."

FIFTY-SEVEN

CALIBAN

I watch the ship go until I cannot see it. There is only the empty blue sky and the sun shining on the sea.

Miranda is gone.

She is gone.

Gone.

There is an emptiness inside my heart as big as the sky. Miranda is gone.

But she will send for me.

She did promise.

I go to the palace. It is empty, too. The gardens seem quiet, and I cannot think why until I do see that the fountains are stopped.

Quiet.

So quiet.

Master is gone; the little undines are free. No more splish-splashing fountains. The little gnomes are free; no more emptying chamber-pots and digging in the garden.

I am free.

Oh, but Miranda is gone.

In the kitchen, the larder is empty, but outside I see they did leave the chickens and the nanny-goat behind. "Hello!" I say to the chickens that do peck and scritchety-scratch in the dirt, to the nanny-goat with her full udder who looks at me with her yellow eyes. "Hello, hello! Do not worry, I will take care of you."

They do not say anything, the poor dumb animals. But I will take care of them until Miranda does send for me. I milk the nanny-goat and scratch her ears the way she does like.

In the hearth, there is only grey ashes, but I dig in them and find embers underneath the grey. I bring kindling from the woodpile and blow on the embers until they do glow and catch fire.

I will tend the fire.

I will take care of the animals.

All until you do send for me, Miranda; only I wonder how long it will be. But you did promise.

(Oh, but he held your hand in his and you did let him, Miranda.)

No.

No, I will not think thoughts that will make my poor empty heart sick with hatred and badness.

I look through the palace to see what else they did leave behind, and *waah!* In Master's sanctum—no *Prospero's* sanctum, I am free and I will not think that servant-word anymore—the walls are black with soot. All of Miranda's paintings that were so beautiful are gone.

I wish they were not gone. I would have looked at them every day and thought about Miranda painting them.

Oh, but I go to Miranda's chamber, and what do I find on the window-ledge? There is Umm's mirror that I did give to Miranda so long ago, bright and shiny. I know Miranda did leave it here for me to find, and I am glad; only I do not want to look into it and see my face anymore.

No, I do not.

That night I sleep in Miranda's bed. They did take the linens, but not the pallet that smells of her and the dried grass it is stuffed with.

There is no one to greet the dawn.

It is so quiet.

I gather eggs and milk the goat.

I tend to the fire.

Then I go to the high place.

I am not so foolish that I think there will be anything to see, no. I know that it will be a long time, a very long time. It is only that I do not know what else to do.

Setebos watches.

I watch, too.

"La!" Ariel's voice says behind me. "Dost thou imagine they'll return for thee? Surely not!"

I do not turn to look at him. "Go away."

Ariel steps around in front of me. "Thou art a guileless fool and a dreamer," he says with pity. "And 'tis only by the grace of God that thou art not a murderer."

I do look at him then; I look at him and think how much I hate him. "I wish I had never given Setebos's name to Master," I say in a hard voice. "None of this would have happened if he had not freed you."

"Nor would it if thy mother had not imprisoned me in the first place," Ariel says. "And Prospero would have had the name from thee one way or another. Still, I suppose I do owe thee for it."

"I want nothing from you," I say.

"And yet thou shalt have it," Ariel says. "Do thyself a kindness and heed my counsel: Forget the maiden and put her out of thy thoughts, for she will surely do the same."

I shake my head. "No. Miranda will send for me. She did promise. One day, she will send for me."

There is oh, such pity in Ariel's gaze that I look away again. "As thou wilt, Caliban," he murmurs. "On thy head be it."

When I look back, he is gone.

I watch the sea.

Behind me, Setebos laughs at the sky.

Oh, Miranda! I do love you and I will wait for you always. One day, you will send for me.

Until then, I will think of you and remember.

You in the sunlight.

You on the grass.

You with the yellow flowers.

ABOUT THE AUTHOR

JACQUELINE CAREY is the author of the *New York Times* bestselling Kushiel's Legacy series of historical fantasy novels, the Sundering epic fantasy duology, postmodern fables *Santa Olivia* and *Saints Astray,* and the Agent of Hel contemporary fantasy series. Carey lives in western Michigan.